DARK WATERS

VIOLET FENN

First published by Harker House Publishing 2024

Cover design by GetCovers.

HARKER HOUSE

"If Liverpool did not exist, it would have to be invented."

Felicien de Myrbach, 1898

Witch-Hunt On The Wirral

"GET YOUR FAT FURRY ASS OFF MY NICE CLEAN BED," I yelled, throwing a tea towel in the offender's general direction for emphasis. "I just put those sheets on this morning, for fuck's sake!" The enormous grey cat had been happily snoozing in a nest made of my pyjamas until I'd stuck my head in through the door and spotted him. I'd been looking for my aunt, who has a tendency to curl up on my pillows when she fancies a nap. I once asked her how she ever felt tired enough to sleep, considering she didn't technically exist.

"It's a comfort thing," she'd said, a trifle sniffily. "Ghosts have feelings too, you know." I was only too knowledgeable on the topic of ghosts and their emotions, on account of how several of them make their emotions my problem on the reg. I'd have argued that if anyone needed a nap it was probably me, but knew it was doomed to failure. Mostly because Aunt Kitty is very good at smiling and nodding understandingly, before carrying on with whatever it was she was doing before I rudely interrupted. Anyway, I'd come home late to a suspiciously quiet flat after spending the evening over at Izzie's. We'd been packing up the last of her things ahead of her move from Button Street down to the Royal Albert Dock. I'd miss having my bestie around the corner, but no one could blame her for wanting to swap pissy town centre doorsteps for the security doors and concierge desks of the fancy apartments down on the waterfront. I'd snuck through the living room and into my bedroom hoping to catch Kitty snoozing, only to find Grimm asleep on my new Beetlejuice pyjamas. They'd been an online bargain—probably because it was currently July and therefore nowhere near Halloween season—and I hadn't even had a chance to wear them yet. Grimm opened one eye at the commotion and then casually yawned in the manner of a toddler who was already an expert at winding up their parents and was prepared to put some serious work into developing the talent. "Get off," I repeated, flapping my hands at him. "You heard me. Go shed on the sofa instead."

"That's not possible, I'm afraid," said the cat.

"Why not?" I asked. "And I told you already, I don't like it when you talk to me. It's fucking creepy."

"Finn threw up a furball earlier," said Grimm. "I've been waiting for you to get home so you can clean it up."

"Ohhh," I groaned, "you bunch of absolute mingers. Now stop talking to me."

"There you go again," he said, "shutting me down. You really should consider therapy, Lilith. You're far too easily unsettled."

"You'd be fucking unsettled if random creatures started talking to you," I said. It was less than two weeks since Grimm had first spoken, and I still wasn't entirely comfortable with it. For one thing, he didn't speak in the way humans did—instead, his words dropped, fully formed, directly into my head. My head's a busy enough place as it is. My other issue was that he kept breaking off to lick his own backside. It was late evening, and all was quiet in Liverpool Town. Well, as quiet as a city centre ever gets, which actually means 'mostly quiet with occasional shouting and police sirens'. I'd been over at Izzy's flat for the evening, helping her pack up the last of her things. She was about to move from Button Street down to the Royal Albert Dock. I'd miss having my bestie around the corner, but no one could blame her for wanting to swap pissy town centre doorsteps for the security doors and concierge desks of the fancy apartments down on the waterfront. "Where's Kitty?"

"Transported herself off to Shrewsbury to see that man of hers."

Grimm's tone was disapproving. "She didn't say when she'd be back. Anyway," he went on, "as we're already having a conversation, perhaps we could discuss You Know What?"

"Absolutely the fuck not."

"Lilith," wheedled the cat, "we need to talk. There is trouble brewing, and you need to prevent it."

"There is always trouble brewing," I pointed out. "If it isn't people accidentally walking into time slips, then it's the vampires getting themselves barred from Coopers."

"They haven't been barred again?" Grimm raised a furry eyebrow. "I thought they'd promised to behave after the last incident?" The Edge Hill vampires had only recently been allowed back into the pub on Cases Street, after promising they would never again attempt an acapella version of Sabbath's War Pigs. Apparently, the manager's ire had been less at the choice of song and more the fact they'd sung it at a group of off duty squaddies, who'd taken it badly as you might expect and tried to start a fight. But vamps can disappear quickly when they need to, and the soldiers ended up fighting themselves. At least one had managed to give himself a black eye.

"They're popular with the female customers," I said. "Girls hang around them like flies on rancid honey and end up drinking enough to make up for the fact the vampires don't drink at all. They're the karaoke equivalent of those strip clubs where women get free cocktails in return for bringing men in with them. And you're still not supposed to be talking." I flopped onto my bed and checked the phone that lay on the bedside table. I'm not a complete Luddite, but I've purposely not allowed myself to get into this modern habit of carrying a phone everywhere I go. For one thing, the less contactable I am, the less aggro people can drag me into. More pragmatically, I have a history of breaking phones almost as soon as I acquire them, and it's an expensive habit. I was currently using an old iPhone that was at least five iterations out of date and had been lurking in Izzy's junk drawer until she'd thrown it at me and told me to rejoin the human race. I'd pointed out that whilst I was, technically, human, the fact I'd been dead for quite some time made integration into society that bit more complicated. Her reply had been to throw the matching charger at my head, before going back to packing the contents of her knicker drawer into an impressively large cardboard box. She'd used tissue and everything. If I ever needed to pack up my pants, I thought idly, I'd probably just throw them into a carrier bag and hope for the best.

Perhaps, said the city that lives in my head, ***you'd have better luck with men if you put more effort into your appearance***.

And perhaps, I retorted silently, *you need to learn how to be less sexist. Anyway*, I added, *I'm also shit out of luck with women.*

At least you're consistent. I ignored the urge to bite back, having learned long ago that arguing with esoteric beings that no one else can hear only leads to confusion, and checked my messages. Then I put the phone back down and stared at the ceiling in annoyance.

"No messages?" asked Grimm.

"Nope," I sighed. "And I'm still not talking to you."

"I really don't understand you, Lilith," said the cat. "You live with a ghost, a shape-shifting roofer, and a talking cat. You yourself are a dead woman walking. And you're telling me you don't want to talk about the possibility that one of the most important artefacts of the modern age is somewhere in the vicinity? Just waiting for you to discover it?"

"I really, truly don't want to talk about it," I said. "So, yeah. Spot on."

"But it's the Holy—"

"SHUT UP."

The cat shut up, opting for glaring resentfully at me instead. I stalked into the kitchen and made a cup of tea, then took it back to my room and banged it down onto the bedside table hard enough that most of the contents spilled out. Ignoring the mess, I sat on the bed and stared glumly at my knees. They were currently clad in an ancient pair of grey jogging bottoms over the top of the kind of knitted slipper-socks that get handed out to patients on emergency hospital wards. It's only a couple of minutes to Izzy's flat from mine, so I rarely bother making myself presentable for the short walk. It wasn't quite a fortnight since my cat—my fucking cat—had informed me that not only was the Grail real, it was about to make itself part of my life whether I liked it or not. I'd greeted this announcement by deciding to ignore it entirely. Grimm had made periodic attempts to speak to me in the intervening days, but

I'd shut him down every time. Having a talking cat was mad enough—I was definitely not going to let it drag me down the road of conspiracy theories and ancient aliens. The problem was that I could feel it lurking. The Grail, not the cat. At least, I assumed it was the Grail. Something was skittering around the edges of my mind, trying to find a way in. It scritched and scratched with sharp little claws, making sure I couldn't ignore it for long. Sometimes I think Liverpool is a giant oyster shell and I'm the creature tucked away inside—occasionally a bit of annoying grit gets in and I have to decide whether to clean it out, or just grow more layers in the hope of protecting myself. After rocking back and forth for a bit, I lifted my head up and sighed heavily. "I'm going to have to do something about the Grail," I said. "Aren't I?"

"Yes, Lilith," said Grimm. "Yes, I'm afraid you are."

"And what exactly do you suggest I do?" I asked. "Go on an Indiana Jones-style rampage? Steal it for myself?"

"Theft of the Grail is the very last thing you should attempt," said Grimm. "That thing is a disaster just waiting to happen."

"Same old, same old," I shrugged. "Okay," I sighed, flopping dramatically onto my back, "hit me with it."

And then the entire world went black.

~

"What the fuck?" I opened my eyes to find myself standing in the middle of a room lit only by candles. There was a circle of people surrounding me, all wearing—and I swear I'm not making this up—hooded cloaks. Heavy black cloaks with bloody great cowls that hung down and hid their faces. They were all kneeling in what appeared to be supplication, their hands outstretched on the floor in front of them. "Get up and bloody well look at me," I snapped. No reaction for a moment, then a quiet shuffling as members of the circle glanced sideways at each other, as if wondering what to do. "ON YOUR FEET. ALL OF YOU." Aah, the joy of being able to compel humans to obey your orders. Comes in handy, that does. A dozen confused faces became visible as their owners slowly clambered to their feet against their will. I swivelled on the spot, pinning each of them with my beady gaze. It had not escaped my notice that the candles were placed in a circle, and I was at the centre. "Would one of you idiots like to explain exactly what the fuck is going on?" No one spoke. A couple of them shuffled backwards and dropped their heads, as though hoping they might somehow become invisible. Finally, a cloak in the corner took a very small step forward.

"We, ahhh," the voice hesitated, "we were expecting someone else. Actually." The voice was male and, at a guess, in his early twenties. "Someone more..." he coughed politely, "impressive?" He gave a polite shrug, hampered by the weight of his cloak. He looked like a sentient blanket.

"You do realise you look like a sentient blanket?" The blanket considered this for a moment. Then it straightened up and pushed its hood back, revealing a worried looking young man with straggly blond hair. He had what looked suspiciously like eyeliner smudged around his watery eyes. "They do good waterproof eye makeup these days," I said helpfully. "You should probably try it."

Blanket Man put a hand up to his face without thinking, then dropped it and narrowed his eyes at me. "Who are you?" he asked.

"I might ask the same," I retorted, "as I'm the one who's been dragged away from their cuppa with zero warning. I was trying to have an important conversation with my cat, for fuck's sake." The other members of the circle were audibly shuffling now. Several had grouped in the far corner and were whispering to each other about how it wasn't supposed to work like this, I wasn't what they were expecting, they should have known Derek was a fake... "I can hear you, you know?" I said, turning on them. They all cowered back except for one. It was the smallest Blanket Person in the room, and as they stepped forward, they too pushed their hood back, revealing a short, stocky woman in her thirties. She had dyed black hair pulled back from her face and wore an old Sisters of Mercy t-shirt over a long hippy skirt. You know the type of thing—endless fringing, and bells if you're really unlucky. It was a wonder I couldn't smell the patchouli from here. "Don't you work in the craft market down in Baltic Triangle?" I asked her.

"Don't you run the cafe on Harrington Street?" she returned. She had what I thought might be a faint Glasgow accent and a clever twinkle in her eye. "I always knew there was something weird about that place."

"There is nothing weird about Flora's," I snapped. "How very dare you." I looked around the large, square room, the occupants of which were now pressed back against the walls, as far away from me as possible. There were thirteen in total, most of whom had now removed their hoods and were openly gaping at me. "Roger?" I looked in astonishment at the oldest of the group, a man in his sixties with closely cropped grey hair and a round, friendly face that was currently scrunched up into an expression of confused anxiety. I saw that face several times a week, on account of him being a regular in Flora's. "What on earth are you doing here?"

"Well," he said, trying to sound braver than he clearly felt, "I could ask you the same, couldn't I?"

"But I asked first," I pointed out. "You're one of my favourite customers, Roger! What on earth are you doing with this…" I looked around at his companions, "this bunch of bloody weirdos?"

"We were summoning the King of the Underworld," said the man I thought might be Derek, as though it was obvious. "In order to worship and do his bidding. But there has clearly been some mistake."

"I should fucking well say so," I snapped. "For one thing, I am clearly female." I gestured up and down myself. "Under my pyjamas I am, anyway. So it's Queen, not King, thank you very much. Not that I'm bothered about gender, you understand, but. Well." I frowned and pulled my thoughts back on track. "Anyway," I went on, "I'm a woman. Obviously. And," I glared at Derek, "who the fuck are you?"

"I am head of this coven," he said, in a voice that definitely wasn't naturally that deep, "and as I said," he coughed self-consciously, "there has been a mistake."

"He's Derek Johnson," said the women from the craft market. "From over Kirkdale way. And I'm not sure this is a mistake," she said, turning to Derek. "Why would she be here if she wasn't the chosen one?"

"She's a faker," snapped Derek, "and she has to be sent back to wherever she came from."

"Harrington Street," I said helpfully. "And that would be grand, actually. With any luck, my tea will still be hot."

"You are clearly a duplicitous demon," said Derek. "And as such, you must be cast out into the depths of Hell." There was movement behind me, and I lifted an arm in time to knock Roger off his feet.

"What did you do that for, you idiot?" I glared down at Roger, who was now lying on the floor and clutching his nose.

"Ooo boke my dose!" he wailed. I bent to inspect the damage.

"No, I haven't," I said. "It's just bleeding a bit. Anyway, you shouldn't have been trying to attack me."

"Roger is a devout member of this group," said Derek, "and as such, will do all in his power to ensure our safety."

"Well, he doesn't have very useful powers," I said. "You should maybe get some fitter members. And some better manners. Because if this is how you treat guests, it's no wonder you've been struggling to find one who'll put up with you." A flash of light in the corner of the room made me whip round to see who else was going to have a go at me, but there was nothing but shadows.

"As I said," Derek was clearly having trouble remembering to use his Serious Voice, because he occasionally squeaked like a small and very frightened mouse, "you were not our intended, ummm, target."

I turned to look at him again. "So who was?"

"I told you," said Derek impatiently, "the immortal king. Leader of the dark forces." Amazingly, he appeared to be completely serious.

"I'm sorry," I squinted at him, "did you just say 'dark forces'? Really?" Derek shifted uncomfortably. "Did you have any particular dark forces in mind? Cos I can give you a list, if you're looking for suggestions? There's this bloke in the pharmacy on Castle Street, for a start."

"David is one of our trusted informants," said Derek. "It was he who confirmed the existence of the undead."

I gaped in astonishment. "David Mansoor?" I asked.

Derek nodded. "We tricked him, of course." He looked smug. "He thinks we're witch-hunters."

"That, that..." I struggled to find a suitable word, "...that asshole is nothing but a pain in the fucking backside! How the fuck he's kept his pharmacy license when he spends half his time annoying perfectly civilised members of society, I do not know." David Mansoor had been responsible for me having to fight a pack of vampires in Anfield cemetery the previous year, and I bear a good grudge. "Hang on," I belatedly registered what Derek had said. "Witch-hunters?" He nodded. "But you're not hunting witches?"

"On the contrary," said Derek, "we merely wish to show our support to the Dark Lord."

"Jesus fucking Christ," I murmured, "I've landed in an episode of Doctor Who. Where," I jabbed a finger at Derek, "are you expecting to find this Dark Lord?"

"Within the summoning circle," said Derek, pointing at my feet. I looked down and saw I was standing within a chalk circle that had been drawn on the carpet. "But we got you instead."

"That's because there is no Dark Lord," I said, pacing the edge of the circle. Poking one foot tentatively over the line, I established that I wasn't going to collapse into dust and stepped over it. The nearest blanket people all stepped backwards away from me. "There's just me."

"It can't be you," said Derek. "You're just, well," he trailed off.

"A woman?" I squinted at him. "That's what you were going to say, isn't it?"

"Look," said Derek hurriedly, "it's not what it sounds like. I'm all for equality. Everyone knows that. Don't you?" He looked around at his hooded friends, who were giving him looks that suggested Derek possibly wasn't quite as egalitarian as he liked to make out. "It's just that we know there's stuff going on and we want in. But in order to do that, we have to commit ourselves to the Dark Lord."

"You keep talking about this lord," I said. "What makes you so sure it's a man?"

Derek looked sheepish. "David told me there was a woman involved," he said, "but that she couldn't be the one in charge. Because she was, well," he coughed. "He said this woman was unhinged."

"Oooh," I said, "the cheeky fucker! Just wait til I get hold of him. Anyway," I said, "this has been lovely and all, but I need to get off home. The cat's going to be wondering what happened to me."

"Not until you tell us how to find your leader," said Derek.

My patience finally snapped. "I AM THE BLOODY LEADER," I intoned, the Voice in full effect. "BUT NOT ACTUALLY YOUR LEADER. LEADER OF THE UNDEAD. Not humans," I went on, reverting to my normal voice. It's tiring having to boom like that. "I try to leave humans alone." There was no answer. Looking round the room, I realised this was because they were all on the floor and apparently praying. "Oh, for heaven's sake," I said, "get up!" The only response was a hushed murmur, as though the group were all whispering prayers. "GET UP." They got up. "You," I said, pointing to the woman from the craft market, "what's your name?"

"Siobhan," she said. "Pleased to meet you, m'lady." She bobbed a small curtsey.

"Who are you?" I demanded of the man standing next to her. He was in his early twenties and dressed in the sort of generically alternative clothing everyone used to buy from Quiggins. These days you could probably get an entire emo wardrobe from Primark on Church Street and still come out with change from a twenty.

"George," he said, and bowed.

"Will you please stop doing that?" I said. "I hate it when people bow and scrape. It's fucking weird. Oh," something jogged my memory, "is your nan called Judith, by any chance?"

"Erm," George stuttered, "yes? Why? Has she done something wrong? You're not going to hurt her, are you? Take me instead, I beg you!" Before I could say a word, he threw himself at my feet. I stared down at him in confusion and took a step backwards. George grabbed my ankles in response. "Take me," he pleaded, "feed off me and make me one of your true followers!"

"You can let go now," I said, shaking my foot in an attempt to make him let go. George just clung on harder. "Get off!" I kicked out and George went flying across the room, knocking two of his companions over like skittles. To my horror, the rest of the group had fallen to their knees again and were crawling towards me like something out of a horror movie. "Stop it!" I turned around to look for an escape route, but they were all around me. "STOP IT NOW." They stopped crawling, but didn't get up. "Can someone please tell me where the fuck we are?"

"Across the water," said Derek, from his position on the floor.

"You'd better be joking," I snapped, "because otherwise I am going to be absolutely justified in kicking your arse into the fucking Mersey."

"Of course I'm not joking," said Derek. "I will always speak the truth to our ki—queen. We have powers of our own, you know."

"Well, Derek," I said, stepping forward, "I do not appreciate being dragged out of bed, however devoted you all are." Derek was careful not to crawl backwards, but he was doing a very good impression of a rabbit in headlights. "And second," I jabbed a finger at him, "since when have witch-finders been based in Birkenhead?"

Like many people on the Liverpool side of the Mersey, I rarely give Birkenhead much thought. I mean, obviously I know it's there. And there's nothing technically wrong with it, it's just that it's not Liverpool. Me and Izzy had been to gigs at Future Yard on Argyle Street a few times and always had fun, but then the gig ends and you're stuck on the wrong side of the river late at night and it's a pain in the arse to get home. It's mostly easier to just not bother, although Izzy had recently informed me that the night bus was running again. I'd pointed out that as I am no longer capable of getting pissed, I would just drive us the next time we made the effort. I did offer to stick her on my back and swim it, but she hadn't been keen. I certainly hadn't expected my next visit to the One Eyed City to involve standing in what looked suspiciously like someone's living room whilst being surrounded by a rag-tag team of would-be Buffys. Buffys who unfortunately resembled the Klan if they turned goth and bought their outfits from Home and Bargain. "I told you," said Derek, "we're not witch-finders. There is no evil here."

"Then you haven't spent enough time in your own town centre," I said. "All I know right now is that this isn't Liverpool. Or Harrington Street. And it definitely isn't my nice, cosy bed.."

Siobhan got to her feet and came to stand next to Derek. I couldn't help noticing the pitying look she gave him. "There's clearly been some kind of mistake," she said. "We were seeking a conversation with the leader of the underworld."

"Yeah," I said, "that'd be me. I mean," I shrugged, "I haven't been in the job very long, so don't be asking complicated questions. Although I could check with the others, if there's anything specific you need to know. Hang on," I said, remembering where I was, "why did you have to go to the effort of dragging me over the bloody river? Couldn't you have just popped into the cafe? You know, 'Hey Lil, got some questions about the afterlife, don't suppose you've got five minutes to chat?' That sort of thing."

Siobhan stared at me with an expression of utter amazement on her face. "You?" she said finally. "You're really their leader? Head of everything dark and demonic?"

"I'd hardly describe us as that," I said, looking down at my clothes. Slipper-socks do not a glamorous immortal make. "We're just like you, really. Just with, ummm, extra talents." Like not having to breathe, or eat. And being able to suck the life force from humans if we decided they were getting too annoying.

"Well, you're here now," said Derek, clearly rallying himself. "And we demand the right to worship."

"Are you shitting me?" I said. "You think I want people following me around like, well, followers?" In my defence, it had been a very confusing night and I wasn't at my most eloquent. "Don't you think people might notice if the local cafe's suddenly filled with a goth cosplay team?"

"We know about the vampires," said Derek doggedly. "And the cats. If you don't allow us to join you, we'll have no option but to make sure the authorities know what you're up to."

"Ummm," I rubbed my face hard and eventually managed to stifle the cackling noises that were fighting to get out. "Wouldn't that defeat the object?" Siobhan rolled her eyes and gave me a look that roughly translated as 'men, huh?'. "And which specific authorities are you talking about, Degs?" Derek looked annoyed, but didn't say anything. "Cos the government already knows about us. You're looking at a fully authorised demonic immortal." Okay, so that was something of an exaggeration. My brushes with the law hadn't exactly been friendly so far. And there was at least one civil servant down in London who'd very much like to fit me out in a pair of custom-made concrete boots before dumping me far out to sea. "Although I'm not actually demonic," I went on. "Some would say I'm quite cute, really." Derek was just opening his mouth to speak when there was a crashing noise outside the door. It burst open to reveal a very pissed off vampire.

"How dare you treat the Queen like this," Aiden boomed, striding into the room and picking Derek up by the scruff of the neck. "Do you have any idea who you're dealing with?" He shook the man like a rat, and the rest of the would-be Shadwells backed themselves up into the corner en masse. "I should rip your head off for this level of dishonour, you pathetic little—"

"I thought we were going to be calm and sensible about this?" said Gaultier Mapp, strolling in behind him. It might have been more impressive had he not been wearing a crocheted mini dress over gold booty shorts and matching platform sneakers. "'Lil's in a bit of bother, best go see if she needs our help' was what we said. And that," he went on, looking at the man Aiden had pinned up against the wall, "is one of the porters from the Titanic Hotel, if I'm not mistaken."

"Head porter," said Derek. Aiden shook him again and Derek wisely shut up.

"Head porter, then," said Mapp. "Terribly important job, that is. World would fall apart if it wasn't for the selfless sacrifice of the head porters. You okay, Lil?"

"How did you know about this?" I asked him.

"Aah," said Mapp, "I have my spies. Nah," he shrugged, "Heggie overheard someone talking about plans to kidnap the local ruler of the undead last time he was down Red Brick Market. He told me about it at the time, but it sounded so ridiculous that I assumed it wouldn't come to anything. I called round to see if you fancied a round of crazy golf and that cat of yours was losing his shit, so I got Kitty to find out where you'd disappeared to." That must have been the flash of light I'd seen. My great-aunt Kitty is far more independent these days, but reassures me we still have a psychic bond that she can tug if needs be. I'd really rather she didn't tug anything of mine to be honest, but it definitely comes in handy at times.

"Never underestimate the stupidity of humans," said Aiden, who had Derek pinned to the wall. The shorter man's feet were struggling to stay in contact with the ground, and his eyes were bulging.

"For god's sake," I said, "put the idiot down before he chokes." It took Aiden a few seconds to realise I was referring to Derek. When the penny finally dropped, he let go so suddenly that Derek hit the floor with a thud. "You," I gestured around at the blankets, "get over there where I can keep an eye on you." The motley crew shuffled sideways until they were ranged around an old, moth-eaten sofa that had been pushed into the corner of the room. Derek went to sit on it, but changed his mind when he saw me watching him. He stood in front instead, his formerly aggressive expression swapped for one that looked horribly like awe. The rest of the group wedged themselves into the space behind the sofa, presumably hoping eighty pounds of wood and perished foam would offer some protection in the event of a vampire attack. Mapp and Aiden stood either side of me, ever the loyal henchmen. "You'll have to excuse me," I said politely, "but I'm leaving now. We must do this again another time. Actually," I thought about what I'd just said, "let's never do it again. It's very kind of you to offer your services," I smiled at Derek and he looked like he might faint, "but as you can see, I've already got a support team. Although if any of you knit," I went on, "you're very welcome to come down to Flora's on a Wednesday evening. Gaultier here is always happy to see new faces."

"We provide a welcoming and inclusive environment for all enthusiasts of the yarn arts," said Mapp, nodding amiably. "Good coffee, an' all. Maybe you could join us one of these weeks, Roger?" Roger made a coughing noise in response.

"Is there a problem, Roger?" I asked.

"My name's not Roger," he said defiantly. "It's Frank."

I gave Frank a sharp salute. "Roger that," I said, and stalked out into the daylight.

Ferry 'Cross The Mersey

The second we were out of sight of the house, I rounded on Mapp. "I am perfectly capable of saving myself," I said. "I don't need your help, thank you very much."

"Charming," said Mapp, who didn't look remotely put out. "I take time out of my very busy day to rescue a damsel in distress, and this is the thanks I get." His eyes were squinting against the sun, but I could still see the twinkle.

"I am not a damsel," I snapped, "and I do not need rescuing."

"Of course you don't," he said. "Everyone knows that."

"Also, it's only just daytime."

"Doesn't mean I'm not busy," said Mapp. "Could've been up to all sorts of interesting shenanigans, for all you know."

"Were you?"

"No," he admitted. "But it's a nice thought."

"Where's Aiden gone?" I said, looking around for the third member of our party.

"Probably turned into a bat," grinned Mapp. "Come on," he turned in the direction of the river, "I'll race you to Seacombe."

. . .

I'd expected the first ferry of the day to be quiet, but by the time we got to the pier a small crowd had already gathered, waiting to be allowed onboard. Mapp waved at a small, jolly-faced man as we approached. "How y'doing, Mack?" he asked.

To my surprise, the man flung his arms open and grinned. "Get here and hug me, man!"

Mapp grabbed him and the two men hugged tightly, thumping each other on the back in as manly a fashion as can be achieved considering one of the pair was wearing heels and a see-through minidress. "Long lost friends, innit," Mapp said to me when they finally straightened up. "I don't get the ferry as much as I used to."

"Thinks he's above all this, doesn't he?" said Mack, still grinning. "But I remember the days when mister Mapp here used to spend hours going back and forth."

"What were you doing that for?" I asked Mapp.

"Never you mind," said Mapp, tapping his nose. "Ask no questions, get no lies, as they say. Anyway," he turned to Mack, "we're here now. Fancy giving me and Lil a free pass back over to the homeland?"

"As if you have to ask," said Mack, gesturing to where the passengers were now boarding. "On you go."

"How do you know Mack?" I asked Mapp as we made our way up onto the viewing deck. It's only a ten minute trip across the river on the commuter boat, but on the rare occasions I made the journey, I always found myself a spot on the deck. If friends ever asked why, I said it was because I was a poor traveller and less likely to get seasick if I stayed where I could see the horizon, but in truth I'd never been seasick in my life. The real reason I insisted on staying outside was so I could wave hello to the Liver birds as the boat neared the city. I'd always done it, ever since I first moved up to Liverpool for university as a teenager. The Mersey was as darkly opaque as ever. People often assume it's because the river's filthy with pollution, but it's actually one of the cleanest waterways in the country. There are porpoises, seals and even some species of shark hiding out in its depths, if you know where to look. And I know exactly where to look, because I'm friends with the local Asrai and those water-women keep tabs on everything that goes on in their waters. There was no sign of Daisy or her friends this morning, though. They were probably out in the bay, busily disconnecting the underwater cables that powered the offshore wind farm. I quite enjoyed seeing the serried ranks of huge white blades rising out of the water just offshore, but I got the distinct impression Daisy thought they were messing with her sub-aqua aesthetic. She certainly liked to cause their management company as much annoyance as possible. Shifting my gaze towards the approaching city, I saw my beloved birds on the skyline and wondered idly whether Bella would recognise me from such a distance.

"If that bird launches herself off the building at the sight of you," said Mapp, as though reading my mind, "Eadric is going to lose his ever-elegant shit." I leaned over the boat's high railings and rested my chin on my hands, gazing happily as we neared the giant building.

"I don't think other people notice when she does things like that," I said, not taking my eyes off the approaching city. "All this talk about how the birds can never be allowed to fly away or the city will fall," I went on. "That's just sentimental bollocks. The birds are here because they want to be—they don't have to be forced. Bella came all the way to Chester to rescue me, remember? I'm pretty sure not one person noticed anything different up here while she was away." I'd never forget the awe-inspiringly terrifying sight of a full-sized Liver bird heading towards me through the glass roof of my temporary prison. That version of Bella had been cast in fire and powered by fury, and I still wasn't entirely sure how I'd managed to sit on her back for the journey home to Liverpool. Nor how we hadn't been spotted by the control tower at Speke airport, despite having been well and truly within their air space. Bella had swerved to avoid an EasyJet plane at one point and we'd been close enough for me to see the terror in the pilot's eyes, but there hadn't been so much as a whisper of local gossip about it. And this is a city in which people genuinely think they might drop through a time slip if they walk up Bold Street too often. I mean, *I* know it's a definite possibility and people really ought to be more careful where they're walking, but the general public doesn't. Anyway, there really hadn't been a single peep about the flying firebird from any quarter, so I could only assume the pilot had put it down to sun flare and tried to forget it. "My theory is that it's only those with extra powers who see the really weird stuff," I said. "Y'know, people like us."

"Good old Netherweird," grinned Mapp. He'd long picked up on my nickname for what Eadric preferred to call the netherworld. It seems to amuse him. It's definitely more apt, though. Netherworlds are the kind of thing you find in books about dragons and Vikings, and Liverpool is way too weird in itself to bother with any of that boring stuff. We've got enough spooky shenanigans going on in this town to power the National Grid, but we try to keep it to ourselves. Since I'd become one of the literal walking dead, I'd learned that most towns and cities have some level of supernatural oddness going on in the background—it's just the intensity that changes, depending on the source. Some tiny little villages, no more than a dozen houses wide, have more ghosts than Borley Rectory. Then there are entire towns that would struggle to find a spirit anywhere other than behind the bar of the local Wetherspoons. Mortals tell their spooky tales and get a thrill of terror, without realising that most of us on the dark side of the veil are walking around like normal people and they're probably passing ghosts a dozen times a day without even realising. Chances are, if you've seen an apparition late at night down a country lane, said apparition will also be telling their mates about accidentally frightening you and how they hope you've just put it down to a trick of the light. "You think we've got superpowers, then?" said Mapp. "Do I get a cape? I'd rock a cape, I reckon." He did a twirl on the deck to demonstrate, and a smart woman in a business suit glanced over and smiled at him. She caught me watching her and blushed, whipping her head round to stare out to sea instead.

"As if you don't have power," I snorted. "You've got more power in your little pinky than most people have in their entire bodies, and you know it."

"Ooh, but I'm not one to boast," said Mapp. "Prefer to keep my talents to myself, innit."

"Says the man dressed as...well." I peered at his outfit. "What are you dressed as, exactly?"

"Aah," said Mapp, looking down at his clothes as though seeing himself for the first time. "Wasn't expecting to go out in public, was I?" He plucked at the lace dress he was wearing. "Owain asked me to model his work," he went on. "Just so's he could figure out how to do the sleeves." Owain was a member of what was commonly known as the

Renshaw Street Knitting Club, on account of how they'd started out in Mapp's shop on that very street. "I wasn't kidding when I said I was busy. We'd been up all night with this," he tugged at the hem, "and there'll be murder if I don't get it back to him sharpish."

"I haven't seen Owain in ages," I said. "He's still around, then?" I'd only actually met Owain a couple of times, always in Mapp's shop. A quietly spoken Welshman in what looked to be early middle-age, he used to be a fisherman but swapped making nets for the finer arts. Mapp had one of Owain's shawls framed and hanging in his shop, and refused every request to buy it. It wasn't my decor style of choice, but I could see why Mapp was so attached to it. Owain's work-worn hands somehow transformed his thread into the sort of gossamer-light streams of fabric a Nottingham lace-maker would envy.

"Just because you haven't seen someone," said Mapp, "doesn't mean they're not around. We don't go into standby mode until you reappear. Sorry about that." He raised an eyebrow before relenting. "You might be busy ruling the underworld, Lil," he winked, "but the rest of us go through our days in the same boring ways we always have. Owain comes over and sits with me every week, same as always."

"As if your life is ever boring, Gaultier Mapp. Hang on," I frowned. "The knitting group meets at Flora's now. Why doesn't Owain come to that instead?"

"Some of us are not the cafe sort, Lil," said Mapp. "I mean," he grinned, "obviously I myself am very much a proponent of the cafe lifestyle. I'm probably better suited to Parisian cafe life than that of our beloved city, like. But a cafe's a cafe and beggars can't be choosers."

"What's wrong with Flora's?" I might not get much chance to work behind the counter these days, but the cafe's my baby and always will be. "People seem to like it well enough."

"Aye," said Mapp, "that they do. And rightly so. But you have to remember that not everyone is a joiner, Lil. We don't all have that urge to be part of the wider community. Owain's happy keeping himself to himself. As is his right."

"What do you do whilst Owain's busy knitting spider webs?"

"Tatting," corrected Mapp, "not knitting. I've told you a thousand times."

"All looks like knitting to me," I shrugged. "I've never got the hang of any of it myself."

"You should get Jenny to show you," said Mapp. "She's almost as good as Owain himself, these days." 'Jenny' was Jenny Thompson—a local woman who worked as a special constable in the city centre. Despite being thoroughly mortal, Jenny had helped us out with inside information often enough that I suspected she knew more than she was letting on. But I'd never bothered querying it, because, well. You don't look a gift police horse in the mouth.

"I thought she was mostly quilting these days?" I said. "That's what she's been doing in the cafe every week."

"Aah," said Mapp, "but she comes to the private group as well. Don't look so shocked, darling. There isn't any rule against humans joining in."

"I'm not bothered about Jenny learning to knit," I said, "or whatever it is she does. What I'm bothered about is that you're still running the old group and you didn't even tell me!"

"And?" Mapp looked genuinely curious. "Why would you mind? Or even care?" That stumped me. I didn't actually know why it bothered me so much to hear Mapp still had his little private crafting group up in the Renshaw Street shop. It wasn't as though I was desperate to join—I'm about as crafty as a sloth and have never felt like a lesser person because of it. The ferry began turning for its approach to the jetty, and the breeze whipped my hair across my face so I couldn't see properly. I flapped at it in annoyance and opened my eyes again to find Mapp grinning at me.

"What?" I scowled at him. "And you never answered my question."

"You didn't answer mine, either," he replied.

"I asked first," I said. "How do you know Mack?"

"He told you himself," said Mapp. "I used to travel on the ferry a lot."

"What for?" I genuinely couldn't think of any good reason that Mapp, of all people, might choose to spend time on the Wirral. There's nothing wrong with the Wirral, you understand—it's just that it isn't Liverpool. So near and yet so far, as they say.

"None of your beeswax," said Mapp lightly. "I'm not obliged to tell you everything about my life, queen or no. So," he went on, "why are you annoyed about me having a private social group with my friends?" The ferry bumped against the jetty and the rest of the passengers began making their way to the exit.

"I'm not annoyed," I said. Mapp walked ahead of me as we got off the ferry and held out a hand for me to steady myself as I stepped off after him. I might be supernatural, but I'm still not super-elegant. Which is annoying. "Oh, I don't know," I sighed as we turned to walk up the jetty and into town, "I'm just being silly."

"You're not being silly," said Mapp. "You're just trying to find your place in the world, is all." We stopped to wait for the traffic lights on the Strand, and Mapp turned to look at me. "It'll be okay, Lil," he said. The green man lit up and we stepped out onto the road. A horn beeped, and we both turned to see a pair of workmen wolf-whistling out of the open windows of their battered white van. Mapp curtsied and blew a kiss in return. "I've got faith in you," he said, as we reached the other side.

"Huh," I said. "If only I had faith in myself."

Hey Mister Pharmacist

Mapp invited me up to the shop to have coffee with him and Owain, but I said I'd better go home in case Grimm was worried. He gave me a strange look, but didn't say anything. We parted at the turning for Harrington Street, and I tucked myself out of sight until I was sure he was gone. Then I turned and headed determinedly back down to Castle Street. I banged through the door of the chemist shop with such force that it smacked into the wall behind it and the glass pane made an audible cracking noise. There was a gaggle of customers waiting to be served, all of whom turned to stare as I entered. The pharmacist had his back to me as he checked a prescription, clearly far too busy and important to be distracted by something as minor as the front door being broken off its hinges. "Morning David," I called cheerily, "I'd like a word in your shell-like, if I may." His expression as he spun around to face me was so delightfully horror-stricken that I wished I had a camera. I'd have printed that face out and stuck it to my kitchen wall for posterity. And also to use for darts practice.

"I am quite busy at the moment, unfortunately," said David. He was going for 'smooth and professional' in the face of customers' curious glances, but was mostly achieving only 'surprised and caught in the act'. "Perhaps you could come back later?" His smile was bright, but his eyes glinted with fear. Good-oh.

"Don't you worry," I said, matching his friendly tone, "I can wait. I'll just pop the 'closed' sign up," I turned and flipped the hanging sign on the door, "so no one disturbs us. Ooh hi, Mysha," this was to a woman in the queue who was smiling in recognition at me, "didn't see you there. How's your Ruby getting on?"

"Morning, Lil," said Mysha. "She's doing well, thanks. Getting the cast off this week. We're hoping to be back at knitting club before the end of the month."

"Brilliant news," I said. "I'll let Mapp know. He was asking after you both only the other day."

"Such a lovely man," cooed Mysha, who was clearly as under Mapp's spell as everyone else I knew. "Old beyond his years."

"He certainly is," I said. I turned back to David Mansoor, who appeared to be frozen to the spot. One hand was outstretched towards the customer in front of him, a tube of athlete's foot cream in his visibly shaking palm. "I'll just wait here," I said, stepping into a corner of the shop that housed the orthopaedic foot supports. "Don't mind me."

To his credit, David managed to work his way through the customers with only a couple of furtive glances in my direction. Okay, so they were the sort of glances small rodents give to a falcon they've only just spotted sitting on a fence post above their head, but still. I stood with my arms folded and head resting casually back against the wall, occasionally humming the Star Wars Imperial March under my breath. The first time I did it David's head shot up to glare at me, but I just smiled beatifically back and switched to Danse Macabre by Saint-Saens. To be honest I only really know the tune because it's used in What We Do In The Shadows, and I bloody love that programme. In my more whimsical moments I like to think of myself as Nadja, wafting around the afterlife with a nifty range of mourning frocks and a sick and ridiculous sense of humour. I'd once made the mistake of admitting as much to Izzy and she'd said I was more like Colin Robinson, whose lookalike was still doing nightly guard duty up on the roof of my flat. Aiden had brought pseudo-Colin in to replace Katja, who'd been staked on my doorstep. I was still quietly seething about her death, and David Mansoor would be an excellent target on which to vent some of my undead spleen. Not that David had been responsible for Katja's demise—that was entirely down to Ivo Laithlind, twat of this parish. Actually, Ivo isn't of this parish at all—his territory is further east—but he'd spent a long time in it since I'd died and found myself on the wrong side of the mortal coil. Mostly because he was under the misguided impression that I was his fated true love and that only our eternal union could save the netherworld. Save it from what, I still wasn't sure. And I was pretty sure that Laithlind himself was its biggest threat, on account of how he was incapable of fucking off and letting people get on with their afterlife in peace. Anyway, the last time I'd seen him he was disappearing under many tonnes of rubble as the Chester Steam Mill came crashing down around his stupid ancient ears, and I was really hoping that was going to be the end of it. I mean, there's no denying Ivo's innate hotness—I often had to close my eyes whilst talking to him in order to not get distracted and risk forgetting what I was about to say in favour of imagining him without his clothes on—but there's only so many times someone can attempt to hold you prisoner or steal your most valuable treasures before you're going to get a bit fed up with them.

I idly twisted the gold band on the ring finger of my left hand. Plain and simple to look at, to me it was a symbol of my commitment to the city. I never took it off. Okay, so I didn't take it off because I wasn't entirely sure it wasn't sentient and I was a bit worried it might go off on adventures of its own if I didn't keep it on me at all times. But Izzy was still wearing the gold chain necklace I'd given her at the same time I'd had the ring made and she didn't seem to be having any problems, so maybe I just had an overactive imagination. Mind you, Izzy's still mortal and might not notice any spookiness hanging around her neck. But I'd had to split the crown up—yes, that crown, the one that was supposedly melted down by Oliver Cromwell but was in fact stolen before he could destroy it and then passed to me, centuries later—in order for it to be less of a target. There were too many fools who thought owning the crown also meant owning its power. And Ivo Laithlind was the biggest fool of them all. So I'd had the most famous crown in British history melted down by a talented Mercian queen of my acquaintance, and she'd then transformed some of the resultant liquid gold into the ring and chain. I should probably have worn both items myself, but I secretly hoped that letting Izzy wear it would give her some level of protection. From what, I wasn't entirely sure. But there's no fear quite like realising you're going to live forever (or at least several hundred millennia, which basically amounts to the same thing) to make you terrifyingly aware of the fragile mortality of your friends and family. Me and Izzy were thirty-three now, and had been best friends since we'd met at primary school, aged eight. But I was frozen at thirty-two and would stay that age until the end of time. Whereas Iz would gradually get older and eventually die. Or succumb to disease, or an accident, or… I snapped myself out of that train of thought as soon as I realised what I was doing. One of the first things you learn as a revenant is that because you don't need to sleep, you have an awful lot of time available for thinking. And it's way too easy to disappear down a depressing rabbit hole of 'things your loved ones might die of and you'll have to watch'. Izzy had actually bought me a t-shirt with 'DEATH BY OVERTHINKING' written across the front for my last birthday, and was far more amused by it than I was. She doesn't always buys me t-shirts—sometimes I get doormats or a mug instead. But always with the 'funny' slogan on it. Izzy could find humour in just about anything, it was one of the things I loved most about her.

"Bye now," I said to the bloke who was David's last customer. He'd been engaged in conversation about ingrown toenails for longer than he might have expected, as David frantically tried to put off the moment he'd have to face me. He looked relieved to get out of the shop. As the door clanked shut behind him, I flipped the sign to 'CLOSED' and turned to face him, smiling horribly as I did so.

"Why are you always bothering me?" whined David, his immaculate eyebrows scrunched up as if in pain. "I have done nothing to upset you."

"You are a lying snake, David Mansoor," I said amiably, not moving from the doorway. "You are a constant thorn in my delightfully pert backside, and quite frankly, I am sick to fucking death of you."

"Why do you always talk like that?" David frowned.

"Like what?"

"Like you are finding everything amusing," he said. "Many smart comments and smug jokes." I was flattered. As far as I was aware, my conversational skills mostly consisted of random streams of consciousness that often made people glaze over before I'd got to the point.

"Maybe I'm practicing for open-mic night over at Blackstock Market," I said. "Or maybe—just maybe—I'm just really fucking fed up with you putting your stupid fucking oar into my fucking life at every fucking opportunity." I'd stepped closer with every insult, and we now stood glaring at each other on either side of the narrow pharmacy counter.

"You are not alive, though, Lilith," he said. "Are you?"

"I'm alive enough to be standing here in front of you," I narrowed my eyes at him, "and that's enough for most people. It's certainly enough for me to be capable of making your life very, very difficult."

"You are strange," he said. "And everyone knows it." He had some fully gold-plated balls, I had to give him that.

"This entire city is built on strange, David," I said, leaning even closer. "Liverpool is pretty much the capital of strange. You're going to have to learn to live with it, I'm afraid. Because we're not going anywhere. And," I added, "we'll still be here a long time after you're dead and buried. I can promise you that much."

"Not if I have anything to do with it," he muttered. His grumbling turned into choking noises as my arm flashed across the counter to grab him round the throat. "Aeerrrghh!"

"David," I said calmly, "if you don't leave me and my friends alone, I am going to feed you to the vampires." His eyes flashed, but he didn't say anything. Mostly because I still had a firm grip on his neck and his eyes were bulging. "We all know about your involvement with that nasty little bloodsucker that used to be in charge." Until I'd staked him up at Anfield, after David had nearly got me killed. "But he's gone, and now my friends are in control. I know Aiden would very much like a polite word in your fragile little ear." A flash in David's eyes confirmed that he did indeed know only too well who I was talking about. "Or I could just feed you to the cats." I let go, and David fell gasping to the floor behind the counter. "They'd enjoy a new squeaky toy." Flipping up the hatch, I stalked around it and loomed over him. Which, I'd like to point out, is a nifty talent when you're only five-foot-six in your slippers and dressed like an escapee from the local psych unit. As if to reinforce the image, my grippy-socks chose that moment to snag on the tiled floor. I shot out a hand and grabbed the nearest solid object in order to avoid falling on top of the flailing pharmacist. Unfortunately for David, the nearest solid object was the cash till, and I'm stronger than I look. It crashed down onto the tiles next to his head and only narrowly avoided wiping him off my list of People I'd Like To Throttle. Which was a shame, but I guess we can't always get what we want.

But sometimes—just sometimes—we get what we need. I heard the shop door open behind me and was just turning and trying to think of an excuse for why I was standing over the pharmacist, having apparently just attempted to smash many kilos of electronic equipment into his face, when the newcomer spoke. "Need any help, Lil?" It was Jenny Thompson, appearing as though I'd summoned her through the power of thought. She was followed into the shop by a handsome-looking woman in her mid-fifties, who was dressed in wide-legged jeans over white sneakers, topped off with a fitted red shirt with cropped sleeves. Her grey-blonde hair was piled on her head and tied in place with a polka-dot headscarf. She looked like the sort of woman who knows how to do victory rolls and can probably jitterbug with the best of them. But there was an air of casualness about her that made me think she'd just dressed for genuine comfort. When I dress for comfort you know about it, because I end up walking the streets in outfits like the one I was currently wearing. I'm pretty sure people sometimes wonder if I'm a rogue sleepwalker who needs pointing toward home. But as I'd said to David, Liverpool is used to strange behaviour. We only bother staring if the person in question actually looks as though they might be a danger to themselves or others.

"Can you lock the door?" I asked. Jenny's been around long enough to know that things aren't always quite what they seem, and appears to have taken it in her stride. We can certainly rely on her to help us out in a sticky situation. And she's good at passing on the sort of inside information that isn't quite breaking the law as a police employee, but enables us to get out of difficult situations without the general public realising there's a real life episode of the X Files going on right under their noses.

"This is Freya," said Jenny over her shoulder, as she latched the door closed. "She's from over the water."

"I'm kind of busy right now?" I gestured to where David Mansoor was still lying on the floor, clearly hoping it was a fever dream and he'd wake up soon. "Shit." A confused face had popped up in the window behind Jenny. It was the pharmacy assistant, who must have been out running errands and was now clearly wondering what on earth was going on. She'd been working in the shop on a couple of the times I'd popped in to annoy David, and she definitely knew who I was.

Jenny followed my gaze. "Aah," she said. Unlocking the door, she stuck her head out. "Someone was taken ill," she explained to the confused woman, whose name I thought might be Sue. "I just happened to be in here at the time. I've promised David I'll look after the place until he gets back."

Sue looked unconvinced. "I'll better come in and make sure everything's secure," she said, stepping towards the door. Jenny gripped the door firmly and blocked Sue's way.

"No need to worry," she said. "I'm on duty soon, so I've said I'll take charge until officers arrive."

"I thought you said someone was taken ill?" said Sue. "Why are the police involved? Look," she tried to step forward again, "just let me in. I need to make sure the controlled drugs are secure." Jenny didn't budge.

"No need," repeated Jenny with a bright smile. I really liked Jenny a lot, I decided. "Just take the rest of the day off. We'll be making sure it's all safe, don't worry about that."

"Why's she here?" asked Sue, pointing at me. "She's not police."

"Lilith was here when the incident occurred," said Jenny smoothly. "As was this lady here." She inclined her head to where Freya stood in the corner of the shop.

"What incident?" Sue was beginning to sound panicky. "And where's David?"

"He went with the patient," said Jenny. "It all happened ever so quickly, didn't it Lil?" I nodded mutely, waiting to see what she was going to come up with next. "One minute he was standing here just waiting for his prescription," she went on, "and the next he was on the floor. Blood everywhere, we had to close the shop."

"Blood where?" said Sue, looking past Jenny to the immaculately clean tiles of the shop's floor. "I can't see any blood."

"It happened out the back," said Jenny blithely. "David dragged the poor chap through in order to give him some privacy and he'd just got him behind the counter when POP!" Me and Sue both jumped, but Freya stood blithely watching events unfold, a faint smile lurking. "Red stuff everywhere," shrugged Jenny. "Must have burst an artery or something."

"I haven't heard anything from David," said Sue doggedly. "I need to check with him before I leave you here without supervision."

"Sue," said Jenny, "I'm the police. Therefore, I am the supervision. I'm sure David will be in touch as soon as he gets a moment." David chose that particular moment to attempt to get up from the floor. He opened his mouth to shout, but I was faster. Before he could alert Sue, I dropped down behind the counter, landing astride him with my knees on his arms and a hand clamped over his mouth. His eyes widened in panic, and I could feel him instinctively trying to bite me. I gave his face a warning squeeze and heard a horrible crack. Like I said, I'm stronger than I look. David made a gurgling noise and stopped trying to fight me off.

"Where has that woman gone?" asked Sue, craning to look past Jenny into the shop. Jenny must have realised I'd disappeared, because when she next spoke, it was with firm urgency.

"Oh dear," she said, "maybe the same thing's happened again."

"Same thing?" said Sue. "Aneurysms aren't catching, Jenny."

"Well, I'd better go see what's occurring anyway," said Jenny. "Go home, Sue. I'll tell David to call you as soon as he gets back from the hospital."

"Which hospital did they go to?" asked Sue, but Jenny was already shutting the door. I heard her slide the bolts across, followed by a clattering noise from near the shop window.

"I'm closing the blinds, Lil," said Jenny. "It's safe to get up now." I clambered to my feet and then leaned back down to roll David onto his side. He lay there moaning quietly, one hand gingerly holding his face.

"I think I've hurt him," I said, gazing down at David. "I didn't mean to, though. Not that he didn't deserve it."

"Aah, he'll be okay," said Freya from behind me, making me jump. At least I didn't smash anything this time. "Won't you, David?" She came to stand next to me and we both stared down at the man on the floor. "Get yourself up, love," said Freya, poking David with the toe of her sneaker. "It's not hygienic to lie on floors." David managed to shuffle himself upright until he was sitting with his back to the display unit behind the counter. "That reminds me," said Freya, "I promised to pick up some Gaviscon for Norman in the village. Pass us a bottle, will you? The big one." David looked at her as though she was insane, but used his free hand to reach backwards and pull out a large brown glass bottle. "Cheers, love," said Freya, taking the bottle from him. "Suffers terribly with his bowels, does Norman." She tucked the bottle into her shoulder bag and tilted her head sympathetically at David. "Can I have a look at that?" she asked. "I promise I won't do anything awful." David grunted and gave the tiniest of shrugs. Freya leaned down and gently placed her hands on either side of his face. Then, without warning, she made a sharp wrenching gesture and David let out a guttural howl. Stepping backwards, Freya dusted her hands off on her jeans in a businesslike manner. "It was just a dislocated jaw," she said. "It'll feel better now."

"Neat work," said Jenny approvingly, coming to stand with us. All three of us gazed down at David, who glared back in outraged fury.

"How dare—" he started, but Freya was too quick for him. Leaning forward, she slapped him shockingly hard across the face.

"You listen to me, David Mansoor," she said. "We all know you're a devious little sneak who likes to meddle in other people's business. This is what happens to devious little sneaks, David—they get found out. And they get punished. Do you really want to keep pushing your luck with this?"

"I don't understand," said David. His voice was muffled slightly because he was carefully keeping his mouth almost closed, but he was speaking well enough. Phew. The last thing I needed today was to have to find an alibi for causing actual bodily harm to a local shopkeeper. "Why are you sticking up for them?"

"Who's them?" asked Freya. She smiled down at him. "It's rude to dehumanise people, David, you know that. And some of us are more human than others."

"You are all freaks," he spat. Clearly, the feeling was coming back into his face. Shame. "All of you are demons walking this earth and you should not be here."

"I have no idea what you're babbling on about," said Jenny, "but you clearly didn't take history at school. Because if you had, you'd know that this city has form for accepting pretty much anyone, so long as they're nice to others. And that goes for you as well, David Mansoor. You need to learn how to play nice, and you need to learn fast. Because if you don't, I will give Lilith here a list of all the blind spots in the town's CCTV cameras, along with a copy of the patrol routine for this entire city. And you will spend the rest of your life unable to walk down a quiet street without constantly checking over your shoulder. Won't that be fun?"

"Sounds cool to me," I agreed. "I could do with a new hobby."

"Give up now, David," said Freya. "Before you regret it. Ooh," her face brightened, "don't suppose you've got some insoles while I'm in here? These pumps are playing havoc with my bunions."

Do You Want To Know A Secret?

"I've been trying to get Freya to come to knitting club," Jenny said to me. The three of us were sitting at a table outside the cafe opposite the pharmacy. It had been an intentional choice, and David clearly did not appreciate this supervision. He occasionally stopped what he was doing in order to glare out at us through the glass. One of us would wave now and then, just to keep him on his toes. He must have called Sue as soon as we'd left, because she'd stomped down the street and back into the pharmacy within minutes of us leaving. We hadn't bothered trying to bully him into a cover story. As Jenny had pointed out, both the lies and the truth were so ridiculous as to be unbelievable, so it didn't really matter what he said. It can't have been flattering though, because it wasn't long before Sue was also taking time out to scowl at us across the street.

"You know I'm not good with people," said Freya.

Jenny snorted. "Give over," she said, "you get on with everyone! Look how they all rely on you down your way. Norman would struggle without you running errands for him, for one."

"Where do you live?" I asked. We were going to have to discuss the whole 'I'm not entirely normal, but you seem to know that already' aspect of things, but I wasn't in a hurry to broach the topic. "Jenny said you're from over the water?"

"Near Prenton," said Freya. "Nowhere anyone's ever heard of."

"She lives out in the sticks," Jenny informed me brightly. "Over Bidston way."

"That's hardly the sticks," I said. "Bidston's Birkenhead, pretty much."

"Not where this one lives," said Jenny, in the tone of someone who has inside information and is hugging it to themselves for as long as possible. "Didn't even know the house was there till I gave her a lift home one night, did I?"

Freya rolled her eyes. "I told you I could make my own way home," she said. "You didn't need to drive me all the way back."

"How were you going to get back over the water at that time of night?" asked Jenny. "It was well late."

"There're these things called buses," said Freya. "You should try them some time. And I've got feet, you know. I'm perfectly capable of walking home from the bus station."

"Whereabouts in Bidston?" I asked. I knew the hill area, but only from a trip to the city farm many years earlier. I'd made the journey over with Devin, who I'd been dating at the time. I wondered idly how Dev was settling into his newly undead lifestyle, and whether he'd met the Golem of Olde Glasgow Town yet. Dev himself hadn't even realised he was dead until he'd turned up for work as usual and created such a drama that I'd heard it from down the street and staged an intervention. Eadric had arranged for him to move up to Scotland for a while, in the hope that he'd learn to manage his newfound paranormal abilities. It helped that the ghost of his dead mother had appeared at the same time, and had happily accompanied her only child on his mystical journey through the underworld. Not that there was actually anything particularly mystical about it. Devin had just woken up dead one morning, in much the same way that had happened to me a year or so earlier. The only thing Dev and I had in common—apart from our dating history—was that we'd both died from a blow to the head. Mine was thanks to a rogue vampire barrelling me off the top of the fire escape outside my flat, but Devin's had been more mundane. He'd gone out with friends after work and got absolutely hammered before heading off to walk home alone. After somehow ending up on Vauxhall Road near the junction with Tithebarn Street, he'd decided to attempt a one-man rodeo on the back of the giant Lambanana that sits outside the university library. One accidental slip later and Devin was headfirst on the concrete pavement, dead as the proverbial dodo. The problem was that Devin's brain didn't register the message, and just carried on as normal. I'd talked to Eadric and Nik about it several times since, but try as we might, we couldn't find any reason why Devin had been the next revenant to join the happy gang. And, as Mapp likes to say, coincidences are more common than you think. In all of Eadric's thousand years on the planet, he'd never met more than a handful of revenants in any of the cities he'd visited. When he'd finally settled in Liverpool a few centuries earlier, he'd thought he might be the only one in the entire city. Mapp had eventually followed him up north, the two men having been friends since the thirteen-hundreds. Then Missy, who lived up at Anfield cemetery, had arrived soon after. She knew Mapp from his time in London and fancied a change of scenery—as well as a marginally lower risk of being executed as a witch—so north she went.

It's important to note here that, despite being the literal walking dead, we are definitely not zombies. I'd once asked Mapp—probably the most intelligent person I knew—if he thought zombies did possibly exist somewhere in the world. He'd said no. "Probably just poisoned," he'd said, as we'd sat swinging our feet off the edge of the top dome of the Liver Building one summer evening. "Lots of poison can be made from plants, 'specially the hallucinogenic ones. I'm thinking those poor flaky bastards are still alive, just semi-comatose."

"Do you think they know what state they're in?" I'd asked with morbid fascination. The thought of going through life semi-conscious was bad enough—the prospect of also being aware of what you were doing, but being unable to stop it made it even more horrifying. "And why the flaky skin?"

"Probably don't have time for a decent moisturising regime," Mapp had shrugged. "What with being so busy terrorising the townsfolk, and all that."

"It's never had an official name," shrugged Freya, bringing me back out of my daydreams. "Where I live, I mean. I get mail delivered to the post office and pick it up from there."

"How can anyone send you mail if you don't have an address?"

"I've got a name myself," said Freya. "That's usually enough."

"Freya Spragg," said Jenny, ignoring Freya's frown. "Have you ever heard anything like it in your life, Lil?"

"It's a very nice name," I said. "And unusual enough for the post office to remember you, I'd imagine."

"Exactly," said Freya. "And I get heat and hot water from a wood-burning range cooker, so no utility bills either."

"The water must come from somewhere, though?"

"There's an old spring water well," said Freya proudly. "Comes up right in the middle of the kitchen."

"Freya here is one of those off-grid types," interrupted Jenny. "Knits her own lentils, sort of thing."

"Don't you start," said Freya. Her amused tone suggested they'd had this conversation many times. "Just because you can't live without satellite television and hot and cold running electricity."

"That's impressive, though," I said. "Living completely off-grid, I mean. How long have you been there?"

"A long time now," said Freya. "Can't remember exactly. Anyway," she got up from the table, "I need to be off. Got a few chores to do before I head home." She held a hand out to me and, after a second's confusion on my part, I shook it. "Nice to meet you, Lilith," she said. "Perhaps you could pop in for a chat about Derek when you have an afternoon free. Jenny can give you directions, I'm sure." Before I had chance to ask how the hell Freya knew about Derek, she gave us a quick wave and was striding off towards Derby Square.

"Who's Derek?" asked Jenny.

"Just someone I vaguely know," I said. "He's very annoying."

"I didn't think Freya knew anyone over this side of the river." Jenny frowned. "She's a funny onion," she went on, "but nice with it."

"A funny onion?"

"Something my nan used to say," grinned Jenny. "Ridiculous, when you think about it. What's funny about an onion?" We both considered this for a few minutes, taking time to gaze over into the pharmacy so that David wouldn't get too comfortable. "I know you're not normal, Lil," said Jenny suddenly. "Oh god," she clattered her coffee cup down onto the table, "that didn't come out right. I meant," she mopped at the spilled coffee and I handed her a spare napkin, "not like everyone else. Oh, fuck it." She gave up trying to clean the mess and sat back in her chair to look across at me. "You know what I mean."

"It's okay," I said, if only to break the awkward silence. "I know I'm a bit weird at times."

"Yeah," said Jenny, squinting across at me, "you're proper weird at times, Lil. Definitely weird. But there's something more, isn't there?"

"What do you mean?" I asked, not liking the way the conversation was going. "More than having an actual fist fight with the local pharmacist?"

"Yeah," said Jenny, "about that." She gazed across at David's shop. "What's his beef with you? And more to the point," she turned to fix a beady glare on me, "why did Freya just back you up without question? She'd never even met you before today."

"So did you," I pointed out. "You immediately covered for me, even though I'd clearly just had a violent altercation with a shopkeeper on his own premises. Why would you do that?"

"I'm loyal to my friends," said Jenny, sounding sheepish. "I'm sorry," she went on. "I shouldn't be nosy. I like you, and I like Mapp's lot. Well, most of them, anyway." I wondered which one of the Renshaw Street crew had rubbed her up the wrong way. "I think you're all good people." She looked across at me, a determined expression on her face. "And that's enough for me. Anyway, when I was growing up, people liked to say my family was weird, and I didn't like it. So I stand up for others."

"Thank you," I said. "I mean that. And I know I'm weird, if that helps. More coffee?"

Jenny looked carefully at me for what felt like a very long time. "Go on, then," she said eventually. "One more, then I'd best be off. Although," she gazed thoughtfully across to where we could see David and Sue watching us through the shop window, "I'm rather enjoying myself."

~

I got back to the flat to discover Grimm had taken advantage of my absence by curling up on my pillows for a snooze. "Are you fucking *shitting* me?" I yelled, throwing a scatter cushion at his rapidly retreating furry backside. "Jump in my bloody grave as quick, would you?"

"How was I supposed to know you'd come back?" came a muffled voice from under the bed. "You might have gone forever. No point wasting good pillows."

I decided to ignore the implausibility of his voice sounding muted considering he spoke directly into my head, and did what I always do when I need uninterrupted thinking time—I ran a bath. Even Kitty knows better than to disturb me when I'm in the bathroom. Izzy was busy in the cafe downstairs and I hadn't seen Finn since the previous evening, when he'd gone out to visit his mum. I'd once asked him if she ever wondered where he disappeared off to for days on end. "She's used to my ways," he'd said, and that had been the end of the conversation. Mostly because he'd spotted an unwitting pigeon landing on the living room windowsill and had barrelled into the glass before I'd had chance to stop him. "Sorry," he'd said sheepishly from his prone position on the floor, "been mostly cat recently. I sometimes forget which body I'm in." I cracked open the tiny bathroom window and peered out. No sign of Finn's van, so he must have gone straight to work from his mum's place. Rachel and Alan were sitting at the old and cracked patio table they'd installed at the back of my scrubby car park. I was relieved to see that Rachel wasn't drinking anything for once. She liked to sit outside with Alan and have a glass of fresh rat blood in the evening, when the weather was fine. Alan doesn't partake on account of how he's a ghost, but he likes to see his girl happy. Me, I'd rather not watch my neighbour sipping warm haemoglobin, especially as the viscosity means it sticks to her teeth. I spotted Grimm curled up underneath the table. He's usually the provider of Rachel's liquid refreshment—he gets the fun of the chase, she gets a glass of something warm and sticky. Just as I was ducking back inside the bathroom, Alan looked up and saw me.

"A'right, girl?" he called up. "How're you doin'?" Rachel glanced up at the window and smiled nervously. I gave her a little wave.

"I'm getting in the bath," I said. "And I'd really appreciate it if I wasn't disturbed."

"No worries," said Alan. "We'll look out for you. Won't we, princess?" Rachel would have blushed, but she lost that ability along with her pulse. Instead, she lifted her hand to wave back. In it, she held a travel cup with a straw. The straw looked pinkish, and I didn't think it was from the colour of the plastic. Sighing, I closed the window. Why couldn't anything in my life be normal?

"Why can't anything in my life be normal?" I repeated, out loud this time. I was lying under the bathwater with my eyes open, looking up at the ripples on the surface. Talking underwater amuses me more than it probably should, mostly because it makes my voice sound weirdly robotic. I sighed and watched the bubbles rise to the surface. Baths can be quite the zen experience when you don't have to breathe. Unfortunately, I gulped in my panic and ended up coughing water all over the place, all whilst feeling blindly around for something to dry my eyes. "Here you go," said the voice. A clean, dry flannel was placed in my hand, and I dried my face before glaring at the person currently sitting on the lowered toilet seat.

"What the fuck are you doing in here?" I asked.

"Nice to see you too, dear," said Gran.

"I am in the fucking bath!" I yelped. "Couldn't you wait til I was sitting having a cuppa? Pop up when I'm dozing on the sofa? Or maybe —just fucking maybe—you could actually give me some fucking warning so I can put some sodding clothes on before I'm confronted with dear old granny sitting on the lav?" I stood up to reach for my towel, then immediately sat down again and settled for glaring instead.

"Here you go, love." Gran's eyes twinkled as she passed me a towel from the rack on the back of the door.

"What's happened?" I said, as I clambered out of the tub whilst carefully holding the towel in front of me.

"Why does something need to have happened for me to visit my granddaughter?" Gran said. "Can I not just pop in for a quick visit when I'm in the area?"

"You are a fucking ghost, Gran," I said, wrapping the towel tightly around myself and reaching for the bathroom door. "You are in all areas at once. Or at least," I gave it some thought, "presumably whichever area you want to be in at any given time. I keep meaning to ask Kitty about it. Oh god," I turned back to look at her, "Kitty is going to lose her shit if you're here when she gets back."

"Off with her fancy-man again, is she?" sniffed Gran. "It's a wonder you remember what she looks like, she's away that often."

"What's it to you what Kitty gets up to?" I asked. "And how would you know how often she's away? Have you been spying on me?" Gran had helped me sort out the mess with the time slips, and I would always be grateful to her for that. But she also winds her younger sister Kitty up to insane levels of hysteria, and it's me who's left to pick up the broken crockery. Which is why I hadn't been particularly sad when Gran had disappeared again. She hadn't told me where she was going, other than to potentially visit long-lost relatives. I was curious, but hadn't asked for details. I still wore the ring she'd given me, though. The gold band with its glittering amethysts had sat firmly on my finger ever since. But now Gran was back, sitting in my bathroom and chatting away as though we did this all the time. Which we kind of did. The first time Gran had reappeared in my life had also involved her materialising in the bathroom when I was attempting to soak away the stresses of the spooky lifestyle. The concept of personal space has never overly bothered the O'Reilly clan.

"Just making assumptions," said Gran. "Bet I'm not wrong, though."

"I'm going to my bedroom to put some clothes on," I said, refusing to bite. "I'll tell you when it's okay to come in."

"Okey dokey, dear," she said amiably, making herself comfortable on the loo seat. I'd always found it weird how Gran's ghost seemed more solid than Kitty's, despite her reappearing more recently. Perhaps it was because she hadn't been dead as long. Although Kitty had died in the sixties, her older sister had managed to hang on until I was well into my teens. "I'll just wait here."

"Out with it, then," I said. We were in the living room. I'd got myself dry and dressed in record time, hoping Gran could be gone again before anyone else came home. It was rare for me to have the flat to myself, and I was having to try very hard not to resent Gran for choosing this particular moment to reappear. "And how did you know I was home alone?"

"I didn't," said Gran. "If anyone had been here and had a problem with me, I'd have dealt with it." She sniffed the air. "That cat's still around, then?"

"How can you smell Finn?" I frowned. "You're a ghost!"

"How observant of you," said Gran. "I can see you, can't I? And clearly I can hear you, because we wouldn't be able to hold a conversation otherwise." It hadn't actually occurred to me that ghosts must still have some of their senses. I guess it's difficult to haunt people if you can't hear their terrified screams. But a sense of smell seemed unlikely. Even to me, the living dead girl.

"So," I tried again, "what brings you back to my neck of the woods?"

"Just checking in on my favourite granddaughter," said Gran.

"I'm your only granddaughter."

"Same difference," Gran shrugged. "If you really want to know, things seemed...different, somehow. Something in the air. Is there something going on, Lilith?"

"You mean other than me being dragged across to Birkenhead by a bunch of would-be occultists and the fate of the entire underworld apparently being in my hands? I dunno, Gran," I shrugged, "seems like a pretty normal week to me."

"What happened to that man who thinks you should be in love with him?"

"Which one?" I said. "There's at least two." And possibly a third, but I didn't say that out loud. Sean Hannerty—'Sean Hannerty, the famous crime writer', no less—was still trying his best to persuade me that human-revenant relationships weren't as doomed as I insisted they were. Considering he'd nearly died on at least two separate occasions purely because we were in the same vicinity, you'd think he'd have learned to stay well away by now. Mind you, I couldn't really blame him. Hanging around with me had given him the source material for a new paranormal fantasy series that his agent had high hopes of translating into a Netflix deal. Should just film my day-to-day life, I thought. They wouldn't even need to budget for the CGI.

You'd have to make Aiden sign an agreement promising that none of his underlings would bite the film crew, said the city in my head. ***And I'm not sure the Williamson Tunnels volunteer group would be happy to see their beloved excavations on television, complete with local madwoman bouncing around in them.***

Joe's in the bits they don't know about, I said. *They probably wouldn't even recognise it as the same place.*

We think you doubt their ability to identify underground Victorian brickwork, it said. ***Anyway, what's your grandmother doing here? We thought she'd disappeared for good.***

Hoped, you mean.

Same difference. I practically heard it shrug as I gazed over to where Gran was sitting in the armchair, watching me with interested eyes.

"I don't currently have any love life to speak of," I said out loud. "If that's what you're asking."

"I was thinking more about what danger you might be in," said Gran. "If you don't have a man around to keep an eye out for you. What about the one from up north? He seemed very keen."

"Oh yeah," I snorted. "Keen enough to think that trapping me with him in a room outside of time and space was a way to my heart. This isn't the nineteen-forties, Gran! Women can keep themselves safe these days."

"Oh yes?" she said politely. "And how has that been working out for you so far, Lilith O'Reilly?" She sniffed. "Seems to me you're getting a bit big for your boots, my girl."

"That's enough," I said, getting to my feet. "I love you dearly, Gran, but I will not tolerate you appearing without warning in my home—in my bathroom, for fuck's sake—just so you can criticise my life choices. Death choices," I corrected myself. "Whatever. I think you need to go. Let me know where you're staying and I'll come visit you sometime."

"I'm a ghost, Lilith," said Gran, getting to her feet, "I don't 'stay' places. I just appear when I'm needed and disappear when I'm not."

"And now it's time to disappear," I said firmly. "Come back when you can accept that maybe I neither need nor want a man in my life. And nor," I went on, fixing her with a sharp gaze, "do I need my dead relatives telling me what I'm doing wrong."

"Well, if you want to be like that," said Gran huffily. "I guess I'll be—"

"Lil!" called Kitty from the kitchen. "Can we talk?" I leapt up off the sofa in a panic. There wasn't enough crockery left to risk another family spat. "Who are you talking to in there?" I whipped round, hoping to persuade Gran to disappear before Kitty saw her, but she'd already gone.

"Myself," I said, flopping back down on the sofa. I was sure all this stress couldn't be good for my heart, dead or not. "It's the only way to have a sensible conversation around here."

"Oh Lil, you're so funny," said Kitty, wafting in from the kitchen. And yes, 'wafting' is absolutely the correct word in this context, thank you very much. I looked it up one day after Izzy objected to my usage. According to Merriam-Webster, it means 'go lightly by' or 'as if by the impulse of wind', and if that doesn't describe Kitty's ghostly floating to a T, I don't know what does. Izzy obviously found the idea of being 'impulsed by wind' highly amusing and spent the next half hour pondering whether ghosts ever farted, but that sort of thing's pretty normal for Iz. Considering how delicate she looks, the woman is ninety-per-cent smut and terrible jokes.

"Can you smell cats in here?" I asked her.

"I can't smell anything," said Kitty, looking puzzled. "Why?"

"No reason," I said. "Just wondering, is all. Finn spends so much time sleeping on the furniture, I just thought maybe I wouldn't notice if it whiffed a bit."

"I think even Finn would draw the line at peeing on the furniture," said Kitty. She stood in the middle of the room and gazed down at me.

"Out with it, then," I said.

"Out with what?"

"Kitty," I sighed, "you're about as good at keeping secrets as I am at cooking Heston Blumenthal recipes. Also," I eyed her beadily, "you're hovering above the carpet and you have a worried expression on your face. What's happened now?"

"Well," said Kitty, perching on the side of the armchair, "you know Jonny's family used to own that big place just outside Whittington?" I nodded. She meant Halston Hall. Shropshire seat of the Myttons, it had been in the family for generations, until Jonny had done his level best to bankrupt both himself and anyone who might later inherit from him. They'd somehow clung onto it for a decade or so after his death, but eventually gave into the inevitable. The estate had been broken up in the mid-eighteen-hundreds, but the Hall is still a family home—if you can describe a massive Grade-I listed mansion set in six hundred acres of land a 'family home'. These days the upkeep is funded, like so many old buildings, by it being rented out for events and film shoots. "What if I told you," Kitty went on, "there used to be hidden treasure there?"

"What sort of treasure?" I asked. "And didn't you just say it used to be there? Which implies it isn't anymore."

"That's because it went missing," she said.

"Well, that's hardly surprising," I said. "If there'd been any hidden treasure in Jonny's old stomping grounds, I'd imagine his family used it to help pay off the debts he left them with."

"No need to bring up people's pasts," said Kitty with a frown. "You wouldn't like it if people kept going on about things you'd done in your youth."

"Kitty," I said patiently, "the worst I ever did was drink too much cheap wine and throw up down the back of the seats in the Pilgrim. And it was only the once." Unfortunately, I did it whilst on a date, and the poor unfortunate soul I was with never asked for a second meeting. His name had been Caleb. He had dyed black hair and fancied himself as a musician. It was coming back to me now. Everything comes back to me if I give it time. "And that's not quite the same as drinking oneself into penury and dying in a debtor's prison, is it?"

"Well Jonny's not dead," scowled Kitty, "as well you know. Anyway, that was a very long time ago. Things are different now."

"You're taking this the wrong way," I said. "I like Jonny, you know I do. I was just pointing out that treasure being hidden there in the past is not as interesting as treasure absolutely, definitely being hidden there now."

"Thing is, Lil," she worried at the hem of her pale green shift dress, "I think there's more to it than that. Jonny's always talked about there being secrets on the estate. He says his papa told him the family was the guardians of the true faith." I tried my best to ignore the prickle that was crawling slowly up the back of my neck.

"And your point is?" I said. "What's this got to do with any of us?"

"The point," she said, "is that I think Eadric had something to do with it going missing." The prickles were increasing in intensity now. Fairly soon I was going to be twitching like my mum used to when she stuck those weird slimming pads to her stomach and gave herself electric shocks.

"Eh?" I stared at her in genuine bemusement. "What on earth makes you think that Eadric—of all people—might be connected to the disappearance of Jonny's family fortune?"

"Well," she looked embarrassed, "I might have overheard him on the phone. The other day. And I was down in Shrewsbury with Jonny yesterday and we were talking about Whittington—oh," she smiled, "I forgot to tell you! I'm remembering things again. That's why we were talking about the castle—Jonny and I had a picnic there once."

"There's lovely for you."

"It was," she agreed. "Anyway, we were talking about the castle, like I said. And I suddenly remembered Jonny's old stories about the missing treasure. So I asked him if he'd ever found out what happened to it, and he said no."

"Okay," I said slowly. "So far, so completely not following this at all."

"Well, I remembered what Eadric had said on the phone," she said. "I didn't really think about it at the time, especially as he didn't know I was watching him."

"Hang on," I frowned, "so now you're telling me you were spying on Eadric? What the fuck, Kitty?"

"I was not spying," she said indignantly. "I was here in the kitchen!"

"So where was Eadric?" I asked, as confused as I'd ever been. "And more to the point, where was I when all this was going on?"

"It was the other day," she said, "when you were out looking for Finn." I knew exactly when she meant. Finn had gone walkabout in cat form and left his mobile phone switched on in my kitchen. I'd got sick of answering calls for his roofing business and went out to give him a good talking to and/or a kick up his furry backside, depending which version of him was unfortunate enough to get caught.

"Eadric was here?" Kitty nodded again. "What the fuck did he want? And why didn't you tell me?"

"Should I have?" she pulled an apologetic face. "I didn't think much of it at the time, I just assumed he'd tell you himself when he saw you. He'd popped in to see how the decorators were getting on, I think. But they'd gone off for a tea break. When he realised you weren't here either, he muttered something about no one being reliable anymore. Then his phone rang, and he stood on the fire escape to take the call."

"And you just casually listened through the wall?"

"Well, he hadn't noticed me," she said, "so I thought I'd just stay out of his way." Kitty had always been shy around Eadric. She'd once said it was because he was so old, and hadn't understood why I laughed.

"Who was he talking to on the phone?"

"I don't know," said Kitty. "I could only hear his side of the conversation. Something about him being sure it was safe and not to worry. Then," she broke off, looking thoughtful.

"Then what?"

Kitty pulled a face. "Then he said, did they think he was stupid. And then," she paused. "And then he said 'she won't find it, we both know that. Even if it comes looking for her.'"

"If what comes looking for who?"

Kitty appeared to take a deep breath, which seemed somewhat unnecessary for someone who'd been dead since nineteen-sixty-five.

You breathe plenty for someone who doesn't need to, said the city. ***Glass houses, and all that.*** Christ, it was like being a teenager trying to have a sneaky cigarette round the back of the bike sheds, only to be caught by the headteacher's CCTV. Never unmonitored, never alone.

We close our eyes when you're in the bath, said the city, ***if that helps***.

Shut up, I snapped silently. *If I wanted to be judged all the time, I'd have let Gran stay.*

"If whatever it is comes looking for you," said Kitty. She spoke in a rush, as if hoping to get it over with as quick as possible. "He said that if you got hold of it, 'only the gods knew what might happen.'"

"He's hiding something from me, isn't he?"

"Literally," said the ghost of my great-aunt.

"Then," I said, standing up, "that's all the more reason for me to find it. I'm going to need to speak to Jonny."

Fishy Business

"Wait there," said Kitty, "I'll be right back." I paced up and down my small kitchen while I waited, seething quietly. Eadric bloody Silverton was going to have a lot of explaining to do when I got hold of him. Every time I thought I was finally getting to grips with the afterlife, something happened to make me realise just how little I really knew. Call me naïve, but I'd assumed that my begrudging acceptance of the role of presumptive leader of the underworld meant I finally knew all the secrets. How the hell could Eadric expect me to rule the sodding place when he was still hiding things from me?

Technically, said the city, ***it's not a place. More a state of mind***.

You know what I meant, I snapped back. *Stop being so bloody obtuse*.

The inevitable smart-ass response was stopped in its tracks by Kitty reappearing. A couple of seconds later, Jonny materialised next to her. "Where the fuck did you come from?" I asked him.

"It's Kitty's new trick," Jonny said, indulgently. "She likes to pick me up and drop me in random places."

"Could you do that with me?" I asked, turning to her. "Cos that would come in handy, I don't mind telling you." Was that how the Birkenhead demon hunters had got me over the water? Some kind of spooky teleportation? I doubted it. Derek came across as an old-school geek—more black-painted bedrooms and Aleister Crowley quotes, than a modern-day Captain Kirk.

"I don't think so," said Kitty apologetically. "I tried it with Finn the other day—he was late for work and asked if I could give him a lift. But however much I concentrated, all I could do was make him slightly transparent. He said it gave him a headache and ended up cancelling his jobs for the day."

"So what makes ol' lord of the manor here any different?" I nodded at Jonny. "And do not tell me you have a cosmic connection, or I will be forced to throttle the pair of you with one of his lordship's silk cravats."

"We don't know," said Jonny, "and that's the truth. But Kitty's... abilities," he looked to her for confirmation, and she nodded, "have definitely been getting stronger recently."

"Much stronger," she agreed happily, doing a twirl.

"I'm not sure I'm entirely happy with the current state of affairs," Jonny went on. "We don't know where this new power's coming from, and I'd hate anything to happen to my Kitty-bell."

"Bleurgh," I made vomiting noises for emphasis. "You're the reason she's dead in the bloody first place!"

"Lilith!" Kitty's voice was sharp, to match the expression she was pulling. "We agreed not to talk about that."

"That's in the past," said Jonny, patting Kitty's arm reassuringly. "And we're looking to the future."

"You're looking at an eternity in a psych ward for traumatised immortals," I informed him, "if you ever harm a hair on Kitty's head again." Just then, Grimm bounced in through the kitchen window. He dropped onto the floor and sat watching us with an annoyingly human-like smile on his face. "And you can butt out," I told him.

"What on earth's the matter with you?" Kitty frowned. "It's not like you to pick on poor Grimmykins. Here, pusscat," she hunched down and held a hand out to him, "come to mummy, baby." I glared at the cat as he slowly padded forward into my aunt's ghostly arms. She scooped him up and kissed the top of his head before turning back to me. "Honestly, Lil," she said, "I don't know what's got into you today."

"I've been spending too much time with idiots," I said, stalking into the living room and flopping onto the sofa. Kitty didn't bother responding. She waited for Jonny to follow me in and sit in the armchair before perching herself on his lap. God, their constant public displays of affection made me want to puke. As if the rest of society really needed to have their self-satisfied happiness rubbed in their faces.

Jealous? murmured the city. ***When's the last time you played coochie-coo with another human being?***

Shut the fuck up, I hissed silently, *or I will get Mapp to suck my mind right out of my head and you'll be a homeless little city with no one to annoy.*

We'd find someone, it replied. ***Maybe we'd take over the cat***. I looked at Grimm splayed backwards in Kitty's arms and thought it would take more than the sentient ghosts of an entire city to get that devious scrote under any sort of control. ***Or Isobel.***

"Oh no you fucking won't!" The words came out before I could stop myself. I clapped my hand over my mouth and looked across to where Kitty, Jonny and Grimm were all staring at me.

"What is that delightful companion of yours suggesting now?" asked Grimm.

"It's telling me that talking cats should probably be taken to the vet for a thorough check-up," I snapped. "See if they're not just losing the plot."

"I think it's you who's losing the plot, Lil," said Kitty. "Are you sure you're okay?"

"Yes," I sighed, "I'm fine. For a certain variable of 'fine', obviously. Jonny," I sat up and looked him in the eye, "tell me about your family's missing treasure."

~

"I'm not sure Papa was being entirely truthful, though," said Jonny. He'd given me a potted history of the Mytton family, and most of it had been depressingly similar to every other wealthy family history. Family becomes rich through marriage and inheritance, starts collecting land, gets even richer by doing not very much at all. So far, so sociologically annoying. In Jonny's case, however, the family history included dalliances with the Knights Templar, and all the religious and historical weight that conveyed.

"Let me get this straight," I said slowly. "You're telling me your father believed that the Grail—the actual, honest-to-literal-God Holy Grail—was brought to Britain in the sixth century? And they just stashed it away in Shropshire?"

"That's about the sum of it." Jonny nodded. "As I said, I'm not convinced of the veracity of his claims." He gave a rueful smile. "There was definitely treasure of some sort," he went on. "Mama used to tell me stories about it. But it was long gone by the time I took over."

"And if it hadn't been," I muttered to myself, "it would have rapidly disappeared when you got hold of it anyway. So," I said, ignoring Kitty's indignant expression, "what made your pops think the root of all religious mania might have been hidden somewhere in the family vaults?"

"Well," said Jonny, "there are the stories, of course. Legends, all about the Grail and its magical properties. And the Templars were definitely protecting something."

"Their stashes of stolen wealth, I'd imagine."

"Why else go to all that trouble?" he went on, ignoring me. "Something important was there. And if it wasn't the Grail, then what?"

"Okay," I sighed. "Say we accept the Grail is real. Fucksake. Why," I said, "does this bloody country always think it's in charge of everything?"

"I don't follow," said Jonny. "What does the country itself have to do with the Grail?"

"Oh, come on," I said. "You've just told me yourself that the Knights fucking Templar set up shop on your estate and that the Holy Grail just happens to be tucked away somewhere, but no one knows where. And you expect me to believe it's nothing to do with Britain itself? This country is so fucking arrogant." I sighed. "Always thinking it's better than everywhere else, even the supposed bloody Holy Lands. You realise the Grail is literally a fairy story?"

"But it's a real thing," started Jonny. "It's a symbol—"

"I don't care what it's symbolic of," I said. "It was made up in the twelfth century. And what it actually is changes depending on who's telling the story. Sometimes it's a cup. Or a tray, or a book. It could be a three-foot platypus called Gerald, for all I fucking know. Do you believe in the Bible, Jonny?" He thought about it for a long minute, then finally nodded. "Then I'm happy for you," I said. "It must be lovely having the reassurance that there's something else after all this." I gestured around the room. "After an eternity of talking to ghosts and trying to keep tabs on idiot vampires and having bloody were-cats vomiting on my sodding bloody sofa," I said, "it would honestly be refreshing to discover the Elysian Fields were real, and I was free to spend another bloody eternity just staring at clouds. What I'm saying, Jonny," I leaned forward for emphasis, "is that I do not believe in organised religion. Not yours, not the Templar's, not anyone's. I just believe in what I can see in front of my own dead eyes. Even if," I frowned at the cat, who was chewing his own feet, "what I see in front of my own poor eyes is mostly scenes of absolute madness."

"I don't think it would have mattered which country it got taken to," said Jonny. "The belief would have travelled with it."

"Then it would have been better off going to Scandinavia," I said. "They really know how to write an ancient belief system. Maybe the Vikings could have caught Christianity. Might have saved a lot of bloodshed."

"They did," said Grimm, from where he was lounging on Kitty's lap. "Catch Christianity, I mean." Jonny and I both stared at Grimm. Kitty stared back at me and Jonny.

"You can hear him," I said to Jonny. "You can bloody well hear him!"

"Hear who?" asked Kitty.

I looked from her to Jonny and back again. "You didn't hear anything?" Kitty shook her head, looking confused. "Jonny did, though." Jonny was staring silently at Grimm, a dumbstruck expression on his face. "Didn't you?"

"Would somebody like to tell me what's going on?" Kitty rose upwards suddenly, dumping Grimm onto the floor. She always loses control when she's upset. If she gets really wound up, she can be off through the ceiling before you know it. I once spent an entire evening watching television whilst trying to ignore the bare feet dangling through the living room light fitting, all because I'd disagreed with her suggested answers for Only Connect.

"Your beloved Grimmy-wimmy-baby-cakes is secretly a talking cat," I said.

"He is not!" Kitty stared down at Grimm in horrified fascination.

"Oh, he is," I said. "A walking, talking, listening cat." Grimm was gazing implacably up at me with enormous amber eyes. "Kept that from you, didn't he?"

"But, but," Kitty's face scrunched up, "I've told him everything!"

"Aha!" I said in response to Jonny's worried expression. "You've clearly got no secrets round here, Jonny-boy! As for you," I poked a finger at the cat, "perhaps you'd like to apologise to Aunt Kitty?"

"She already told you, Lilith," said Grimm. "She can't hear me."

"Why not?" I asked. "If me and the squire here can hear you, why can't Kitty?"

"She's a ghost."

"So?" I said. "Are you telling me there's such a thing as selective cat audio?"

"No idea," he shrugged. "Different creatures hear things at different frequencies, perhaps? And what you're forgetting," he glanced upwards to where Kitty was now hovering several feet above the floor, "is that Kitty is actually dead. Toast. Brown bread." I frowned at him, then turned to Jonny.

"Did you know already?"

"No," he said, "but I've met talking cats before. There used to be a big ginger tom living behind my place in Shrewsbury. I had some really interesting chats with him. I'm sorry, Kitty-cat," this was to the soles of Kitty's feet, which were just above his head, "please don't be upset. Owwww!" A ghostly heel had connected sharply with his face, and by the expression on Jonny's face, it was solid enough to hurt. Kitty disappeared silently up through the ceiling, leaving me with her confused boyfriend and an overly smug cat.

"She'll calm down," said Grimm. "She always does." Jonny stared worriedly up at the ceiling, which was now empty of everything except stripped plaster and a solitary hanging lightbulb.

"Never mind Kitty," I sighed. "Who else knows about the Grail?"

"Most don't know anything concrete," said Grimm, "just the legends. But plenty suspect it might be real. And if it's about to make its presence known again, I'm thinking there's enough of those who know for life to become very difficult indeed."

"Does Eadric know?" I asked, thinking of the conversation Kitty had overheard.

"He's clearly more aware than most," said Grimm, nodding. Which is a really fucking weird thing to see your cat do, in case you were wondering. "But whatever's stirring, he's clearly yet to do anything about it." Which sounded like a very Eadric reaction. Not that he's risk averse; it's more that he works to the mantra 'if it ain't broke, don't fix it'. Although he'd word it more like 'if nothing is untoward, change nothing'. To be fair, that approach had worked for him for almost a full millennium, so he might be forgiven for thinking it was the sensible way forward. It was only since the Scouse netherworld—and with it, the rest of the country—had begun ramping up the weirdness that a proactive approach might have been more appropriate.

"What about Ivo?"

"I suspect so," said the cat. "Why else," he shrugged, "would he be showing such interest in someone like yourself?"

"Cheers," I scowled. "Thanks for the vote of confidence. And if Ivo knows, we can assume Liam does as well." Nod. Well, that was just brilliant. My sworn enemy and my ex-lover knew the legends were real, and neither had bothered to mention it. It was lucky I wasn't speaking to either of them, or I'd have been forced to have Sharp Words. "Mapp and the Renshaw Street mob?" Gaultier Mapp is one of my very favourite things about being undead, and not just because he's the most deliciously naughty man I know.

"Just Gaultier," said Grimm, "as far as I am currently aware. Joseph Williamson doesn't know. I'm confident about that. The impression I get is that they think he's a bit, erm," he frowned. He actually fucking frowned. "Flaky? A sardine short of a full catch, you might say. At least, Gaultier seemed relieved that he didn't know. Said he couldn't trust Williamson not to get his vampires to steal it out of pure curiosity."

"Hang on," I said. "You seem to know what everyone thinks about this. Is the Grail like some weird cousin everyone acknowledges but mostly tries to ignore? And if so, why hasn't anyone told me about it?"

"This is no open secret, Lilith. I was merely informed of their conversations by an acquaintance who is in close contact with Silverton Properties."

"Who was that?"

"He doesn't have a name," said Grimm. "He lives in the building's basement and wanders where he pleases. It can be useful."

"Is he," I said slowly, "by any chance a cat?"

"Yes, Lilith," said Grimm, "he's a cat. Is that a problem?" He gave me a beady-eyed look that reminded me very much of Salem, the cat from Sabrina the Teenage Witch. You know those GIFs that have Salem casually filing his claws? I was pretty sure Grimm would have very much liked to be in possession of a nail file at that precise moment. Just for the look of the thing, you understand. "As for the rest of them," he went on, "Gaultier Mapp actually told me about it himself, before I got word from my contact down at the waterfront. Can you believe that?" He shook his head in despair. I could totally believe that, as it happened. Mapp bloody loved a gossip. "He came to visit you one day and happened to walk past me on the outside stairs. Bent down to pet me and muttered about things being hard enough without the 'Holy blessed Grail' complicating matters. As for the rest of them," he sighed, "news travels. People ignore cats, Lilith. Can you believe that?" I could very much believe it, although I wasn't going to admit as much to Grimm. After all, who takes any notice of a cat? Cats are everywhere—on the streets, in people's houses, strolling along the rooftops. No one ever thinks 'Ooh, better not talk about secrets when there's a cat in the room', on account of how cats aren't listening. But I was beginning to realise that the cats were indeed listening. And they'd clearly been doing so for a very long time.

"How do you know about Ivo?" I just couldn't help myself.

"News travels," he shrugged. "Especially now the big cats are coming back. Fast paws and loose lips, you know how it goes."

"I don't, actually," I said. "Not had much previous experience with the social lives of were-cats."

"I'm sure you'll figure them out eventually," said Grimm.

"But they're all hunting it down?"

"They know it exists," said Grimm. "What they don't know is where it is. Or, I suspect," he gave me a thoughtful look, "what good it might do them to find it."

"Why," I frowned, the most obvious question in the world only just occurring to me, "do they even want it? Surely it's a symbol of Christianity? Which, if you don't mind me saying, doesn't generally approve of undead creatures of the night."

"Christians consider the Grail a symbol of their religion," said Grimm, "because the history books are wrong. Oh, they had their own grail, back in the day. But it wasn't this Grail. The stories got muddled and mixed up and now everyone thinks the one tiny little cup is the epicentre of their belief system. Or something like that." He gave a very feline shrug. "I must have missed theology class." He tilted his head to look at me closely. "Have you ever wondered how you people came to exist?"

"You people?" I said. "What the fuck's that supposed to mean?"

"It may have escaped your notice," said Grimm, "but I am a cat. A talking cat, Lilith. So I'm sorry if my terminology is not entirely to your liking." He narrowed his eyes at me the same way he looked when he thought I was being tardy with the sardine can. "And you know exactly what I meant, so you can save your breath."

"Don't have any breath to save," I muttered.

"Again," said the cat, "you knew what I meant. And you haven't answered my question." His mouth never moved except to change expression, yet he really was talking to me. Sitting there on the rug in front of me and actually bloody talking. Maybe I really was finally going utterly mad. It was probably well overdue. I looked at Jonny, who was listening with interest but not showing any signs of incipient madness. Mind you, this is the man who loved his animals so much that he used to let his favourite horse sleep on the rug by his fireplace, so he probably wasn't the best barometer of sanity. "Okay, so I'll tell you," said Grimm, clearly losing patience. "You are still human, yes?"

"Of course I am!"

"No need to get testy," he said, blinking at me with annoying casualness. "So you're human, just on an epic scale."

"Well, I'm glad to hear at least one person thinks I'm epic," I shrugged. "It's about time."

"I'm not a person," said Grimm, "I'm a cat. And I meant it literally. Those like you have lifetimes measured in epochs, rather than decades. Yes?"

"Yes," I grumbled. "And fucking tedious it's going to be, an' all."

"You weren't always the odd ones out," said Grimm. "There was a time when your long lives were the norm. As were your abilities to run and jump and do a lot of other things that are mostly stupid, if you don't mind me saying."

"Well, you've already said it now," I pointed out. "So it doesn't really matter whether I mind or not."

"I have a theory," said Grimm. "If you're interested."

"Of course I'm bloody interested," I said. "You're a talking cat who apparently knows the truth about the Holy Grail. I don't know many people who wouldn't be interested." And a lot of them would be most interested in putting him in a science lab and running some very invasive tests, but I kept that bit to myself. "Out with it then," I said. "Tell me exactly what it is we're dealing with."

"We are not dealing with anything," said Grimm. "This is a You problem. It's nothing to do with us cats."

"Ooooh," interrupted Kitty, dropping back through the ceiling without warning. "Your chap up on the roof is so lovely, Lil!" She smiled at me. "We've had a good chat, I feel so much better now." She perched on Jonny's lap as though nothing had happened, and he looked so relieved that I was almost embarrassed for him.

"He can speak?" I raised an eyebrow. "I was under the impression he only communicates in grumpy hisses."

"That's because you don't give him enough time," she said, a hint of reproach in her voice. She'd clearly been reading Izzy's old copies of Cosmo again. "Everyone has feelings. They just need to be allowed the space in which to express them." Yup, definitely Cosmo.

"Oh, he expresses his feelings alright," I said. "He mostly expresses just how much he resents being up on my bloody roof." I'd been trying to persuade Aiden to drop the 24/7 vampire roof guard thing, but he'd flatly refused to even consider it. It was too soon after losing Katja, he said. And far too dangerous, with Ivo potentially still on the prowl. He had a point. However much my pants region argued with my brain over the thorny topic of Ivo Laithlind, there was no getting away from the fact that the world's shittiest Viking had murdered Katja in cold blood. I mean, obviously her blood was already cold on account of her being a vampire, but my point still stands. He'd killed my friend in his attempt to get to me. And he'd only wanted to get to me in order to then get to the crown, which he somehow saw as being symbolic of power over, well, pretty much everything. Everything in this country, at least. I wasn't sure how the Americas would feel about being once again ruled by someone over on the colonial side of the pond, and I had no plans to find out. I turned back to Grimm and glared silently until he stopped licking his unmentionables for long enough to register my existence. "You don't think the resurgence of were-cats in the north-western area is anything to do with the Grail, then?" I asked. News reports about big cats being spotted in the British countryside were becoming a regular part of local news reports, and I wasn't happy about it.

"How am I supposed to know?" said Grimm, twitching his shoulders in what was clearly a shrug. "I'm just a cat." I opened my mouth to say something that would definitely have been very sharp and witty had I actually managed to speak, but he cut me off. "I must get on," he said, stretching out and springing his claws with evident satisfaction. "Business meeting at Pier Head. You know how it is."

"I don't know how it is, as it happens," I said to the back of his head, as he jumped lightly off the arm of the sofa and stalked towards the door. "What sort of business?"

"Fishy business," said Grimm. He paused and turned to look at me. "Daisy has acquired an otter. We cats have come to an arrangement with him."

"Daisy's got a pet otter?"

Grimm nodded, and I swore to myself that I would never, ever get used to a sentient nodding cat. "She's training him to go hunting and bring the catch back to her," he said. "That way she gets to sunbathe with her friends on the buoys out in the bay and still have a nice fish supper when she's done."

"Why would it do that?" I asked. "Surely otters would want to keep their catch for themselves?"

"The impression I get," said Grimm, "is that's it a choice between sharing a fish or losing a flipper. Personally," he raised a paw to straighten his ear, "I'd give up a limb before I bowed down to anyone."

"I don't doubt it," I said. "So what's your...arrangement? With this friend of Daisy's?"

"He shares a portion of his catch with us cats," he said, "and in return we protect the holt during kit season. Humans are far less likely to do something stupid when there's a risk of getting their faces ripped off by a hundred pounds of angry were-cat. Anyway," he went on, before I could ask how many humans had faced off with a shape-shifting feline, "I must be off. Apparently Gary's got a nice bit of eel waiting for me." I couldn't help but notice that his accent occasionally veered off into Cockney and wondered where it came from. The rescue centre I'd got Grimm from hadn't known anything about his background. The girl in charge of the cattery section had told me he'd just been sitting on the doorstep one morning when the manager arrived to open up.

"Hang on," I said, "who's Gary? Oh fuck right off," I went on, realisation already dawning, "you're not telling me Daisy's pet attack otter is called *Gary*?"

"Everyone's entitled to reinvent themselves, Lilith," said Grimm, already heading out of the door. "You of all people should know that."

I Did Not Lobotomise That King, Actually

The next day was dawning bright and warm when I got up from my overnight meditation. I've been practicing enough that I can now lose a good eight hours to mindless nothingness, which I feel is an achievement of sorts. Okay, so I might not sleep like a normal human, but I can at least pretend. And after the first couple of times I'd lost my shit at fellow spooks who'd dropped in for a cuppa in the early hours 'because they were bored', people had learned to leave me alone until morning. Grimm was snoring on top of the duvet and didn't move, even when I clambered out of bed and started banging around getting dressed. The room smelled faintly of fish, so I opened a window whilst silently cursing the otter delivery service. Kitty and Jonny had gone back to Shrewsbury after we'd established that yes, weird shit was once again brewing, and no, I didn't know what to do about it. Kitty informed me brightly that she 'trusted whatever decision I made' and I hadn't the heart to tell her my only plan so far was to pretend nothing was happening. With that aim in mind, I settled in for a morning of choosing colours for the bathroom. The decorators Eadric had insisted on hiring had finished stripping the walls a few days earlier and were eager to move on to actual decor. I hadn't even wanted the bloody place doing up in the first place, but Eadric had forced my hand.

It was my penance, he'd said, for not accepting the 'suitably elegant and well-appointed' (his words) apartment he'd offered me in the Albert Dock. Apparently, he considered a flat above a shop to be an embarrassing location for one of his co-directors to live in. I'd pointed out I wasn't actually a director yet, so it didn't matter. My inability to keep my stupid bloody mouth shut was the reason I was currently avoiding the Liver Building, because Eadric had taken matters into his own hands and had the legal paperwork drawn up. I'd got away with it so far, but at some point in the not-too-distant future, I was going to have to sit down at the enormous desk in his office and sign my life away. That all I was actually signing up for was a ridiculously high monthly pay cheque for nothing more than existing didn't make it any easier. I wasn't used to having money, and I still wasn't sure I liked it very much. I made a coffee and had just sat down on the sofa to leaf through the pile of interior decor magazines that Missy had dropped off for me when there was a knock at the kitchen window. "Yo," said Izzy, coming in through the kitchen door before I'd even got to my feet, "wanna come play janitor for a bit?"

"Don't tell me," I sighed. "The dishwasher's acting up again." We'd always had issues with plumbing and electrics in Flora's. This was no doubt caused in part by the fact the entire place sat on top of tunnels that had been dug without a care for any pipework that happened to be in the vicinity. I'd have been well within my rights to demand financial contributions from Joe Williamson for the endless repair work, because it was his adventures underground that caused most of the problems. But Joe's been dead a couple hundred years now and the insurance company would probably ask questions if I demanded reparation from a dead man. And like I say, I'm not short of a bob or two these days. So I generally suck it up and get someone in to fix things—if I can't kick whatever it is into submission first.

"Yurp." Iz flopped down into the armchair opposite. Then she got up, removed a copy of House Beautiful from the seat, and sat back down. "Gawd," she said, looking at the cover, "money definitely doesn't buy taste, does it?" She waved the magazine at me so I could witness the full horror of the blandly beige house on its cover. "You decided what to do in here yet?"

"Pink and leopard print. Maybe some dark forest green," I shrugged. "Like I said from the start." Eadric had pulled a face when I'd excitedly shown him the wallpaper samples I'd been collecting, and asked if I wouldn't actually prefer something more classic. I'd pointed out that it was him who'd insisted on the refurb in the first place, and he should probably learn to be careful what he wished for. Nik had taken one look and asked when Joan Collins was moving in. "Who's looking after the shop?"

"Oh," said Izzy, looking distinctly shifty, "I was kicking the dishwasher, and Sean was in at the time. So he offered to look after the place while I nipped up here."

"Izzzzz!" I wailed. "We talked about this!" Sean already knew far too much about my ridiculous life and, to make it worse, had funnelled this knowledge into a new paranormal book series. His publishers hadn't been keen on this new direction originally, but it was now attracting worryingly enthusiastic interest from the streaming channels. Everyone was happy—except me. I'd have been more cross about it had he not split the royalties with me. As it was, I could probably have lived off my share of book profits alone. In fact, I was planning to do almost exactly that. What Eadric didn't yet know was that, if he was going to insist on paying me ridiculous money purely for being dead and unburied, I planned to divert the vast majority of it to charity. Not that I'd decided which charities should benefit as yet. I wasn't so altruistic that I didn't change my mind every time I thought about it, depending on who had annoyed and/or pleased me recently. A local cat rescue organisation had been top of the list for a while, but that depended entirely on how irritating Grimm and Finn were between now and whenever I actually signed the paperwork. Anyway, all that apart, Sean Hannerty has a crush on me and he doesn't care who knows it. But I refuse to do anything about it—despite once going on a date with him and knowing from personal experience that he is an excellent kisser—because I am way too clumsy and I would very much like not to kill him by accident. "Sean isn't allowed to help," I said. "I don't like feeling beholden to him"

"Oh, get over yourself," she said. "He's just being sweet."

"And now I owe him," I said.

"How?" Izzy asked. "It's me he was helping, not you."

"It's not you he's trying to seduce though, is it?"

"Seduce?" Izzy snorted. "He's just being nice, Lil. Remember what it's like to be nice to people?"

"I am nice to people, thank you very much." I glared at her. "Who said I wasn't?"

"No one," she said, getting to her feet. "I'm just saying that not everyone is like your ridiculous immortal suitors."

"It is not my fault the undead idiots are in love with me," I said. "Life would be a lot easier if they weren't. Anyway, I haven't seen either of them since Chester."

"That'll be because you lobotomised one and dropped a building on the other."

"I did not lobotomise Liam," I said. "I merely threw a stone at his head. And he got away without being spotted, so he can't have been hurt that badly."

"What about Ivo?" said Izzy. "An entire steam mill fell on him. No wonder he's been quiet."

"Well, he's not dead," I said. "I can tell you that much."

"How do you know? Ooh," she grinned, "do the two of you have a cosmic connection? True love pulling you towards each other, even through the falling rubble of an historic building?"

"They're already rebuilding it," I snapped, "so you can pack that in. It wasn't my fault it fell in the canal."

"Bella's been full of herself ever since," said Izzy. "Gleaming with pride up on that tower, so she is. I hear she threatened to give Bertie a kicking if he didn't stop whining."

"What's the matter with him now?" In theory, I'm friendly with both Liver birds, but everyone knows me and Bella are BFFs. Anyway, Nik generally looks after Bertie—he heads up to the eastern dome each evening and reads him a bedtime story, which is Bertie's daily reward for behaving himself and watching over the city like he's supposed to. Bella faces out onto the water, and I was sure that was a good part of the reason she had a much friendlier demeanour. Although Mapp said she once pecked a chunk of his hair out because she didn't like him putting feathers in his dreadlocks, so maybe it really is just me she's nice to.

"Nik's insisting on choosing their next book," she said. "Says he's fed up with witches and wants to do the Tiffany books for a change."

"Ooh," I said, "I like those. Maybe we could paint Bertie's face blue and teach him a Scottish accent."

"People would assume he's an Everton fan," said Izzy. "You can't do that to the poor bird. Anyway," she went on before I could say anything, "you didn't answer my question. How do you know Ivo's still alive? Not that he's actually alive, obviously. You know what I mean."

"He's as alive as I am," I said. Izzy just raised her eyebrows. "I don't know how I know," I sighed. "I just do. I'd know if he wasn't around anymore. I'd sense it, I think."

"Like a bad smell," said Izzy. "How romantic. Anyway, are you going to come kick this dishwasher or not?"

"There you go," I said, putting a cup of tea on the table in front of one of our regulars. "Nice waistcoat." I nodded towards the red and gold jacquard weave he was sporting. I thought his name was Bob, but couldn't be entirely sure. Bob apparently had an endless wardrobe of fancy waistcoats and I'd yet to see the same one twice. He nodded silent thanks and went back to reading the newspaper. I like customers best when they just crack on without bothering me.

"It's nice to see you down here for a change," said Sean, as I headed back behind the counter. "Hanging out with the normal folks."

"Got to slum it occasionally," I said. "Wouldn't want to be getting too big for my boots, like."

"As if that's ever going to happen to you," he said. "So, when are you going to let me take you out again?"

"There you go," I sighed, "always spoiling things." Sean looked unrepentant. "Don't you have work to do? I thought your agent was after the new book soon?"

"Already sent it off," said Sean smugly. "This one practically wrote itself."

"Helps that you just have to narrate Lil's actual life," said Izzy, wriggling past us with a tray of dirty mugs. "Bloody hell, Lil," she said, looking at the dishwasher, "you really told it this time, didn't you?"

"It didn't want to behave," I shrugged. "So I gave it a hoofing."

"I can see that," said Izzy, staring at the deep dent in its door. "I'm just wondering exactly how many hoofs one kitchen appliance can take."

"Finn's going to get someone in to fix the electrics," I said. "Hopefully everything will work better after that."

"You're trusting the feral roofer to find you an electrician?" said Izzy. "I'd have thought rat-catching would have been more his area of expertise."

"Oh, he's good at that as well," I said. "But he still works in the trade, don't forget. Got lots of handy mates. Apparently one of them knows about his, erm," I trailed off, remembering that I was standing within earshot of several customers.

"Less salubrious habits?" asked Izzy. "Oh, he's got plenty of those, alrighty."

"So?" I turned to Sean and pulled a confused face. "You haven't answered my question," he said. "When are you going to let me take you out again?" He was wearing an old Nirvana t-shirt over faded jeans and ancient trainers. Bronze-brown hair flopped into his eyes as he spoke, and he shook his head to get it out of the way. He reminded me of an eager spaniel, waiting loyally for its next orders.

"When you've invented a safety suit that stops me from accidentally injuring you," I said. "Then we can discuss it. No," I saw him open his mouth to argue, "it's not happening. Look, Sean," I went on, "I really am flattered. Honestly, I am. But no. Final answer."

"You'll change your mind," he said, flapping a cloth cheerily at me as he headed out from behind the counter to wipe down the tables. "Eventually."

"He's accepted Celebrity Bake Off, you know," said Izzy, coming to stand next to me. Because I'd stayed downstairs to help out, we didn't actually need him anymore, but he'd insisted on staying. "Apparently he's been practicing his macarons."

"Well, they're wasted on me," I said. "Maybe he'll impress someone from Love Island and they'll live happily ever after."

"I don't think they have the Love Island lot on Bake Off," mused Izzy. "They don't really look the cake sort."

"No one on the celebrity version is the cake sort," I pointed out. "They're there for comedy value, not their talents with a flan case."

"Sean doesn't look the comedy type," said Izzy. We both watched as he broke off from cleaning a table to talk to a customer. The woman was in her fifties at a guess, with elegantly coiffed grey hair and the sort of patterned jumpsuit that you just know cost a fortune from some upmarket online hippy store. She reached into her bag and pulled out a book, which she proffered to him.

"Hang on," I heard him say, "just need to find a pen. Got a pen, Lil?" he asked, turning to us. I picked one up from beside the till and held it out to him. "Thanks," he grinned, and turned back to the woman. Izzy and I watched as he opened the book and signed it before handing it back. The woman thanked him and left, looking noticeably flustered.

"Still got it," he said, coming back to the counter.

"Maybe she's single," I suggested. "She'd certainly appreciate you more than I clearly do."

"Aah," said Sean, "I know you don't really mean it."

"I really do bloody mean it."

"Children, children," said Izzy. "Can I leave you to it, Lil?" she asked. "Only I need to go sign paperwork for the flat. It wasn't supposed to be ready until tomorrow, but Eadric's just texted to let me know it's been finished early."

"Yeah," I said, "go on. It's nice being down here for a change."

Izzy looked from me to Sean, then back again. "Try not to fall out while I'm gone?" she asked, her voice doubtful. "It would be nice if the place was still standing when I got back."

"I'll do my best," I said, "but I can't promise anything. Oh, for fuck's sake!" A small group of people were standing outside Flora's and staring in through the front windows. This was clearly causing concern to the customers sitting nearest the glass, because they all turned to look at us. "Yes, yes," I told them, "I'll sort it." Izzy followed as I stomped out of the cafe and stalked towards the unwanted visitors. There were two young women in their twenties, and a man barely out of his teens. They were all dressed in various shades of black, and the man had ringed his eyes with badly drawn liner. Presumably this was the cadet branch of Goths Anonymous. "Can I help?" I asked. "Or are you just here to gawp?" To my horror, the nearest woman bobbed a curtsey. The bangles on her wrists jangled like wind chimes and she caught hold of them hurriedly.

"Sorry, er," she started, looking to her friends for help, "ma'am."

"We were told we'd find you here," said the man, "but we didn't believe them." I narrowed my eyes and held a finger up to silence the second woman, who was clearly about to say something equally stupid.

"No," I said firmly. "No, no, no. You can pack this shit in right now. You hear me?" A noise behind me made me turn, and I found Izzy struggling to stifle her laughter.

"I'll leave you to it, Lil," she said. And then to the group, "I'm sure your lady here will be pleased to see you another time." They looked at her blankly. "It's just that right now she's got a cafe to run." She turned and headed off down Harrington Street, but I could hear her snorting before she'd even got to the main road.

"Look," I said to my unexpected visitors, "this is very flattering, but I'm really not interested." A thought occurred to me. "Maybe go visit that bookshop," I said, "up on Renshaw Street. I hear the owner of that likes to be worshipped by strangers."

"It was mister Mapp who sent us here," said the second woman. "He didn't tell us you might actually be in Flora's, though."

"Where did he think I would be?" I asked, unable to stop myself. Never mind dishwashers, it was Gaultier Mapp who was next in line for a kicking. And I'd be swapping my Converse for DMs before I did it.

"In your apartment, of course," she said. "We weren't going to bother you, Li—ma'am."

"You can use my name," I said. "It doesn't wear out. Can I ask what you were planning to do?" This seemed to stump them. They gave each other blankly confused looks, before all turning back to me.

"We, ummm," started the man. "We were just going to, I dunno," he thought about it, "hang around? Maybe see if you needed help with anything. That sort of thing."

"Help with what?" I turned to check on Flora's and discovered we had an audience. The occupants of the window tables were all gazing out at us with interest, and Sean was standing behind them with an annoying grin on his face. I gave him a scowl on general principle and turned back to my immediate problem.

"Ruling the, erm," the young man tried, but trailed off. His female friends weren't so cowed down.

"Thing is," said the one with the bangles, "we want in. To the supernatural stuff. It's all very well Maya here pretending she can read Tarot cards," the second woman started and went to speak, but her friend ignored her, "but we all know it's not the real thing."

"And I am?"

"That's what they say." She bobbed another curtsey. "Ma'am." I'd had enough.

"No," I said again. "Absolutely the fuck not. Life's complicated enough without the Scouse wing of the Cure fan club trailing around behind me. Don't you have anything better to do?" I looked at each of them in turn. "Homework? Drinking cheap wine in the park? Anything other than annoying me?"

"He said you'd be like this," said Maya. "He said we should stay in the background and not let you know we were here. 'Just keep an eye on her from a distance'," she went on, "that's what he said. Make sure you're safe, without you knowing we're doing it."

"It's just that we didn't expect to see you down here," said the man. "In the cafe. Don't you have people to do that for you?"

"We can help," said Bangle Woman, "if you're short staffed? We don't need paying or anything."

"Actually," started Maya, but I was ahead of her.

"Gaultier—mister—Mapp told you all this?" I'd string him up by his own lace neckline, the absolute scrote. Presumably this was his idea of a joke. I was going to put live mice in his stockroom next time I was up Renshaw Street. Just see if I didn't.

"No, this was master Aiden," said Maya. "He was there as well. He said you might like the company, but would probably complain to start with."

"Too right I'm bloody complaining!" I was trying to remember how best to kill a vampire. Aiden might be the cleverest blood-sucker I knew, but I was pretty sure even he wasn't immune to decapitation. It was clearly time to sharpen my knives. "Who else knows about me?"

"Oh," shrugged Bangle Woman, "everyone, pretty much. They were talking about you up in the Swan the other day. Grenville here overheard them."

"Grenville?" I glared accusingly at the man. "Who the fuck's called Grenville?"

"Well, aah," he stuttered, "I am? My mum and dad are quite old, to be fair. In their fifties, at least. Maybe they thought it was fashionable." I thought of my seventy-something mother and how she would never have dreamed of calling a child bloody Grenville.

"I'm not sure your parents would appreciate being called old," I informed him. "And," I belatedly registered what he'd said, "who the fuck was talking about me in the Swan? I haven't been in there for years." The Swan sits halfway up Wood Street and is legendary for its refusal to modernise. The last time I'd been in there, the floor was sticky under my feet and the barman struggled to hear my order over Zeppelin playing at top volume. None of it appeared to bother the collection of ageing bikers lined up at the bar drinking pints of bitter, all lost in worlds of their own.

"It was the vampires," said Bangle Girl, her jewellery rattling with excitement. "They're not really vampires, of course," she added hurriedly, "but they don't half look like them."

"I just bet they do," I murmured, making a mental note to check with Jenny whether there'd been any reports of neck injuries in the Wood Street area recently.

"Anyway," the jangling started again, "it doesn't really matter who they are, does it? They know the truth, and that's the important thing."

"Important for who?" I asked. "And where did these ridiculous rumours come from in the first place?"

"We know you don't want publicity," said Grenville. "Mister Mapp said so. But we'd like to offer our support."

"Why," I started slowly, "would I need support? From anyone?"

"In case anyone tries to attack you," said Maya brightly. "We could help you fight them off."

"That's enough," I said, "we're done. I'm out. It's very kind of you to call, but I'm not actually in the market for cafe staff just now. I'm sorry you've wasted your time. Now if you don't mind, I've got a cafe to run. And I'd prefer it if you didn't scare my customers off. Shoo!" They shooed. Only as far as the turning for North John Street, but it was better than nothing. I turned around to head back inside and noticed Grimm sitting on the bottom step of the fire escape. "Do not say a single word," I warned him. "I can do without your input today, thank you."

"I'm sure I have no idea what you're talking about, Lilith," said the cat. "I'm not as interested in your life as you seem to think." I didn't bother dignifying it with an answer.

"How much is Izzy's new place costing her?" asked Sean, when I'd bashed around in the staff kitchen long enough to calm myself down. We were standing on either side of the cafe counter, chatting idly. There's always a lull in trade during the early afternoon. "I'm assuming you've given her a raise?" I had indeed put Izzy's wages up, and they were now way higher than the standard rate for a cafe manager. I figured she deserved the extra in return for her tolerance in the face of supernatural madness. And my own outgoings were near to nothing anyway, so it wasn't as if I couldn't afford it. Eadric had signed the Flora's building over to me shortly after realising I was going to be a thorn in his side literally for all eternity. I'd pointed out I hadn't actually asked to become one of his undead cohort and that he should probably do the right thing and stop charging me rent, considering I'd have been paying it for centuries and he was already rich as Croesus. Then there'd been the thing with the crown, and the depressing realisation that not only was I now a citizen of the underworld, I was also possibly head of the entire damn lot of it. And supreme rulers aren't known for paying their own bills. So I now owned my entire building outright, and no longer had any need to pay rent on either my home or my business. I also had no grocery bills, on account of how I didn't eat anything. Which was a pisser, in all honesty—I really, really missed cake. But the payoff was that I could run at the speed of light and leap tall buildings in a single bound, so I figured it evened out in the end. Okay, I'm exaggerating about the speed and the leaping, but it's as close as to make little difference.

"Nothing," I said. "The new place, I mean. And yeah, she's had a raise."

"Are you paying her rent as well?" Sean looked perturbed. "I know you care for your mate, Lil, but that's excessive."

"I meant she is literally paying nothing for it." Picking up a clean tea towel, I started polishing the cutlery that had been left to drain next to the sink. "She owns it outright."

"Fuck me," whistled Sean, "that must have been one hell of a pay rise."

"No money's changed hands," I said. "There's a clause in all the leases down at Albert Dock that the places can only be owned, not rented out. It's to stop people turning them into holiday lets, I think. So it was simpler for Eadric to just sign it over."

"He gave her almost a million quid's worth of apartment?" Sean's voice was incredulous. "Just gave it to her? She's not even dead!"

"Will you keep your bloody voice down?" I hissed. "We still have customers, for fuck's sake."

"Who just gives someone a ridiculously expensive apartment?" Sean hissed back. "Are you sure he isn't losing his marbles?"

"You can go ask him yourself if you like," I suggested. "See how many limbs you still have by the time he's finished answering you."

"He wouldn't hurt me," said Sean smugly. "He likes me."

"He feels sorry for you," I said. "He thinks you should go find yourself a nice human to settle down with. Have yourselves a brood of tiny little crime writers."

"I already tried that, remember." Sean had dated a woman called Sophie the previous summer, but it hadn't lasted long. About as long as it took him to call her by my name, in fact. I knew about it because the row had kicked off in Flora's and Izzy was not one to miss any spilled tea.

"Anyway," I said, not wanting to get into a discussion about Sean's love life, "Eadric is not losing his marbles. And it's only the penthouses that are worth that kind of money. Izzy's is on the third floor."

"Not one of those with the 'all original brick interiors'?" He made bunny ears with his fingers. Sean had clearly been reading a lot of estate agent blurbs.

"Might be," I shrugged. "Haven't seen it myself, yet. How do you know what they look like?"

"Saw a listing for one a while back," said Sean. "Pretty sure that was third floor. I was thinking about buying it at one point, had a viewing and everything. Thought it might be more suited to the crime writer's life, you know?" I shrugged, implying that no, I did not know. "Then I decided it was a daft idea. I'm fine where I am."

"Where exactly are you?" I asked. "I've never thought to ask."

"And I thought you'd never ask," he grinned. "I live in Vauxhall. Got in just before they started gentrifying the place."

"Vauxhall's been gentrified?" I raised an eyebrow. "Which bit? Cos some of it's definitely missed that memo."

"Okay," he said sheepishly, "maybe just my bit. So far, anyway. I'm near the comedy club. I guess being overrun with tourists will make anywhere safer, eventually."

"That'll be because tourists are easier picking than locals," I said. "You think it's safer, but really you're just further down the priority list for potential muggings."

"I do love your positive outlook on life. Anyway," he grinned, already knowing the answer, "when's the last time you even visited Vauxhall?" I huffed in response. Why would I bother heading out of town, when everything I needed was within a ten minute walk of Flora's? "Why don't you come for a visit?" Sean asked. "See it as a field trip. Map out your domain, that sort of thing." Before I could tell him that nowhere was my sodding domain—least of all the north end of town, which had always had a mind of its own—when two women walked in through the door and I nearly dropped my coffee cup in surprise.

"Delphine?" I asked. The taller of the two women gave me a slightly embarrassed nod of recognition. "And if it isn't Judith Pargeter, as I live and breathe." The second woman blushed crimson. I grinned manically at them. Next to me, Sean was giving a good impression of a choking hyena. As well he might, on account of how Sean had been present the last time we'd met, when Judith had tricked Delphine into attacking me on my own doorstep. They'd been dressed as ninjas at the time. And as they're both well over retirement age, it was truly a sight to behold. It had been a very interesting day. "What the fuck are you doing in here, Jude?" I went on. "Thought you were planning to stake me like the demon I am?"

"No need for language like that," Judith mumbled.

"I meant it," I went on. "I'm surprised to see you in here, after what happened."

Delphine either didn't notice her friend's embarrassment, or didn't care. By the determined expression on her face, I was going with the latter. "Well," she said, "I wasn't very happy with the way Judith treated you last time we met. And I like the coffee in here. So I didn't want to have to avoid it just because ol' muggins here," she nodded at Judith, "got onto all that silly vampire nonsense."

"It's very nice to see you back," I said to Delphine. "You too." I chirped brightly at Judith. "Welcome."

Sean grinned. "Said the spider to the fly."

Hear No Weasel, Speak No Weasel

As Sean seemed more than happy to be left in charge of Flora's, I decided to pay Mapp a visit. Partly for a change of scenery, but also because Judith was looking increasingly uncomfortable in the face of my bonhomie and I didn't want to be responsible for her having a heart attack. Not while she was on my premises, anyway.

"Why don't you put the kettle on and make us both a cuppa?" Mapp said as I banged through the front door into the shop. He barely looked up from his laptop. "You can keep me company whilst I check through this." He nodded at the computer. "According to this list," he said, "I've got fourteen different stuffed weasels somewhere in this shop. All we have to do now is find them."

"Ooh," I said an hour later, after we'd finally located the last of the weasels, "I nearly forgot to tell you! I met a really interesting woman yesterday."

"Ooh," said Mapp, looking up at me with an interested gleam in his eye, "tell me *all* about it! Did your eyes meet across a crowded cafe table? Did sparks fly?"

"Give over," I said, flicking a duster at him. I was working through a box of wooden shoe lasts that we'd found underneath a shelving unit in a far corner of the shop. I wasn't convinced anyone was ever going to buy them, but Mapp had been insistent there was a market for shoe-related weirdness, and not just on pay-to-view fetish sites. "Nah," I went on, "just a friend of Jenny's. No romance, soz like."

"Aah, one can live in hope," grinned Mapp. "So who's this friend? Should we adopt her? Make her one of our own? Mwahahahahahaaaa!" He held clawed hands aloft and pulled what I could only assume he thought was a vampiric face. To be fair, the dark purple lipstick he was wearing did at least make him look like an actor in a nineteen-twenties horror movie.

"You're not as scary as you like to think," I said. "This lot are done," I dropped my cleaning cloth onto the table and surveyed my handiwork. "Where do you want them?"

"Stick them on the counter," he said, "and I'll sort them tomorrow. Might make a little procession of them inside the main window," he looked thoughtful. "Like a ghostly chorus line. Anyway," he turned to look at me, "who's your new friend?"

"She's not my friend," I said. "Not yet, at least. I did like her, though. And I think she might be one of us."

"You mean dead?" Mapp asked. "Or just weird?"

"I don't think she's dead," I said, carefully not mentioning that I'd checked. "But there's definitely something odd about her. And she knew about the incident with Derek and the Wirral weirdos."

"What did this woman look like?" Mapp sat back in his chair and looked at me. "Old? Young? Got a hooked nose and a black cat sitting on her shoulder?"

"None of those things," I said, "so up yours. No," I hoicked myself up onto the counter next to the till, "just really normal. Middle-aged, grey hair, dresses like a rockabilly who can't quite be bothered anymore."

"Oh no," said Mapp, getting to his feet. "No, no, absolutely not!"

"Absolutely not what?" I frowned at him. "Do you know her?" I asked. "Freya, I mean?"

"Yes, Lilith," he said, his face ashen. "I know Freya."

"What's wrong with her?" I'd never seen him so visibly stressed before. "Is she evil? A demon?"

"It's worse than that, Lilith," Mapp said.

"Worse than a demon?"

"Yes," said Mapp, visibly shuddering. "She's my ex-wife."

"Your wife?" I'd been out to buy us both proper espresso from a nearby late-night cafe, having realised instant really wasn't going to cut it in the circumstances. When I got back to the shop, Mapp was still sitting exactly where I'd left him, gazing into space and looking worried. "Your actual, real *wife*?" I was struggling to get my head around the idea of Gaultier Mapp being married. Actually, I think it was more that he'd married a woman. I've got nothing against traditional heterosexual marriage, you understand. So long as it doesn't involve me, at least. It's just that Mapp seemed the most unlikely person to ever do such a thing. "Did you get married in church?"

"Do we really have to talk about this?" he asked, a pleading look on his face. "Can we not just forget she was ever mentioned?"

"Well I liked her," I said defiantly. "So there."

"You would. Sometimes," he sighed, "I think you exist just to wind me up, Lilith O'Reilly. You and that, that..." he trailed off, then shook himself. "That *bloody* woman."

"So," I tried again, "did you? Get married in church?"

"Heavens, no!" Mapp hunched his legs up onto the chair and sat hugging his knees. "What church would have married a couple like us? Had we even wanted to do it in a church. Which we didn't."

"So, where *did* you get married?" I asked. This was the most interesting gossip I'd heard in a very long time, and Izzy was going to expect all the information. "St George's Hall?" The registrar's office had been inside St George's for as long as I'd lived in the city.

"This was long before the hall had been built," said Mapp. "It wasn't a formal thing, anyway."

"Freya looks to be all of about fifty," I said. Mapp nodded. "And she's not dead." Another nod. "But you got married before St George's Hall opened." Nod. "Which was in eighteen-fifty-four."

"I married that woman," said Mapp, "in seventeen-ninety-six. No," he shuddered, "I'm not going to talk about it. What's done is done."

"Mapp," I said, "you can't leave me hanging like that! I've just discovered you have a wife—"

"*Ex*-wife," he interrupted.

"You have an ex-wife," I said, "and I didn't even know you'd ever been married!"

"No one knows," he said. "Not really."

"Eadric must have been around back then," I said. "Does he know?"

"Eadric," said Mapp, "is a better friend than most. He knows when to leave well alone."

"I'm your friend as well," I pointed out, "and I'm just showing an interest in your life. It's not my fault I bumped into her, for heaven's sake."

"She never comes over here," he muttered, "never. Something's going on if that woman's travelling over the water."

"The only thing that seemed to be going on was her neighbour's dodgy belly," I said. "She was just running errands."

"Running errands," he said. "Running errands. Ha!" He spat the words out. "As if she ever does anything for another being."

"Mapp," I said, "can we get back to the bit where you explain how I just met a completely normal, human woman who you apparently married over two hundred years ago?"

"She's not normal," he said. "There's nothing normal about Freya."

"I dunno," I shrugged, "she seemed pretty normal to me. I liked her."

"Look," he turned his big, pleading puppy dog eyes on me, "I really don't want to talk about it."

"Do not give me that look," I said. "I'm not falling for it. You are avoiding the issue, Gaultier Mapp."

"Yes, Lilith," he said. "Yes, I am. And I'd appreciate it if you could show some understanding, for once. Why should I explain my personal life to you? Or anyone, come to that." He gestured around the shop. "I've got my work and I've got my Heggie, and I've got you and my other friends. These are things I am happy to talk about. I no longer have a wife and that pleases me more than you could possibly imagine. Now," he got to his feet and dusted himself down, "if you've got any heart, Lil, you'll leave me be. And you won't go discussing this with anyone else. I didn't ask for my past to be dredged up, and I'd thank you to remember that."

I got up slowly, reluctant to leave things on a sour note. "Can you not just tell me why it's such a touchy subject?"

"No."

"Even after all this time?" I tried. "Two centuries later and she still holds power over you?"

"Freya does not hold any power over me." Mapp's voice was dangerously quiet. "She never did. I tied my world to that woman," he went on, "and thought she would be with me forever." He trailed off.

"And?" I said encouragingly.

"And," he looked me in the eye and smiled sadly, "it was the biggest mistake of my life."

"What?" Izzy stared at me as though I'd told her aliens had just landed in Williamson Square and popped into the LFC store to buy souvenir scarves. "Mapp's married? To a human? A human *woman*?"

"Yurp." We were sitting in the living room of her Button Street flat, packing up the last of her belongings. I'd left Mapp to his fretting in the early hours and had spent the rest of the night waiting for dawn to break, so I could risk waking Izzy in order to fill her in on my news. Apparently I should have looked at a clock first, because as Izzy pointed out, dawn at this time of year was actually a good few hours before most human alarms went off. "That's what I said."

"I'm actually less surprised by it being a woman," said Izzy, "and more than he ever got married in the first place."

"It was a handfasting," I said. "Pagan rather than Christian."

"That makes more sense," said Iz. "I couldn't really imagine Mapp standing in a church in his best suit."

"Especially as his best suit is made of purple sequins." I went back to wrapping mugs in paper, while Izzy rooted through her kitchen cupboards.

"Christ," she said, peering at the label, "this salt went out of date five years ago." She frowned and gave it a shake. "Do you think salt actually goes stale?"

"Doubt it," I said. "Considering it's used as a preservative. Is there anything crawling in it?" She pulled the top off the plastic tub and looked inside. "Nah," she said decisively, "it's fine." She pressed the lid back on and put the tub into a cardboard box on the worktop next to her. "Damon wants to get married," she said. Her head was inside a cupboard and it took me a minute to register what she'd said. "Turmeric definitely goes off." A small plastic jar hit the floor with a solid-sounding thud.

"Really?" I looked up to where she was now kneeling on the work surface in order to get to the back of the top shelves. "Like, *married* married?"

"Yup," she said.

"Are you going to marry him?" I asked. "I can just picture you in one of those enormous meringue dresses, all flounces and frills."

"Fuck off," said Izzy, throwing a jar over her head. I caught it, took one look at what was left of the contents and dropped it into the bin bag.

"I'm surprised garlic goes off," I said. "You'd think it would be strong enough to kill any lurking bugs."

"Not when it's more than a decade old," said Izzy, turning so she could slide back down onto the floor. "And I'll have you know I would wear a very stylish dress if I ever got married."

"If?" I raised an eyebrow at her. "Come on," I said, "you and Damon are a match made in heaven. Why on earth wouldn't you get married if he wants to?"

"That's the thing, innit." She shrugged. "It's Damon who wants to get married, not me. I can't see the point."

"Well, I can't argue with that," I said, "given I'm always telling people what a stupid idea it is to even live with someone, let alone marry them. Urgh," I shuddered, "I can't imagine having to ask another person's permission for decorating. Let alone relying on them to remember to pay the gas bill and to put the bins out on the right day."

"Exactly!" Izzy said. "That's exactly it. I like living on my own.

Always have. And if I'm being absolutely honest," she grinned, "I'm really looking forward to having this new flat to myself."

"Poor Damon," I said. "Demoted in favour of a tasty bit of real estate."

"Cheeky mare!" I ducked as a jar of dried coriander flew past my head, but Izzy was laughing. "Yeah," she said, "it sounds really shallow when you put it like that. It's true though." She walked across to the small kitchen window and peered out. "It'll be nice looking out and seeing the river, instead of Dave the Teeth pissing up next door's front steps." Dave the Teeth was a rough sleeper who favoured a spot outside Izzy's building and refused any offers of help to find support and housing. He'd once told me he was born on the streets and was fully prepared to die there as well, and he worked diligently towards making that happen sooner rather than later. He was known as 'the Teeth' because he only had two teeth in his entire head, and both were brown and rotten. We like to put a bit of lateral thinking into nicknames in this city. "Anyway," said Izzy, banging the cupboard door closed and opening the next one, "I'm not getting married. Not yet, anyway."

"What does Damon think of that?" I asked, looking around for more newspaper. A two-day-old copy of the *Echo* was tucked underneath the bin bag and I began pulling it apart. Then I put it back together and started reading an article on page five.

"He said he understands my reasoning," said Izzy, "but wants to discuss it again in a year's time. Are you even listening to me, Lil?"

"Yeah," I said, "that's nice. It'll be fun."

"What will be fun? Lilith O'Reilly," Izzy stamped a foot in front of me for emphasis, "you're not listening to me."

"Have you heard anything about a burglary on Water Street?" I asked her. "The old Martins Bank building?"

"Isn't it empty?" She frowned. "Can't be much left in there for anyone to nick. Why are you interested, anyway?" I was interested because I was pretty sure at least one of the tunnels that no one knows about ran underneath the old bank, but I didn't say that. I'd only get a lecture on leaving things well alone, if the vampires were going out on the rob that was Joe's problem not mine, blah blah.

"I'm not really," I said. "Just curious. Always liked that building." In fact, I had a sneaking suspicion it might well be part of the Silverton Properties portfolio, just hidden underneath a maze of shell companies. When I'd first started going through the company's books—at Eadric's invitation, I might add, I'm not that bloody nosy—I'd noticed the endless references to companies that didn't seem to fully exist. These days I knew it was less to do with tax avoidance and more to do with having to cover up the fact that the company's owners still looked exactly the same, over two centuries after it was founded. Back then I'd panicked and demanded reassurances from Eadric that he wasn't secretly a criminal mastermind. He'd pointed out that, had he really been up to no good, he probably wouldn't have chosen to run his nefarious empire from the top of one of the most recognisable buildings in the world.

"Have you finished that lot?" Izzy asked, nodding at the box I'd been filling with crockery. "And are you ever going to finish telling me about Mapp and his unexpected lady wife?"

"Yeah," I said, getting to my feet, "this box is done." I lifted it up onto the worktop and started hunting in the drawers for the sticky tape.

"Here," said Izzy, holding a red plastic tape dispenser out towards me, "I decided to bring out the big guns." I used the dispenser to noisily close up the box, then handed it back.

"Not much else to tell about Mapp," I said, "just that he apparently used to be married to this Freya woman, but clearly isn't anymore."

"Didn't he tell you about her?" Izzy picked up the bin bag and shook it down so she could tie a knot in the top. "It's not like him to miss out on spinning a good yarn."

"It was weird," I said. "He seemed really surprised by me having met her. But she only lives over the water, and clearly comes over to town now and then. So why hasn't he told anyone about her?"

"Maybe it happened before the others were here?"

"Eadric was in Liverpool before Mapp got here," I pointed out. "And they were friends from the start. Also, Freya isn't dead. I'm sure of it."

"Then how could she have married Mapp so long ago?"

"That's what I don't know," I said. "Anyway, she said she'd like to chat with me again at some point, so I'll see if she tells me anything herself."

"What does she want to catch up about?" Izzy asked. "Is she cute?"

"Don't you start," I said. "Not everything revolves around whether people are fanciable. Sometimes they're just being nice." I hadn't told Izzy about the Birkenhead incident. It had turned out okay in the end—if we ignored the fact that random people now bowed and scraped if they saw me in the street—and she only worries. "We just agreed to have a cuppa together at some point, that's all."

"Uh huh," said Izzy, "whatever you say. Now, are you going to carry this lot down to the waterfront for me?"

"On my own?" I asked, looking at the stack of boxes that were waiting to be moved.

"No point having a super strength zombie for a best friend," shrugged Izzy, "if you have to carry your own bags."

~

The Albert Dock didn't get its 'Royal' moniker until the start of the twenty-first century, despite being built in the mid eighteen-hundreds. Constructed entirely from brick, cast iron and stone, it was the first dock in the world to be almost entirely fireproof. This proved useful during the city's later economic slump, as it merely deteriorated, rather than going up in flames like so many other abandoned buildings in the city. As soon as money started creeping back into town, the docks became the obvious place to stick the incomers who had more money than sense. And thus, the Colonnades sprang into life. Over one hundred luxury apartments complete with twenty-four-hour concierge service and the sort of underground parking Batman would envy, the development sits over and around such upmarket commercial ventures as the Tate gallery and, well, Premier Inn. It's a fancier Premier Inn than most, to be fair. I once had a wander around it with my mum, who was staying overnight in order to indulge in a bit of joint literary wankery with Nik Silverton. I don't call it wankery to her face, obviously. But when those two get together it's honestly like trying to sit in on a conversation between Hemingway and bloody Chaucer—endless incomprehensible in-jokes that only make sense if you're a renowned flouncy poet who's been around for over two centuries, or a retired woman who's decided to keep busy during her twilight years by doing a PhD on the impact of eighteenth-century literature on modern socio-cultural traditions. Me and Eadric usually just go sit with Bella and leave them to get on with it. Anyway, the hotel is full of random dock machinery that the leaseholders aren't allowed to remove because the entire place is Grade I listed, and the apartments are no different. "Is yours the one with a brick corner library area?" I asked Izzy as we carried boxes down Paradise Street. Actually, it was only me who was carrying anything—Izzy was using a slab trolley she said Damon had borrowed from a construction site.

"If you mean the bookshelves," she said, slowing down to manoeuvre the trolley around a group of gossiping tourists, "then yes. How do you know that?"

"Sean went to view it at some point," I said. I stopped to wait as she got the trolley stuck on a lifted kerb stone. "Where's Damon?" I asked. "I'd kind of assumed he'd be at your beck and call for the move, considering how he clearly worships the ground your dainty little feet walk on."

"Away working," puffed Izzy, finally dragging the trolley off the kerb. "Mate of his was short staffed for a music festival and asked him to help out." Izzy and Damon had met when he was doing security outside Flora's, after a tunnel fell in and exposed Liverpool's somewhat shaky foundations for all to see. It hadn't taken long for him to expose himself as yet another academic—this time in the field of plant biosynthesis, no I don't know either—who just does security as a side-gig on account of how he's built like the proverbial brick shithouse. Given Izzy's the size and shape of a porcelain doll, they make an amusing couple. Well, it amuses me, anyway. Izzy says I'm just envious because she can hold down a steady and committed relationship whereas I am a flibbertigibbet who can't even decide what her type is, but what does she know.

"Good job you're not moving far then," I said, "innit?"

"Sean's welcome to have a proper look around," said Izzy, "if he's still thinking about moving down there? Ooh," she grinned, "we could have a dinner party! Me, you, Damon and Sean. Wouldn't that be fun?"

"You're forgetting the bit about me not being able to eat anything," I pointed out. "It isn't much of a dinner party if one of the party can't eat dinner."

"It's fine," she said airily, "you can just sit around looking beautiful and intellectually curious. Leave the actual conversation to the rest of us."

"I have a bloody degree, you know," I pointed out. "Which is more than *some* of us can say."

"Whateverrrrr," she said blithely, "it's not like a First in History has got you any further than running a cafe, now is it?" I didn't reply, but couldn't help smiling to myself as we slogged our way down towards the waterfront. Me and Izzy had bickered our way through most of our childhood and most of the adult years, but things had felt a bit dislocated recently. I wasn't sure whether it was down to me spending less time in Flora's, or because she was usually with Damon when she wasn't working.

"This is nice," I said, as we stopped to wait for the lights to change so we could cross the Strand. The sun was shining and tourists were already crowding their way around Albert Dock ahead of us.

"What is?" Izzy asked. "Dragging my worldly goods around the city centre like an upmarket hobo?" The green man popped up, and I helped her pull the trolley over the kerb and into the road. "You might want to look like you're struggling a bit more with those boxes," she said as we crossed. I'd rearranged my load so I was carrying two large cardboard boxes on one shoulder, one on top of the other. I attempted to look like I was being weighed down and almost lost a box in the process.

"Doing stuff together," I said, after I'd rebalanced myself. "You know. Just being normal."

"Lil," Izzy said patiently, "I'm having to remind you to stop looking like one of the sodding Gladiators, casually carrying a box of crockery like it's actually filled with feathers. There isn't anything about you that's normal, love." I sighed as we walked past the Victorian carousel that stood next to Salthouse Dock. It was crowded with families, small children clinging to the horses' necks and shrieking happily. I eyeballed the nearest horse warily. The last time I'd ridden the carousel, I ended up being unceremoniously dumped into the cold and stinking waters of the seventeenth-century Mersey. Izzy was right—there really was nothing normal in my life.

"Oh well," I said, more brightly than I felt, "at least you've got a flat out of it."

"Yes," said Izzy with a grin, "yes, I have. And a very nice flat it is, too. Come on," she headed towards the private entrance that was tucked away between the tourist shops along the dockside. "Let me give you the tour."

Hot Gossip

"Okay," I said, sitting down on a stack of boxes, "this place is incredible."

"Isn't it?" Izzy skipped happily around the enormous living area that formed the centrepiece of her new home. "I absolutely bloody love it." It was no surprise she was happy. The apartment—and this place was definitely an apartment, not a common-or-garden flat—was utterly gorgeous. Almost entirely original brickwork, the only modernity came from where partition walls had been used to break up the space into smaller areas. Off to the right of the living area was an archway into a smaller area, which I thought was probably what Sean had meant by a library corner. It was certainly begging for a chaise longue and as many bookshelves as could be squeezed into the tiny space. I'd been surprised to discover the bathroom only had a walk-in shower, until Izzy had gleefully shown me the ensuite for the master bedroom, which came complete with an enamel, claw-footed bath.

"And this is one of the cheaper places," I marvelled, gazing around me. Although, perhaps surprisingly, I still wasn't jealous of Izzy moving into such an amazing place. Okay, so the atrium down at ground level had been impressive, and the concierge at the desk was friendly without being too much. And I'd felt a tiny twinge of envy when I saw the beautiful brass mailboxes that lined the corridor on each floor—it was definitely a step up from having post dropped through a letterbox onto a soggy doormat. But however fancy it might be, it wasn't town. I like living in town. The fact that Flora's is pretty much as central as it gets is a lot of the reason I love it so much. Even on the busiest days or nights, when Mathew Street is packed with tourists and drunks all jostling together like old friends, Harrington Street is peaceful. This is relative, of course. I still hear the screams and shouts, and the sirens that often go with them. But living above the cafe means I can oversee all the activity without having to actually get involved. And I still live within a ten minute walk of the best baklava in town. Not that I can eat baklava, of course. Revenants do, technically, have the full range of bodily functions, but it all works at such a slow pace that any food I dared eat would be fully rotten before my body made any attempt to even consider digesting it. It's the principle of the thing, though. I fully believe you can judge a neighbourhood by the type and standard of the food available. Take Bold Street, for example. Its array of cheap and cheerful franchise outlets is broken up by upmarket 'street food' outlets that are twice the price of any comparable food on the actual streets of the countries they came from. And dotted within them all is the occasional outlier that's been around seemingly forever and has probably had the same clientele for all that time. The offerings down at Albert Dock are more generic, for the simple reason that smaller companies simply can't afford to rent space there. Whereas Harrington Street is nothing like either of them. Flora's is the only food outlet, unless you cross the main road and go into one of the pubs on the bottom half of the street. And pubs don't count. But you can find pretty much everything you could ever hope or wish for within a casual five minute stroll of my fire escape. Harrington Street is in the city, but not entirely *of* it—it has an air of otherness than isn't purely from the fact it's inhabited by several members of the supernatural underworld. At least, that's what I told myself. Maybe it was subconscious wishful thinking, just trying to distract me from the fact Izzy now had an intercom and private underground parking.

"I've even got underground parking," she said, like the creepy fucking psychic she is. In reality, Izzy is so far from being psychic that it's laughable—we once played a game of 'guess what I'm thinking' and almost came to blows, because she wouldn't have it that I wasn't actually thinking about raccoons eating bananas. According to Iz, 'everybody likes raccoons eating bananas'. And she got even more annoyed when I asked how often she'd actually *seen* a raccoon eating a banana. Apparently, I was being disingenuous.

"And yet you have no car." Izzy had passed her test more than a decade earlier, but I'd only witnessed her driving on two occasions that I could remember. And the second one ended with her driving into a hedge and leaving the car—her dad's beloved Audi, no less—wedged into the greenery because, apparently, 'parking sucks'.

"Damon will use one of them," she said. "And I thought you might like one." She threw what looked like a small piece of grey cardboard at me and I caught it in my hand. It was actually made of plastic, and had a small computer chip embedded into the top surface. "Automatic recognition," she said, "for the access gates. You're number three-five-seven—should be signposted when you get down there. Not that you need it," she added, "now you've got the magic key." I had, in fact, lived on Harrington Street for over three years before it had occurred to Eadric to give me a key for the barriers that block it off from the main road. When I'd queried this with him, pointing out I'd actually been using his own parking spaces under the Liver Building and wouldn't it have been easier to give me a key in the first place, he swore he'd somehow just entirely forgotten the barriers even existed. My theory was that he'd liked being able to keep tabs on what I was up to, but he'd politely informed me I wasn't actually that interesting. "I get three spaces," Izzy went on, "so I've given you the one in the middle. Thought it was safest." I narrowed my eyes at her, but took the plastic anyway.

"Thanks, love," I said, "it's really kind of you."

"I can give you a spare key for the flat itself, if you like?" Her voice sounded strained, and I realised she was on the verge of tears.

"Oh Iz," I said, getting to my feet, "what's up?" I stepped forward and she gave a short, tight hug. Then she stepped back and smiled.

"Just weird," she said, "innit? We moved up here as not much more than kids, and now here we are."

"Here we are," I agreed. "You're living in the fanciest tower block in the city, and I'm dead. I think you got the better deal, in all honesty."

"Oh, I don't know," said Izzy, "I—"

"Hellooooo!" We'd left the front door wedged open while we were moving the boxes in. A familiar voice sang out from the communal hallway. "Is m'lady accepting visitors?" Nik Silverton's face appeared around the edge of the door. "Oh hi, Lil," he said, "I didn't realise you were here. Are you helping Isobel settle into her new digs?"

"Come in," said Izzy, "and shut the door behind you, there's a good little fop."

Nik grinned and did as he was told. "You're going to need more furniture," he said, turning on his heel in order to take in the entirety of the flat. "Or more friends to help fill it."

"I've got all the friends I need," said Izzy. "And yes, I'm including you in that, before you get all overdramatic and silly."

"As if I'd do such a thing," said Nik.

"As if," said Izzy, rolling her eyes. "Now, come tell me and Lil what you know of Mapp's ex-wife."

Nik stopped staring at the vaulted ceilings and looked at her, a suspicious expression on his face. "What ex-wife would that be?" he asked.

"Nik," I said, "don't even bother attempting to lie about this." I knew his carefully neutral tone of old. It was the sort of voice he put on when he was determined to not give any useful information whatsoever, but wanted to seem as helpful as possible whilst doing so. "You know her, then?"

I saw it on his face as he considered lying, then immediately gave up the idea. "Yeah," he said eventually, a study in self-composure, "I know her. Or rather, I *knew* her. Haven't seen that woman around for decades now. Shame, really," he went on, "I rather liked her."

"When you say you haven't seen her for decades," I said, "just how long are we talking?"

"Oh," he said airily, "you know. About a century, I'd say. Maybe a fraction longer. Anyway," he looked from me to Izzy and back again, "why do you want to know? And more to the point," he frowned, "how did you find out about her in the first place?"

"Lil met her," said Izzy.

"Yesterday," I added. "In the chemist in town."

"You can't have," said Nik. "She's been gone for years!" He frowned. "I'm sure Gaultier would have said something if he thought Freya was still around. And," he eyeballed me suspiciously, "how did you know she was Mapp's ex?"

I explained the incident in the pharmacy, and how I'd asked Mapp about Freya, but he'd refused to discuss it. "She's cool," I finished. "I really liked her."

"And Lil doesn't like many people," Izzy pointed out. "So why all the secrecy?"

"It's no secret," he said. "I just don't like discussing other people's private lives." It was a valiant effort, but one we all knew was doomed to failure. Nik can no more resist the opportunity for a good bit of gossip than I could compete at the Horse Of The Year Show on the back of a retired llama. "She's not who you think she is," he said eventually.

"So what is she?" Izzy asked. "Cos from what Lil says, she's clearly not one of you lot. Ooh," she raised her eyebrows, "don't tell us—is she a Tory? Is that why Mapp's embarrassed?"

"Christ no," said Nik, rolling his eyes. "Even Gaultier has his limits."

"If she's a United fan," I said, "you'd better tell us now. Because that is a line even I can't cross."

"Anyway," said Izzy, "whatever Freya actually is, it can't be anything that awful or you lot would have known about it by now." I wasn't entirely sure she was right, considering I'd only a few days earlier been abducted by the amateur occultists from over the water, and I hadn't known they existed until it happened. But I appreciated her loyalty. "And if she *isn't* anything awful, then why won't Mapp talk about her?"

"Yeah," I agreed, "it's not like ex-wives are a rarity. You and Eadric have them."

"Theirs are dead, to be fair," shrugged Izzy. "Point still stands tho, Nikolaus. Why doesn't Mapp want to talk about his ex-wife?"

Nik sighed. "Will either of you accept that I don't want to talk about it either?" We both shook our heads vigorously, and he sighed. "You are a pair of absolute wretches," he said. "I don't know what I did in a previous life to deserve you two as companions."

"Something utterly marvellous and deserving of reward," said Izzy, "clearly. Now, out with it."

"You are not to tell Mapp where you got this information from," said Nik. He wagged a finger at us for emphasis. "Understand?"

"Yes, dad," I singsonged at him.

"Of course Mapp doesn't want to talk about Freya," said Nik, ignoring me. "He's probably concerned about what she might do to him if she found out. I did warn him," he went on. "I mean," he shrugged, "what kind of idiot marries a witch?"

The kind of idiots who then realise they've bitten off more than they can chew and don't quite know whether to spit or swallow, as it turns out. According to Nik, Mapp had first met Freya when he was selling trinkets from a little shop on Hockenhall Alley, and she happened to walk past. "He tempted her inside to peruse his wares," said Nik. "What's so funny?"

"You of all people should recognise a euphemism when you use it," said Izzy. "'Peruse his wares', indeed! I bet that's not all she perused, eh Lil?"

Nik scowled as we cackled like witches. Personally, I thought our reaction was appropriate under the circs. "I'm not going to tell you anything if you insist on behaving like children," he said.

"Get on with you," said Izzy. "You love a bit of gossip."

"Yeah," I said. "And this is *excellent* gossip."

"High tea indeed," agreed Iz. She dropped onto the floor next to me and we both looked at Nik, who was perching on the solid stone sill of Izzy's front window. "Go on," she said. "We promise to behave."

"I do not trust a word that comes out of your delicately vile little mouth, Isobel," said Nik. He was smiling, though. "Where was I? Okay, so Gaultier had the misfortune to meet Freya and he was immediately infatuated. I gather Eadric attempted to reason with him, but he wouldn't listen. Spent all his time on the ferry, going back and forth to visit with her, before he finally persuaded her to move into the shop. Actually," he looked thoughtful, "I'm pretty sure Eadric only met her twice, and one of those occasions was their wedding."

"When was the other?" I asked.

"She turned up at the Liver Building one day," he said, "a few years later. Just walked into Eadric's office as cool as you like, apparently, as though she'd been issued a personal invitation."

"What did she want?" Izzy asked.

"To inform him she'd told Mapp she no longer considered herself married," he said. "And to deliver a box of his possessions. Things he'd left in her house over the water."

"Why did she take his stuff to Eadric?" Izzy asked. "Couldn't she have dropped them off to him herself? Or asked him to collect them?"

"You have to remember," said Nik, "that I am relaying this information secondhand as it is. I'm not clear on all the details. I gather Gaultier had disappeared off the scene for a while and Eadric had simply assumed he was busy playing happy families. You know how Eadric is." I did indeed know. Eadric was so insular as to be almost rude at times. Now that I knew him better, I thought he probably just felt safer in his own company. But he and I had had some spectacular disagreements in the time since I'd died, mostly started by me accusing him of not caring about anyone except himself. These days I suspect Eadric actually cares so much that it's almost painful, so he shuts himself away and avoids the issue entirely. "As it transpired," Nik went on, "he was hiding out at his old shop, too ashamed and embarrassed to speak to anyone."

"Ashamed and embarrassed about what?" I asked. "It must have been something pretty appalling." As Mapp was the most open-minded person I'd ever met in my life, I was struggling to think of anything he might feel shame about.

"About having married in the first place," said Nik. "Although he didn't admit that until much later on. I gather he felt foolish. And as someone who has had their romantic overtures rejected more than once, I can understand that."

"Depends what you consider romantic, I guess," said Izzy. "Cos I'm not being funny like," she raised an eyebrow, "but I know for a fact you once hand-delivered a poem to that Japanese place on Duke Street cos you fancied one of their waiters. That shit tends to freak people out, in case you haven't noticed."

"Well, I know that *now*," said Nik, pulling a face. "But what else was I supposed to do?"

"Go into the restaurant and book a table like a normal person, maybe?" said Izzy. "Instead of standing outside and gazing wistfully through the window like a sodding lunatic."

"What is the point of booking a table when I can't eat?" said Nik. "That would look even stranger, no?"

"Well, Lil manages to—" started Izzy, then broke off. "Actually no," she went on, "don't use Lil as an example of how to date."

"Thanks a bunch," I scowled. "Can we get back to the topic of Mapp and his dramatically ill-fated marriage?"

"No, we absolutely cannot," said Mapp himself from behind me. I whipped around to find him standing in the open doorway, looking as angry as I'd ever seen him. "How dare you discuss my personal life behind my back? How *dare* you?" He turned and left before any of us could say anything and without thinking, I ran after him. There was a squeak of shock from behind me as I shot up so quickly that the boxes we'd left on the floor went flying, but I was already out of the door and racing down the corridor after Mapp. I leapt down the stairs on the principle it was faster than using the lift, and got to the main entrance just in time to see the heavy doors slowly closing. Zipping through the gap, I got out onto the cobbles of the dock itself and almost bowled over an elderly woman who'd stopped to let her dog have a wee up the iron railings. I apologised profusely and forced myself to stand still against the wall while looking for Mapp. There was a flash of reflected light from over by the lock bridge—Mapp's silver jacket. Tourists immediately blocked my view, but I kept looking and sure enough, Mapp reappeared in the distance, walking at a brisk pace along the Strand. Not wanting to cause a scene, I walked at a carefully human pace in the other direction, leaving Albert Dock through the side exit onto Gower Street. As soon as I was back out onto the road, I launched myself at full speed up towards the Strand. I try not to run in public when humans are around in any numbers. It's not the running itself that draws attention —I can move so fast that most people don't notice anything more than a slight breeze. It's the starting and stopping that causes problems. I'd used Izzy as a guinea pig once and she'd politely informed me that, from a human perspective, it is very unnerving to witness someone apparently disappearing into thin air. She also said that the stopping was even more disconcerting, because, "one minute there's an empty space and the next you're standing in it like some creepy portal dude and honestly mate, can we *please* not do this again?" With her sage advice in mind, I'd chosen Gower Street because it's usually the quietest side of the dock. And even if there are people hanging around, they're mostly guests from the Premier Inn who are generally distracted and/or hungover enough to not actually care what's going on around them.

Once I'm on the move, it's simple—if by 'simple' we mean 'runs so fast and dodges people so quickly that I've been and gone before anyone notices'. And I've practised enough over the past couple of years that I've now got favourite stopping places. If I'm heading down Toxteth way, I often go via Duke Street and through St James Gardens, because I can be reasonably confident of no one hanging around by the St James Road exit. I rip through the greenery like Speedy Gonzales and come to a screeching halt just before the gates, before sauntering casually out onto Upper Parliament Street, ready for a good nosey around Red Brick Market. Today's destination of choice was St Lukes, aka the Bombed Out Church. I ran at full tilt along Wapping, dodging people and traffic until I got to the turning for Blundell Street. A left turn sharp enough that I felt the soles of my trainers rip, then through the back streets of the Baltic Triangle until I hit Duke Street. From there it was just a quick bob and weave round to Roscoe Street, where I finally came to a halt next to the railings that surround the remains of the church. "Got any change, love?" I looked down at the man who was sitting on the pavement, wrapped in an old sleeping bag. He looked middle-aged, but I suspected he was probably only in his mid-thirties. He reminded me of Billy. I was so taken aback by the memory that I just shrugged at him, lost for words. "Suit yer fuckin' self then," he said without malice. I forced myself to walk off purposely, heading down Leece Street with a confident stride that didn't match how I was feeling.

I was tucked into the shop doorway and safely hidden from view when Mapp arrived back at the shop. He turned into the doorway with such determination that he walked straight into me. The force nearly took the door itself off its hinges, and we automatically clung to each other while regaining balance. Then Mapp shoved me hard and stepped backwards onto the pavement. "What are you doing here?" His eyes were narrow and his face furious. "Haven't you got gossip to be getting on with?"

"Mapp," I started, "I'm—" he held a hand up to stop me.

"No," he said. "No. I don't want to hear your bullshit, Lilith O'Reilly. I don't want to hear about how you didn't mean it, you were just curious, oh dear, you didn't know you weren't supposed to tell Isobel. I don't want to hear it."

"This is ridiculous," I said. "Completely and utterly fucking ridiculous. What the *fuck*, Mapp?"

"You heard me," he said. "I don't want to talk to you."

"Well, I'm talking to you," I said firmly. "Get in the shop right this minute or I will get up on the bloody roof and start throwing the pigeon shit down through that broken window frame."

"You wouldn't."

"Just fucking try me," I said. "Now get inside and put the bloody kettle on like a good little shopkeeper."

~

"But what I don't understand," I said, "is why all the drama? Yes," I nodded, "I know I shouldn't have been talking behind your back. But we're your *friends*, Mapp! Of course we're going to be fascinated by finding out something like that!"

"I don't see why," he said. We'd locked ourselves inside the shop and turned the sign so it read 'closed'. Then I'd pushed Mapp bodily as far towards the back of the shop itself as possible and dragged two chairs out from behind a stack of boxes marked 'FISH - FRAGILE'. Knowing Mapp, it could have been anything from live goldfish to ancient and valuable taxidermy, so I put the boxes safely out of the way in a corner before dropping the chairs down onto the floor facing each other. We were sitting close enough that our knees almost touched, and I could literally feel the stress emanating from him.

"Because it's a normal thing to talk about," I said. "It would be like me finding out Sean was married and just hadn't mentioned it."

"I thought you said Sean was married."

"Yes," I said. "'Was' being the operative word. He got divorced years ago."

"Well, so did I," said Mapp. "So why the interest?"

"Because I just met your bloody ex-wife in the middle of Liverpool, you idiot! And I thought she was really nice. I knew there was something different about her," Mapp made a quiet snorting noise, "and that made me like her even more. I just thought she might turn out to be an interesting new friend, that's all. And now everyone's upset with everyone else and you're trying to tell me she's a fucking monster from the deep, or something."

"She's certainly a monster," he sniffed. "A heartless, cold-blooded harpy."

"Come on," I said, "you know you can tell me anything."

"Yeah," he said, "and then you go and tell Izzy and Nik and anyone else who'll bloody listen."

"Don't start that again," I said. "None of us were being malicious, and you know it." He made a quiet harrumphing noise, but his anger finally seemed to be fading. "What on earth can she have done to make you this angry, all these years later?"

"If I tell you," said Mapp, "you have to promise not to laugh."

"That depends if it's funny or not."

"Promise me, Lilith." His face was deadly serious, and for a brief second I panicked that I might be about to get more than I'd bargained for. Mapp really was the most broad-minded person I'd ever met, with a curiosity that regularly led him into trouble even when he wasn't looking for it. I couldn't think of anything Freya could have done that might make him this stressed, short of human slavery or a major fetish gone wrong. And I definitely wasn't a therapist. What if I'd accidentally brought up an ancient trauma that led to Mapp having a breakdown? Heggie would knock me into the middle of next week if I upset his boyfriend. Not that he was capable of knocking me into the middle of anything, but I'd probably let him do it out of sheer guilt.

I looked Mapp straight in the eye. "I promise," I said. "I promise I will listen and I promise I won't judge."

"That'll do," he said. "I guess." Then he told me what Freya had done to him—and I laughed. I laughed and laughed until I thought I might choke. And I was still laughing when he threw me bodily out onto the street and told me to never darken his door again.

It's Curtains For You

"Curtains?" Izzy asked. I'd gone back down to Albert Dock and found her silently unpacking, worry written all over her face. Apparently Nik had left not long after I'd gone racing after Mapp, saying he was 'too old for all this hysteria'. He wasn't too old to ask her to fill him in as soon as she heard anything, though. "You're telling me that whole drama was over a pair of bloody curtains?"

"Yup," I said, "I am. Freya made curtains out of a cloak Mapp had planned to keep for himself, and he never forgave her." I was pretty sure no one could blame me for laughing when Mapp had finally told me the story behind the breakdown of his marriage. Already in the business of buying and selling knickknacks and curiosities, he was offered the cloak on a chilly November day, somewhere around the turn of the nineteenth century. Mapp thought it might have been 1801, but couldn't be sure. He remembered the time of year clearly, because it was soon after All Saint's Day. This was the original shop down in Hockenhall Alley, and I hadn't been remotely surprised when he'd confessed that some of his stock perhaps had less than trustworthy purchase histories. 'A lot of it was dodgy as all fuck, love,' had been how Mapp himself had described it whilst telling me the story. A bastardised mix of antique dealership, pawnbroker and middleman for fencing, the shop had been popular with thieves and vagabonds, as well as officers on shore leave from the ships that were crowding the burgeoning docks. Mapp had done a roaring trade in clothes and jewellery that were sold at bargain prices, but only to those who knew better than to enquire about their provenance. The cloak had been brought in by a regular supplier of his. Tom was a kitchen boy from Everton, who supplemented his meagre earnings by relieving his employers of a few valuable items here and there. 'Nothing they'd miss,' Tom had told Mapp. 'Them toffee-nosed buggers don't even know what they've got half the time.' This wasn't just any old cloak, though, at least not according to Mapp. He'd gone into great detail about the quality of the fabric, and how it had supposedly been taken from the corpse of a Prussian nobleman who'd died whilst visiting with Tom's employers. According to Mapp, the cloak had been made of rich blue velvet, had a lining of magenta silk satin, and was quite the most beautiful thing he'd ever seen. His eyes had lit up as he was describing it to me, and even I couldn't deny that it really did sound like the most Mapp-esque item of clothing ever.

"Didn't she know how important it was?" Izzy asked.

"I get the impression Freya wasn't easily impressed by rich men's fripperies," I said. "Thought it was more important to have heavy curtains to keep in the warmth during winter." The couple had been living over the shop and, according to Mapp, their quarters had been little more than a couple of rooms—one behind the shop counter, the other on the floor above and accessed by a rickety ladder. 'Like sleeping in a hayloft', according to Mapp. Not that they'd done much sleeping, by the sound of it. The only time he'd sounded fond of his ex-wife had been when he sidetracked into telling me what she looked like on their wedding day, and how he'd barely been able to wait until their guests had left before ripping her dress off and consummating the marriage good and proper.

"I thought you lot didn't feel the cold?" Izzy said. "Why would Freya be worried about staying warm?"

"That's the thing," I said. "Nik was telling the truth. Freya isn't a revenant—she really is a witch."

"According to Nik and Mapp, you mean." Izzy was busily emptying bags of pasta into the storage jars she'd bought in honour of her new kitchen. Despite having managed perfectly fine with just shoving packets into cupboards all her life, she'd now decided that an apartment as upmarket as this deserved better. So, to prepare for her promotion up the social ladder, she'd ordered an entire family's worth of crockery and storage. There'd been so much of it that the sales staff in John Lewis had personally delivered it to the Colonnades that morning. They'd left it in the custody of the concierge, who'd apparently lugged it all upstairs in the lift while I'd been off kicking information out of Mapp. "Don't feel too sorry for him," Izzy had said when I'd returned to find her sitting inside the world's most expensive cardboard box fort, "he's got a fancy trolley. And I got the distinct impression he was enjoying checking out the apartment. Apparently he lives in St Helens."

"That explains a lot," I'd said. And then we'd both sighed quietly in sympathy.

"Anyway," said Izzy, "is Freya really a witch, do you think? Or are Mapp and darling Nikolaus just being judgmental little bitches?"

"I think they mean it literally," I said. "Although I'll be the first to admit I had no fucking idea witches were living on the Wirral."

"Wirral witches," grinned Izzy. "Got quite a ring to it, no? Ooh!" She swung around to look at me. "While we're talking alliterative weirdos, what about the Vauxhall vampires?"

"We don't have any vampires in Vauxhall," I pointed out.

"Not that you know of," said Izzy darkly. "But there's been some weird stuff happening over there recently."

"Like what?"

"Like people saying there's vampires." Izzy eyed the half-empty bag of orzo in her hand. "People losing track of time on a night out, only to wake up the next morning looking pale and not wanting to go outdoors. Why did I buy this stuff?" she went on, before I had a chance to point out she was describing the symptoms of a hangover as much as a vampire attack. And I knew which was more likely. "More to the point, when did I actually *use* half of it?" She sniffed the contents. "Urgh," her delicate face screwed up in distaste, "I'm pretty sure there's mould growing in there. Oh well, one less jar to worry about." She threw it in the general direction of an open bin bag and missed. Tiny bits of pasta scattered across the floor in all directions. "For fuck's *sake*," she muttered.

"People always think there's vampires lurking in random places," I said. "Been stories about it for years. As far as I know, the Edge Hill lot are the only ones that are actually real."

"And now witches are real as well," said Izzy. "Where the fuck did the dustpan go? Oh fuck it," she grabbed a broom and swept the shards of pasta into a corner, "that'll have to do."

"Singular witch, I think." Picking up a small kitchen knife from the windowsill, I cut the tape on the next box in the pile and opened it up. "Surely," I said, with my head half inside the box, "this can't be entirely filled with towels?"

"Probably," said Izzy brightly, "I bought three of everything in the range."

"There's only one of you," I pointed out.

"Yes," she said slowly, "but towels need time to air out. And they do get washed occasionally. Anyway," she went on, "there's one each for me and Damon, and a spare for the wash. It was a very sensible purchase, actually."

"If you say so," I said doubtfully. "I'm just not sure you needed three of every single size they offer. Where are they going?"

"In the storage unit in the small room next to the main bathroom," she said. "But it needs putting together first." She pointed to where an intimidatingly large IKEA box was propped against the wall. "Here," she threw something at me and it jangled as I caught it, "I bought a new set of allen keys. That should keep you busy for a while."

~

"And just this one last form," said Eadric, sliding a sheet of heavyweight paper across the desk towards me. I'd long lost count of how many pieces of paper I'd signed already. I wouldn't have been in the office at all, except Izzy had remembered I was supposed to be sorting the paperwork and had kicked me out of her flat. There'd been stern warnings about not coming back until I'd sorted my shit out, and all sorts. Picking up Eadric's heavy ink pen with a sigh, I scribbled an approximation of my name across the bottom of the sheet. Then I sent it skidding back to him across the polished mahogany.

"Why are we bothering with paperwork?" I said. "It's not as though anyone can be allowed to see who's in control of the company." I still wasn't convinced it was a good idea to accept a directorship. Most people would be thrilled by the prospect of being offered a seat on the board of a massively profitable company, and they'd be even more thrilled by the frankly obscene wage that came with it. Because I am clearly an idiot, I'd actually tried to persuade Eadric to lower the amount of money that was about to start flowing into my bank account each month. He'd refused, arguing that it would look strange having one board member earning far less than the others. I'd countered with the argument that as he and Nik were the only other shareholders, no one would care. Eadric insisted that his accountants would, which then led to a lengthy conversation about how to keep such business connections running for years, without anyone realising that their client didn't appear to be ageing.

"Avoid ever meeting them in person," he'd said. "That way you can pretend to be your own granddaughter if needs be." "We have a lawyer who looks after that side of things for us," said Eadric. "You signed to say you're happy for him to undertake legal enquiries and the like on your behalf. Here," he went on, flicking through the stack of forms and pulling one out to show me. The letter heading bore the name of a legal firm with an address near Nottingham.

"And they never query your requests for fake identities?" I asked. "No one's ever wondered why you need forged documents on the reg?"

"As I have told you many times," Eadric had said with a faint smile, "the need does not arise very often. Besides," he held the papers up on end and tapped them against the desk until they were neatly stacked, "money means freedom. Not only from general daily worries about life's expenses, but also from the law. You may not like it," I screwed my face up a bit to illustrate that he was correct in this assumption, "but it is necessary in order to survive." When I'd expressed confusion as to how one person could ever hope to spend even half the amount I was going to be earning each year, Eadric had suggested I should consider giving it to good causes. And so I rang the company's accountant, a stern-sounding man known only as Dave, who'd insisted on first phoning Eadric in order to confirm I was who I claimed to be. I was pretty sure that Dave himself wasn't being entirely open as regards his personal identity, but hadn't bothered arguing. When he'd called back a few minutes later, Dave's voice had held a slight but noticeable air of deference. This didn't, however, stop him from snorting incredulously at my suggestion of sending twenty percent of my income to charity.

"But, erm," he'd eventually managed, "that is a sizeable sum of money, Miss O'Reilly."

"Yup," I'd agreed, "it is. Hopefully it will do some good. Did you get the details I sent you?"

"It's in front of me right now," Dave had said. "Am I to believe this is the, erm," he'd coughed, "'good cause' you wish to donate the funds to?" The quotation marks were actually audible.

"Yes," I'd said firmly. "Doesn't it say 'send it to these people' at the top of the page?"

"It most certainly does," he'd said. There was a brief silence, during which I could practically hear his thoughts. "The Society for, erm," I could hear paper being shuffled in the background, "Feline Rescue and Rehabilitation?"

"Is that a problem?"

"No, no," he'd said hurriedly, "it's just that, well." A pause. "It's not a very...glamorous thing to give such large amounts to, is it?"

"What's wrong with cats?" I'd asked. Both Grimm and Finn had been asleep on the sofa at the time, and two pairs of beady eyes cracked open at my question. Actually it was one and a half pairs, because whilst Finn is like a bouncy toddler who's interested in everything, Grimm is a born cynic who refuses to show curiosity about anything that doesn't affect him directly. One slow-blinking eyeball is about as much as he'll give to anything that doesn't involve food.

"Oh, oh," Dave had spluttered, "I didn't mean to imply it wasn't a very worthy cause. I'd just been expecting something less....esoteric, perhaps."

"Research into the abandonment of big cats in the British countryside doesn't seem particularly esoteric to me," I'd said. Finn had squinted suspiciously at me from under his blanket. Quite how a fully grown man could curl up into such a small space was beyond me. I'd noticed that, despite being in his human form, he still had slit-pupil cat eyes. Not quite awake yet, then. "If they're really out there," I went on, "then it's better that funds are available to those who wish to care for them, no?"

"Do they look for yetis as well?"

"Excuse me?" The coughing that echoed down the phone suggested Dave had belatedly realised his mistake in speaking his thoughts out loud.

"Nothing," he'd said hurriedly. "I'll get on that immediately." And he'd put the phone down without another word. So, yeah—I'm now one of the biggest contributors to the funds of a very secretive charity. I'd been having thoughts about expanding it to dogs, having heard one too many rumours about potential canine incursions into Sefton Park, but when I risked mentioning it to Grimm, he'd informed me it was only acceptable if the money went towards a neutering programme. Somehow I'd managed not to mention that he himself was noticeably sans bollocks. Maybe he'd just been trying to even things out a bit.

"One last thing," said Eadric, interrupting my daydreaming. He slid a small cream envelope across the table towards me. The flap was open and I could see something metallic inside.

"What's this?" I asked.

"Look inside," said Eadric with a smile. Nervously, I picked up the envelope. Knowing my luck, it probably contained Semtex. As I tipped it up, a small silver key slid out and onto the desk with a heavy clunk. "That," he said, "is the key to the last secret we've been keeping from you."

"You've been keeping secrets?" I frowned. "Rude."

"We couldn't risk it until we were sure about you," he shrugged. "Although in truth, we meant to tell you about it quite some time ago. But so much has been happening that we forgot."

"Who's 'we'?" I was suspicious. Keys meant secrets that had needed locking away, and that was never a good sign.

"Our lord and master and me, myself and I, of course," said Nik, appearing through the door that led to his private rooms. "Don't worry,

Lil," he dropped elegantly into the armchair that sat alongside Eadric's desk, "we're not going to drop any unexpected relatives on you."

"Thank fuck for that," I muttered, picking up the key. It was for an old style barrel lock, and looked very much like it had been taken from a wardrobe. "Please tell me there isn't an entrance to Narnia in the basement?"

"Well, it's funny you should say that," said Eadric. He pushed his chair backwards and got to his feet. "Come with me?"

"Where?"

"Oh god, Lil," said Nik, "stop being so dratted suspicious of everything! Surely you can trust us by now?"

"I have learned not to trust anyone," I said, but I stood up anyway. "Apart from Izzy. And maybe Grimm."

"Good lord," said Nik, "I wouldn't trust that animal as far as I could throw him. Isobel is reliable though, I'll give you that."

"If you tried to throw Grimm anywhere," I said, "he'd rip your face off. And shit on it before you could grow it back."

"Children, children," sighed Eadric. "Can we get back to the subject at hand?" Nik and I broke off from glaring at each other and glared at Eadric instead. "This was supposed to be a pleasant surprise," he said. "Please don't spoil it by bickering."

"Yes, Dad," I said. Nik just grinned. "Where are we going?" I asked him.

"I'm going nowhere," said Nik. "I've only just put on clean socks and they're my favourites." He thrust a foot in the air and waggled his toes, which were encased in pale blue knitted silk. "You two can go visit the bowels yourself."

"So we are going down to the basement, then?" I turned to Eadric. "There's nothing but a car park down there. Ooh!" I had an exciting thought. "Have you bought me a car?"

"No," sighed Eadric, "I have not bought you a car, Lilith."

"Well that's disappointing."

"You drive the Alfa more than I do," he said. "And you also own that ridiculous German box that has cost me a ridiculous amount of money already. I really don't think we can justify another car."

"If I had an Alfa of my own," I pointed out, "I could run errands for you. Maybe zip down to London, drop in on Elizabeth, see how the boundaries are getting on. That sort of thing."

"Lilith," said Eadric patiently, "can we please leave the car discussion for another time? I was rather looking forward to surprising you today, and you've already made it very clear it's not what you wanted."

"I don't know what it is yet," I said, "so I can't know I don't want it. Lead the way, guv'nor." I shooed him with my hands, and he shook his head as he turned for the door to the private reception room. "Gonna get me a car," I said to Nik as I passed. Without looking up from his book, he held up a hand and I high-fived him. "Gonna get me a caaaaaar," I hummed to myself as I followed Eadric out into the lobby. He stopped at the doors of the small lift that gives us private access to street level and pressed the button to open the doors. "Are we going outside?" This lift only went to either the car park or the plant room through which we get out onto the street. "It's not like you to go outside with the proles," I went on. "Is it a special occasion?"

"We're not going outside," said Eadric, "and nor are we heading for the car park. Do you have the key?" I waggled it at him, and he nodded. Then he turned to the control panel of the lift. "Come closer," he said, "and put your other hand here." I did as he asked, pressing the palm of my hand against the blank steel below the lift buttons. There was a distinct click beneath my hand, and I felt the panel pop away from the backing plate. As I pulled my hand away in surprise, the panel dropped on hidden hinges to reveal a lock.

"What the fuck?" The lift itself was modern and sleek, all metal and LED lighting, and I used it all the time. The button panel hadn't changed—it still looked exactly like every button panel you ever find on a private lift. Actually, it's only in the last couple of years that I've come into contact with any private lifts, but I'd rapidly become blasé about it. I'd know I'd finally settled into the life of eternal luxury that Eadric and Nik were so used to when I hired a private jet to get to London, instead of borrowing the Alfa. Actually I'd probably never hire a jet because I think about the environment and carbon footprints more than the others do, but the principle still stands. "I'm pretty sure I've put my hand against that before now," I said, nodding at the panel. "Why hasn't it done this before?"

"It wasn't programmed to give you access before." I gave him a suspicious look. He likes to give the impression he's above thinking about modern technology, but it clearly hadn't bypassed him entirely. "Nik sorts it out," he went on, clearly reading my mind. "He gets a man in."

"I bet he does," I snorted.

Eadric rolled his eyes. "Can you keep your mind out of the gutter for once?"

"Not if the rest of me is going to be in the gutter," I said. "And how did you get my hand print?"

"You spend a lot of time shouting at me with your hands on my desk," said Eadric. "It was a simple matter of taking a copy using fingerprint powder."

"You need better cleaners then," I said. "Where are we going, the storm drains?"

"Wait and see." He grinned at me. "God," he said, "you are so frustrating at times, Lilith O'Reilly. Now will you please use the key you've been given? You'll find everything out soon enough."

"I don't know why I should trust you, old man," I said, but I was already putting the key into the lock. "If this drops us into a sewer, I am not going to be happy."

"As if I'd walk around in a sewer," snorted Eadric. I turned to look at him. He had an impish smile on his face and suddenly looked about twenty years younger. "Trust me, Lilith," he said. "Just this once." I held his gaze as I turned the key in the lock. Nothing happened for a second, then the motors clunked into action and the lift began a slow descent.

"The floor numbers aren't coming up," I said, pointing to the control panel. The small screen that usually showed the numbers was resolutely blank, except for a small flashing arrow pointing downwards.

"That's because it's not stopping," said Eadric. "We've bypassed the usual controls."

"A'right, Willy fucking Wonka," I said, "so you've got a magic lift. Where's it taking us?"

"Patience," said Eadric. "You'll see in a minute." It actually only took another thirty seconds for the lift to reach its apparent destination. It made the same pinging noise as usual when it stopped, but the doors didn't open. "Turn the key back," said Eadric. "You have to take it out and keep it safe. We'll need it to get back up to the surface."

"Surface of what?" I asked. "The fucking moon? Jupiter? Hey Jupiterrrrrr," I sang, "I'm the moon!" Eadric nodded silently at the lock, clearly not appreciating my awareness of retro popular culture. Sighing, I turned the key back to the 'off' position before pulling it out of the lock and tucking it into the pocket of my jeans. Finally, I thought, a use for that ridiculous tiny pocket that's always sewn into the front of jeans. Kids at school used to say it was for condoms, but I'd never bought that. Apart from anything else, even a solitary condom would pop back out of that pocket eventually. Although I guessed that's why people used to do it, in the hope of making it seem like they might, at some point in the not-too-distant future, have sex with an actual human being. As I was pondering this, the lift doors finally opened. Finally, I understood why Eadric had made me wait. In front of us, its surface glittering like liquid stars in the darkness, was a lake.

The last time I'd found a lake underneath Liverpool city centre—this shit really does happen to me way more often than I'd like—it nearly ended in half of Mathew Street taking an unexpected journey to the centre of the Earth. But that had been an old, abandoned cavern, complete with stalactites and rough walls. What lay in front of me now was absolutely glorious in its intentional beauty. The lift had opened onto a narrow stone pier, just wide enough for a person to step out onto. "Go on," said Eadric. "Take a look."

I turned to him and narrowed my eyes. "You first," I said. "I've had bad experiences with Silvertons in caves." The Mathew Street incident had been caused by Eadric's then-wife, who would have very much liked to have left me down there forever. That sort of thing stays with you.

"Fine," he said, and stepped past me out onto the plinth. "Look," he went on, "it's completely safe." Before I could say anything, he dropped into the water. It had looked bottomless in the gloom, but didn't even come up to his knees. "This is our secret," he said with a grin. "What do you think?"

"I think," I said, as I finally stepped carefully out onto the walkway, "you are all entirely, amazingly, insane." The—what? Room? Cavern? Basement was too mediocre a word for what lay in front of me. The lake was wide and dark, but now my eyes were adjusting, I could see defined edges in the gloom. Huge stone arches reared out of the water at regular intervals, disappearing up towards a ceiling hidden high above us in the darkness. It looked very much like a crypt. I turned slowly on the spot and saw that the lift shaft was built into a stone wall that looked very much like the external skin of the Liver Building itself. "Hang on," I said, cogs finally beginning to turn. "Are we underneath the building itself?"

"Yup," said Eadric with a grin. "Actually, we're technically in the river. The stone pilings filter the water before it gets in here."

"I'm glad to hear it," I said, eyeballing the tidemark that was gradually soaking its way up his trouser legs. "Can immortals catch cholera?"

"There hasn't been cholera around here for a long time," said Eadric. "You can thank Kitty for that."

"Kitty?" I frowned. "She lives in my flat, Eadric. I think I'd know if she'd been working in public health?"

"Not that Kitty," he grinned. "The one I'm talking about is long gone. Shame, really," he looked wistful. "She'd have been a force to be reckoned with as a revenant."

"Can we do the local history lesson another time?" I asked. "Only I'm wondering how you've got an entire spooky lake underneath the Liver Building and no one apparently knows about it?"

"Oh, they know about it," he said. "Or rather, they suspect. The local history department at the library has got the original plans tucked away somewhere in the archives. But it's been closed off almost since the building first went up, and I suspect most have forgotten it even exists. No one can get down here now."

"Apart from us."

"No one else can be trusted with it," he said. "It's too dangerous to allow humans into places like this." He turned away from me and spread his arms wide, as though greeting the void.

"Obvious question alert," I said to his back, "but what's so dangerous about an underground paddling pool? I mean," I looked around again, "you could probably do with better lighting. And the health and safety bod from the council is going to want handrails on this step. Bit of investment and you could have a nice little tourist trap down here."

"Which is exactly why we cannot allow anyone else to know about it," said Eadric, turning to face me. "This is more than a pretty tourist attraction, Lilith. Much more."

"Okay," I said slowly, wondering if he'd actually gone mad. Existing for a thousand years allowed an awful long time for the old brain cells to start fraying at the edges, after all. "So what is it?"

"You are aware of the City itself," he said. It was a statement rather than a question, and the capitalisation was audible. "You talk to it."

"I do," I said. "Sometimes. We're not what I'd call besties or anything. More like reluctant colleagues."

"It has never spoken to me," said Eadric. "I wonder why that is?"

"Maybe you're too formal," I shrugged.

"I feel it sometimes, though," he said. "Like a defensive dome, covering the city. It feels alive in a way nothing else does." He turned to look at me. "Is that how it feels to you?"

"Protective," I said. "Not defensive."

He nodded. "Listen," he said. "Close your eyes and listen." I closed my eyes and immediately wobbled. So I opened them again and moved so that my back was firmly against the stone wall. "Don't even think about playing tricks on me when I'm not looking," I warned Eadric, "or I'll drown you in your own basement, so help me."

"Just close your eyes and concentrate, Lilith," said Eadric. "I promise it's worth it." I sighed and did as he asked. For a long moment, nothing happened. I could hear the faintest movement of water as it rippled against the stone, but nothing else. "I'm going to sit down on the step next to you," said Eadric quietly, "just stay where you are." Water sloshed quietly as he waded back towards me, and I heard the rustle of fabric as he turned and presumably sat down. "Let it come to you," he said. "Don't chase it." I wanted to tell him I wasn't chasing anything, and in fact had absolutely no idea what on earth he was talking about. But this was clearly a big deal to him, so I decided to indulge. If nothing else, it gave me time to assimilate this fresh addition to my list of weird shit going on under the streets of Liverpool. We couldn't be right down at the riverbed, surely? Although perhaps it wasn't actually that deep. After all, the Strand and all the docks and buildings attached to it were built out from the river bank, over what was once a shingle beach. And the cavern underneath Mathew Street had been carved by hand from the sandstone bedrock. So yeah, maybe it really was possible to create an underwater lagoon that nobody knew about. As I stood in the strange underwater vault and allowed my mind to wander, I felt something else creeping into my head. Something old and comforting and safe. Something caring and warm, but also traumatised and abandoned. Something that was feeling its way carefully, trying to work out if I was friend or foe. Something—

Whoah, I said silently. It's generally considered polite to introduce yourself before clambering inside someone's mind. The weird creeping feeling stopped, but there was no reply. Which was actually a bloody relief, because the two voices that liked to pop into my head on the reg were already two too many. Do you have a name? I tried. Nothing. Remembering what Eadric had said about not chasing, I kept my eyes closed and slowly slid down the wall until I was sitting next to him on the plinth. At least, I thought I was—he could have disappeared into thin air, for all I knew. But somehow I knew I had to keep my eyes closed or it wouldn't work. Just as I was beginning to think I'd imagined the entire thing, the creeping feeling started again. It was tentative and soft, and not remotely scary. It's okay, I said, I won't hurt you. A warmth began to wrap itself around me, as though trying to snuggle in for comfort. It curled and coiled around my shoulders and down my legs, as though working me out. Then it widened and became more blanket than rope, enveloping me in a warmth and hunger and a desperate desire to be—what? My eyes blinked open and the feeling drained away instantaneously, leaving me staring blankly into the darkness.

"You felt it," said Eadric. "Didn't you?"

"Does it do that to you?" I asked.

"Do what?"

"It tried to, I don't know," I trailed off. "The best way I can describe it is like a lost dog or something?" I turned to look at him. His eyes were interested and curious, and it occurred to me he seemed more at peace down here in the watery darkness than I'd ever seen him. "An abandoned dog," I went on, warming to my metaphor, "that's been abused and ignored and isn't sure whether or not its rescuers are going to be kind."

"Incredible," breathed Eadric. "You really do feel it."

"It would be bloody hard not to," I said, my usual cynicism finally making a reappearance. That was a relief—for a second I'd been worried I might have had some kind of religious experience and might be doomed to just smile beatifically at everyone and be a pro-level kind person for the rest of eternity. And that wouldn't do. "How do you cope with it?" I asked him. "Do you come down here a lot?"

"Not recently," he said.

"Cities are for life," I admonished him, "not just for Christmas. You can't just leave it down here all alone without checking on it! Where's your heart?"

"I didn't abandon it, Lilith," he smiled. "It abandoned me."

"What do you mean, it abandoned you?" We were still sitting on the stone plinth in the crypt, the dark water still casting galaxies onto the stone from the reflected light coming from the open lift door. "People abandon cities, not the other way around. Anyway, it's still here. I felt it."

"As did I," said Eadric, "until fairly recently. Roughly until you arrived on the scene, in fact. It wasn't as you describe it, though. Not for me."

"What was it like?"

"It was just," he looked thoughtful, "a presence? I think that's how I'd describe it, anyway. Nothing specific, just an awareness that something else was there. It was bigger and older than me, and it didn't seem to care whether I was here or not. I found that comforting in a way."

"You were comforted by the fact it didn't care?" I asked. "You should probably consider therapy."

"I know myself better than any therapist." Eadric smiled. "I liked the fact that whatever it was, it clearly considered me irrelevant. Sometimes it's nice to feel utterly unimportant—just a minuscule atom in the maelstrom of existence."

"Nihilism, thy name is Eadric Silverton."

"It was friendly," he said, ignoring my witty comebacks as usual. "I could tell that much. But nothing real enough for me to credit it with any sentience. And although I was fascinated by it, it never seemed very interested in me."

"Oh it's sentient alright," I said. "I don't think it's the city itself, though."

"Well of course I wouldn't know what that was like," said Eadric. "So I'm not in a position to make comparisons." He looked thoughtful. "Perhaps it's the land itself."

"I don't think so." I said. "When I speak to the city—*the* City, the one with a capital 'C'—I always get the impression that it's, ummm," I frowned. "It's *everything*. If that makes sense?" Eadric shrugged as if to say we both knew nothing made sense whatsoever but hey, we're used to that now, right? "It's the buildings and the history and the land and, well. Everything. But this is different." I turned to look across the crypt. "It feels deeper. Both metaphorically *and* literally."

"We'll have to head back up in a minute," said Eadric. "But now you've got the key, you can come and go as you please." He put a hand on my arm. "Lilith?"

"Sorry," I said, turning to him. "I was in a world of my own for a minute." I was beginning to get an inkling as to what the water spirit might be, but didn't want to say it out loud in case it sounded stupid.

Don't worry about that, said the city, ***we're all used to it***.

I'm right though, I said silently, "*aren't I?*"

Yes.

"Are you okay, Lilith?" Eadric asked. I screwed my face up and wriggled around a bit, as if that might help things settle.

"Yeah," I said, turning to him, "I'm fine. Don't be fretting about me, grandad."

"I'm not fretting about you," said Eadric. "It's just that when you go quiet, it's usually because something terrible is about to happen."

"Cheeky fucker," I said, getting to my feet. "Just for that, I'm going to tell Nik you think his poetry's shit."

"I'd really rather you didn't," said Eadric, waiting for me to step into the lift before following me in. "Mapp once criticised something Nikolaus had written many decades previously and it didn't end well."

"Ooh," I said, turning the key in the control panel and watching as the doors closed on the darkness, "handbags at dawn!"

"More like quills," said Eadric with a grin. "Those Romantics were always a strange bunch."

Keep Your Friends Close - And Your Enemies Closer

When we got back up to the top of the clock tower, there was a visitor waiting for us in the lift lobby. She was tall and elegant, with cropped black hair and sly, cat-like eyes. Her emerald green silk blouse fastened tightly at the neck and wrists and dropped loosely over her skin-tight black jeans. Long legs ended in spike-heeled black ankle boots, one of them swaying gently in the air as she lounged cross-legged on the red velvet sofa. "Good to see you again, Lilith," said Eve, getting to her feet. I had no idea what the British government's Head of Weird Shit was doing back in Liverpool, but it was unlikely to be a good omen. I shook her outstretched hand, which was as soft and supple as always and definitely did not feel as though it belonged to someone as old as I knew her to be. "Eadric," she nodded. He shook her hand politely. "You rarely leave the tower," she said, "unless it's urgent. I often think of you as the northern equivalent of the London ravens." She smiled. "If you go outside for too long, is the building at risk of collapse?" *She doesn't know about the crypt*, I realised.

Which is interesting in itself, said the city. ***Don't you think?***

"How can we help you, Eve?" Eadric asked, refusing to bite. "I hope nothing untoward has occurred?"

"It was actually Lilith I was hoping to speak to," said Eve. "If that's acceptable?"

"It's not my decision to make," said Eadric. He was being perfectly polite, but I could tell he'd been knocked slightly off-balance. Eve didn't know about the crypt, and Eadric really didn't want her to know. "Lilith makes her own decisions. As I'm sure you're well aware."

"Of course," said Eve smoothly. "Lilith?" She looked at me. "Could we perhaps walk outside for a while?"

"I'm pretty sure it would be easier to just talk in here," I said. "There can't be much you can say to me that Eadric can't hear."

"It's fine," he said lightly. "I'm sure I can trust you to keep the family secrets." The ghost of a wink. "You're not to bully our visitor, though. Understood?"

"Aye aye, cap'n." I gave a mock salute, and he walked off into the office. As he turned to close the door behind him, he was out of Eve's line of sight. He raised an elegantly curious eyebrow and closed the doors. I turned on Eve. "What the fuck are you really doing here?" I demanded. "Because I'm pretty sure this isn't a social visit?"

"Of course it's a social visit," said Eve. "You're far too cynical. As I said to Eadric, I thought we might go for a walk."

"What for?" I eyed her suspiciously.

"Let's call it a corporate induction," she said. "Or introduction, if you like."

"Introduction to what?" I said, pressing the button to open the lift doors. I'd met Eve on a couple of previous occasions and although she could be annoyingly intrusive in matters of a paranormal nature, she was safe enough. She'd actually backed me up in the face of her colleagues on more than one occasion, and I value that sort of thing in my friends. She didn't open any secret compartments in the lift or open a door to Narnia; instead, she merely pressed the very normal button for the very normal ground floor. We stepped out into the main atrium of the Liver Building and I followed Eve out onto Canada Boulevard. It was a muggy and overcast day, the sun trying and failing to burn its way through the cloud cover. There seemed to be more people around than usual, and I realised it must be school summer holidays already. Time's weird when you're immortal. I'd only been dead a couple of years, but I was already losing the human habit of keeping track of the seasons. I guess the weather isn't as important when you don't sweat or feel the cold. Winter or summer, it's all the same to us. I still tied my hair up with the scrunchie I always keep wedged in my jeans pocket for emergencies. It didn't matter that I was immune to heatstroke, if I let my hair hang free in this sort of weather it would still frizz itself up into a puffball the Hair Bear Bunch would be proud of.

"To the background of revenants," Eve said. "The truth about how we came to exist." She flashed a grin at me. "That sort of thing."

"In all honesty," I said, "I decided a long time ago that we're just humans with some kind of extra freak gene added."

"Is that what you think?" Eve asked. "That humans came first and we're an offshoot of them?"

"Yup," I said, pausing to check for traffic before we crossed the Strand. "We're throwbacks, I reckon. Where are we going, anyway?"

"Right now," said Eve, "we're going for coffee. That way we can have a chat without other people involving themselves."

"What other people?" We got to the top of Brunswick Street and Eve turned left. I was expecting her to cross the road to the coffee shop I'd been to with Jenny and Freya, but to my surprise, she kept walking until we were outside Cafe Nero.

"Why don't you sit down," she indicated an empty table outside, "and I'll get coffee. Black?" I nodded and she disappeared inside. I realised it was the table that was making me suspicious. I knew for a fact there were usually at least three tables outside this particular branch, and they were never empty. But today, just as Eve had decided to visit for a spooky heart-to-heart—or whatever it was she was really after—there was no one else around. I wondered just how far Eve's influence reached. "They're bringing it out to us," she said, reappearing through the doorway. "Do you not want to sit?" So I sat, and Eve took the chair opposite me. She didn't say anything; rather, she just gazed across the table at me with an expression of friendly yet somehow resigned amusement. I was about to open my mouth and break the silence when a barista appeared with our order. "Thank you, my darling," Eve said, taking the tray. "You're an angel." The woman blushed and nodded her head in sheepish acknowledgement before disappearing back inside.

"Want to tell me what this is all about?" I asked, after Eve had arranged the table to her satisfaction and propped the empty tray up against the wall behind us.

"Eadric tells me you've finally agreed to join the family firm," she said without preamble. "So I figured this was as good a time as any to bring you up to speed on a few things."

"Like what?" I stirred my coffee for no other reason than to give me something to do. Also, I'd drunk way more coffee over the last couple of days than I ever normally consumed, and I was concerned it might start seeping back out. Revenants can—and need to—drink liquids in order to make up for natural evaporation, but one mocha latte too many and you're leaking coffee out of your eyeballs. Which can take some explaining if you're in a public place when it happens.

"How much has the cat told you?" I gaped at her silently. "I know that you have been in communication with that animal of yours," she went on, when it became clear I wouldn't be replying at any speed, "and now I'm wondering just what he's been telling you."

"I don't know what you're talking about," I managed eventually. "How can anyone have a conversation with a cat? Ridiculous idea."

"Oh," said Eve, "I don't know. Probably in much the same way they can talk to a metal bird. Or a were-cat. Or a city, maybe." She smiled. "I know more than you realise, Lilith," she said. "And perhaps more than you'd like. But that's the nature of the beast, isn't it? We're all trying to keep our balance in a world of things that go out of their way to keep us off balance."

"I have absolutely no idea what you're talking about," I said truthfully.

"What about the Grail?" She took a calm sip of her green tea. "I'd imagine that's causing you quite some confusion at the moment." She put her cup down and it clattered against the saucer. "Never did see the point of saucers," she said. "They always seem like an unnecessary affectation to me."

"Okay," I said finally, "I give up. You win." Eve raised a questioning eyebrow. "I have absolutely no idea what you're talking about," I said, "and I think you're doing it on purpose."

"Why would I do that?"

"I have absolutely no fucking idea," I said. "But you lot like putting people on the back foot, don't you?"

"'You lot'?" Eve smiled. "I think you'll find you're actually one of 'you lot', Lilith. Whether you like it or not."

"Oh, don't start with that bollocks," I said. "It's boring. You expect me to be all 'I didn't ask for this' and then you can give it the old 'but you're here now and you'll just have to deal with it', same as always. You forget, Eve," I leaned towards her slightly and lowered my voice, "I've been dead a good while now, and I've had time to come to terms with it. And what I've mostly realised in that time is that everyone has an ulterior motive. You, Eadric, absolutely bloody everyone. Including me."

"Can I ask what your motive might be?" She was smiling again, and I was beginning to find it very annoying.

"My sole motive," I said, "is to keep on living."

"But you're dead, Lilith," she said. "We keep having to remind you of that."

"I don't need you to remind me," I said. "I am well aware of my deceased status, thank you very much. I'll rephrase it for you. My motive, Eve, is to carry on with my life whilst doing what I think is best with the rest of it. The spooky shit. The vampires and were-cats and sodding bloody witches, all of it."

"Witches?" Eve's voice betrayed her curiosity. "The witches are back in Liverpool? That's very interesting."

"It was just a turn of phrase," I said, suddenly deciding it might be better to keep Freya to myself. "I have no fucking idea whether there are actually any witches around. And neither," I added, "am I interested in finding out."

"Well I would be," said Eve lightly. "They're a fascinating breed. Anyway," she went on, "back to the matter in hand. I don't have much time," she checked her watch for emphasis, "and I won't be back this way for a while."

"You were asking me about the Grail," I said. "That bastion of historical romance, that I'm pretty sure never even existed. Yet you're all somehow attached to the myth. This shit might be important to you, Eve, but from where I'm standing it's just another stupid drama waiting to kick off. Why the hell," I was warming to my subject, "can't anything be simple? Why can't you just have a conversation, instead of going off on tangents about sodding tea cups or spirits or holy sodding artefacts?"

"Human memories are short," said Eve, "and liable to conveniently ignore any events that don't fit their preferred narrative." She took another sip of her tea, gazing at me over the top of the cup. "Do you know how old the Grail actually is, Lilith?"

"You're telling me it's real?" I asked her. "Really real?"

"Do you think it's real?"

I thought about it for a moment. "I think it's real in the heads of those who believe in it," I said finally. "And I think it probably did exist at some point."

"But?"

"But what?"

"This particular 'but' is written all over your face, Lilith." Eve smiled. She really did have the most beautiful smile I'd ever seen on a human being. It wasn't a particularly broad smile, or one that showed lots of perfect teeth. It was a kind smile. Eve radiated goodness. Which was interesting, because Eve worked with the government. And goodness has never been on the list of required qualifications for civil servants.

"Are you human?" I'd blurted it out before I could stop myself.

The smile widened. "What a strange question," she said. "But then you've always been full of questions, haven't you?" She leaned back in her seat and gazed levelly at me. "What does 'human' even mean?" she asked. "You believe you're human, Lilith. And yet you don't fit any of the parameters that usually apply in order to qualify someone as such."

"What do you mean?"

"You're human because you hold on to humanity, Lilith. You cling to it like a life raft on turbulent waters." She paused and looked thoughtful. "I sometimes wonder what would happen if you let go."

"Let go of what?"

"Let go of your own expectations," she said. "Allowed yourself to just...be. What would happen then, Lilith O'Reilly?"

"I'd probably lose what's left of my marbles and tear the city up in a fury," I said.

"You really would," she said, "wouldn't you? I'd like to see that one day, I think. It would be an interesting experience."

"Not for anyone who happened to be in the city at the time."

"True." We sat silently for a while, but it wasn't uncomfortable. I usually find long silences really awkward. It feels as though you're just waiting on the terrible thing to happen, even when nothing terrible is expected. Although in my experience, the point at which nothing terrible is expected to happen is usually when the terrible thing happens. So I fill the silence with inane chatter in order to stave off the terribleness. I had no urge to fill the silence with Eve. There was something monumentally solid about this slender, dark woman—a definiteness about her entire being. I'd only met her a handful of times, but the idea of a world without Eve in it was as unimaginable as a world without the breeze that blew in from the Mersey, reminding everyone that the sea was waiting for all of us, eventually.

"I don't think it's very old," I said eventually. "The Grail, I mean." I turned my head to see Eve watching me with interest. "Or if it is, then that's a different Grail. I think," I said, warming to my theory, "the Grail—our Grail, if you want to call it that—is old. But I think the conventional one—the one everyone thinks of, that held the blood of Christ and all that jazz—is a newer invention. Or," I shrugged, "maybe it never existed in the first place." I turned to find Eve grinning at me, amusement crinkling the corners of her eyes. "What?"

"'All that jazz,'" she said. "The origin story of one of the most powerful religions in history, and you describe it as 'all that jazz'." She made an inelegant snorting noise that was at odds with her appearance.

"I'm not big on religion," I said defensively. "Never have been. So if you're expecting me to be in awe of anything that involves a church of any denomination, you've got the wrong person."

"It wasn't a criticism," she said. "It was merely an observation. If more people were less impressionable when it came to the gods," she went on, "I think the world might be a much nicer place. And it's interesting," her eyes didn't leave me for a second, "that you so readily suggest the existence of another, more solid Grail. One that is older than the world could imagine. The source of our existence, perhaps."

"You're one of us, then?" I asked. "A revenant, I mean?"

"What do you think I am?" she said. "I'm sure the Silvertons must have theories. And Gaultier Mapp always did like the opportunity for a good gossip."

"What do I think you are?" Eve nodded. "I mean," I floundered, "apart from seriously fucking hot?"

"That's very sweet of you," she said, "but I meant more on a biological level."

"I dunno," I shrugged. "It's about the same thing from where I'm looking at it. Okay, okay," I'd seen her expression of amused tolerance with just a twitch of impatience, "I think you're one of us. But maybe at a higher level. Got your prefect badge, that sort of thing. Am I close?"

"Not about the prefect badge." Eve smiled. "But not far off with the rest of it. What do you know about the Sumerians, Lilith?"

"The King List?" She nodded. "They were around a very, very long time ago," I said, "and they all lived for a very, very long time. That's about the sum of my knowledge, I'm afraid." I'd long ago mastered the art of shutting irrelevant memories tightly down in mental boxes, because after I'd died my brain decided to dredge up every fact and figure and memory and embarrassment and, well, pretty much everything I'd ever witnessed. And it had dumped the lot right at the forefront of my mind, as though I wanted nothing more than to spend the rest of eternity chewing over why the fuck I'd turned Stef Woodson down when they'd invited me out on a double date back when I was eighteen. I was about to leave home for university and was still boringly sensible enough to think it wouldn't be a good idea to potentially start a relationship just as I was moving away. But there was no denying that Stef was as hot as the surface of the sun. I can only assume I'd been going through a phase of dramatic self-sabotage at the time, because that was one of the most ridiculously stupid decisions of my entire adult life. Especially as Stef had gone on to become a television producer and occasionally posted photos from fancy celebrity events on Instagram. Not that I'm shallow, you understand. Anyway, my reincarnation as an immortal had brought with it every memory I'd ever had, and I'd had to shut that shit down hard to avoid losing what was left of my marbles. But sometimes little bits pop back up, whether I like it or not. "Oh!" I said, as just such rogue thought popped up and tapped at the door of my memories. "Are you suggesting we're Sumerian?" I boggled my eyes at her. "Cos I'm pretty sure I'm just from Shropshire, in all honesty."

"You're not, though," she said, "are you? Yes, you were born in the borderlands. But your family is Irish, I think?"

"On one side," I said. "Just Mum's lot."

"Your father grew up in a family of witches," said Eve. "That isn't as common as you might think."

"I didn't think it was common at all," I said honestly. "And I'm pretty sure I'd have heard about it already if there were witches in the family tree." Actually, I wasn't as sure about that as I hoped I sounded. A lot of family secrets had bubbled to the surface since I'd died, and witches weren't even the weirdest one so far. "I just assumed I'd lucked out with the weirdo genetics. Maybe that was why I didn't die when I fell off the roof."

"You died as a human," Eve said. "But your true nature carried you through."

"What sort of nature might that be?" I was feeling indignant now. Eve was discussing my family's bloodline as though we were in some kind of breeding programme. "I'm still me, dead or not."

"So I ask you again," said Eve, "what do you think I am?" I gazed levelly at her, giving myself time to think. It didn't matter how old or important Eve might be, she didn't get to play me like a cat with a sparkly new toy.

"I think," I said eventually, "you're just Eve. And I also think," I considered my words carefully, "you might just be the oldest person I have ever met in my life." And I know people who were born when the years were still only in three digits.

"And you'd be right."

"So what does the Grail have to do with it?" I asked. "Our Grail, I mean. Is it Sumerian? Or are you—we—just an evolutionary offshoot that no one really understands?"

"The Grail is what endows immortality," said Eve. "There are conditions, of course. But those who meet those conditions are granted eternal life, as well as healing of all wounds."

"Mental or physical?" I asked.

"Both," she said. "You were right, Lilith. The Grail—as modern humanity knows it, at least—is entirely fictional. You've read the Arthurian legends, I assume?"

"Some of them," I shrugged. "They're a bit bloody wet, if you ask me."

"They really are very wet," agreed Eve with a grin. "But that's what comes of leaving overindulged young men in the company of pen and paper without appropriate supervision. They get carried away by the dramatic romance of it all. Geoffrey of Monmouth had a lot to answer for." She sighed. "And don't even start me on Beowulf."

"Grendel should have bitten his head off at the start," I said. "That poor dragon."

"Indeed."

"So, did you drink from the Grail?" I asked her. "The real one—our Grail? Back when...whenever you were still human?"

"Do you think I'm not human now?"

"Well, you work as a civil servant," I said. "So I'm honestly not entirely sure."

"Touché," she smiled. "But no, I didn't drink from the Grail. I was the last of my line, Lilith. Every one of my family and friends died. Or were murdered, or simply went missing. It happened over a very lengthy period of time, and it took a while for the realisation to dawn on me that I would, indeed, be alone forever." She paused for the briefest of moments, then turned to look at me with a determinedly bright expression on her face. "So I travelled. I travelled to countries where no one knew me, where people were just getting started with the world and inventing and learning and oh! So many wonderful things." She smiled. "So very many wonderful things."

"When was this?" I asked.

"Time before time," said Eve. "The passage of days wasn't considered as important back then, so it wasn't marked. At least, not in the way we mark it these days. Back then we had the seasons and we recognised certain weather patterns, but not where they'd come from. So people assumed it was magic. And modern historians assume it's all been wrongly translated. Which just goes to show how foolish modern historians can be."

"It's true, then?" I frowned. "You're telling me that the Sumerians were real?"

"Of course the Sumerians were real," said Eve. "That's an established historical fact."

"I know that," I said, "it's Mesopotamia. Modern Iraq. But," I squinted my eyes and looked up towards the sun, as though it might give me some answers, "you really did all live for centuries at a time?"

"I'm still here, aren't I?"

"When were you born?" I dropped my gaze back down, green and red blurs dancing across my vision from the sun.

"Like I said," Eve smiled, "before time."

"A thousand years old?" I persisted. "Two?"

"More than I can remember," said Eve, "and that's the truth. You stop worrying about how fast the weeks and months are going when your life span is measured in millennia."

"Yeah," I shrugged. "That's what Eadric says."

"He's still a baby," said Eve. "He's got a lot to learn." She saw my raised eyebrows. "What?"

"If Eadric's a baby," I said, "what am I?"

"You're thirty-two years old," said Eve. "And you'll be thirty-two years old forever. It's not a bad age to be stuck at. And," she gave the ghost of a wink, "you're still more mature than Eadric Silverton."

I frowned at her. "What makes you say that?"

"'Mature' might be the wrong word," said Eve. "More pragmatic, maybe? There's a level of bloody-minded determination in you that doesn't happen often."

"Just lucky, I guess. So you're telling me anyone could drink from the Grail—like, literally drop their vodka-Red Bull in it and give it a slug—and become immortal? Although," I frowned, "maybe I'm thinking of a film. Please tell me the killer rabbit's real?" Eve looked blank. "Never mind," I sighed. "You'd remember if you'd seen it."

"I can't say I recall that one," said Eve. "But yes, immortality is granted to those who drink from the Grail. It's not that simple, though."

"Quelle surprise."

Eve smiled. "If it really was just a case of drinking from the Grail and becoming immortal," she said, "the world would have been overrun with revenants centuries ago. No, the Grail is, to all intents and purposes, nothing more than a small and insignificant cup. You probably wouldn't even notice it if I put it on a shelf with other crockery." She looked thoughtful. "Assuming the rest of the crockery was also handmade several thousand years ago, of course."

"Of course," I said. "So, what's the magic word?"

"What magic word?" asked Eve. "This isn't wizard school, Lilith. I didn't say I'd never watched any movies," she said, seeing my expression, "just not the ones you were referencing. I have friends at work who are huge fans and I've been to the cinema with them occasionally. Can't say they're really my thing," she went on. "Too much dodgy politics bubbling under the surface, if you ask me. I have enough of that in the office."

"So it's not magic?" I asked. "We're not secretly actually witches and wizards?"

"Oh," said Eve, "they exist, for sure. But I prefer to call them scientists. And no, we're not scientists."

"What's scientific about any of it?" I frowned. "None of it makes any sense, not on a scientific level."

"Humans have an unfortunate tendency to ascribe anything unknown to the powers of magic," said Eve. "What you all forget is that things are not automatically impossible, just because you haven't thought of them yet. Humanity can be terribly arrogant at times."

"Humans are arrogant most of the time, in my experience," I said. "Always trying to control things and bend the world to their will. Destroying anything that doesn't do what they want it to."

"Or simply ignoring it entirely," said Eve. "Which I think is somehow worse. Do you know how magnetism works?"

"I'm not entirely stupid, thank you very much." I frowned as I realised I wasn't actually entirely sure I did know. "North pole, south pole," I said. "Law of attraction, and all that."

"The supposed law of attraction is that positive thoughts and behaviour attract similarly positive responses in others," said Eve. "It has nothing to do with polarities."

"A'right, Einstein," I snarked. "We're not all centuries-old geniuses, thank you."

"I'm no genius," said Eve. "Just open-minded. You understand that everything is made of atoms, yes? And those atoms are always moving, even though the item they make up isn't?" I nodded. "Magnetism is caused by the activity of the electrons within those atoms. Most materials are made of atoms within which roughly half the electrons spin in one direction, and the other half spin the opposite way. They cancel each other out and the item is inert. Or magnetically neutral, if you like. But in some things, the electrons all spin in the same direction—and that creates enough physical force to give them magnetic power. I'm oversimplifying here, obviously."

"Obviously," I said, trying not to drool. I always did find intelligence attractive.

"So," she went on, "magnetism is an invisible force which is absolutely scientific and provable, but invisible. And for a very long time, that invisibility—the fact that it cannot be physically seen to happen—persuaded people that magnetism was a form of magic. As I said," she smiled, "magic is merely science that hasn't been discovered yet."

"Okay," I said, "magic isn't real, but science is. And we're real, even though no one knows how or why."

Eve nodded. "There are theories," she said, "but nothing provable. Not yet, anyway."

"But it has something to do with this Grail?" I could feel my eyes beginning to squint with the strain of trying to work things out in my head. Not even exaggerating—they do it when I'm tired, concentrating or pissed. Izzy always said she could tell when I'd had too much to drink, because my right eye goes wandering. It's not the most attractive quirk, but it could be worse.

"It involves drinking from the Grail," she said, "yes. But something else has to happen at the same time. Care to take a guess at what that might be?"

"You have to dress as a clown and ride a unicycle whilst reciting the last three pages of the Mabinogion?" I shrugged. "Honestly, Eve," I said, "it could be anything. This ridiculous underworld of ours might need people to hop on one foot whilst making a sacrifice to the Death of Rats, for all I know."

"You have to be wearing something whilst drinking from the Grail," said Eve. "A very specific something. Something few people have seen, let alone touched." A horrible thought began crawling its way up the back of my neck in order to scratch at my brain with ominously sharp claws.

"This…thing," I started slowly, "does it have a name?" Shit, shit, shit. I was pretty sure that the key to immortality was currently divided up between me, Izzy, and the void space beneath my bedroom floorboards.

"Want to tell me where you got that ring from, Lilith?" said Eve, nodding at my hand. Even as she said it, I felt the gold band vibrating against my skin, as though it was scared of being discovered.

"It was a gift," I said, with more confidence than I felt.

"I'm sure it was," said Eve, "but that doesn't mean it was yours to destroy." I opened my mouth to speak, but she held up a hand. "No, you don't need to make up excuses for my sake, Lilith. In fact, I'm not entirely sure that I don't approve of what you've done. It might be better for the power to be broken up. Although I perhaps wouldn't have done it quite so literally."

"You're supposed to disapprove, though," I said. "Aren't you?" Eve nodded.

"I am," she said, "yes. The crown was so much more than the sum of its parts." It still is, I thought, feeling its warmth spreading up through my hand. But you don't know that, do you? Which is interesting. "But sometimes I wonder whose rules I'm living by, after all these centuries. I've already outlived everyone who attempted to tell me what to do. And I'm not planning to break that habit any time soon."

"What's your point here, Eve?" The ring was getting hotter, and it was taking a lot of concentration to not wedge my hand into my lap in order to hide it from Eve's calm gaze. "If you already knew what I'd done, why have we been sitting here talking in circles for so long?" I was sure the metal was burning my finger. Glancing down, I was horrified to see my hand was glowing. I hid it behind my back, clenching and unclenching my fingers in the hope it might dissipate some of the heat.

"Because I had to know," said Eve. "I had to see for myself."

She's dangerous, said the city. Its sudden arrival in my head made me jump, and Eve didn't bother hiding the fact that she'd noticed. ***But probably not to you.***

What about to the city in general? I asked it. *What are her motives?*

She's too old for anything as basic as motives, it said. ***She goes beyond that. Right back to the dawn of measurable time. Back to the beginning, as the books say.***

You're not telling me she's—

We're not telling you anything, Lilith. Other than how real she is. You can be her enemy, or you can be her ally. Each option is equally dangerous.

What would the others do? Eve was gazing at me silently, the ghost of a smile twitching at the corners of her mouth. I was pretty sure she knew damn well I was having a full-blown conversation in my head.

It doesn't matter what the others would do, said the city. ***All that matters now is what* you *do.***

What would the big cheese say? I asked it.

Ask it yourself, said the city, and faded away.

"What does the city think?" asked Eve. I didn't bother asking her how she knew who I was talking to.

"It thinks I have to make up my own mind," I said.

She smiled and stood up. "Come with me," she said. "I want to show you something."

Enemy Of The (Undead) State

The Martins Bank building on Water Street is as famous for its history as its imposing architecture. Built in the late nineteen-twenties in the classical style, the building has long lost its purpose as a banking hall in favour of looming blankly over Water Street. One of those places that's too fancy to demolish whilst also being too big and expensive for most businesses to risk taking on, Martins Bank is best known for being the onetime guardian of the British gold reserves. During the first year of WWII, the decision was made to move Britain's wealth out of the country, in order to keep the national coffers safe in the event of Hitler and his cronies actually managing an invasion. London's stash of the gold stuff was therefore transported in secret up to Liverpool and stored in the hastily repurposed vaults of Martins Bank. It makes for a thrilling story, but the riches were only in Liverpool for a short time. Within weeks they had been moved again, this time onto ships bound for Canada. Hardly anyone involved in the manoeuvres—codenamed Operation Fish—knew what it was they were actually transporting across the ocean. Which is probably why the entire cargo—worth over thirty billion of your English pounds, in twenty-first century money—made it safely to Halifax, Nova Scotia, without a single sailor becoming suddenly and suspiciously wealthy along the way. Those sailors really earned their wages on that trip, by the way. Still unaware of the true nature of their cargo—although possibly suspicious, when they realised they were being joined by a heavily armed fleet of escort ships—they sailed safely to Canada, only for one of the 'treasure ships' to develop engine trouble and drift to a halt in foggy seas. Unable to risk the entire fleet, MS Batory was left to sit in open waters with only a single warship—HMS Bonaventure—for protection. I'm sure military historians would tell the story as an illustration of British pluck under duress, but for one thing, the Batory was Polish; and for another, I'm pretty sure no one was feeling very plucky in the moment. I suspect there was an awful lot of brown trousers by the time repairs were made and the ships finally followed their compadres into Halifax harbour several days later. Martins Bank continued as a boringly normal bank until it was finally closed and vacated in 2009. And as far as I knew, it had lain empty ever since. "Why do you think it's been empty for so long?" Eve asked, as if reading my mind.

"Because it's huge and expensive?" I suggested, really hoping she couldn't actually read my mind. "And it's a listed building, so they probably can't carve it up into tiny student flats like they've done with everything else." I frowned. "Why has it been empty all this time?" I asked. We stood looking up at the vast building that towered above us. "Water Street is as central as it gets," I went on, "and this is one of the most famous buildings in town. How come none of those ridiculous hedge-fund companies have taken it over?"

"Hedge funds don't really exist outside the capital," said Eve. "In fact, they don't really exist at all." She sighed. "It's all just imaginary numbers, Lilith. Endless numbers, pushed and pulled around by people who think they're more intelligent than they really are. Ones and zeros, bouncing between nonexistent places and risking boom or bust with every transfer."

"I've never understood that side of finance," I said. And, seeing Eve's mouth opening to speak, added "and I don't need to know about it now, either."

Eve smiled. "I'm going to show you something few people get to see," she said.

"I've heard that one before." Eve rolled her eyes but didn't bother replying. Instead, she beckoned me to follow as she headed down Exchange Street West, to where construction hoardings blocked off an entire side of the bank building. A scruffy-looking man in old work clothes and a high-vis jacket was leaning against a large, hinged access panel. To my utter astonishment, when he saw Eve, he jumped to his feet and saluted.

"Morning, Miss Eve," he said. "Come to check we're up to scratch?"

"Do you think you need checking up on, Joachim?" she asked, one eyebrow raised in apparent amusement.

"Oh no, of course not," said the man. He looked like any of the hundreds of anonymous workers who crawl up and over the buildings of Liverpool on a daily basis, but for some reason he was clearly flustered by Eve's mere presence. "It's all under control. As always." He pressed buttons on a small metal box on the access gate and it opened with a solid-sounding clunk.

"Glad to hear it," said Eve, as he pushed the gate open for us. "We'll let ourselves in." She strode ahead, and I had to do a little skip to keep up with her. Poor Joachim, who was red-faced and staring determinedly at the floor, actually gave me something approaching a bow as I passed. The gate closed again behind us, and I was pretty sure I heard Joachim let out a sigh of relief.

"What's all this about?" I asked. Eve didn't reply until we'd reached a door at almost the far end of the building. It was old and heavy and set well back, so the stonework formed a porch around it. A small brass plaque on the door read 'Eden Enterprises Inc.'.

"Some things," she said, taking a small key from her pocket and unlocking the door, "are so important that I cannot allow anyone else to be involved. To that end, I keep offices in certain of the more..." she squinted into the darkness before finding a light switch, "relevant cities." She flipped the switch, and a harsh yellow ceiling light illuminated a bare concrete corridor. "Life is so much easier if you don't trust anyone, don't you think?"

"Sounds pretty miserable, if you ask me." I followed her inside and pulled the door shut behind us. It didn't seem to have much more than a standard Yale lock protecting it from, well, whatever it needed protecting from. Maybe Eve booby-trapped it each time she left.

Nothing would have surprised me at this point. I stared at the back of her head as I followed her down the corridor. Her dark hair was cropped as short as ever, and pomaded firmly into place. A single rogue curl had escaped and was sitting behind her right ear like a concealed earpiece. I thought she would probably end up with ringlets if she ever let it grow out, and wondered idly whether she ever had to cut it. Contrary to what you probably think you know from endless terrible movie depictions of the undead, our bodies still function and our hair still grows—it just happens at a glacial pace. Her heels clicked confidently on the bare grey floor of the corridor and I muttered my regular hex against those who can somehow walk in skyscraper heels. I know they're no good for your posture and I've heard all the theories about them being a male invention designed to keep women at a disadvantage—most of them via Izzy, who insists that shoes are a feminist issue—but I've always envied anyone who can teeter around on five-inch stillies without looking like a baby deer that's been at the gin. It had just occurred to me I should perhaps be making small talk when Eve stopped walking and I nearly bounced into her back.

"It's about time you saw this for yourself," she said, turning towards a door that was set back slightly into the rough grey wall. She slid a slender hand into her jacket pocket and produced another small key. I expected her to unlock the door—that's what keys are usually for, in my experience—but to my surprise, she held the key out to me. "Why don't you go in first," she said. "See what you make of it." I'd put my hand out automatically, and she dropped the key into my palm. Close up, it was nothing more than a very normal-looking key of the sort used for front doors up and down the land. There was a matching Yale lock on the door, which was cheaply made and painted an institution-like magnolia colour.

"Nah," I said, holding the key back out to her, "you can do it." She raised an eyebrow at me in response. "For all I know," I shrugged, "you've got a literal pit of vipers tucked behind that normal-looking door and you're just waiting for an opportunity to hoof me in with them."

"Why would I want to do that?" she asked. Faint creases of amusement fanned out from the corners of her eyes.

"Plenty of people would like to dump me into a pit of snakes," I said. "And some of them have been people I thought were friends. So you can go first." In answer, she took the key back from me, unlocked the door in a totally un-sinister way and pushed it open for me to see inside. The room was, as far as I could tell, completely empty.

"It's a nice room?" I said, unable to think of anything else. "Very...spacious."

"Excuse me," Eve pushed past me into the room. "What the fuck?" she spluttered, turning on her heels to look around the entire space. "What the fuck?"

"Mind telling me what we're what-the-fuck-ing about?" Reassured that the room itself must be safe enough if Eve was standing in the middle of it, I stepped forward to join her. "I assume something's missing?"

"Missing?" said Eve. "Missing?" For a brief second I could see actual raging fury visible behind her eyes, but then she got a hold of herself. "Yes, Lilith," she said, "something is missing. Something really fucking important is fucking missing. And what I want to know," she went on, turning to me, "is where the fuck it has gone."

"Whoah," I said, taking a step backwards, "back up there, lady! I don't even know what it is that's missing, okay? So don't be accusing me of anything." Eve narrowed her eyes suspiciously, and appeared to take a deep breath. I very much doubted she actually needed to breathe.

"No one knows what is in here—was in here," she said, "except me." *And Eadric*, I thought. *But you think I don't know. Which means he doesn't want me to know. And why might that be?*

Because neither of them like the idea of handing over power, said the city. ***Despite both considering themselves above such tedious emotions as envy***.

They've both had a lifetime to get used to being in control, haven't they? And now they can't quite let go. However much they like to moan about the responsibility.

For different reasons, it said. ***Eadric is concerned for your safety—Eve is simply looking out for herself***.

Aren't we all?

I sighed. "So why were you about to show it to me?" I asked.

"Because," Eve said, "I am slowly coming to terms with having you around, and I thought it would be safer if you knew what you were dealing with. But it's gone."

"Can we just stop beating around this particular bush," I said, "and accept that the Holy Grail was in the basement of Martins sodding Bank, but you've somehow managed to lose it?"

"You knew the Grail was here," said Eve, swinging round to stare at me. "You bloody well knew."

"No," I said, "I didn't. But we'd just been discussing it and then you wanted to show me something important, and now the important thing has disappeared and you're considering whose head to lop off first. Correct?"

"Correct," said Eve. There was no inkling of amusement in her tone, which was worrying.

"You've been away from humanity for too long," I said. "We're brighter than you think."

"I work with plenty of humans on a daily basis."

"You work for the Home Office," I said, "which is not the same thing. When's the last time you hung out with the common people, Eve? Took some time out of your busy working schedule to dance and drink and screw? After all," I shrugged, "there's nothing else to do." She looked at me as though I'd lost my mind. It was probably a fair response.

"The Grail is missing," she said. "The Holy fucking Grail. And all you can do is make ridiculous jokes about song lyrics?" Aah. Not as disconnected as she made out, then. "Do you have any idea how dangerous it could be in the wrong hands?"

"Yup," I said. "We'd be overrun by undead despots. Probably a good few in your own office who'd fancy their chances with immortality. They'd maybe even like to take over from you." She frowned, but didn't say anything. The ring on my finger was sending static shocks up my arm as though I'd been rubbing balloons on my hair. Back when we were kids, Izzy had found it highly amusing to blow up a balloon, then rub it against my curls until they stuck out in all directions. Somewhere back home in Shrewsbury there was a box of aged photos of the pair of us, several of which showed me looking like a resigned mad scientist. Izzy was usually nothing more than a blur next to me, because she couldn't sit still long enough for photos. I glanced down. The glow had dissipated and my hand looked reassuringly normal—except for the faint blue sparks dancing on my fingertips. I closed my fist quickly and held my hand behind my back. "But you need the other half of the magic recipe," I went on. "Don't you?" She gazed at me silently, and I didn't like the way her expression had changed from one of friendly curiosity to something more akin to the last thing an injured baby wildebeest sees before the cheetah launches in for the kill. "Eve," I said slowly, wondering how the fuck I kept managing to get myself trapped in secret hideouts with undead psychopaths, "you've lost the Grail. You. Have. Lost. The Holy. Fucking. Grail, Eve. Perhaps you'd be better off trying to find that, before you start trying to intimidate me." I could hear the tiniest of clicking noises behind me, as the fingers of my left hand tried their best to spark into life. I don't know if you've ever found yourself in mortal fear of part of your own anatomy, but let me tell you something —it isn't as much fun as it sounds. Desperate now, I felt for the ring on my other hand—the one Gran had given me in the middle of the time-slip farrago that I mostly try not to think about. Still keeping a sharp eye on Eve, I managed to twist the ring so its stones faced inward, and clutched my palm closed around it. Come on, I thought to myself, don't let me down now.

"Give me that ring," said Eve suddenly. She was far too close for my liking, her dark eyes intense.

"No."

"It's not yours," she said. "Breaking down the crown wasn't your decision to make."

"And yet I did it," I said, somehow managing to sound calmer than I felt. Come on. The words repeated themselves over and over inside my head, willing Gran to appear. Come on, come on, come on. "I think you'll find this city doesn't mind too much about the destruction of symbols of oppression, Eve."

"I've been here so much longer than you," said Eve, her voice dangerously quiet. "How dare you disobey my orders, Lilith O'Reilly? How dare you!" She shut up suddenly, and for a brief second I thought she was having second thoughts about her tirade. And then, "what the fuck are you doing here?"

. . .

Gran launched herself so hard and fast that even Eve didn't see it coming. One second she was staring at the ghost of my dear departed grandmother; the next, she was flying head first across the room, having been socked in the jaw so hard it sent her airborne. "Try threatening my Lilith, would you?" Gran hissed. "You lay one single finger on that girl and I will have you ripped apart by wolves." I didn't have time to ask Gran where she kept her wolves before she turned her gaze on me. "You okay, Lil?" I nodded. "Still got the rings on?" Another nod. "Looks like you're out of luck, missy," she said to Eve, who was slumped against the opposite wall but glaring up at us in mortified fury. "I reckon it's probably best if you leave now. Don't you think?"

"Oh no," said Eve, "no, no, no. You don't get to swan in and take over, you—"

"That is enough," Gran interrupted. "No one here cares what London thinks, Eve. You're confusing us with people who give a shit." My eyes widened in surprise—I'd never heard Gran so angry before. Mind you, I'd never seen her punch anyone before, either. Just shows you can never tell a person's true personality until you've got yourself stuck in a life-threatening situation and need them to rescue you. "Get out," she went on. Eve struggled to her feet, and I wondered just how hard that punch of Gran's had been. I've been smacked a few times since I woke up dead—it's pretty standard behaviour in the netherworld; no one really means anything by it—but had never suffered much more than a brief light show behind my eyelids. Eve looked like she'd just gone seven rounds with Mike Tyson. And I'm talking glory days Tyson, not the version that comes out of retirement in order to get beaten in return for a giant pay packet.

"You won't get away with this," Eve scowled. "You think you're clever, but you're not. You have no idea who you're dealing with."

"Oh," said Gran, "I'm pretty sure I do, actually. It's been a long time since you got evicted from that paradise of yours, hasn't it, girl?" An expression of pure rage flashed across Eve's face. "And you've been envious of Lilith ever since." Eve visibly shook herself and straightened up. It was as though she was growing taller, even as I watched. "Because she," Gran went on, not moving from her spot in the middle of the room, "well now. She stood up for herself, didn't she? Got herself vilified for it, of course," Gran shrugged, "but what else can you expect from a society that believes women are lesser creatures? Whereas you," she took a barely noticeable step towards the younger woman, "you got suckered into doing as you were told. Being revered with as much intensity as you were feared. It's difficult being a woman in a man's world," she went on, "isn't it? And I'd wager you know that better than most."

"What do you want from me?" Eve managed. I was shocked—I'd fully expected her to fight back, probably using weird superpowers I hadn't known even existed. Shit like that is par for the course in my world.

"I want you to leave Lilith alone," said Gran. "Nothing more, nothing less. Do you think you can manage that?" She smiled thinly, and I wondered at the ability of little old ladies to look absolutely fucking terrifying when the mood took them.

"You know I can't promise that," said Eve.

"Then the best I can offer," said Gran, "is that you leave right now. Before I change my mind and decide to have you for breakfast." She looked Eve slowly up and down. "Delicious you look, too." Oh, this was just fucking brilliant—not only was my Gran an undead superhero (albeit on a personal level), she was also a letch.

"What the hell is going on?" I asked the room in general. Both women turned to glance at me briefly before deciding their counterpart in the middle of the room was more interesting. "I know I say this with boring regularity," I went on, "but this is all entirely mad. She," I pointed at Eve, "has lost the Holy fucking Grail. And you," I stabbed a finger in Gran's direction, "have lost what's left of your tiny fucking mind. So if it's all the same to you," I looked at Eve, who glared silently back, "I'll be leaving now. And I'm taking my grandmother with me."

"That woman isn't—" Eve started, but I held a hand up.

"To be trusted? Oh," I said, "I am well aware of that, believe me. But she's my grandmother, so I'm keeping her. And you," I raised an eyebrow at Eve, "will be fucking off out of my city."

"Your city?" Eve snorted bitterly. "You've been in this world for five minutes and you think this entire city is yours?"

"You have to remember," I said, stepping fractionally closer, "this isn't London. Everyone here thinks Liverpool is *their* city. We're protective of it, and it protects us in return. It doesn't think it's the centre of the bloody universe, and it doesn't take its residents for granted." I gazed thoughtfully at her. "But you've been taken advantage of, haven't you? Even as you work to convince yourself that you're doing good. Watching over your undead kingdom like a vulture, making sure no one gets in or out without you knowing about it. But it's sucking you dry, isn't it? Isn't it, Eve?" She scowled at me, but stayed silent. "Sucking the life out of you," I went on. "Taking your passions and personality and desire to help, and twisting it round so it can use you as a tool. That's all you are," I went on. I felt a faint smile twitching at the corners of my mouth, but it was a bitter one. "You're nothing more than a vessel, Eve. A vessel for adoration, yes—but also for hatred. You're a symbol of everything that could be good in this world, but in reality is all that is bad." My right eye twitched, and it took me a second to realise that my idiotic undead body was trying to cry. I can actually cry quite well when occasion demands, but this particular soppy episode came as a surprise, even to me. "I feel so sad for you," I said. Eve gave me a wry smile in return. "We could have been friends, you and I."

"Who knows," shrugged Eve, "perhaps more."

"Perhaps," I said. "And now we'll never know."

"Never say never," she countered.

"Right now," I smiled, "I would be thrilled if I never had to see you again. I assume you can make your own way back to London?"

"We'll take her," said a familiar voice behind me. I spun around and gaped in shock at the newcomer.

"Elizabeth," I said, "what the fuck are you doing here?"

"Nice to see you too," said Elizabeth, undead Queen of London. "You know how fast news travels in the underworld, Lilith," she went on. "We heard trouble might be brewing, and decided to help you head it off at the pass, so to speak." Even as I opened my mouth to ask who 'we' was, the answer stepped into the room. Jude is tall and slender, with cropped hair and a neat line in loose-fitting suits that make them look as though they're on their way to the local dojo. I've never heard them speak, but that doesn't stop them making it very clear that their opinion of me is close to zero. Unfortunately for Jude—but luckily for me—their loyalty to Elizabeth means they have no option but to back her up when she decides to help me out. And that happens more often than you might think, despite our respective cities having delighted in endlessly antagonising each other over the centuries. But undead is undead, and we stick together. Especially when it comes to those who might threaten what tenuous stability we manage to keep between our territories.

"That was quick," I said, "even by your standards." I'd have put good money on there being a helicopter waiting patiently on a nearby rooftop.

"We like to be efficient," Elizabeth smiled. "Jude?" Jude stepped towards Eve, who glared back but didn't move.

"I'm not a prisoner," said Eve. "So you can pack it in with the bodyguard bullshit."

"Of course you're not," said Elizabeth smoothly. "Jude is just here to escort you safely to our transport back to London." I was openly gaping at them all by this point, and Elizabeth noticed. "If you'd like to get going, Jude," she said without turning around, "I'm just going to have a quick word with Lilith in private." Without a flicker of response, Jude turned to head back out of the door and to my surprise, Eve followed without a murmur. She stopped in the doorway and turned to look back at me. For a moment, I thought she was about to say something. But she clearly thought better of it. With an almost imperceptible shake of her head, she walked out after Jude and disappeared down the corridor. "Lilith," said Elizabeth, "perhaps your grandmother might like to leave us for a moment?" I turned to look at Gran, who shrugged and disappeared. Sometimes I really wish I could do that. Stupid corporeal undead bodies. Ghosts have it much easier, I reckon.

"Thank you," I said when we were finally alone. "You appear to be making a habit of rescuing me. I'm sorry."

"Don't be," said Elizabeth. "You'd do the same for me, I'm sure." And I probably would. But it was hard to imagine Elizabeth getting into any situation that would require me to take over. She might have been one of the younger members of the undead gang, but I always had the impression she was a kind of mother hen to the rest of them.

"I'm assuming you know why Eve brought me here?"

"Of course I do," she said. "She wanted to show you her precious little prize." Elizabeth's tone was almost mocking. "As though that was the reason for all," she shrugged, "this. I don't know what's happened to the Grail, Lilith," she went on, "and I'm not sure I really care. It's done nothing for me, and I have no loyalty to it."

"I think it's more a weapon than a treasure," I said. "It needs to be kept safe because of the risk of what might happen if others got hold of it."

"Well, I suppose it's both." She smiled. "It just depends which side of the power balance you're on. Eve isn't a bad person," she said, "you need to know that. But she's seen too many bad things and lived for far too long. And that affects people's minds eventually, however much they think it doesn't. Power is important to her, and for very good reason—she was under the control of others during her lifetime and she won't ever let that happen again."

"She let you tell her what to do just now," I pointed out. "And she went off with Jude without arguing."

"That's because she knows it's time to hand over control," said Elizabeth. "She's old and tired and will benefit from the support of others for a while."

"You make it sound like she's some kind of doddery old granny," I said, thinking of the handsome and forceful woman who'd just walked out of the strongroom meek as a pussycat. "She isn't going to just switch off like that, whatever you think."

"Oh I know that," said Elizabeth. "She'll be back in her office by tomorrow and probably making life hell for the minions around her. And we will make her feel involved and support her from a distance. But it's time she left you—" she broke off as a loud crashing noise erupted outside. We both ran for the corridor at the same time and narrowly avoided jamming ourselves in the doorway like something out of a Laurel and Hardy skit. Elizabeth shoved me without malice and shot through the door at full tilt, with me close on her heels. In fact I was running so fast that I had to jam my heels into the ground when I got outside in order to have a hope of stopping in time. I still crashed into the hoardings that shielded the site from public view. Picking myself up off the floor, I turned to find Elizabeth pulling Jude out of the crumbling stonework of the bank. They appeared to be uninjured, but their clothes were dusty and torn and their expression was one of furious embarrassment. I took care not to catch their eye in case they decided to take their fury out on me. A groan to my left made me turn to where Joachim slumped against the entrance.

"She ran off," he said, as I slid him carefully away from the broken hoardings and onto the floor. A large tarpaulin covered a stack of bricks next to me. I ripped it off and folded it into a makeshift pillow before laying him down in the recovery position.

"I don't suppose you know which direction she went?" The metal panelling of the gate behind was pushed out into what looked suspiciously like the shape of his hunched body. Eve must have thrown him with some force to get that kind of result—it resembled one of those novelty tins you can buy to make overly complicated birthday cakes for ungrateful four-year-olds. He lifted his hand high enough to point vaguely over his head, before dropping it again and appearing to lose consciousness. "Shit, shit, shit," I muttered, frantically trying to remember how to check for a pulse. Was it two fingers behind the ear, or three on the wrist? And which bit of his wrist was I supposed to be pressing anyway? A weird noise was rumbling in my ears and I didn't know whether it was an alarm going off or whether I was just brewing a panic attack. I was still debating it when I felt a hand on my shoulder.

"Let me do it," said a calm voice from behind me. I swung around in astonishment.

"What are you doing here?" I asked.

"Heard the commotion from out on the street," said Freya. "Norm had a reaction to that cream I got for him. Spent last night sitting on a bag of frozen peas, so his sister tells me. Had to come back into town for a different one, didn't I? Come on," she pushed me gently out of the way, "I'll sort him out. You'd better go after the lunatic." The noise was getting louder. *Fucksake*, I thought, *this really isn't the time to be developing tinnitus.*

It isn't in your head, said the city. ***It's the birds.***

Top Cat

As I raced towards the waterfront, I thought how handy it would be if Gran reappeared before I got there. Death had certainly given her a sense of aggressive protection that she'd never shown in life, and right now I was sorely lacking in the wing-man department. Elizabeth and Jude were nowhere to be seen, and I'd left Freya tending to Joachim. As I bounced over moving cars on the Strand at lightning speed, the noise of the birds screeching from the top of their towers got louder. The really weird thing was that no one else seemed able to hear it. Even as I was darting across the car park in order to speed-climb the side of the Liver Building, I could see members of the public wandering along the waterfront in the sunshine, as though everything was absolutely normal.

It's you they're calling for, said the city, ***no one else***.

Fucking brilliant, I hissed as I bounced over the parapet onto the roof, *so now I'm full-time bird-nanny on top of everything else?*

You always were, it replied. ***You just didn't know it***.

Bloody marvellous, I snapped. *Just bloody sodding arsing marvellous.* The worst of the noise was coming from Bella's end of the building, so that's where I headed. She was still perched safely on top of her dome, but the noise coming off her was incredible. Something had seriously pissed her off, and I was fairly confident I knew what—or who—it was. Even as I was thinking it, there was a crashing sound from inside Eadric's rooms at the top of the tower. Forgoing the usual route, I leaped in through the nearest open window. Unfortunately for me, I hadn't taken into account the internal layout in my hurry. I crashed down right in the middle of Eadric's enormous mahogany desk and went skidding over it onto the floor. Luckily for the man himself, he wasn't sitting at it. *Un*luckily for him, that was because he was stuck in a corner being yelled at by Eve. It appeared to be along the lines of her screaming at him about 'what the fuck do you think you're playing at' while Eadric leaned casually against the wall with his patented calm expression glued onto his face. I knew that look of old. It was the sort of look that says 'I can keep this up for hours, just carry on making an idiot of yourself' whilst doing absolutely nothing to actually fix anything and also totally avoiding any form of conflict. Something about the scene in front of me made me snap. I was sick to death of secrets and lies, and idiots thinking I didn't need to know what was going on. It was always, 'Oh poor Lilith, she's new to it all, you know' and I was absolutely fucking done with being patronised. Also, that cow Eve was threatening Eadric and however much he annoys me, I'm loyal to a fault. Without thinking, I picked up the heavy Bakelite phone that sat on Eadric's desk. For a long time after I first met the Silvertons, I'd assumed it was an ornamental affectation, but these days I knew it to be both original and fully working. Wrenching it off the desk, I stood up and hurled it with all my strength at the back of Eve's head. I moved so quickly that even Eadric didn't see me until the phone was already flying through the air. His suddenly panicked expression was enough to make her turn, but it was too late. The body of the phone crashed into the side of her head, the handset swinging wildly at the end of its cable and narrowly avoiding taking Eadric out at the same time. He somehow ducked out of the way in time, and it smacked into the stone wall instead, sending a fracture crawling up the stonework towards the window. "What the hell are you doing?" he shouted as I launched myself at Eve and kicked her hard in the back. "Lilith!" Eadric grabbed me from behind and I saw red. Spinning around, I smacked him across the face hard enough to send him sprawling across the floor. Hoping it would be enough to put him off trying again, I turned back to Eve. She was groaning and trying to push herself upright, so I clearly hadn't done too much damage. Which was a shame.

"What the *fuck* are you playing at?" I said, giving her another kick in the shins. I'd been foolish to think I'd get the better of her so easily. A hand shot out and she grabbed my ankle, pulling my leg out from underneath me. I landed hard on my backside and shrieked loudly, but it wasn't from pain. Standing on the ledge of an open window on the river side of the building—a window I knew damn fine was in full view of the public—was Finn. Before I could do anything to stop him, he launched off the windowsill and charged. Eve had just enough time to roll out of the way as Finn barrelled into the room, his face a mask of wild fury. "How did you get up here?" I asked him stupidly, but he ignored me. He rounded on Eve and snarled—and it didn't sound remotely human. "Finn," I yelled, "I'm okay! I can deal with this myself."

"This isn't about you," he said without looking at me. "It's her I'm after." Eve was getting to her feet and backing away, her gaze fixed on Finn. Her expression was that of terrified fascination.

"You're one of them," she said slowly. "Aren't you? You've been hiding out up here all this time." I gaped at Eve, then Finn, and then back again. "Nasty little fleabags," she said. "Evil, vicious creatures, the lot of you. Just you wait until London hears about this. You," she pointed at Eadric without taking her eyes off Finn, "are responsible for this. This is what happens when you let a pathetic little girl take over without so much as an attempt to make her follow the rules. You get a city overrun with freaks and monsters."

"Finn is not a monster," I said quietly. "And this city loves its freaks."

"Of course it does," Eve spat. "The entire place is a freak show. I've always made a point of standing up for all the territories and treating them equally, but there are limits. This cannot be allowed to carry on. Eadric," she risked a glance to make sure she had his attention, "you will rid this city of anything supernatural that is not human, and you will do it immediately. We can no longer take the risk."

"I'm not going to do that," said Eadric. "The cats aren't hurting anyone."

"So you *did* know." Her tone was triumphant. "All these centuries you've been denying the existence of the cryptids, and you were harbouring them here in your ridiculous city all along."

"I'm not harbouring anything," said Eadric. "No one's hiding. Not from the netherworld, at least."

"You're not even trying to hide from the *public*," said Eve. "You have cats running wild and idiot girls ruling the roost. You do realise, Eadric," she went on, "Lilith here has her own little fan club? They're sitting outside her pathetic little cafe even as we speak."

"What the fuck is wrong with you?" I said. "We were friends a couple of hours ago, and now you're insulting me and everyone around me."

"Two hours ago," said Eve, "I thought you were more intelligent than you actually are, Lilith. Two hours ago, I wasn't being attacked by that, that *thing* that claims to be your grandmother. And two *fucking* hours ago, Lilith O'Reilly, you weren't attacking me for no reason. We have *rules*, Lilith," she spat in my general direction. "Rules that exist for good reason. Rules that keep us *all* safe."

"No one's safe though," I said. "Are they? Not really. We're all freaks, Eve. All of us. You included. None of us are supposed to exist, yet here we are. What do you think you're doing?" She'd pulled a phone out of her pocket and was already dialling a number.

"I'm calling for backup," she said. "The Natural History Museum will be interested in him." She nodded towards Finn. "Or at least," she smiled, "what's left of him when the scientists are finished." I launched at her without thinking, blind fury powering me forward. The phone went flying out of her hand and I saw Eadric tread on it hard. I hit her from the side and she toppled awkwardly, taking me with her. For a few confusing seconds, we rolled and scuffled like kids in a playground. Eve grabbed a handful of my hair and I screamed as she ripped it out by the roots. In revenge, I bit down hard on her shoulder and she howled in pain as I forced my teeth down to the bone. I could taste blood in my mouth, and for a terrifying second it overwhelmed me. Then...peace. Along with the blood came the scents of incense and citrus, heavy rain and warm sand. My mind was drifting off into another world and suddenly I wasn't fighting anymore; instead, I was clinging to her in the hope of being saved. I wrapped my legs tightly around her waist and sucked hard against the wound I'd inflicted, even as she screamed in horror and tried her best to scrabble away from me. I couldn't let go—she was me and I was her and this was my salvation, if only the gods willed it...There was a roaring noise in my head and then I went flying across the room hard enough to hit the opposite wall with a creaking thud. I opened my eyes and tried to remember what it was I was supposed to be doing. Eve was on her feet and stalking towards me with pure hatred in her eyes. "How *dare* you," she hissed. "You always did think you were better than me, didn't you, Lilith? I should have finished you off back then. Back when you were throwing your weight around and wondering why everyone hated you for it. You thought I was stupid, remember? It never once occurred to you," she was only a few short paces away from me now, "that maybe I was playing the long game. That perhaps, just perhaps, I—" I never did find out what Eve perhaps did. Because that was the moment approximately eighty kilos of black panther smashed teeth-first into the side of her face.

Shape-shifters are such a popular trope in television and other media that we all think we know what they'd look like in real life. On one side you've got the terrible fake-fur-and-dodgy-claws of old movies, and on the other there's the CGI creepiness of the modern werewolf. The only human-cat hybrid I'd ever seen before was Michelle Pfeiffer, and her feline turn was a lot sexier than the chaos of hair, teeth and eyeballs that was whirling in front of me right now. Finn had not just 'turned cat'—he'd turned fully feral. Eadric and I were on opposite sides of the room, both of us pressed back hard against the walls as far away from the carnage as possible. The air filled with the nauseating sound of tearing flesh as Finn ripped Eve limb from limb, right there in front of us on Eadric's very expensive Persian rug. It took a horribly long time for her to give up. She was still kicking and screaming even as he ripped her arm out of its socket and flung it across the room with a swing of his massive head. The disembodied limb hit something breakable behind me and the melodic chimes of shattering china tinkled through the air like a sound effect in a horror movie. I gazed in transfixed horror as Finn threw what was left of Eve across the floor before dropping down to stalk his now-immobile prey. She turned to me and I held her gaze as the big cat made his final attack. And I was still looking into her eyes when Finn's jaws locked around her head and ripped it from her body. There was movement in the corner of my eye, and I turned to find Nik standing in the open doorway, his mouth opening and closing silently like a confused guppy. Behind him, wearing matching expressions of pale horror, stood Elizabeth and Jude. "I don't suppose," I said weakly, "any of you have the number for a decent dry-cleaner?"

Beware Old Ladies, For They Be Dangerous

Elizabeth took over, of course. Her grey eyes were paler than usual as she gave Jude instructions, but her tall, willowy frame never wavered. There was no way of cleaning Eve's remains up neatly, so Jude settled for rolling them up in what was left of Eadric's beloved rug. There's good reason why beheading a revenant is the only way of getting rid of them for good. Once the connection to the brain is fully severed, the entire body collapses into a mess of sticky—and thankfully mostly unidentifiable—ashes. Fellow immortals delight in telling me tales of revenants who've somehow managed to reattach their own head before cellular collapse kicks in, but I'd always got the impression it had to be done *really* quickly for it to have a hope of working. And as Finn had refused to let go of Eve until she was spread around the room like vomit at a freshers' party, she hadn't stood a chance. "We will make...arrangements," said Elizabeth, as Eadric, Nik and I joined her to watch Jude slinging the horrible parcel over their shoulder like a sack of soggy potatoes and adjusting the weight to their liking, before moving to wait by the private lift. Finn had lost interest when his prey finally stopped fighting back. He was currently snoring on the floor in the corner of the office. At my suggestion, Nik had draped a large, woollen blanket over him, in case he woke up human and we found ourselves with a naked roofer on our hands. "London will expect an explanation, of course," she went on. "I think the safest approach is for all of us to simply pretend that none of this ever happened. I assume our late colleague was merely visiting the city for social reasons?" One of us must have mumbled assent, because Elizabeth nodded sagely. "Then I will inform them she had left Liverpool before I arrived and that none of us knew her next planned port of call. I have to admit," she said, "I thought better of her. But then she never could resist stamping her authority over everything. Making up for a lack of autonomy in her youth, poor thing. Where did you grandmother disappear to, Lilith?" The unexpected question threw me and I gaped blankly at her for a few seconds before remembering how to speak.

"Gran's a bit mad," I said apologetically. "Sorry about that. She probably won't show her face again for a while."

"That's a shame," said Elizabeth. She gave me a curious look and then smiled. "She seemed interesting."

"The novelty of Gran's company wears off fast," I said. "You're not missing much."

"So," said Elizabeth, "if we're all in agreement that the details of this little incident go no further, we'll be off. Thank you, Jude." She nodded, and Jude pressed the call button for the lift. "Oh, I'll need the car keys," Elizabeth went on. We all stared blankly at her in return. "For your car, Eadric? Even I can't get onto a plane without having my baggage checked, and I'd rather not risk carrying unauthorised human remains in the back of a hire car."

"What are you going to do with her?" I asked, as an unhappy-looking Eadric went to get the keys. "It's not as if there's much left to bury."

"We'll rinse her off into the Thames," said Elizabeth. "Let her spread out across the waters, as she always liked to do." Eadric reappeared and rather begrudgingly dropped the keys for the Alfa into her hand. "Thank you, Eadric," she said, "I will arrange to have it returned to you, of course. Although it's been a while since I had cause to drive one of these model machines." Her face broke into an unexpected smile, and it was as though the sun had suddenly switched to full beam in the sky. "I rather fancy seeing how fast one can go."

We saw Elizabeth and Jude off, and I then spent several minutes reassuring Eadric about the safety of his beloved car. Finn was still in cat form and still asleep, so the Silvertons had no option but to leave him where he was until it wore off. I finally managed to leave and headed down to ground level in the lift. As I walked out onto Canada Boulevard, I was greeted by polite clapping. "Thought you'd gone for good," I said, as we dropped into step next to each other. "Could have done with the extra help up there, to be honest."

"Aah," said Gran, "you were grand. From where I was standing, it sounded like you had it under control well enough."

"You could hear us down here?" I asked. Shit.

"Don't panic now," said Gran. "It's only the more unusual of us that can hear that sort of thing. The public didn't even notice," she went on. "Too busy with their own noisy self-importance. Me and the girls just sat out there," she indicated the river, "and watched from a distance. Nice move with the telephone, by the way."

"Hang on," I said, "you sat in the river? How?"

"I'm a ghost, dear," said Gran calmly. "I can sit wherever I like."

"With the girls, though? Oh, for fuck's sake." Realisation dawned. "You were with Daisy, weren't you?" I picked up my pace and began stalking along the promenade. Gran faded from view.

"Daisy wasn't around today," said Gran, approximately two inches away from my ear.

"Fucking hell," I yelled at the empty space where I was pretty sure Gran was standing. Or floating. Or whatever it was she was doing, apart from driving me absolutely up the bloody wall. A group of Japanese tourists were taking photos next to the Superlambanana in front of the Museum of Liverpool. They turned as one to stare at me with polite curiosity. "Sorry," I said, indicating my ear. "I'm on the phone." They didn't look convinced, but I very much doubted I was the weirdest thing they'd seen in Liverpool so far. One of the city's greatest tricks is to deliver weirdness around every corner. "I don't actually care what Daisy was doing," I hissed in what I thought was Gran's general direction. "I just don't like the idea of you buddying up with the mermaids."

"Why not?" Gran asked in an annoyingly reasonable tone. "They're nice girls."

"They eat people, Gran!"

"Not often," she said. "They said the one you dumped in there a while back tasted foul." I cringed at the reminder of my hurried disposal of a corpse, just twenty-four hours after I'd fallen to my death off the fire escape outside my flat. Izzy had helped me and we'd done the best we could, but I hadn't known about the mermaids back then. It was a long time later, after I'd befriended Daisy and learned about the existence of Asrai—mermaid-like water creatures specific to Shropshire and the north-west—that I also learned of their habit of stashing anything edible in order to keep a ready supply of snacks tucked away at the bottom of the Mersey. The corpse had resurfaced a year later, thankfully minus any identifying features. I'd caught a brief glimpse as it was being dragged out by the police, and it definitely hadn't looked appetising.

"We don't talk about that," I said finally.

"Right you are," agreed Gran. "Let's go have a nice sit down in the sun, shall we? It'll do you good to relax for a while."

"What's my mum's name, Gran?" I asked, as we sat gazing out over the river. The skyline of the Wirral looked almost pretty in the early evening light. I wondered if Derek and his crew were gathering to sing my praises tonight. Or maybe they'd finally got over themselves and found something more interesting to do with their time. Macrame, perhaps. Or stamp-collecting. I wondered idly whether the Stanley Gibbons company still made those collector books and the little packs of random stamps. Me and Cally had loved those stamp books when we were kids.

"What sort of question is that?" said Gran, turning to look at me. She was slightly transparent out in the open air. I smiled at her. "What?" she asked. "Did someone say something funny?"

"I was just thinking that you look very pretty today," I said. It was true. There was a faint, shimmery halo around her, as though she'd started her day with that instant breakfast cereal they used to advertise on television all the time. Her blue eyes sparkled as she gazed at me in confusion. "And it's a perfectly straightforward question. What's Mum's name?"

"It's Helen, of course," she scoffed. "What are you dragging through you this time, you silly child?"

"What was Cally's favourite snack?"

"I really don't know what you're talking about, Lilith." Gran sniffed. "How should I remember what he liked? He's been gone a long time now."

"Because it was you who used to give it to him." My younger brother didn't like sweets in the way other kids did. Not for him those sticky bags of jelly bears that supposedly taste of cola, but the flavouring of which never entirely fights its way past the taste of sugar and gelatine. No, Cally liked grapes. He got through several bags of them every week, mostly supplied by my grandparents. Gran used to pull them off their stalks and drop them into a bag, which she'd then put in her freezer until the small, round fruits had turned into balls of sweet and crunchy ice. "How dare you use my own grandmother to spy on me." I'd grabbed the apparition by the arms before it had the chance to disappear and with my hand gripping it tightly, it was stuck. Gran's expression rippled and twisted as though it might rip itself right off her head and yes, it was absolutely as creepy as it sounds. Finally, my intruder gave up and allowed their features to settle into their own grinning face. "What the fuck are you doing here?" I hissed, not letting go. "Why can't you just die and leave me alone?"

"If that bird of yours couldn't get rid of me," said Ivo Laithlind, "I really don't think you're going to manage it." He looked down to where I was gripping his arm so tightly that I could practically feel the bones creaking underneath my fingers. "You know I'll heal if you injure me, Red," he went on. "Sorry about that." I threw him backwards in disgust and he hit the old brick wall with a crunch.

"You were spying on me in the bath!" I paced angrily up and down in front of him, so outraged that it felt like my head might explode from fury. "You grubby little bastard!"

"It might surprise you to know," said Ivo, "that I've seen a naked female body before. Yours is a pleasingly aesthetic example, I have to say." He grinned up at me. "But you know how it is," he shrugged, "seen one, seen them all." His hand shot up to grab my arm before I could land the punch. "You forget," he got to his feet, still gripping my arm, "I know what you're capable of now. Which means I'm better prepared." He saw me glance sideways down the promenade. "The birds won't protect you today, Red," he said. "They know they don't need to."

"Bella knows what a fucking shithead you are," I spat. "She'll come down here if I need her."

"You're not listening to me," said Ivo. "I'm not the danger. Oh," he chuckled, "I was the danger, sure enough. I'd have happily stayed shut in that room in Chester with you until you came to your senses. But I can see now that I was going about things the wrong way."

"You don't say." I glowered at him. "As if there's ever a right way to imprison someone."

"I'm a very old man, Red," said Ivo. "I'm from another time."

"A fucking prehistoric time, you mean."

"Not quite." He smiled. "But not far off. I suppose I, well." He broke off, looking thoughtful. "I suppose I misjudged you, Lilith." I narrowed my eyes at him suspiciously. Ivo never called me by my full name. "I misjudged you and underestimated you, and for that, I am truly sorry. I thought I could wear you down with my innate charm."

I snorted. "What's charming about taking someone prisoner?" I asked. "Where I'm from, right here in the twenty-first century, we call that assault, Ivo. A-fucking-ssault. Ain't nothing romantic about that, mate."

"Aah," he said, "such a way with words. But I'm telling the truth, and you need to listen to me. Because if you don't, we are all going to end up in one hell of a mess. Possibly literally."

"Hell is a theoretical concept," I said. "It isn't real."

"Oh," he smiled again, but it was faint, "it's real enough. We've all got our own personal version of hell, Red. Mine involved waking up in that burial mound and realising I'd been pulled back into this godforsaken living world to fight for my life. Ironic, don't you think?"

"There's a song about that," I said, apropos of completely nothing. "And now I'll have an earworm for the next week. Cheers."

"You're funny," said Ivo. "Do you know that?"

"It has been said, yes." I glared down at where he still sat with his back against the wall. "You trapped me, Ivo Laithlind. You shut me in a room and planned to keep me there forever."

"Not forever," he said. "Just as long as it took for you to see sense."

"Apologise."

"Excuse me?" He raised his eyebrows and smiled faintly at me. "For what?" he said, "trying to make you see sense?"

"You will bloody well apologise," I said. "For tricking me, for trapping me in that fucking steam mill and most of all," I took a step forward, "for sneaking an eyeful in my bathroom like the horrible little pervert you so clearly are."

"I think not." He shrugged. "For one thing, you place far too much importance on your physical body. I'm more interested in your mind. And for another, you don't survive as long as I have by apologising to people."

"Apologise," I said again, "or I will throw you to the mermaids."

"Oh Red," Ivo chuckled, "I—"

"APOLOGISE." The voice isn't even loud these days—it doesn't have to be. No one else would even have heard me, but the prehistorically limbic part of Ivo's brain got the message and instantly tried to obey. He tried his best, I had to give him credit for that. The tension was visible in his face as he fought his own body, his legs moving under him even as he pushed backwards against the wall. "GET ON YOUR KNEES AND APOLOGISE, IVO LAITHLIND." He rose up onto his knees, every fibre of his being fighting against it, even as he moved. His hands rested casually on his thighs, but his expression belied the furiously impotent rage he was feeling inside. "Not much fun being forced to do things against your will, is it?" I said out loud. Ivo glared silently at me. "I asked for an apology," I reminded him. "Now would be a good time."

"I'm sorry," he said finally. "I behaved badly and I am genuinely sorry." He tried to get up but couldn't. "For christ's sake, Red," he said, "this is getting silly now."

"I'll let you move when you've apologised like you actually mean it." I stepped closer and looked down at him. "I quite like the sight of you on your knees," I grinned. "Knowing your place in the world."

"You are such an exasperating creature," Ivo managed. "Absolutely ridiculous. But you know your own mind, I'll allow that. Okay," he sighed, "I really am sorry. Truly I am." He looked up at me, his sharp eyes glittering. I'd become so used to the paleness of revenant eyes that it took me a second to register that Ivo's irises had turned almost entirely silver. "I behaved despicably," he went on. "To others, as well as you. And I truly am sorry for that. But whatever you think of me, I can't survive the modern world without you. And I'm pretty sure you need me as well. That's the truth of it, Red."

"So you admit to being selfish, as well as perverted?"

"I'm not a pervert," he said, smiling despite himself. "I keep telling you that."

"Whatever," I said. My arm twitched, and he saw it. "I'm not going to punch you," I sighed. "You can get up now." He didn't move. "GET UP." He got up and grinned at me. "But," I warned him, "I'm going to need you to explain why I'm so important to your plans."

"And I'll be happy to give you that explanation," said Ivo. "But we appear to have company." I followed his gaze to where two young men stood by the safety railing next to the river. They were staring at us as though they'd just bumped into Lady Gaga in the chiller aisle of Tesco. They were wide-eyed and pink-cheeked, and seemingly stunned into silence.

"Can I help you?" I asked.

"I, ummm, well," started the nearest of the pair. He was in his early twenties at a guess, tall and slim, with sandy-coloured hair that flopped into his face. He looked like a surfer who'd got lost on his way to Porth Neigwl. It's the nearest beach to Liverpool with any real waves to speak of, and is commonly known as Hell's Mouth. For very good reason—more than a hundred ships have wrecked in the area over the centuries and there's still enough debris littering the ocean floor to give divers plenty to look at. I smiled helpfully at Surfer Dude, wondering if he perhaps had a mental condition.

"We're honoured to meet you, ma'am," blurted the second man. To my absolute horror, he dropped to his knees. Then he tugged at the leg of his friend's trousers until he, too, knelt in front of us. "We had no idea. I mean," he risked a glance towards me, "we didn't expect to see you out on the street."

"I'm not on the street," I said. I was thoroughly confused, and their current behaviour wasn't helping. "I'm on the promenade. You know," I floundered, "where they used to walk up and down. Back in the day." I trailed off, now as bemused by my own behaviour as that of the two men in front of me. Next to me, Ivo sniggered. I turned to give him a sharp look, but he was carefully staring in the opposite direction, towards the distant skyline of Ellesmere Port. "It was quite the thing back then," I said. "Want to tell me what the fuck is going on?" The men stayed on their knees, silently facing the ground. "Er, hello?" I tried. "Are you okay? Is there a number I can call?" Ivo's muffled snorting got louder. "Do you have carers around anywhere?"

"There's nothing wrong, ma'am." said the first man, finally remembering how to talk. "You came as a surprise, that's all."

"An amazing surprise," agreed his friend.

"For heaven's sake," I said, "will you please stand up? People are looking." A gaggle of tourists had stopped just behind my strange visitors and were whispering frantically to each other, clearly trying to figure out who on earth I might be. One of them was taking photos on her phone, presumably to reverse-search my image. I was fairly confident nothing would come up—inner-city cafe owners not tending to make the news very often—but it definitely wasn't helping my ongoing attempts to keep the weird bits of my life on the down-low. "GO AWAY." I said it quietly, but the intent behind the words worked. "Not you," I said in a normal voice, grabbing each of the men by an arm. The onlookers dispersed, confused expressions on their faces. "You're going to stay here and explain yourselves."

"I think," said Ivo, making me jump as he appeared next to me, "they're worshippers."

"What the fuck?" I snapped. I bloody hate being taken by surprise. And I really bloody hate it when the culprit is someone who's already got me at a disadvantage. I'd been about to rip Ivo a new one—both metaphorically and literally—when the men had appeared, and I didn't appreciate being distracted from my righteous fury. "Worshipping what?"

"Ummm," said the first bloke, who was clearly having trouble again.

"You, Your Majesty," said the second. "We wish to worship you."

"Oh no you fucking don't," I said. "I've already told the other lot to pack it in. You needn't think you're any different."

"There's more?" murmured Ivo. "My word, you have made an impression." He sounded amused.

"Look," I said, ignoring him "I'm not sure who you think I am, but you're clearly mistaken."

"You're the queen," said the more coherent of the two. "Queen of the Netherworld. Derek told us you were here, but we didn't believe him. Did we, Aaron?"

Aaron nodded. "Yeah," he said, "Derek told us. Thought he was losing his mind, didn't we, Pab?" They nodded in sync for a few seconds. It reminded me of those dog ornaments you used to see in the back windows of cars owned by people who thought they were being cool and retro, but mostly just looked cheap and naff.

"Well, Aaron," I said. "Pab. Pab?"

"Pablo," said Pab, helpfully. "My mum likes to go to Spain on her holidays."

"Well, Pablo," I tried again, "Aaron. It's been lovely to meet you, but I really don't have any vacancies for worshippers just now. You'll have to look elsewhere, I'm afraid. I hear the bookshop up on Renshaw Street is always happy to welcome new members." Mapp would enjoy having a fan club.

"Aah," Aaron looked suddenly sheepish, "I don't think so. Thing is," he shuffled on the spot, "we tried in there yesterday. Didn't we, Pab?" Pablo nodded. "Derek told us you hang out with the bloke in there, so we went to ask him. You know, the tall one who's a bit weird."

"I dunno," said Pablo. "I've always thought he's pretty cute."

"Yeah," said Aaron, "but you're not exactly known for your high standards, are you?" Pablo frowned at him. "Remember the one you met in Furnace a while back?" Aaron went on. "Him with the pink feather boa?" Camp & Furnace is a venue over in Baltic Triangle and, despite its name, not somewhere I'd expect to find many blokes in fully-feathered drag.

"We all make mistakes," said Pablo. "Anyway, he had a cute flatmate."

"So anyway," said Aaron, "we went to the bookshop." I sighed. No doubt Mapp had sent them my way as revenge for me laughing at his curtains story. "And he told us you were at that cafe on Harrington Street, but we didn't believe him."

"Went in to look though," said Pablo.

"Yeah," said Aaron, "we went to have a look. That cute bird was working behind the counter. You know, the one with the scary eyes." That would be Missy—part time waitress, full-time immortal feminist. "Anyway, we asked her if the queen was around."

"We were subtle, mind," said Pablo. "Said it quietly. Under our breath, like. And we ordered a pot of tea." He looked at me with an expression more usually seen on small kids waiting for praise.

"And what did the cute bird say to you?" I asked.

"She told us to fuck off and stop being nosy assholes," said Aaron. "Seemed really angry for some reason. Pabs here lost his nerve, so we left."

"Didn't even get a cuppa," said Pablo. He pulled a face like a labrador puppy who's just been accidentally kicked by its owner and is planning to make them feel guilty for the rest of their days.

"Look," I said with as much patience as I could muster, "as interested as I am in your tea-related traumas, I've got stuff to do. And none of it involves being worshipped."

"Never say never," murmured Ivo, next to me. "I'd happily worship you into the middle of next week if you'd only give me the chance."

"Is this man bothering you, ma'am?" asked Aaron. "We'll be happy to escort you home if you'd feel safer."

"Do I look like someone who needs escorting?" I snorted. "No," I went on, seeing Pablo's mouth opening, "don't answer that. This... gentleman," I side-eyed Ivo, "is a business associate. So if you'd leave us to conduct our, uh,"

"Business?" offered Ivo.

"In peace," I finished, "I would appreciate it. And I really don't need anyone to be worshipping me. Makes things awkward when I'm buying cat food. Sorry about that. YOU MAY LEAVE." The last bit was to fend off Pablo, who was looking as though he might actually cry. It worked. The two men suddenly developed expressions that implied nothing would make them happier than to leave me alone; in fact, it would be their pleasure. They turned on their heels simultaneously, as neat as a pair of guards on parade. "GO HOME," I said. They went, stepping smartly along the promenade in a fashion that was at complete odds with their appearance.

"What the fuck is going on?" I said, spinning to face Ivo. "And don't think I haven't forgotten what a shithead you are."

"As if," said Ivo. "It's growing, Red." I gazed stonily at him, waiting for the unfunny payoff. It didn't happen. "The power," he went on. "It's growing. In you, in the city, in pretty much everything."

"What about you?" I asked. "Your eyes are different."

"I suspect my eyes are just older and wiser." He smiled as he said it, and I had to fight the urge to put out a hand and stroke the creases around his eyes. I'd never so much as snogged Ivo Laithlind, which was more than could be said for my personal history with Liam O'Connor. Yet Ivo had always been the one I felt close to, despite his consistently appalling behaviour. I didn't know why that was, and I didn't like that I didn't know.

"No," I said, "they're different. You used to have a silver ring around the edge, same as the rest of us. But now they're almost entirely silver. And," I went on before he could reply, "do not try to tell me it's the fluorescence."

"Why would fluorescence have anything to do with it?" he asked. "We're outside." I shrugged to convey my disinclination towards explaining modern film references to someone old enough to remember when quill and parchment was considered fancy. Anyway, he'd have only complained about the 'sparkling in sunlight' thing. "It's the power," he said when it was obvious I wasn't going to elaborate. "Like I said, it's increasing. In me, as well as you. As *much* as you, I think." He tilted his head and gazed at me thoughtfully. "I didn't used to be able to persuade magpies to help me out, you know. And I certainly couldn't disguise myself as a ghost. But now I can do this." He raised a hand as if showing me something, and for the briefest second it was Aunt Kitty standing there. "Or this." He turned slowly on the spot and as he faced me again it was Jonny looking back at me. I blinked hard and Ivo was back.

"How the fuck do you do that?"

"No idea," he said, "and that's the truth. I was just sitting thinking one day about how it would be useful to be able to disguise myself as other people, and it just happened without warning. If I hadn't been sitting near a mirror at the time I'm not sure I'd have even realised what was going on."

"Who did you turn into?" I asked, fascinated despite myself.

"Aah," said Ivo, "well that's where it gets a bit embarrassing."

"Ed Sheeran?" I asked. "Barack Obama? Oooooh," I raised an eyebrow, "was it Princess Di? You look like the sort who probably fancied her way back when."

"Sometimes," Ivo said, "just sometimes, I wonder what on earth I ever did to deserve this."

"Laid waste to the British landscape," I shrugged. "Executed our kings. Desecrating and pillaging. Y'know, the usual."

"It was just the one king," he said, "and that was a very long time ago. Do you want to know who I turned into, or not?"

"Oh go on then," I said. "If you must."

"I was thinking about the Bastard," he said, "and what I'd like to do with him. Very entertaining it was, too."

"I'm sure it was," I agreed. "Nothing like daydreaming about your enemies to give yourself closure."

"And then," Ivo went on, ignoring my sarcasm, "something caught my eye in the mirror. I turned to look properly, and found William staring back at me."

"Out of the mirror?" I asked. "Or the actual reflection?"

"That was my first thought," said Ivo. "That perhaps the Bastard had figured out a way of spying on people through silvered glass. It wouldn't be the first time." I raised my eyebrows at that, but decided now wasn't the time to press for irrelevant details. "But no. It was the reflection. It was *my* reflection."

"You'd turned into Liam?"

"My outward appearance had," said Ivo. "I was still myself on the inside. And the same when I was disguised as your grandmother—I looked like her, but she wasn't here with me."

"She must have been," I said, thinking of the fear I'd felt in Martins Bank when I realised Eve was actually mad. "I called her with the ring."

"I'm afraid not," he said. "I was already here when you did that. I did wonder whether she would turn up as well, but thankfully not."

"I'm assuming it's because of quantum," I said, "or something equally ridiculous. Anyway, *why* were you dressing up as my grandmother?" It was an obvious question, but I had to ask it. "Have you been stalking me for long?"

"I wasn't stalking you," sighed Ivo. "Why can't you understand what I'm trying to tell you, Red? I knew my own powers were getting stronger, and something was pulling me towards you at the same time. It doesn't take a genius to put two and two together, does it?"

"I think you're crediting me with more intelligence than I've actually got," I said. "Because from where I'm standing, I can't see any obvious connection."

"You're getting more powerful," said Ivo, "and so am I. I think the two things are connected and I wanted to talk to you about it. But I knew you wouldn't speak to me if I turned up as myself."

"Correct. Oh my *god*," I said, as my memory finally juddered into action. "That conversation in my bathroom!" I glared at Ivo. "You were going on about how I'd be better off with a man around."

"I don't think that's quite what I said." Ivo had the decency to look embarrassed. "But you can't blame a man for trying."

"Oh yes I bloody can," I said. "I can blame you for a lot of things, as it happens. Why am I even standing here listening to you?" I was asking myself as much as anything. "You're a lying, duplicitous bellend, Ivo Laithlind. To accuse you of having the morals of an alleycat would be an insult to alleycats."

"And yet the birds still don't seem to be feeling the need to protect you," he said. He nodded his head behind me to where Bella and Bertie were presumably up on their domes, same as usual. "Which is interesting. Don't you think?"

"I expect they're assuming I'll just rip you to pieces myself," I said. "Save them the bother."

"Or they know there's a bigger threat than me around," said Ivo. "One you might need my help with."

"The day I come to you for help, you'll be needing your snowshoes," I said. "On account of how that hell of yours will be freezing over."

"What if I told you I know about the Grail?" he said. I stared at him silently, lost for words. "And before you ask," he went on, "no. I'm not hunting it for myself."

"Why not?"

"You do know about it, then." He looked smug.

"I know nothing," I snapped. "I just can't imagine you ever not wanting things for yourself. Power, money, even me. Well," I shrugged, "two out of three ain't bad. I'd suggest you give up while you're winning."

"I've learned my lesson with you, Red." A faint smile tugged at the corner of his mouth. "That day in the Steam Mill was the closest anyone's ever got to actually finishing me off. Since I woke up dead, anyway."

"How did you survive?" I asked, curiosity getting the better of me. "I don't know many people who could survive having an entire industrial building land on them."

"Aah," said Ivo with a smile, "I can't give away all my secrets, Red. Especially not to you. Let's just say I'm stronger than you think and leave it at that."

"Tell me about this Grail," I said. If he wanted to play the ingenue, then so could I. "Like in the Bible?"

"The Grail was never mentioned in the Bible," said Ivo. "But I think you know that already." I kept my expression blank. "Well, if you don't know about it already," he went on, "you soon will. It's here. Somewhere. And the Bastard will make a move fairly soon, I think."

"What the fuck does Liam have to do with anything?"

"It still sounds strange to hear you refer to him by that name," said Ivo. "Perhaps you'll decide to take him up on whatever offer he makes you. Because he will, Red."

"Will what?" I was genuinely confused. I hadn't seen Liam since I'd accidentally embedded a stone into his skull down in Chester a month earlier. It had been the same day Ivo had pulled a fast one with the parallel universes and their different rooms in the same bloody tower. God, was it really only a month since I'd been trapped in a room with the man standing in front of me now? I'd sworn that I'd never speak to him ever again, and with bloody good reason. Yet here I was, standing chatting casually as though we were nothing more than friendly acquaintances who hadn't met up in a while.

"The Bastard will make you an offer," repeated Ivo. "We all know it's power he really wants," he tilted his head enquiringly at me, "and he can't get it without you."

"Why not?"

"Have you ever wondered why he gave you the crown?" asked Ivo. "Yes, you have power of your own. But when all's said and done, Red," he smiled, "you're just a cafe owner with aspirations."

"What's that supposed to mean?" I frowned at him. "Aspirations? You cheeky fucker. What's wrong with wanting to be successful?"

"You've always wanted more than that, though," he said. "Haven't you? All this talk of wanting nothing more than your cafe and your cat—albeit a very unusual cat—but really you wanted more."

"I have no idea what you're talking about," I said sharply. But I did know. And he was right. For all I'd told myself—and anyone else who'd listen to me—that all I wanted in life was to run Flora's and have Izzy and Grimm around, there's always been a tiny niggling voice in the back of my head telling me I could do better. That I could do more. I did a degree because I thought that might make me finally feel like a 'proper' adult, but all it gave me was an expensive certificate and a lot of mostly irrelevant knowledge. I'd stayed in Liverpool after university because it was definitely more interesting than Shropshire, even back then. But it was also because I could feel the potential oozing out of its concrete pores. Liverpool's the sort of place that makes you feel you could achieve anything, if you only tried hard enough. But Liverpudlians rarely become successful from hard work alone. There's a layer of rage behind the determination. Fury at the way in which they've been treated over the decades, and anger in the face of prejudice and assumption. A lot of scousers would probably admit publicly to being powered by spite. Not the nasty, sneaky kind, though. Nope, this is the sort of spite that sticks both middle fingers up at the world and says See? We didn't need your support, you mealy-mouthed cynics. We can get by without you. I'd felt it as soon as I'd moved in for Freshers Week, and it had seeped ever deeper into my bones over the intervening years. And what had I done with that inner power? Sold coffee and cake and made small talk with tourists. And it had been fun—but it wasn't enough. It seemed ridiculous now that I'd ever thought it might be. But I still didn't know what that had to do with the crown. "How would giving me the crown help Liam? Surely if it was that important, he'd have kept it for himself."

"You overestimate the Bastard's morals, Red," said Ivo. "You're not his ultimate target."

"Then what am I?"

Ivo smiled thinly at me, then shrugged. "You're the bait."

I Am The Bait, But I Am Also The Trap

"Bait for what?" I stared at Ivo. "Who's coming for me now?" I was getting really bloody tired of things trying to kill me. Okay, so being the immortal ruler of a supernatural realm inevitably carries risks, some more dangerous than others. But could I not just go maybe two months without having to fend off yet another assassination attempt? "Is the Headless Horseman due in town?" I went on. "Or maybe Cthulhu's planning to rise from the deep and throttle me with his tentacles?"

Ivo arched an eyebrow at me. "I'm not sure even Cthulhu would want to take on those sirens of yours," he said.

"Daisy's not a siren," I snorted. "Sirens aren't real. Anyway, the Asrai spend most of their time out in the bay during the summer—Cthulhu could definitely sneak past them if he went deep enough."

"And then clamber out of the mud and onto the waterfront," said Ivo. "And do what? Torment the locals? Munch on a passing narrowboat?"

"Good fibre in a narrowboat," I said. "All that wood."

"Lots of it is actually fibreglass these days. Listen to me, Red," he said. "This is important."

"So is the digestive health of the mythical sea monster," I said, desperately trying to put off the moment I discovered just who was after my head on a spike this time. "Care and feeding of your pet underwater leviathan, sort of thing."

"It isn't a 'who' that's after you," he said. "It's a 'what'."

"What do you mean, what?"

"That isn't a correct sentence in any iteration of the English language," he said, clearly struggling to hide his impatience, "and you are prevaricating. You have to listen to me, Red."

"Why?" I scowled at him. "Why should I do anything you ask, Ivo? The last time we met, you imprisoned me." Something else occurred to me. "Why did you trap Jonathan?" Jonathan Hulls was—and still is—your basic-issue mad scientist, if said mad scientist lived in the Cotswolds and wore an elaborate wig in place of the usual electric-shock hair. But that was three hundred years ago, back when he was still technically alive. These days he occupies a small house tucked away next to the old steam mill in Chester and his once luxurious wig is home to a small white mouse called Horace. Horace is a particularly cute mouse, to be fair. In fact, Horace often makes more sense than Jonathan, despite not being able to actually speak. Ivo had taken Jonathan hostage when he was still alive, and used him to create a very weird alternate dimension that was connected to the 'real' world whilst also being disconnected enough for bits of it to survive the mill's collapse. No, it doesn't make any sense to me, either. Not even after slogging my way through a copy of 'Quantum for Beginners', which I'd borrowed from Nik. When I'd expressed my surprise at such a book even existing within Nik's usually more, shall we say, stimulating collection of faded and battered romance novels, he'd reminded me he had, in fact, attended Cambridge university in his youth, and was perfectly capable of intellectual endeavour, thank you very much. And I reminded him that his time as an undergraduate was widely remembered for involving more bears than one might usually expect to find in student halls. At which point he'd thrown a copy of Jilly Cooper's 'Riders' at me and stalked out of the room. Me and Nik are basically dysfunctional siblings divided only by class, money and centuries. And even the money side of things was beginning to balance itself out. "Do you want me to answer your question," said Ivo, "or shall I leave you to carry on the conversation with your inner demons?"

"Of course I want an answer," I said, embarrassment making me snappy. Not that I wasn't fully entitled to be snappy, considering I was talking to the biggest idiot I'd ever met in my life. Although he was also, just possibly, the most dangerous. And definitely one of the cutest, I thought to myself, tilting my head slightly to gaze at him. Why the fuck was every hot man I knew an absolute bloody psychopath? Other than Sean, who was so sweet that I was beginning to suspect he must have ulterior motives. No one's that nice without good reason. Mind you, for all I knew, the 'good reason' might just be that he fancied the arse off me. It does happen occasionally. Unfortunately, I suspected Sean's loyalty was simply down to the endless plot lines he could 'borrow' from my life, and which were slowly making him even more successful than he was already.

Definitely financial motives, said the city helpfully. ***Far more likely than physical attraction***.

Thanks a fucking bunch, I hissed silently. Yes, it is possible to have a snippy conversation inside your head without making a sound externally. Ask me how I know.

"Talking to your friends again?" Ivo smiled politely. I sighed. I really needed to work on the blank expression. Eadric always said he could read me like a book. Nik said it was probably an utterly filthy book considering I had a mouth like a fishwife, but luckily Daisy had appeared at the office window and distracted me before I could throw something heavy at his stupid head. It had been mid-afternoon and not only had she scaled the front of the Liver Building above a promenade dotted with tourists, she'd done it stark bollock naked. Only without the bollocks, obviously. Eadric had dragged her inside and hastily wrapped her in a throw from the armchair, before shutting all the windows tightly and making me promise to deliver her back to the river after dark. Which is how I came to spend an entire afternoon shut in Nik's private rooms with a mermaid who stank of seaweed and insisted on pushing her webbed toes into my face at regular intervals. Daisy found it funnier than I did.

"They're better company than most people," I said. "Now tell me about Jonathan." I expected him to argue, but he just shrugged and leaned back against the old brick wall.

"What do you want to know?" He slid his hands into his trouser pockets and adopted the casual stance of a catalogue model displaying the new autumn collection. Casual and smart, with just a soupçon of erotic potential. Nik would have been impressed. "He had something I needed, and I took it. Sometimes it really is that simple."

"You took his ideas," I snapped back. "You took his dreams, Ivo. You took his inspiration and his invention, and you locked him away with them." Jonathan had told me himself that he couldn't remember how the 'trick' worked—how he'd trapped the Queen of Mercia in the walls of her own city on Ivo's instruction. Ivo had clearly figured it out for himself eventually, but had never let Jonathan go free. Four hundred years after his official death, Jonathan Hulls had still been living a gloomy half-life in a non-existent glass room attached to the old Chester Steam Mill. Like I said, quantum's weird. These days he was happily ensconced in the little house next door to the mill, along with the now-freed Mercian queen—better known as Fred—and her daughter, Elf. Neither Fred nor Jonathan like leaving the house very much, but I'm working on it. Elf sometimes helps in Flora's. She's fast and efficient, and an excellent waitress. It might have helped if she wasn't almost entirely invisible. But you don't always get what you want, as someone wiser (or possibly just more patronising) than me once sang.

"What else was I supposed to do, Red?" Ivo's left eye twitched slightly, and I realised he was very angry. "Let him go and what? Have him tell everyone what he could do? Do you have any idea how dangerous he could have been in the wrong hands?"

"You're talking about him as though he's a weapon," I said. "He's a person, for fuck's sake! But you don't care about that, do you?" The eye twitched again, but he didn't say anything. "You use people and throw them away. Or worse—you just forget them. Is that what you'd do to me, Ivo?" Silence. "Is that your plan? To seduce me and get what you want, then what? Shove me in a bloody cupboard and throw away the key?"

"No." He spoke so quietly that I almost missed it.

"Say again?" I narrowed my eyes, just daring him to come out with another ridiculously overblown excuse for his appalling behaviour.

"No." His voice was louder this time. "No, I wouldn't throw you away, Red."

"You were quite happy to lock me up in that bloody mill," I pointed out. And had Bella not come to my rescue, I might still be up there. I wondered how long it had taken Fred to realise no one was coming for her. A week? A month? Ten years? She'd been in that room for more than ten centuries by the time I'd dropped in feet first and rescued her. And by 'rescue' I mean 'lost my temper and floundered around angrily until things somehow worked out'. Fred's freedom—along with that of Jonathan and Elf—was nothing more than a lucky side-effect of my own escape on the back of a raging Liver bird.

"I love you."

For a second, I thought I'd misheard. "What?" I managed eventually.

"You heard me." I forced myself to look at him. He hadn't moved, but to my horror there was what looked terrifyingly like a tear brimming in the corner of one eye. Fucking hell, I thought, he's finally gone and done it. He's toppled over the edge of insanity.

Or he's just being honest. I was reasonably sure the city was shrugging. ***That's a first.***

That's fucking terrifying, is what it is.

You don't have to do anything about it, it said. ***Pretend you didn't hear him***.

"I'm sorry," I said out loud, "but did you really just say you love me?"

Oh well, the city sighed to itself. ***No one can accuse us of not trying.***

"Yes," said Ivo, more loudly now. "Yes, I did. I love you, Lilith O'Reilly. Is that so hard to believe?"

"Actually yes," I said. "Yes, it's really fucking difficult to believe, Ivo. This might have passed you by, mate, but we are currently in the twenty-first century. People who have a romantic interest in other people generally tend to, I dunno, be nice to them to start with?" I shook my head in disbelief. "They don't trick or trap them, and they definitely don't sneak into their bathrooms in disguise. You dressed up as my grandmother, for fuck's sake!"

"Good disguise, though," he said. "Don't you think?" A faint smile played at the corners of his mouth.

"How do you change into other things?" I asked. "I can kind of get the Gran thing, if only because you're both humans and a similar size. But a magpie?" I frowned. "Where does all the extra stuff go?"

"Extra stuff?" Ivo looked amused. "Which bits of me are extra, Red?"

"Bones and eyes and teeth," I said quickly, trying not to blush. "The stuff birds don't actually have. Hollow bones. Where does it all go?"

"It doesn't go anywhere," he said. "You call it my 'trick', yes?" I nodded. "Well," he went on, "they're different tricks. I've never changed my appearance to that of a magpie, for one thing."

"Are you telling me it wasn't you flapping at my kitchen window that time?" I asked. "Fighting with Grimm in the car park?"

"Did he really?" He grinned. "Excellent stuff."

"You nearly injured my cat," I said. "And that is something I would never forgive."

"Oh, I absolutely did not," he said. "And that cat is tough as old boots. Anyway, like I say, I wasn't pretending to be a magpie. It was doing me a favour, that's all."

"What sort of favour?" I frowned. "Were you mind-controlling that poor bird?" This was all getting a little bit too wizard-y, even by my standards. "Do you have a friend who likes to sing about hedgehogs?"

"I have no idea what you're talking about," said Ivo, instantly proving that, whatever he thought to the contrary, we were absolutely not made for each other. "I merely asked the bird to help out, and it did. And before you accuse me of animal cruelty, Red, let me assure you that no one gets to tell a magpie what to do. Do you know why single magpies are considered unlucky?"

"Because they get hijacked by wazzocks like you?"

"Very funny. No," he said, "it's because they're independent. Society doesn't like independent creatures, Red. Society likes everything and everyone to depend on each other, because that's how society stays cohesive. Sometimes that codependence takes a wrong turn, and the society in question turns into a fascist hellscape. But more usually, it just kind of rubs along. The majority are safe if the majority toe the line. That sort of thing."

"What does this have to do with birds?"

"How well do you know your bible stories?" Ivo asked.

"Vaguely," I said. "Did religious education at school, but not well enough to take any exams. Pretty sure I've got the gist of it, though. Interesting story. Over-egged in places, people take it far too seriously, but most of them only really know Genesis and Revelations. Being chucked out of Eden, behold a pale horse, all that jazz. Two out of five, probably wouldn't recommend. Am I close enough?"

"So you know Genesis?"

"Yes," I sighed. Here I was attempting to divert this unexpected and exceedingly uncomfortable situation with my usual hilarious commentary, and Ivo was mostly just ignoring me.

He knows you better than you think.

Shut up.

"Do you know why there were no magpies on the Ark?" asked Ivo.

I frowned at him. "Must have missed that bit," I said. "Anyway, we all know there's no boat big enough for two of everything. And the lions would have eaten most of them, anyway."

"There were no magpies," he said, "because they refused to be told what to do."

"Knew I there must be a reason I liked them so much."

"It's why I like them, too." Ivo smiled, and this time it was genuine. "Magpies know their own minds, Red. Many religious folk will tell you they were cast out of the Ark, but that story's been changed to suit them over the centuries. The original story was that, when all the other creatures dutifully clambered aboard the big ship to freedom, the magpies refused to enter. They preferred to cling to the mast," he smiled, "outsiders through and through. Whilst the rest of the animal kingdom hid away and hoped for it to be over, the magpies were up above it all, cackling at the storm. Of course," he went on, "that's the modern version. The Ancient Romans believed they were magical."

"And are they?" I asked. "Magical, I mean."

"I think so," said Ivo. Even as he said it, a large glossy bird landed on top of the wall behind him. He smiled without turning to look at it. "As you can see," he said, "they certainly know when they're being talked about."

I gazed up at the bird. It looked back at me with interest, its head bobbing from side to side as if giving me its full consideration. "You're the bird that came to my flat, aren't you?" I asked it. I half expected it to answer me, but instead it bobbed its head up and down in response. "Was it you in Chester as well?" Another bob. "You were using it as a spy," I said to Ivo. "Weren't you?" The bird began waggling its way up and down the wall, as though purposely showing off.

"As I've already explained," said Ivo, "it was doing me a favour. That's all."

"Wanna tell me why you're working for this complete asshat?" I asked the magpie. It did a little hop on the spot. "Don't be getting offended at me," I warned it. "I'm not the one helping idiots who should be staying out of other people's business."

"But it was my business," said Ivo. "I had to make sure you weren't going to disrupt anything."

"Uh huh," I said. "How did that work out for you?"

"You're better than I thought," he shrugged. "I underestimated you. Which is a mistake I won't be making again."

"Noted," I said. "Are you ever actually going to answer my question?" Then, in response to his confused expression, "I'm the bait, apparently? Liam's bait. Like a little worm, dangling on a hook."

"Aah," he said, "so I was."

"So what is it he's trying to catch?"

"The Grail," he said, as if it was obvious. Which it probably should have been, on account of how it was clearly turning into 'Hunt The Grail With Lil' week, whether I liked it or not. "He wants the Grail, and he thinks you're going to help him find it."

"Why would I help anyone find anything?" I frowned. "None of you are much of an appealing option, no offence."

"None taken." He gave me a wry smile. "If I'd have known back then what a handful you'd be, I'd have put stronger plans in place."

"Back when?" I eyed him suspiciously. "Back when you fucked around with time itself in order to have things your own way?"

"Yes." His voice was calm and his gaze steady. "And I still believe it was the right thing to do," he said. "For both of us."

I raised my eyebrows. "And what about everyone else?" I said. "What about all the people whose lives might have been destroyed if Eadric hadn't dragged me back into the twenty-first century?" I still sometimes had flashbacks to when Eadric had appeared in the nineteenth century and shoved me without warning under the wheels of a heavy delivery cart. I could remember the split second of horrified fear as the wagon had rolled towards me—then, nothing.

"He didn't pull you back," said Ivo, as though reading my mind. "He killed you off. And that's not the same thing at all."

"Killed me?" I shook my head. "He clearly did nothing of the sort," I said, "because I'm standing here in front of you now."

"Red," Ivo said patiently, "you've been dead for over two years now. Eadric knew he needed to kill that version of you in order for this one," he gestured up and down me with his hand, "to come back to us."

"Whoah there, Neddy," I said, something horrible having just occurred to me. "How many other versions of Me might be wandering around in the ether?"

"I have no idea about ether," said Ivo, "but there might be more of you in other realities, yes."

"No. No, no, no," I began pacing up and down, "I am absolutely the fuck not getting into that shit again. One reality is enough for anyone. This is the one I'm staying in and youse can all fuck right off if you think that's going to change at any point."

"No one's asking you to change anything," said Ivo. "No need to panic."

"I'm not panicking," I said, coming to a halt in front of him. "I'm debating whether to just throw the fucking lot of you into the bloody river. I'm sure Daisy could invite her friends over for an alfresco buffet."

"I dated an Asrai once," said Ivo. "Long time ago. Nice girl."

"Girl?" I frowned at him. "Oh," I said, realisation dawning. "Oh, no. Nope. Do not tell me you had sex with a mermaid, Ivo Laithlind." His grin answered my question. "Ugh," I spat. "Ugh, ugh, you vile creature!"

"You're not as open-minded as you'd like to think," said Ivo. "Clearly."

"My mind is going to stay permanently shut forever, if this is the sort of shit people are going to tell me. Anyway," I said, "why are you telling me?"

Ivo tilted his head and looked at me quizzically. "Because you asked."

"Yeah," I said, "but you wouldn't have been telling me any of your personal secrets just a few months back. Weeks, even." I frowned suspiciously at him. "So what's different now?"

"I realised I'm going about things all wrong," he shrugged. "You're right, Red—force doesn't work. Not in situations as important as this. My mother used to have a saying about it that she liked."

"If in doubt, chop their heads off?" I'd done my research over the last couple of years, and these days I knew the story of Ivo's parents well. His mother had been fierce and proud, and a legend in her own right.

"She'd have liked you," he said. "But no, it was more subtle than that. She used to say that it was easier to catch flies with honey, rather than vinegar."

"Who the fuck even wants to catch flies?" I snorted.

"Maybe it was bees," he shrugged. "It was a long time ago."

"Can we get back on topic here?" I asked. "Only I've got things to do. Places to be. You know how it is."

"I apologise," he said. "I'm wasting your majesty's time."

"Don't you fucking start," I warned him. "If you ever try bowing at me, Ivo Laithlind, I promise I will punch you square in the face." I thought about it for a second. "Again."

"I don't doubt it," he said. "As for the Bastard, it's simple enough. He wants the Grail more than anything. And he thinks he can get it through you."

"In order to cultivate an army of undead supporters, I assume?"

"Of course," said Ivo. "As things stand, there is no knowing who or what might become immortal. Which means—and I must apologise for this in advance—there is no quality control." I scowled, but he ignored me. "If one has control of the process, then one can shape the future to one's own desires."

"One needs to be stopping with the one thing," I said. "It makes one sound like a pretentious little prick."

"You say the nicest things." Ivo gave me a crooked smile.

"So," I said, ignoring the confused hormonal meeping going off in my pants region, "Liam gave me the crown in the hope that the Grail would somehow find its own way back to it?" Ivo nodded. "But he'd already had the crown for centuries before he gave it to me," I frowned. "Why didn't he just find the Grail waiting on his doorstep one morning? It's not very good at its job, is it? Bad Grail. Naughty Grail. Shove it in a corner til it learns its lesson."

"The Bastard doesn't deserve the Grail," said Ivo, wisely ignoring my ramblings. "And I suspect it knows that."

"The Grail's a sentient being now?"

"In as much as anything created by man can be sentient," said Ivo, "yes. You can feel it in the crown, I'd imagine?" I thought about how the crown had almost overwhelmed me the first time I'd put it on, a terrifying mix of fear and exultation, fury and excitement. It had wanted me to wear it, for sure—but it had also wanted to take me over and use me for its own ends. And I wasn't entirely convinced its own motives were any purer than Liam's. Or Ivo's, come to that. Which is why I'd eventually had it broken up. I rubbed my thumb against the back of the gold ring on my left hand. Nothing. And yet it had tried to turn me into some kind of sparking bloody Power Ranger when I'd faced off against Eve in Martins Bank. Presumably the ring at least thought I was safe enough for the time being. Or maybe it had just gone off for a tea break.

"Yes," I said eventually.

"Then you know what I'm talking about," said Ivo. "I suspect the Grail has the same power. I also suspect that this is precisely why our forebears had the sense to keep the two items very much apart."

"The crown came into existence much later than the Grail," I said. "So how does that work?"

"The ancients wore crowns to denote authority," said Ivo, "same as every other civilisation that has ever existed. If not of gold, then of laurel, or holly leaves. Or flowers, for those more romantically inclined."

"Like those fake flower crowns you can buy online?" I asked. "I always thought those were more symbolic of having hippy tendencies and spending too much time at music festivals."

"Nothing like those," said Ivo, but he was smiling. "I've always thought the crown—the crown, the one the Bastard so foolishly gifted to you—might have been made from gold originally stolen from our ancestors. Probably during one of those interminable crusades this country was always going off on."

"And that's when the Grails got mixed up," I said.

"If there were ever two of them in the first place," said Ivo. "As with crowns, symbolism goes a long way when it comes to holy chalices and the like. They're more often a product of wishful thinking, rather than a real item in themselves."

"I'll leave that argument to the church, if that's alright with you," I said. "Got enough on my plate without grumpy bishops turning up. So," I squinted at Ivo, "you think Liam gave me the crown in the hope the Grail would come chasing after it on its little tiny Grail-y feet?"

"Probably not the feet," he said with a grin. "But yes, to the rest of it."

"And you're here to save me from him?"

"Absolutely not," said Ivo. "I have confidence in you, Red. I believe you are more than capable of saving yourself, should the need arise. However," he went on, "I am a pragmatic man. And if I have to save you in order to claim the prize for myself, then that is what I will do."

"So you'd only actually save me in order to save yourself?"

"Pretty much." He shrugged. "I've learned the hard way that I can't force you to care for me, however much I'd like you to. And I can clearly no longer rely on my innate charm convincing you to save both of us together. Which means I have no option but to prioritise myself. I cannot allow the Bastard the opportunity to combine the power, Red." His voice was urgent now. "None of us can take that risk."

"You think you'd be a safe pair of hands?"

"I'd be safer than that monster," said Ivo.

"From where I'm standing," I said, "anyone would be safer than either of you. In fact," I narrowed my eyes at him, "maybe I should just give it to the cats as a plaything. Let them bash it around Sefton Park for a bit, see how the ancients like that for a game of Roman soldiers."

“You’ve got to find it first,” said Ivo. “And you’re not the only person looking for it.”

~

I left him down at the waterfront, after making him promise faithfully that he’d never trick his way into my bathroom again. I wasn’t sure his promises actually meant anything, but that was just par for the course these days. I could count the people I’d trust fully on the fingers of one hand, and I wouldn’t even need the entire hand. Lost in thought as I wandered toward home, I belatedly realised I’d overshot my turn and was instead heading up Paradise Street. I kept walking. The bristling on my neck started as I got to Whitechapel, and suddenly I knew where I was going. A right turn onto Hood Street and within minutes I was outside the Royal Court Theatre. Standing against the wall with my head back against the bricks, I thought carefully about what I was about to do. There was still time to walk away—to head home as I’d planned and pretend none of this stupidity was even happening. The bristling on my neck got stronger, as though a static current was running up my spine. “I’m here,” I said finally. “Did you want something?”

SHE NEVER RINGS, said the City, **SHE NEVER CALLS. SHE DOESN’T EVEN CHECK IN TO MAKE SURE—**

“Yes, yes,” I said, more sharply than intended, “I know, I’m useless at keeping in touch. I kind of assumed you’d be too busy to speak to me unless it’s really urgent.” This was both true, and also an excuse. I did indeed avoid speaking to the City—the real, true, honest-to-god spirit of the City itself, not its annoying underling with all the people that like to chatter inside my head and make my brain hurt. This was mostly because I didn’t like to bother it, what with it being an important ethereal embodiment of a landscape’s soul and all that. But I also avoided it because, truth be told, it scared me a bit. Okay, a lot. You try having a conversation with an invisible being that’s bigger than anything you can comprehend whilst also capable of dropping its comments directly into your brain without visiting your ears first, and then tell me it doesn’t make you nervous.

I AM MERELY INTERESTED IN YOUR WELLBEING, LILITH.

"Fuck off," I said, before I could stop myself, "you are so not! You'll have a hidden motive somewhere along the line. Everyone does." I huffed a bit, just for the show of it.

IT IS UNFORTUNATE, said the City, **THAT YOU SEEM INCAPABLE OF UNDERSTANDING THAT I DO NOT INDULGE IN DECEIT.**

"Why not?" I said. "Everyone else does."

I HAVE NO NEED, it said. **HUMAN EMOTIONS ARE IRRELEVANT TO ME.**

"You seem to have picked up sarcasm well enough."

SOMETIMES I LIKE TO AMUSE MYSELF.

"All sounds a bit human, if you ask me."

I DIDN'T ASK.

"Anyway," I said, knowing better than to get into a battle of wits with an entire city, "if you're talking to me, then something's wrong."

OR RIGHT.

"Well, which is it?" I asked. A man wearing work clothes and a high-vis vest gave me a sideways glance as he passed, clearly thinking the nutters had been let out early. "Right or wrong?" I went on, lowering my voice. "It's to do with the bloody Grail," I sighed. "Isn't it?"

YES, said the City. **AND IT IS, INDEED, BLOODY.**

"Metaphorically or literally?"

HISTORICALLY. MANY A WAR HAS BEEN FOUGHT FOR ITS POWER. AND WARS WILL BE FOUGHT AGAIN.

"And what am I supposed to do about it?" I asked. "Shove it in my knicker drawer and tell everyone to just forget it ever existed?"

YOU'D NEED TO FIND IT FIRST.

"And then?"

FIND IT, repeated the city. **THEN DESTROY IT.**

All My Friends Are Lunatics

"Oh dear," said Izzy as she walked in through the kitchen door the next day, "are we having another 'why me?' moment, by any chance?"

"What makes you say that?"

"Because you're mumbling into the table with your head in your hands," she said. "I'll put the kettle on, shall I?"

"S'pose." I pushed myself upright and sighed. "I'll have an espresso," I said. "Double shot. Maybe that will make me feel slightly more alive."

"It'd be a fucking miracle if it did," said Iz, "considering you're dead as the proverbial dodo."

"Do you have to keep reminding me?" I got up to find an espresso cup in the cupboard. The decorators had got as far as painting the kitchen walls bright green and were due to start on the woodwork any day now, so I'd had to tuck everything away out of paint-splashing range. "Sometimes feels like it's the only thing about me anyone's interested in these days. 'Still dead, Lil? Glad to hear it,' blah blah fucking blah."

"Ooh," said Izzy, "we are a mardy-pants today, aren't we?" She took the espresso cup I was holding out to her and put it under the nozzle of the coffee machine. "Is this thing behaving itself now?" she said, gazing nervously at it. "Only I'd quite like to not end up in A&E again."

"That wasn't the machine's fault," I pointed out. "You're supposed to move your hand out of the way before it starts dispensing."

"Wasn't expecting it to be so bloody fast, was I?" She pressed the button and leapt backwards, almost knocking into me. "Aah," she said, as the coffee began to pour, "there we are. Dunno what you were worried about." I didn't bother responding. Years of experience have taught me that Izzy's meandering thoughts are best left well alone. "So," she handed me my drink and started pouring her own, "what's up? Tell Aunt Izzy all about it."

"You can tell Aunt Kitty as well, if you like." Izzy swallowed down a garbled screech and determinedly did not turn to shout at Kitty, who'd appeared in the living room doorway. She was carrying Grimm like a baby, curled up on his back. I raised an eyebrow at him and he gave me a slow blink in return before uncoiling and leaping out of Kitty's arms. He strolled out of the kitchen door without a backwards glance, presumably to take his embarrassment out on the local wildlife.

"I thought you were with Jonny," I said accusingly. "When did you get back?"

"Ooh, ages ago," said my aunt, settling herself opposite me at the kitchen table. The fact she did this by simply walking through the chair before sitting down on it was not lost on Izzy.

"Kitty," she said, "I love you dearly, as you well know."

"Awww," said Kitty, "That's a lovely thing to say! I love you too." She beamed at both of us in turn. "Isn't this nice?"

"I hadn't finished," said Izzy through gritted teeth. "What I was trying to say was that, although I do indeed adore you, Kitty, my nerves cannot take much more of this," she groped around for the right word, "this utter fucking mentalness."

"Subtle as usual there, Iz," I said.

"She just walked through the bloody chair!" squeaked Izzy. "At least you try to act human."

"Oh god," said Kitty, "did I do it again?" She looked crestfallen. "I'm so sorry, Izzy love. I really don't mean to do it. It's just that I'm comfortable here with you two and I suppose I let my guard down a bit."

Now it was Izzy's turn to look embarrassed. "It's okay," she sighed, "I didn't mean to be cross at you. There's just something about the ghost side of things that freaks me out occasionally, you know?"

"Even more than your best friend being a zombie?" I asked. "Cos you keep telling me that's weird."

"It *is* all weird!" said Izzy. "Anyway," she picked up her coffee cup and eyed me beadily over the rim, "tell us what's ailing you, oh spooky one."

"I can't," I said truthfully. "Everything is difficult and stressful and a lot of it's downright bloody horrible, but I can't tell you about it." I shrugged. "Sorry."

"You need to let the negativity go, Lil," said Kitty. "Think about nicer things for a while." She smiled beatifically across the table at us both. "As I always say," she held her hands up as if giving absolution, "if you think good thoughts, then good things will come to you."

"You never really left the sixties, did you?" said Izzy. "God I wish we'd been born back then," she turned to me, "we could have got off our tits on acid and burned our bras, just for the hell of it."

"That was the seventies," I said. "The bra-burning. They were still wearing big beige nanna-bras in the sixties. Acid sounds fun, though."

"Ooh no," said Kitty, "the one time I took acid, I thought the Snow Queen from Narnia was hiding in my wardrobe. I spent all night with my back to the wall, just staring at the wardrobe door in terror. Actually," she added brightly, "Gaultier was there that night."

"What was he doing, while you waited to be force-fed Turkish Delight?" asked Izzy.

"He was just sitting there, as far as I can remember," said Kitty. She had a faraway look on her face. "Because of course it wouldn't have worked on him, as you know." I did indeed know. I'd never been particularly into mood-altering substances of any kind, but it still sucked sweaty balls that now I was dead, none of it would have any effect on me anyway. Choosing not to do something is very different to knowing there'd be no point even bothering. "He said he still enjoyed watching me having fun. And then when it started wearing off, we—"

"No, thank you!" My voice came out sounding faintly strangled. "We don't need to hear what you and Mapp got up to back in the good old days."

"Why on earth not?" asked the man himself, appearing in the kitchen doorway. "We had some good times, didn't we, girl?" He came to stand behind Kitty's chair and put a hand on her shoulder. I tried not to look too obviously relieved that he'd clearly forgiven me for the gossiping thing. "Reckon we could teach these youngsters a thing or two." Kitty giggled like someone who's just spotted Tom Hardy in the local Tesco.

"I'd really rather you didn't," I said. "Anyway, what's happened now?"

"How d'you mean?" asked Mapp, taking the last seat at the table and smiling round at us all. "Can't I just call in on my beloved monarch without any reason other than to show my eternal devotion?"

"Gaultier Mapp," I said, getting up to find him a cup, "you are never without a devious motive. And you're not speaking to me, remember?" He shrugged noncommittally. "So there's clearly something up. Out with it."

"You know me too well," he sighed. He leaned forward with his elbows on the table and his chin resting on his hands. This was accompanied by clattering as the endless chunky bracelets he wore rattled their way down his arms. "Have any of you spoken to the witch?"

"We don't know any witches," I said. "And if we did, we promised never to talk about them. Remember?"

"Yes, yes," said Mapp, "but now I need to talk about it. Her. Or rather, I need to know where she is."

"Where who is?" Izzy asked. "We can't know where someone is if they don't exist, Mapp."

"The pair of you are utterly impossible," he said, leaning back in his chair and flinging his head up to stare at the ceiling. "My ex-wife," he said, dropping his head back down and glaring at us each in turn. "Where has my dratted ex-wife got to?"

"She's here," said a voice from the doorway. "Oh, hello Kitty! How's things with you?" Kitty rose from her chair and greeted Freya with a hug. The rest of us sat staring at the pair of them in utter bewilderment.

"We've already met," said Kitty. "In town. I hadn't quite got the hang of the reappearing and disappearing thing back then. I'd been to see Jonny in Shrewsbury and got my return journey a bit muddled."

"She popped up on North John Street," explained Freya, "and damn near gave me the fright of my very long life. Anyway, we got chatting, and that was that."

"Uh huh," I said. "Did it not occur to either of you that the other was a bit, well..." I shrugged, "odd?"

"No odder than a lot round here," said Freya. "Anyway, I was just popping in to see how you were doing after yesterday's drama." She was completely ignoring Mapp's presence, whilst the man himself just gaped at her in silent fury. "I went into the cafe to start with, but the nice man sent me up here. He looked familiar, somehow. Should I know him?"

I narrowed my eyes at Izzy. "Have you got Sean working downstairs again?" I asked her. "Where's Todd?"

"On holiday with my cousins," said Izzy. Todd is our part-timer in Flora's, and also one of Izzy's many distant relatives. "Elf's helping Sean out. He'll be fine."

"Elf's invisible," I pointed out. "She can't exactly serve the customers, can she?"

"I think you'd be surprised at just what Elf can do when she puts her mind to it," said Izzy. "But no, she's out back doing the dishes. I told Sean to keep the door shut. That way, no one will wonder why the crockery looks like it's flying around."

"Hang on," I said. "Why do you need Sean's help, anyway? It's your day to work."

"I'm busy," she shrugged, "aren't I? You know how it is." I frowned at her in a way that clearly construed that no, I didn't know how it was, actually. "I live in the Royal Albert Dock," Izzy said, as though that explained everything. "I'm not really sure I'm the waitress type anymore." I turned to look at the others and was relieved to see they all looked as confused as I felt.

"You're not a waitress," I said. "You're a manager. A manager who's on a ridiculously high wage, especially when we consider the fact that Flora's is small enough that it really could survive with not much more than a couple of waitresses."

"So I'm managing," she said airily. "Anyway, I've got a manicure booked for this afternoon. And I'm not going to want to put my hands in dishwater after that, am I?"

"Sean isn't a member of staff," I said. "He's a customer who's nice enough to help out when asked. Some might call him gullible. You can't take advantage of him like that!"

"Then get more staff," said Izzy. "Anyway," she got to her feet, "I'm taking tomorrow off as well. Sean's already agreed. I've got a design consultant coming in to help me choose colours for the apartment."

"She's definitely paying you too much," nodded Mapp. "I could have done you a colour consult for free, you know that."

"I appreciate the offer," said Izzy, "but I really think I'm above the hippy look these days. Anyway," she pushed her chair in and headed for the door, "must be off. Toodles!" With that, she was gone. The rest of us stared at each other in confusion for a few seconds, before Mapp and Freya each remembered the other's presence.

"Hello Gaultier," said Freya eventually. "Long time no see, and all that."

"Not nearly long enough," muttered Mapp. And then more loudly, "Why did you have to reappear? I was perfectly happy without you."

"It's been two hundred years," said Freya, taking Izzy's seat at the table. "Some might suggest you should have got over any hurt feelings by now."

"That's enough," I said firmly, getting up from the table. "I've got enough going on right now, without you two kicking off in my kitchen. Coffee, Freya?"

"Thanks love," she said. "Black, no sugar." She grinned mischievously. "Just like Gaultier here."

"Stop that right now," I said, "or you can leave. Mapp is my friend, and we don't pick on friends."

"Thank you, Lilith," said Mapp politely. "It's nice to know some people still have manners."

"Anyway," said Kitty, "I'll be off, I think. Have fun!" With that, she vanished. *Thanks for nothing*, I muttered to myself. *Leave me with the bickering exes here, why don't you.*

We're certainly never short of entertainment, said the city. ***It's***

a laugh a minute with you. I scowled at the wall in front of me and took a deep breath to calm myself, which, as my only company was another revenant and some form of ancient witch, was safe enough. Which is why I was surprised to find myself breathing in the unexpected aroma of pine needles and burning wood, alongside the clear sensation of some form of ancient heartbreak. I swung around to stare at Freya and looked straight into her level gaze. "I'd rather you didn't do that," she said, "if you don't mind."

"You're alive," I said without thinking. "Aren't you?"

"No one said she wasn't," said Mapp. He looked at each of us in turn, his gaze finally resting on me. "There's endlessly different creatures on this side of the veil, Lil, you know that."

"I'm a person," said Freya sharply. "Not a creature."

"We're all creatures in our own way, my love," he said. I raised an eyebrow at that, but he wasn't looking at me. Mapp and Freya were staring at each other across my kitchen table, their eyes locked and both absolutely motionless. I coughed loudly.

"I'll just make this coffee, shall I?" They both turned to look at me as if only just remembering I was in the room. I waggled a cup in their general direction and made a show of starting the coffee machine. "Mapp," I said, determined to break the tension, "how much do you trust Elizabeth?" He blinked as if to clear his head.

"About as much as I'd trust anyone else," he said finally.

"So, not at all?"

"He never did trust people," said Freya. "For good reason, mostly. Remember that young girl who wanted work as a maid?" She raised her eyebrows at Mapp, who grinned. "Said she was an orphan and would do anything to get off the streets."

"You felt sorry for her," he replied. "Made me take her on for a week's trial."

"She'd stolen all our food out of the cupboard before the first morning was out," said Freya, laughing. "I should have listened to you."

"And I should have listened to you, my love," said Mapp. "You were right about the curtains." I stared wordlessly at the pair of them, wondering—not for the first time—whether the entire world had gone completely and utterly insane.

"You never admit you're wrong," I finally managed. "What's wrong with you?"

"Aah," he said, "maybe I'm going soft in my old age."

"As if," snorted Freya affectionately. There was movement at the kitchen window, and I peered out.

"Aah," I said, seeing the figure hunched on my doorstep, clearly debating whether or not to knock. "Heggie's here."

"Oh let him in," cried Freya. "I'd love to meet him." Mapp and I both stared at her. "What?" she said. "He's your friend, isn't he?"

"Yes," said Mapp, "but..."

"I've kept tabs over the years, Gaultier Mapp." Freya was smiling. "I know all about your Heggie. Knew about Lilith here, an' all. Not that I told Jenny that, of course. Can't be having people knowing my business, now can I?"

"But it's okay for you to know ours?" I asked, as Mapp got up to open the door. "Doesn't seem very fair to me. Cuppa, Heggie?" The little man shook his head as he came in, but took the chair Mapp pulled out for him and sat staring at the table. Which is pretty normal behaviour for Hegs, so I left him to it. "Come on then," I said, turning back to Freya, "give me the potted history of witchery on the Wirral."

"Lilith, darling," said Freya, "there really isn't much to tell. I've been around a very long time, and I've spent most of that time tucked away in my little cottage, being perfectly unbothered by the outside world. I've had to adapt, of course. And I've learned not to hide away for too long. Got one hell of a shock when I came over to the city for the first time in decades and the waterfront looked like it had been bombed."

"That's probably because it had been bombed," I pointed out.

"Yes," said Freya patiently, "but this was a good thirty years after the war ended. Terrible looking, so it was. I went back to my little house and decided not to bother again. But then I started getting visitors, see." Freya had a strange way of speaking—the dialect verged on Welsh, but she had no discernible accent. Which meant she probably sounded something like me, because no one notices their own accent. It certainly wasn't like Grimm, who could go between cut glass Brit to Cockney cabbie in the same sentence, and back again. He sounded as though he'd learned how to speak from several different people. Which was perfectly possible, considering cats aren't usually born knowing how to talk. Freya, on the other hand, had the sort of voice that had been carved out of decades—centuries, possibly—of living around endless different dialects. "People started walking for fun," she went on, "rather than pure necessity. Only realised that one when I had a nap one afternoon and woke up to find a couple and their dog staring in through the windows. I'm not sure who was the most scared," she grinned. "Had to put up a fence after that."

"And you've just been tucked away in the middle of nowhere ever since?"

"Pretty much," she shrugged. "I'm quite liking being back in the land of the living again. So to speak." She grinned. "It's turning out to be more exciting than I expected. Ooh," she went on, "that reminds me! What did you do with Eve?" I froze, coffee cup halfway to my mouth. "I do hope she's buggered off back to London for good," she went on. I'd have breathed a sigh of relief if Heggie hadn't been in the room. Despite being the strangest-looking member of my entire social circle, Heggie is actually as human as they come and therefore susceptible to the whole soul-sucking issue. I settled for taking a sip of my coffee, hoping my hands weren't visibly shaking.

"Yeah," I said eventually, "me too. Elizabeth took her back down south with her." It wasn't a lie, at least. "I don't think she'll be back for a while."

"Good," said Freya. "Never did like that woman."

"You already knew her?" I asked. "I thought you lived quietly on the Wirral and didn't have much contact with people?"

"Like I already said," grinned Freya, "I've been keeping tabs on things a bit more these last few years. Realised I was at risk of getting left behind, otherwise. Unusual people, unusual events. That sort of thing."

"You've been spying on us all this time?" Mapp looked offended.

"I have, yes." Freya shrugged. "Would be foolish not to, given the circs."

"What circs?" I asked.

"I'm a witch, darling," she said. "Our history when it comes to dealing with the authorities is chequered, to say the least."

"If you're that worried," I said, "why are you being so open about it now?"

"Things are changing," said Freya. "I can feel it in my water." I frowned at her. Then I frowned at Mapp and Heggie, just to keep things equal. All three people sitting with me at the table appeared completely oblivious to the intense weirdness of the situation. Maybe you just learned to be more tolerant if you lived for hundreds of years. It would certainly make life simpler. Although that didn't explain why Heggie was sitting happily at the table next to Mapp's ex-wife. Just as I opened my mouth to ask if anyone could tell me exactly what the fuck was going on, Mapp spoke.

"Izzy was a bit weird just now," he said. "Don't you think?"

"Oh, shit." In the confusion of Freya appearing, I'd forgotten about Izzy. "I need to go check on Sean," I said. "If I leave you three up here, will you promise not to break anything?" Heggie tugged Mapp's sleeve and whispered something in his ear.

"We'd better be off now anyway," said Mapp. "Coming, Freya?"

"Yeah," she said, to my surprise. "Let's leave poor Lilith to it." I watched as the three of them got up and made to leave, all apparently perfectly happy with these new arrangements.

"Fuck me," I said aloud, as they exited in a flurry of blown kisses and promises to see me later, "it's like living in a Scouse version of Eastenders."

~

"Oh hi Lil," said Sean. Only two of the inside tables had customers sitting at them, but that wasn't unusual at this time of day. Sean certainly didn't appear to be run off his feet, which was probably a good thing. He'd been leaning on the counter when I walked into Flora's, presumably talking to the middle-aged couple sitting in the window seat. The only other customers were, to my dismay, Maya and Bangle Girl. They sat at the small table that's wedged against the wall, between the counter and the door. No one sits at that table unless there's absolutely nowhere else free, mostly because they get knocked into by anyone wriggling their way through to the customer loo at the back of the cafe.

"Hello ma'am," whispered Maya as I walked past her and behind the counter. I pretended I hadn't heard and beckoned Sean into the little back kitchen that serves as a staff room.

"I'm so sorry," I began, but Sean stopped me.

"It's fine," he said. "I wasn't doing much today, anyway. I didn't know you'd handed full control over to Izzy now, though?"

"I haven't," I said. "Which is why I'm down here talking to you." A clattering noise behind me made me jump, and I turned to see a china plate floating past my head. "Fucking hell, Elf," I hissed, "please don't sneak up on me like that!"

"She didn't sneak up on anyone, to be fair," said Sean. "She was here all along." The air shimmered next to me and for a brief second, I could see Elf's grinning face.

"And she enjoys frightening me half to bloody death," I said. "Thank you for helping, though," I said to the room in general. In response, a ghostly hand appeared next to the sink and gave me a thumbs up. "So what's going on with Izzy?" I asked. "Cos my cafe is currently being staffed by a poltergeist and a world-famous crime writer," Sean gave a humble shrug, "instead of the person who's actually paid to do it."

"No idea," said Sean. "Izzy just said she'd had enough of being a skivvy and was taking a break. To 'reconsider her life choices', I think she said."

"I bloody knew this would happen eventually," I said. "She's clearly dealt with too much weird shit over the past couple of years and she's finally lost her marbles."

"She seemed perfectly sane to me," said Sean. "Just calm and determined? I was wondering whether you two had had an argument and she perhaps just didn't want to work for you anymore." I frowned at that. Izzy and I had spoken in the past about how difficult it was to keep our friendship going the same as it was before I'd died, but I'd thought we both understood that it couldn't be helped. There's a limit to how much friends can continue to do together when one of them's literally the walking dead. On the other hand, she'd been managing fine until recently.

"Can you two manage for the rest of the afternoon?" I asked. "Missy will be back in a few days, and I'll ask her to fill in until I sort out what's wrong with Izzy. In the meantime, I can do tomorrow and I'll give Todd a shout about the rest of the week."

"Lil," Sean said, "please don't ask Todd to come in." He caught hold of my arm and I stared stupidly down at his hand. "I'm enjoying myself," he went on. "I talk to more people in a morning here than I do in an entire month when I'm just working at home."

"Yeah," I said, "but you don't have to make other people's sandwich orders at home," I pointed out.

"I've taken sandwiches off the menu," said Sean, "and just ordered in extra cakes. Makes it easier for me," he shrugged, "and you were never selling many sandwiches, anyway."

"How do you know?" I asked. Then the obvious question occurred to me. "Exactly how many shifts have you been doing in here, Sean?"

"Three this week so far," he said proudly. "Five last week, I think? Can't really remember. Can you remember how many shifts I worked, Elf?" A pair of knives rose off the work surface and lifted up and outwards, as though their owner was shrugging. "Elf doesn't know," he said unnecessarily. "She's not here as much as I am."

"I'm going to have to talk to Izzy," I said. "Something's not right."

"It's since she moved into the Albert Dock," said Sean suddenly. "She hasn't been herself since she signed the lease."

"Pretty sure apartments can't change their owners' personalities," I said. "Even the haunted ones. Oh god," a horrible thought had occurred to me, "what if it is haunted?"

"Your own flat's got a resident ghost," Sean pointed out, "and that hasn't changed you."

"Yeah, but Kitty couldn't haunt her way out of a paper bag," I pointed out. "There's got to be endless death and destruction soaked into the walls of the docks, hasn't there?"

"Given its history," said Sean, "that would apply to ninety-per-cent of this entire city."

"Well, maybe that's why everyone here is completely insane." I shrugged. "Or Izzy really has just got ideas above her station since she moved into the fancier end of town."

"That's why I like Vauxhall," said Sean. "No chance of getting airs and graces on the north side."

"There's not many airs and graces anywhere in this town," I said. "It's only the tourist-y bits that get above themselves."

"Like the Albert Dock."

"Yeah." A metaphorical lightbulb was beginning to flicker in my head. "You okay if I disappear for a bit?" I asked him. "Shouldn't be out too long."

"Course," said Sean amiably. "Don't rush back. I know how to lock up."

"Well, you shouldn't," I frowned. "Know how to lock up, I mean. That's Izzy's job, for fuck's sake!"

"Aah, I don't mind," said Sean, missing the point completely. "I'm having fun. Same again?" I turned to look through the open door and saw Maya standing at the counter. She did a sort of awkward bob and nodded. "They've been in here every day this week," he said to me in a low voice. "No idea what the appeal is, there're busier places up Bold Street way that would suit them better."

"Suggest some to them," I said. "They make me nervous. It's like they're sitting around just waiting for something to happen."

"You okay, Lil?" He frowned at me. "Anything I can help with?"

"I'm fine," I said, and meant it. "Just off for a quick dip."

Northern Lights

"What have you done with the Grail?" Eadric looked at me over the top of the latest edition of the Socialist Worker. The first time I'd caught him reading it I'd thoroughly taken the piss, on the solid basis that no one who owned a property portfolio worth many millions of pounds was going to be genuinely interested in the opinions of a publication so left-wing it was practically on another continent. Turns out, he reads *all* the newspapers. Not the Mail or the Sun, though, he was quick to point out. "There are limits," he'd said, and then refused to discuss it any further.

"What a strange question," he said, folding up the paper and putting it down on his desk. "As in the Holy Grail?"

"As in the one Eve thought was tucked away in Martins Bank," I said. "And don't even bother pretending you don't know what I'm talking about."

"But I really don't know what you're talking about." He leaned back in his chair and gazed steadily at me. "Where has all this come from?"

"You're a shit liar, Eadric Silverton." I leaned forward and glared at him. "Always have been."

"That's how we got your prints for the elevator panel," said Eadric lightly. He nodded to where my hands were flat down on the mahogany surface of his desk. "Amazingly clear. It was very impressive."

"Not my fault I have to lose my shit with you so often," I said. I took my hands off the desk, though. "And stop trying to divert the conversation. You're the only person who knows where the Grail is."

"Why would I know the location of an imaginary object, Lilith?" There was a flicker of genuine confusion in Eadric's gaze. "I truly don't know what you're talking about."

"The Grail," I repeated. "The Holy fucking Grail. Or whatever it is that's the immortal equivalent of it." He was still staring at me, but his expression was now one of carefully concealed concern. I knew that look of old. It was the look that meant he was considering whether I might have finally gone entirely mad. I see it on his face quite often. I gave in. "Eve had hidden it," I said, "but it went missing."

"Is that why she was up here?"

"You know that's why she was up here," I said. "You were talking to her on the phone outside my flat."

"I'm sure I don't know what you're talking about, Lilith," said Eadric. "I'm sorry, but the Grail isn't real. There is no hidden treasure, no one gets to be immortal."

"Except us."

"Except us," he nodded.

"Well," I said finally, "isn't that a shame?" I looked at him and shook my head. "I thought you might know. Actually, I thought you might tell me."

"Sorry," said Eadric. He was already picking his paper back up. "I really can't help you with this one."

~

He's lying. I waited until the lift doors had closed, then pressed the button for the ground floor.

Of course he is.

Why, though? I kicked the wall of the lift absently with the toe of my sneaker and frowned at the dent. *You'd think he'd at least get this lift lined with titanium*, I grumbled.

One can only assume the Silvertons weren't expecting to ever have to share their space with a grumpy waitress, said the city. I scowled at my own distorted reflection in the polished steel surface and sighed. ***He's trying to protect you***, it went on. ***He thinks he can keep the really difficult things away from you. For now, at least.***

He doesn't trust me, you mean.

We're not entirely sure Eadric Silverton even trusts* himself, *Lilith. And it is well within his character to refuse to trust others.

He must trust Nik, though, I said. *Surely?* The city made the weird shuffling noise that always made me think it was probably shrugging. *Mapp?*

They all have their own motivations, it replied. ***Everyone does.*** A pause. ***Even you.***

What if, I said slowly, *I've got it all wrong?*

More wrong than usual? The lift was juddering to a halt, and I stepped forward ready to open the door.

Yes, I said. *More wrong than usual. What if*, my hand hovered over the door button, *it's Eadric who's not to be trusted?*

That is, of course, a valid option.

Right, I said, *that's it. We're going to check.*

Check what? I fumbled at the collar of my t-shirt and pulled out the necklace that holds my keys. Yes, I know most people keep keys in their pockets, not around their neck. I even have a row of hooks in the flat where I hang the keys for Flora's, along with the one for the stupid gas meter that never wants to open properly. But the really important ones—those that allow me into places others don't get to see—are kept on a leather cord around my neck. The one for the Harrington Street barriers is also on there, because there's nothing more irksome than starting up the car only to remember you need to lower the bollards in order to actually get out onto the road. And I'd recently added one more—the key for the lift control panel. Pressing my hand firmly against the metal, I waited for the cover to drop. It took some awkward wriggling to get my neck down close enough, but eventually I got the key in the lock and managed to turn it. Then I remembered the key needed to stay in the lock in order to work, so I had to stay put in that position while the lift registered its new instructions and half-opened the door to the plant room before immediately closing it again. Thankfully no one was checking the boilers that day, or they'd have been presented with a strange woman apparently doing yoga in an elevator. I wedged myself into the corner of the lift and waited as it continued its descent.

Brilliant, said the city, and I was pretty sure that was a sarcastic tone I was hearing, ***another adventure into the underworld***.

~

I don't know what I was expecting—apart from the unexpected crypt in the bagging area, obvs—but it certainly wasn't the swirling mass of purple and blue that greeted me when the doors finally opened. Stepping out onto the stone plinth, I gazed in silent wonder. A galaxy of swirling light twisted and turned in front of me, folding in on itself and then back out and expanding to fill the entire crypt.

What the fuck? No response from the city, which was presumably hiding. Again. See now, you'd *think* it would be useful having an entire city lodging inside your head—all that knowledge gleaned over centuries of existence, the sort of wisdom that only comes with age, that sort of thing. But what I mostly get is a bitchy little gremlin when it fancies a chat, and absolutely nothing at all when I could actually do with some support.

No need to be like that, said the city, sounding hurt. ***We were distracted, is all***.

Better late than never, I sniffed. *So? What's going on here, then?*

No idea, it said, ***but it's alive***. Even as it said it, I could feel what it meant. The swirls looked very much like one of those galaxy projector lights you can get for kids' bedrooms, but these lights had a purpose above and beyond helping with insomnia. These lights had a presence. ***What are you doing?*** asked the city, as I dropped down to sit on the edge of the plinth.

Saying hello.

You're getting wet, it pointed out. My feet were dangling down into the water and it was already being wicked up by my cotton leggings. I sat backwards, resting my weight on my palms as I gazed up into the darkness of the crypt's vaulted ceiling. The lights began taking on a more defined shape, swirling around the stone pillars like a child playing hide and seek. Sometimes it rose high and pulled the rest of the light up behind it, until it became an enormous pulsating ball of brightness, hanging like a heavy purple sun up in the eaves. Then it would drop suddenly as though playing tricks, swooping down fast and spinning across the rippling surface of the dark water, before once again folding back on itself and resuming its dance around the pillars. ***What are you doing now?***

I'm getting in the water, I said. *Obviously.*

Is that wise? It sounded worried.

Probably not, I said. *But when has that ever stopped me?* The city sighed as I waded out into the darkness. Once I'd got to what I guessed to be roughly the mid-point of the crypt, I stopped and leaned against the nearest pillar. I thought it was possibly made from granite, to a Gothic design. Mind you, architecture had never been my specialist subject. Once you've seen one groin vault, you've seen them all. The stone was warm to the touch. Putting my palms flat against the pillar, I closed my eyes and let my mind go blank. If you'd told me to do that back when I was alive, I'd have laughed you out of the room. My brain had always churned like a washing machine on its final spin cycle, and I'd never been able to learn the gentle art of mindfulness. But I've been putting some serious practice in since I'd died. Mostly because you don't realise just how long the days actually are until you can no longer offload some of that time by snoring under a duvet. These days I can float myself off into the metaphorical ether with barely a twitch of my mental 'off' button.

At first there was nothing except the indistinct sound of water rippling against stone. It echoed faintly in the enclosed space and the high ceiling distorted the sound into alien shapes that flitted through the air. "It's okay," I whispered. "I'm here." Slowly—so slowly—I felt it creeping towards me. Not as tentative as before, but still careful.

Without consciously deciding to do so, I sat down in the middle of the crypt. The water came up to my waist, and surprised me by being warm. Not quite 'swimming in the Med' levels, but the average human could have happily taken a dip without feeling cold. Wary of frightening off whatever lived down here, I kept my eyes shut. I felt weirdly untethered, as though I might float away into nothing. The city had disappeared. Perhaps it feared whatever this thing was. It certainly hid itself well on the rare occasions I spoke to the City itself, but then anyone with half a brain would be nervous in the City's presence, however closely they might be related. This wasn't a relative though, I was sure of that. It was something different—something less tangible. It was—

hello

"Hello." I didn't know what else to say. I spoke quietly, but the acoustics of the crypt made my voice sound uncomfortably loud. "How are you?"

I am here

"Yes," I said, "you are. Want to tell me who you are?"

what not who

"Want to tell me what you are?"

no

Well, that was helpful. I tried again. "What do you want?"

make it go away

"Make what go away?" I wasn't sure it was even an actual voice I was hearing. After all, I already had two different incarnations of the city that dropped their comments directly into my head and a cat who did similar, just with added physical gestures. I'm not *un*used to paranormal entities making their thoughts known through psychic means, put it that way. But they all had their own voices, each distinct from the other. The city—the one made up of all its people, that spent more time with me than anything else—was gossipy and mostly friendly and not above the occasional sharp comment. The City itself—the spirit of everything that ever made Liverpool into what it is; the land and history and all that went before—is more foreboding and powerful, but still generally on my side. And Grimm is—well. Grimm's just Grimm. This was different, though. I was *feeling* its thoughts, not physically hearing them. It was as if they were my own thoughts, rather than something external. The warmth was folding itself around me, just as it had when I first came down here with Eadric. I wanted to open my eyes in the hope of seeing whatever it was, but remembered the coldness of its sudden disappearance the last time and kept them firmly shut. There was nothing down here except me and whatever this was.

it must be destroyed

I was sensing a theme here. "Do you mean the Grail, by any chance?"

all of it

"All of what?"

the power. The power must be broken

"Why?" I asked. "And what power?"

no good will come of one holding power

"Okay," I said, "so we're talking about the Grail. Right?" Silence. "And the crown?" I ploughed on. "But I've already broken the crown up. And I can't destroy the Grail unless I know where it is."

close

"Close to where we are now?"

no

Well, that was helpful. "Close to me?"

yes

I twisted the gold band on my ring finger. "This?"

that is yours do not lose it

Not the ring, then. "The Grail's close to me?" Silence. "But not close to me now?" Nothing. This was like a really shit game of hunt the thimble. I felt like a little kid being teased by the grownups into finding a packet of sweeties they'd tucked away for me to find. But instead of a packet of jellybeans, I had an unknown supernatural entity giving it all 'hot or cold', as I guessed.

not unknown

Oops. "Sorry," I said. "I was thinking to myself."

yes

"Would I know what you were if you told me?"

of course

"Well," I said slowly, "you could just tell me your name." But even as

I was saying it, I knew. It was so ridiculously obvious, I felt embarrassed at having taken so long to figure it out. "You're the river."

and more

"You're the Mersey," I said, more confident now. "And I think you're also everything and everyone that's ever lived and died in it."

in and on it

"Why haven't you spoken to me before?" I asked. "I'm down by the water all the time, but I've never heard you."

here is clearer

I thought about this for a minute. There was something in its tone that made me think it was speaking literally. "You've filtered in through the stone, haven't you?"

yes

This, I realised, would be the only place where the Mersey was free to be purely itself, untainted by outside influences. The water out there in the river proper is cleaner than it's ever been, but it's also overrun with activity. Countless different species of fish lurk in its depths, never mind the otters and porpoise. And then there was the Asrai, who I was pretty certain no one would ever describe as peaceful creatures. They're not malevolent, but they're *busy*. Always racing around causing what they probably considered harmless mischief, but definitely caused a headache for the port authorities. I'd spotted Daisy and her friends clinging to the bow of the ferry enough times to be fairly sure the crews were well aware of their existence. Then there's the shipping traffic, which ploughs up and down the central passage of the estuary at all hours of the day and night. There was also the human element—dropping things into the water, falling in and drowning, throwing themselves in with intent. And that wasn't counting those who were pushed in unwillingly, never to surface again. Okay, so most of the bodies get swept out to sea on the Mersey's fast-flowing tides. But they go through the river first, all the same.

so much noise so much sadness

"There must be happiness as well, surely?"

sadness is louder

"And you think the Grail is making it worse?"

pulling everything in nothing escapes

"So you want me to destroy it."

yes

"How do I do that?"

find a way

"Thanks for that helpful suggestion," I sighed. "And I've got to find the bloody thing first."

it's close too close

"You can feel it?"

yes

"Well that changes everything," I said. "Just tell me where the feeling's coming from and I'll go find it." And I'd leave the worrying about how to actually destroy it until it was in my hands, I decided. Maybe I'd just take it to Chester and get Fred to melt it down. I could have it turned it into a paperweight and sent to Eve's London office, with my compliments. Of course, there was no way I could ever actually do that, on account of how no one could ever find out what had happened to Eve. It was a nice thought, though.

near the water

"You do realise that is the absolute definition of not actually helpful at all?" I said sourly. "First, you *are* the water. And second, everything in this city is technically near it. Gonna need you to narrow this one down a bit, mate."

connected to the water not in the water

Of course. Mental cogs were slowly beginning to turn, and things were very close to slotting into place. "It's in the tunnels," I said. "Isn't it?"

don't know where just connected I feel it

"Okay," I said, "that's a start. I'm going to go do some investigating," I went on. "Will you still be here if I come back?"

always here

"Cool," I said, getting to my feet. "I need to get changed, anyway." My clothes were soaked through and it doesn't matter how immune I might be to the cold, clammy clothing is never a pleasant experience. "Might borrow Izzy's trench coat and make like Clouseau. Whaddya reckon?" The warmth swirled again, and I thought the river might be about to speak. Then, without thinking, I opened my eyes. I blinked as my vision adjusted to the dull cold light from the open elevator doors, and knew I was alone. "Oh well," I sighed, trudging through the water back to the lift, "it was nice meeting you." Stepping up out of the water and into the lift, I turned to look out into the darkness of the crypt. For some unknown reason, I gave the water a half-hearted wave as the doors closed. There was no response.

Suspicious Minds

"You're wet," said Grimm, when I let myself back into the flat. He was sitting on the kitchen table, with his long tail coiled around himself. He looked like a furry grey ice cream cone.

"You look like a furry grey ice cream cone," I said. "Or one of those poop emojis. Anyone ever told you that?"

"No one that's survived to repeat the story."

"The poop emoji was supposed to be an ice cream," I informed him. "Only everyone assumed it was poop and now it is accepted as a symbol for poop."

"How incredibly interesting," he drawled. "And very human. Where are you going?"

"To put dry clothes on," I said, already heading into the living room. "You'd better not have been sleeping on my bed again, or there'll be—oh you absolute FUCKER!" There was a loud thump as Finn shot up in a panic and fell off my bed, landing face first on the carpet. "Get some bloody clothes on, you vile scrote!" He'd been lying face down on my bed and was not only in human form, but also fully naked. "Ak ak AK!" I yelled, lost for words in the face of naked male genitals that I absolutely did not consent to seeing in my own bedroom. Or anywhere, for that matter. "OUT!" Finn made a panicked rush for the door, scuttling past me as I threw random objects at him in sheer fury. He made it into the living room and ducked in time to avoid being knocked out by the heavy bottle of CK One I'd just thrown at his head. Yes, I know it's old-fashioned, but everyone smelled of it when I was a kid and even revenants indulge in nostalgia occasionally. "Fucksake!"

"Eadric sent him here," said Grimm, following me into the room. He strolled past me and hopped onto the bed, raising one furry eyebrow as he did so, as if daring me to say anything. I didn't bother saying anything. Instead, I concentrated on stripping off my wet clothes and muttering darkly under my breath. "You're going to do what to that cat?" asked Grimm loudly. "I suspect that contravenes human rights conventions somewhere along the line."

"Sorry Lil," said a sheepish Finn from my doorway, "I—"

"Get out!" I yelled, hopping around in my pants with one leg still stuck damply inside my leggings. "What do you mean, Eadric sent him here?" I said to Grimm. "How the fuck did he get here without being seen?"

"I am assuming it was the nearest place Eadric considered safe," said the cat. "And as far as I am aware, he travelled here across the rooftops."

"Cat or human?" Grimm shrugged, his furry shoulders rising and falling in a creepily human way. "And he'd still have had to cross the bloody Strand. He's going to cause an accident one of these days."

"It was dark," called Finn from the living room. "And I was still cat. Went fast, innit. Dunno where my clothes have got to, mind. Got anything I can borrow?" Grumbling to myself, I got out of the last of my wet clothes and pulled on my dressing gown. It's ancient and has Lilo and Stitch on the back, but then I've always gone for comfort over style. The look on Grimm's face suggested he thought I could possibly put more work in towards the style angle, but I ignored him. Then I stuck my head in the wardrobe and rooted through the pile of old clothes at the bottom.

"This will have to do," I said, going into the living room and throwing a pair of oversized grey jogging bottoms and an ancient Pink Floyd t-shirt at Finn, who had thankfully wrapped himself in a blanket. "I'm going to have to go to the charity shop for spares, the way this is going. Not that I should be responsible for clothing an adult man who has a mother of his own to annoy."

"Mum says she's sick of me ripping stuff," said Finn, as he wriggled into the trousers from the safety of his blanket. Once he'd got the essentials covered, he stood up to put the t-shirt on and I saw the scar.

"Did Eve do that?" I nodded at the long red weal that travelled from somewhere near his left armpit almost down to his navel. He looked down and shrugged.

"Guess she must have," he said. "Should have seen the state of her, though."

"I did see the state of her," I said. "And I never want to see anything like that again, thank you very much. I hope you've cleaned your teeth." In answer, Finn poked an exploratory finger in his mouth and felt around.

"I'll get a toothbrush from the chemist," he said, pulling something stringy out of a molar. "There's some bits stuck."

"You are all completely and utterly disgusting."

"Yeah," grinned Finn, "that's what my mum says."

"So," said Grimm, "what are you planning to do?"

"About what?"

"You know what I'm referring to, Lilith. Don't play smart."

"Am I seriously being told off by my cat?"

"Looks like it," said Finn. "What do you need to do about what, anyway?"

"Nothing." Grimm and I spoke simultaneously. Then something occurred to me. "You can hear him as well, can't you?"

"Always could." Finn shrugged. "Assumed everyone could, to be honest."

"Is there anything else I ought to know?" I said. "You know, any other major fucking issues that everyone else knows about and I don't, but you all assume I'm well up on it?"

"Probably," said Finn. "Wouldn't know what they are, though. Anyway, I'm off out." He frowned. "Can I borrow some shoes?"

. . .

"Where's Kitty?" I asked Grimm. Finn had gone to run his errands—which I strongly hoped included the purchase of dental floss—and I was home alone with my cat. It would have been just like old times, except back then the cat didn't talk back. Sometimes I really miss those days.

"Staying out of the way," he said, "apparently. She's down in Shrewsbury, trying to stop Jonny's incipient nervous breakdown."

"Why's Jonny having a breakdown?" I asked, looking up from the paperwork that was strewn across the table. The centrepiece was a small, fold-out city map, of the kind you can buy in any souvenir shop. I was ignoring the neatly labelled tourist sights and concentrating on drawing lines across it in the hope of connecting things up. The map was, right now, a literal interpretation of the questions that were racing round my head. I'd circled the Liver Building and Martins Bank in red pen, because they were both very obviously directly connected to Lil's Great Grail Hunt. There was a pencil circle around Joe Williamson's tunnels up in Edge Hill—circled because they're geographically central to pretty much any supernatural shenanigans in this ridiculous city, but in pencil because I didn't really think they were involved in this particular mystery. Joe's too flaky for anyone to entrust really important stuff to him. Plus, there's the constant risk of rogue vampires deciding to take matters into their own hands and accidentally diverting history down a completely new and even more dangerous track. More pencil circles marked out Flora's and the Cavern Club on Mathew Street, but neither was at the top of my suspect list. I'd already been down to the cellar under the cafe and checked that the entrance to the fallen tunnel was still blocked off. And as the access route underneath the Cavern goes out into the river, I thought Daisy would have raised the alarm by now if something had been going on over there. I also had a list of suspects, which I was carefully hiding from Grimm. Mostly because he was on it. Okay, so I didn't really think a domestic cat was going to be involved in the theft of a valuable ancient artefact. But he was definitely capable of orchestrating it from a distance, so on the list he went. In an attempt at fairness, I'd even added my own name. I was reasonably sure I hadn't been possessed by the spirit of a kleptomaniac goblin, but it's never one-hundred-per-cent definite in my world. Izzy, Sean, and Damon were at the bottom. Despite Izzy's weird behaviour recently, I didn't think it was to do with the Grail. Izzy never did anything at less than full throttle—if she'd been secretly planning a takeover she'd have been sitting on top of Buckingham Palace waving to her joyous crowds by now, not still rearranging towels in her new apartment. Damon was still away working—I had a vague idea he was due back in the next twenty-four hours, but he definitely wasn't in town right at this minute. And then there was Sean. I hated to admit it even to myself, but Sean was beginning to strike me as a bit wet. I know, I'm a cynical cow. He'd been nothing but lovely and tolerated all the madness for much longer than most would have managed, but still—there it was. And before anyone starts wondering, no, this is absolutely not a foreshadowing of the sort you find way too often in dodgy paranormal novels. My life is insane enough already, without any of that bollocks added to the mix. So no, Sean was not high on my suspect list.

But plenty of my other friends were, and it was making me very uncomfortable indeed. Freya was an easy one to stick near the top—she'd appeared out of seemingly nowhere, already knew everybody, and I knew hardly anything about her in return. The only people above her were Elizabeth and Jude, and that was because I distrust them on principle. It doesn't matter how helpful Elizabeth is, she's still the head of another powerful territory and has been around a lot longer than I have. And Jude does everything Elizabeth tells them to, so is absolutely not to be trusted. Liam was below Freya, again by default. I still hadn't heard from him since Chester and none of my spidey-senses were tingling right now, so I was reasonably confident he wasn't in the territory. My personal Liam theory was that he was hiding out up north and wouldn't show his face again until he was sure I was in charge and might be in the mood for some flattery. Given that I wasn't planning to take charge any time soon and was absolutely never again going to be in the mood for his flattery, I'd mostly discounted him from the current scenario.

Horribly, my next suspects were Jonny and Kitty. Jonny was obvious—it was his family the Grail had originally been stolen from, so he had more reason than most to want to find it. And Kitty because she adored Jonny and would do anything to help him. I didn't think she'd assist in anything that risked hurting me directly, but neither did I think she'd be able to stop him if he decided to make a move. And if

Jonny was on the list, then Owain had to be, as well. I'd been digging through my old history books and had a lurking suspicion who Owain might actually be, although I was trying not to think about it. There was enough going on already without bringing ancient border wars into the mix. Next were Grimm and Finn—devious asshats the pair of them, but probably—probably—not capable of such a major heist. Aiden? Nope—too busy and way too polite. Definitely not Mapp, it just wasn't his style. Which also knocked Heggie off the Most Wanted list, because Heggs doesn't do anything that Mapp doesn't approve of. Eadric and Nik would have no reason to meddle in something that might impact their own peacefully privileged lives. Eadric might have had something to do with the Grail having disappeared from Eve's strongroom, but I was only thinking that because of the conversation that Kitty had overheard. And if it had been Eve he was talking to, she'd have been in on the relocation plans. I'd even added Missy, Alan and Rachel to the list, before immediately scribbling them out again. Missy had been working very unsuspiciously in Flora's for several days before heading off to London. And I knew she was definitely down south, because she was with Ifan, our beloved local busker. He was playing some kind of secret gig, but it can't have been very secret because Izzy had informed me it was being mentioned in the music press. I didn't hold out much hope for Ifan's anonymity lasting much longer, if he kept insisting on amusing himself with shit like that. Rachel and Al were away visiting her parents, who were apparently slowly coming to terms with their daughter's strange new look. According to Missy—who knows all this because Alan is her lodger and she's very good at getting the gossip out of him—Rachel's family were under the impression she'd gone briefly and spectacularly off the rails, only to be saved from herself by the love of the delightful, if somewhat eccentric, Alan. Apparently, her mum kept going on about how much he looked like a pop star she had a crush on in her youth and Rachel had to make him promise not to sing for them in case it gave him away.

The nattily dressed elephant in the room was, of course, Ivo Laithlind. He had a habit of turning up at opportune moments. And those moments were usually opportune for him and no one else. From the first time I'd met him just after I died, to our most recent conversation down at the waterfront, Ivo's priority had been Ivo, and no one else.

He did say he loves you, said the city. ***Perhaps he's changed***.

Ivo Laithlind can no more change his attitude than I could pretend to be Kylie Minogue and get away with it.

The hotpants might suit you.

Shut up.

"Do you want to know why Jonny's having a breakdown," said Grimm, "or not?" I looked up and blinked in confusion for a minute.

"Oh yeah," I said eventually, "Jonny. Gimme the goss, my delightful feline fiend."

"He thinks the Grail is rightfully his, and he's the true ruler of Britain." That made me look up. "And that whoever gets hold of it will steal his lands and property. Is there something wrong, Lilith?" It took some time to get my snorting laugher under control. Grimm gazed patiently at me as I rubbed my face hard in the hope of clearing my mind.

"Jonny lives in a small flat in Shrewsbury," I said. "His family estate is long gone and, last time I checked, was being hired out as a wedding venue."

"That's as may be," said Grimm, "but he's always assumed he'd get it back eventually."

"I think the current owners might be a bit put out if a strangely dressed man turned up on their doorstep claiming to be more than two hundred years old and asking for the keys back."

"None of this makes any difference to Jonny's feelings," said Grimm. "And we all know Jonny has a lot of feelings."

"We do," I agreed. "And he makes them everyone else's problem." I sighed. "So Kitty's down there patting his head and telling him what a good boy he is?"

"That's about the sum of it."

"Then that's two fewer people to worry about," I said, crossing Kitty and Jonny off my list. "Because if he's fretting about who might have the Grail, that implies he doesn't have it."

"And does Miss Marple have any other theories?" Grimm asked

drily. "Or are we just knocking people off the list based on how insane they are at any given moment?"

"Don't be ridiculous," I said. "That wouldn't work. Every last one of them is as mad as an entire box of frogs, and we both know it."

"So, what are you going to do about it?" The cat peered forward to look at the map. "I take it you have a plan?"

"Nope," I said, putting my pen down. "But I have a map and a basic knowledge of the tunnel workings of Liverpool. What could possibly go wrong?"

~

I strode up Canning Street, wondering—not for the first time—what the fuck I did in a previous life to deserve this level of absolutely unrelenting bullshit. Who the fuck goes house-breaking in the middle of the afternoon? Especially when a) they're not actually a burglar, and b) the keys were freely available, if I was prepared to explain why I needed them. But there wasn't a single godsforsaken chance that I was going to tell anyone what I was planning. Mostly because I already knew what the various reactions would be. Eadric would forbid it utterly and I'd still have to do it anyway, so there was no point talking to him. Izzy would yell at me for not telling Eadric. Then she'd yell at me for going alone. Nik wouldn't yell, but he'd definitely flounce in a disappointed manner. Mapp would understand my motives, I thought, but would insist on coming with me. And I needed to do this alone. For a brief, mad second, I considered calling Ivo and asking how quickly he could get to Liverpool. Did it really matter what his motives were, if it meant getting what I wanted in the process?

Canning Street was built in the early nineteenth century and was not, I'd been surprised to learn, named for the canning industry. Considering the size and wealth of the houses on the street, this possibly should not have been quite so surprising, factory workers not being known for having the financial wherewithal to buy and live in the enormous Georgian houses that make up the vast majority of the area. It had actually been named after George Canning, the son of an Irish actress who somehow managed to scrabble his way up the greasy political pole to become the shortest-tenured British Prime Minister until the twenty-first century sprouted a batch of Conservative politicians with less staying power than a lettuce. After going into decline during the twentieth century, Canning Street was mostly derelict until new money came into the city and the upstart rich once again needed somewhere suitably fancy to live in order to impress their clients. Silverton Properties had owned one such house from the start, having bought the lease from the Liverpool Corporation soon after it was built. It too had gone through a downturn in its fortunes, but I suspected that had been more to avoid drawing attention to its owners than any intentional neglect. Eadric had certainly made plans for its refurbishment the minute work had started on its neighbours. Counting my way up the right-hand side of the street, it wasn't long before I came to 'our' house. Even from outside, it was clear that no expense had been spared on its renovation. The original brickwork had been immaculately repointed and the woodwork was a glossy piano-black from top to bottom. I'd looked up the aerial view on my ancient laptop and knew I was more likely to gain access around the back, so headed into the narrow jigger that ran alongside the neighbouring house. It led to a small carpark that held only three cars, all of which looked extremely expensive. I could only assume their owners had excellent sensors installed on them, to avoid scraping their paintwork in the cramped access. Then I turned and realised there was actually a short road leading from the car park up towards the other end of the terrace and wondered why I bothered putting so much effort into working out other people's driving habits.

Keeps your mind busy, said the city. ***Wouldn't want you getting into trouble, now would we?***

I can get myself into trouble anyway, I retorted. *Don't need any help with that.* Looking up at my target, I could see that a small window on the second floor was slightly ajar. The current tenants had clearly wanted some air in the house, but knew better than to leave a more accessible window open for potential burglars. I could have scaled the wall up to the potential entry point, but that risked neighbours spotting me and calling the police. In a city as tightly packed as Liverpool, even the most expensive houses are overlooked from pretty much every direction. But if I was really fast, I might manage to get inside before anyone spotted me. Standing back slightly to gauge my ascent, I heard noises from the neighbouring house. Someone was unlocking the door, talking as they did so. "Help me get this table outside," said the voice, "and we'll have a cuppa in the garden. You can help me decide what colour to paint the window frames." Which meant they'd be staring straight up at the building. Marvellous. It was now or never. Before I could change my mind, I leapt at the wall and scrabbled up as fast as I could—which meant the open window came at me quicker than I'd expected. Choking back a pained shriek, I threw myself in through the narrow opening. It turned out, unsurprisingly, to belong to a bathroom. I'd dived in head first and ended up face down in the sink, with the rest of me flopping through the window like a particularly ungainly fish. There was an ominous crack from the porcelain as gravity won, and I flipped backwards onto the tiled floor. I glared up at the white painted ceiling for a moment or two, wondering why nothing in my life was ever straightforward.

Because you are not straightforward, came the answer.

That's not as helpful as you think it is, I muttered. Scrambling to my feet, I tiptoed to the bathroom door and risked a peek. The house sat determinedly silent in the face of my inspection, which was a relief. I knew from the tenancy paperwork I'd seen in Eadric's office that the current occupants were a professional couple by the name of Mrs and Mrs Smith. I'd assumed the entry was a mistake and pointed it out to Eadric, who'd been baffled in the face of my confusion.

"I'm rather disappointed," he'd said, looking across at me curiously from the other side of his desk. "I'd have thought that you of all people would be more accepting of same-gender marriage." At which point I'd started snorting and had to explain I'd been referring to their name, not their gender.

"I mean," I'd said, "as if anyone is actually called Smith these days? Why didn't they go the whole hog and list themselves as Jane Doe?"

"Both of them?" Eadric had asked, looking baffled. And then, "Oh!" as realisation dawned. "You think they're living under assumed names?"

"Yes," I'd said, "that is exactly what I think."

"Then it is my pleasure to disabuse you of that suspicion," he'd said. I can always tell when Eadric is patronising me for his own amusement, because he becomes even more politely eloquent than usual. "The Misses Smith are friends of the family."

"Who's family?"

"Well," said Eadric, "mine, of course."

"You've been dead for a thousand years," I pointed out. "Who on earth do they think you are, their fifteen-times-great grandad?"

"Uncle," he'd said with a smile. "I only have nieces and nephews. Not grandchildren."

"But you might have, though," I'd said without thinking. Eadric and his wife Golda had a child, back when he was alive. But Golda had left him (spoiler: it was his own stupid bloody fault for acting like a nobhead) and taken their son with her. I knew the loss of his boy was still the biggest regret of Eadric's very long life.

"I suppose I might," he'd said quietly. "I prefer not to dwell on it." I'd apologised and Eadric had accepted it politely, but a tense cloud had hung over us until I'd claimed overdue chores back at the cafe and made my escape. And Eadric didn't even bother asking why I went to the expense of employing people if I was going to do all the work myself anyway, which is his usual response to anything connected to Flora's. So he must have been really pissed off. Thankfully for present-day Me, I had at least managed to read through the rest of the lease before leaving the office. Which was how I knew that Mrs Joanne Smith was a forty-something interior designer, and the unlikely-sounding Mrs Ethel Smith was in her thirties and currently on sabbatical from her job as a senior financial advisor with a large high street bank, whilst she cared for their infant son. The baby was the reason I was sneaking into their house in daylight, rather than under cover of darkness. I might not be maternal myself, but I've known enough people with babies to be well aware that nighttime rarely equals sleep time when there's a tiny human in the house.

I was on the top floor, so would at least have some warning if any of the residents returned while I was still inside. The immediate problem was my strong suspicion that any hidden secrets would be down in the cellar, not on the upper floors. I was helped in my quest by a print-out of the floor plans, from the last time Eadric had advertised the place for rent. Despite being below street level, the basement was, according to the advert, ripe for use as a large playroom, a family room, or—rather optimistically, in my view—a home cinema. I ran down the stairs, slowing only to duck as I went through the hallway in case anyone outside spotted me through the stained glass windows. Thankfully, the door to the basement was held closed with nothing more than an old latch. It lifted easily, as though in regular use. I ducked inside and pulled the door closed behind me. There was no way of latching it again from the inside, so I just had to hope no one came home while I was down there. There was a light switch behind the door, but I didn't dare turn it on. Luckily there was just enough light to see by, thanks to the small frosted glass window set high up into the far wall and presumably level with the surface of the front garden. I went carefully down the stone steps into the room proper, and looked around the most depressing play room in history. It had at least been whitewashed at some point, although it was in dire need of redoing. The room was entirely empty, apart from a pile of old newspapers in the corner. When I looked more closely, they dated back to the nineteen-eighties. I knew from the records that the house had been empty at that time. Mostly because the area had been going through its unfashionable phase— for which, read 'dangerous and extremely unsanitary'—but perhaps an enterprising squatter had decided to brighten it up at some point. They'd clearly been put off, because there wasn't any other sign of habitation. Of course, the Smiths might have emptied it themselves and I was just wasting time pondering irrelevant details. What was noticeable was just how damp it felt. No surround sound cinema was going to be built down here without first putting some serious money into a new and heavy duty damp course. Turning around slowly, I finally found what I was looking for. There in a corner, tucked away down the side of the steps, was a trap door. It wasn't much more than a faint square that was only just visible in the painted concrete floor, but I know a door to the underworld when I see one. Sighing, I stepped over to it. I'm not fond of trap doors. In my experience, they generally lead to trouble.

If they led to something harmless, said the city, ***people wouldn't***

bother installing trap doors. There'd be a glossy entrance on Bold Street, a sign saying something ridiculous like 'ABANDON HOPE ALL YE WHO ENTER HERE' and an awful lot of wannabe-hipster students hoping for free shots.

I ignored the far-from-helpful voice in my head and instead inspected the hatch. Close up, the square was clearer and one side rose fractionally to create a lip. Looking around for something I could use as a wedge, I spotted a small piece of wood in the opposite corner. When I picked it up, I discovered it had a row of nails hammered in a line across one of the short ends. Rust from the nails ran down the wood in faint streaks, presumably caused by the damp.

That probably isn't rust, said the city. I looked at the wood again and realised it would have made a decent weapon, should anyone have inadvertently stumbled into its owner's dungeon-like lair. Ignoring both the city and my own lurking nausea at what the thing in my hand might have been used for, I took it back over to the trap door and considered my next move. Hitting it wouldn't work—in a battle of wood versus concrete, the concrete's going to win nine times out of ten—but maybe I could use the nails as a lever. Angling the wood so the nails wedged underneath the lid of the hatch, I pushed hard. And then I went arse over tit straight across the room, because the hatch rose easily as though it was on a hydraulic lift and my own momentum sent me flying. As I was picking myself up off the floor, I heard a voice above me and froze.

"She's definitely in here," someone said. "I saw her go in." It was male, and sounded vaguely familiar.

"Well, she isn't here now," said a second voice, and I recognised it immediately. "Come on, let's get out before someone sees us." It was Derek from Birkenhead, high ruler of the Wirral Weirdos. Fuck, fuck, fuck.

"I'm just going to check the cellar," said the first voice. Grenville. It was bloody, sodding Grenville, part time pub eavesdropper and full time pain in the fucking ass. "The door's open already—oh!" He looked straight down at me, and for a split second, I had absolutely no idea what to do. The sane and rational part of me thought I should stalk up the stairs and yell at them for trespassing. Maybe I could bullshit my way out of this by pretending to be doing a safety check on behalf of

Silverton Properties. But that would mean explaining myself to Eadric, which was absolutely not at the top of my priority list right now. So I went with the second option. Even as Grenville scrambled down the cellar steps, I was leaping for the open trap door. He reached the bottom and swung around to look at me—just as I dropped into darkness.

Down The Rabbit Hole

I hit the ground with far less force than I'd been expecting. This was probably because—as I realised when I looked up towards the dim light of the basement—the void was only about six feet deep. Grenville was staring down at me with a concerned expression on his face. Behind him stood Derek, who was also looking worried. "Are you okay, ma'am?" Grenville whispered.

"What the fuck are you doing here?" I hissed up at the pair of them. "Why can't you just leave me alone?"

"We're obliged to do all in our powers to keep you safe," said Derek, popping up over Grenville's shoulder like the world's shittest parrot.

"But you don't have any bloody powers!" Derek opened his mouth to reply, but then something made them both whip their heads round and stare upwards. "What the fuck are you doing?" I asked as they looked at each other and seemed to come to some kind of unspoken agreement. Grenville crouched at the edge of the hatch and, before I could say anything, dropped into the void next to me. He hit the ground hard and made a muffled squeaking noise as he fell and rolled. Derek was still up in the basement, his gaze swivelling back and forth between me and the steps to the ground floor of the house.

"They're home," he hissed, and jumped.

"For fuck's actual fucking sake," I grumbled under my breath, standing to pull the trap door closed above us. "What the fuck have I done to deserve this?" The hatch closed as easily as it had opened and made barely a sound as it did so. Someone had put a lot of effort into making the access point work efficiently, and I didn't think they'd have bothered without very good reason. At least, I hoped they'd had very good reason. Because if my suspicions were wrong, I might be stuck down here with Eric and fucking Ernie for far longer than my patience could stand. "Have either of you got a torch?" I asked, somehow resisting the urge to literally just suck the life out of the pair of them and be done with.

"Of course," said Derek. I heard shuffling noises in the dark, and then something touched my hand. Swallowing a loud yelp, I took the torch from him. It was tiny, but the light it emitted when I pressed the rubber 'on' switch belied its size. "Wow," said Derek, as the beam illuminated a tunnel with no visible end. I turned slowly and, as I'd expected, found that the tunnel ended just behind where we stood. This was a direct route and always had been. But to where? Truth was, I hadn't actually got as far figuring out exactly where the tunnel ended. But the Mersey had told me the Grail was hidden in something that was connected to it, but not of it. And what better hiding place than a tunnel that could be accessed from the centre of town, but came out down at the water? Too late, it occurred to me that a compass would have been very handy around about now. But the tunnel sloped visibly downwards, which meant it did at least point in roughly the right direction. I stepped backwards and almost fell over something on the floor.

"Sorry ma'am," said Grenville, from somewhere near my feet. I looked down to see him scooting himself backward to lean against the rough wall. He was clutching his left knee and grimacing. "Think I've twisted something," he said.

"I'll bloody twist you in a minute," I muttered. "You," I pointed at Derek, "are going to wait until I've gone, then drag both yourself and old Hopalong here back up into the land of the living. Okay?"

"I can't do that," hissed Derek. "They'll think we're burglars!"

"Serves you right for stalking me," I said. "Tell them you're urban bloody explorers or something."

"In a private house?" Derek's eyes were pleading. "We have to come with you."

"We'll help," said Grenville. "We can protect you." I stared down at him, still sitting on the floor.

"Just a flesh wound, is it?" I said. "Gonna bite my legs off?" My top tier humour was clearly lost on the pair of them, because they both stared at me blankly. "Oh, for heaven's fucking sake," I sighed. "Come on, then."

Which is how I found myself once again under the streets of Liverpool, this time with a pair of eager but utterly useless human sidekicks. Derek had tried to insist he walked at the front, but I'd stopped that argument in its tracks by threatening to insert the torch into an orifice of his own choosing, if he didn't shut up and get behind me. Grenville had no option but to go in the middle, because he was alternating between using me and Derek as mobile crutches. It would have been quicker to carry him, but I wasn't feeling particularly generous under the circs. So it was a very slow stagger down to wherever we might be going, and it wasn't helped by the tunnel roof being low enough to necessitate ducking in places. Childishly, I didn't always warn the others. Grenville was hunched over enough that he missed most of it, but Derek had been making regular garbled noises and was now complaining of a headache. If my calculations were correct—and they might very well not be—we were going to end up in a blocked off section of the cellars underneath the Baltic Fleet pub. Built in the mid-nineteenth-century, the Baltic is notorious for the smuggler tunnels that emerge beneath its bar. Long bricked up, legend has it the tunnels originally also led onwards up into the Cornhill area which was, back then, a notorious red light district. I strongly suspected it wouldn't have taken too much effort to dig out an extra tunnel at the same time, especially if there was a decent amount of hard cash available to lubricate the palms of those in charge of the digging. Which is where Eadric Silverton came in. Underneath the paperwork for the lease of the Canning Street house had been a tattered invoice from a building company with the unlikely name of 'Byron Brothers'. It was dated 1855 and made out for the sum of ten thousand pounds—a huge sum back then, but probably not quite enough to raise any eyebrows at the tax office. Especially if the aforementioned Byrons just happened to be two of the wealthiest men in Liverpool and therefore—in a world that had yet to develop electronic accounting methods and was run almost entirely via the old boys' network—mostly above suspicion. And where better to hide something as valuable as the Holy Grail than in the bricked off cellar of a pub? Hiding in plain sight had been the go-to method for most of the paranormal fuckwittery I'd dealt with so far, after all. I had no reason to think the Grail would be any different.

The tunnel seemed to go on forever, with not even the tiniest of distant lights to indicate where it might end. It also sloped downwards rather more than I'd been expecting. Before we'd set off from underneath the house, I'd taken a minute to try to orientate myself. Then I'd admitted (silently, because I am not entirely stupid and didn't want my human companions panicking and making everything worse than it already was) that I hadn't a fucking clue. I'd just have to wing it. My entire existence had already been peppered with situations in which I'd winged things I absolutely should not have, but right now I had no choice. Either I trudged on into the darkness in the hope of finding what I was looking for, or I gave up and took my chances with the Misses Smith. Which would mean Eadric finding out what I was up to. And then he'd realise I didn't entirely trust him. Which was true—at this particular point in time I didn't trust anyone, including myself. I'd filed that realisation in the 'things to worry about later' thought box, and had no desire to take the lid off just yet. So on we plodded, like a particularly confusing outtake from The Three Amigos. "Where are we going, ma'am?" Derek asked, for what I estimated was the fourteenth time. I ignored him, same as I had the previous thirteen times he'd asked.

"My knee hurts," Grenville whimpered. "Can't you fix it for me?" I stopped suddenly and both men staggered into the back of me.

"And how," I said, turning to shine the torch into their faces, "would I do that?"

Grenville shrugged, his eyes squinting closed against the bright light. "I dunno," he said. "I thought maybe you could do magic?"

"I'm not a magician."

"I kind of, well," Derek coughed, "well. We all thought you were a witch." A brief pause. "Ma'am."

"Are you fucking mental?" I asked, then realised what I was saying. "Don't answer that. No, I am not a witch. Nor an elf, nor a ghost. And I am definitely not a wizard."

"What are you then?" asked Grenville. "If you don't mind me asking?"

"What I am," I said, slowly turning back to the darkness ahead of us, "is sick and bloody tired of stupid questions. Now if you've quite finished," I stepped forward, "we need to keep moving." I thought I could finally see the faintest chink of light further down the tunnel. Hopefully, it would turn out to be the access hatch into the Baltic's secret storage space, known only to the ancients. And also to my idiot sodding landlords and their hidden treasure. Maybe the light was actually coming from the Grail itself. It occurred to me I had no real idea what the Holy Grail actually looked like, but assumed I'd recognise it when I saw it. And it definitely seemed like the sort of thing that should probably glow. Encouraged, I started walking without bothering to check whether my human companions were still with me. By the pained squeaking noises coming from a few feet behind me, I suspected they were. The light grew as we got closer until it was bright enough for even Grenville and Derek to have noticed.

"Where will it bring us out?" Grenville asked. "Do you have warriors waiting to do your bidding?"

"We can fight," said Derek eagerly. "Anything for you, ma'am."

"I'm really hoping it won't come to that," I said. "Mostly because I don't fancy trying to clean your blood off this stonework." The start of the tunnel had been constructed from standard old red bricks, but their appearance was getting older and rougher as the tunnel progressed. Down here near the mystery light source, the brickwork was occasionally dotted with roughly hewn stone, seemingly wedged in for extra stability in places where the bricks themselves were starting to crumble. The ground beneath our feet had also changed. Whereas the Canning Street end of the tunnel was a standard arched roof construction over what looked to be stone flooring, it was now loose shale over what I thought might be compacted clay with a sandy top layer. The light ahead of us was growing even more brightly now, and I could see that it was actually offset to the left. As we got closer, I realised it was coming from an old-fashioned oil lamp that hung from the wall on a wrought-iron bracket. And on top of the bracket was the unmistakable silhouette of a Liver bird. The sodding Byron Brothers had some explaining to do, I thought to myself crossly. Eadric and Nik had been keeping secrets from me. Again. There was a dark patch on the right-hand side of the tunnel, almost exactly opposite where the lamp hung. I sent a silent prayer up towards whichever godly sucker had responsibility for revenants, asking that the river wouldn't choose this particular moment to break through into the underworld. It took me a few seconds to register that the darkness was actually an opening into another tunnel. I slowed my pace and turned to my companions. "Quiet," I whispered. "I need to go check this out on my own." Both men opened their mouths to argue, and I made a slashing motion across my throat in return. "Stay here," I said. "Or I'll feed you to the mermaids." They'd probably appreciate a fresh meal. Grenville and Derek exchanged glances that suggested this was the first they'd heard about the local piscine weirdness, and I could see the tension in their faces as they struggled to stay silent. Just then, I heard something behind me and spun around. The noise had come from the tunnel ahead of us, which was still dark, despite the oil lamp. I switched off my torch and waited. There it was again. A soft slapping sound, as though someone was flapping an empty pair of gloves against a hard surface. And it was getting closer. Incongruously, my brain chose that moment to notice the differences between the two sections of tunnel. We were still standing underneath a standard arched ceiling, a flat surface beneath our feet. But just past the opening to what I assumed was a side exit, the tunnel's shape changed. It became circular, as though something had burrowed a tube down through the rock. Its diameter was almost as wide as the section we currently stood in, but appeared to have been carved right out of the bedrock itself. The brickwork was finished carefully around the opening, complete with a neat circle of keystones. The flapping noise started up again. It echoed slightly and was accompanied by barely audible shuffling, as though whoever was doing it was walking as fast as they could, but still taking a long time about it. There was a whisper of movement in the darkness, and I thought I saw something heading towards us, close to the floor. "We're going to step closer," I whispered over my shoulder.

"Why?" Both men spoke at once. "Shouldn't we be stepping backwards," said Derek, "not forwards? What if it's something dangerous?"

"Derek," I said calmly, "the most dangerous thing down here is me. And we're moving forward because I am pretty sure that's an exit tunnel on the right, and I'd like to be able to get to it if this turns out to be a zombie."

"Why did you have to say that?" Grenville's voice carried an audible tremor. "I wasn't scared until you said that." A pause. "Ma'am."

"For heaven's fucking sake," I turned to glare at them both in turn, "will you stop calling me Ma'am? I'm not even that old!"

"Sorry Ma—Lilith," said Derek. "It's just that we really would like to be your loyal and devoted followers, and it's difficult not to be overwhelmed in your presence."

"I wish I'd had this effect on people back when I was alive," I sighed. "It would have made my love life easier."

"Better now than never," said a voice behind me, "surely?" I spun around, hands already bunching into fists as I did so. Liam O'Connor stood in the side tunnel, leaning casually against the wall. He was smiling at me. "Who are your friends?" He nodded towards Grenville and Derek, who were instinctively trying to hide behind me. "Did you bring a snack?" Both men made noises like panicked mice and shuffled further backwards.

"What are you doing here, Liam?" I dropped my hands and flexed my fingers. "You're lucky you didn't get a smack in the face, surprising me like that."

"Wouldn't be the first time you'd attacked me," he said. Pushing himself upright, he took a step forward. "And I suspect it'll happen again." He reached a hand out as if to touch my face, but I stepped sharply backwards out of reach. Right onto Grenville's good foot, as it happened.

"Owwwww," he wailed, "that hurt!" Then he remembered where he was and who he was with. "Sorry Ma'am. Lilith. Lil." Derek, Liam and I all stared at him. "It's fine, nothing broken," he trailed off.

"In answer to your question, Lilith," said Liam, "I'm down here looking for something that's been lost. You wouldn't happen to know where I might find it?"

"That depends what you're looking for," I said carefully. The strange slapping noise had started up again and seemed to be getting closer. I stepped sideways, so I was closer to the wall. This left Grenville and Derek exposed to both Liam and whatever was heading slowly towards us, but sometimes you've just got to make sacrifices for the greater good. "Attack ships on fire off the shoulder of Orion? Pot of gold at the end of the rainbow?" I asked him. "Best recipe for Scouse? Actually," I went on, "that last one just starts an argument, whoever you ask. Everyone thinks it's something different, and they're all convinced they're the only one who's right."

"Amusing as always," said Liam. "Perhaps we could discuss this further over dinner some time." I raised an eyebrow at him. "Over coffee then," he said.

"Where does that tunnel lead?" I asked him, nodding over his shoulder. "Did you get in through a drain cover or something?"

"Heavens, no." Liam chuckled. "As if I'd climb down into a sewage pipe. No," he went on, "it goes to the cellar of that little pub down near the river." That would be the Baltic Fleet. Which meant the tunnel that was still in darkness led—where? Even as I thought about it, the shuffling noise from the tunnel got louder and I remembered we had other problems to deal with.

"Any idea what that is?" I asked Liam, indicating the direction of the shuffling noise. "It doesn't seem in any hurry to get here, but I'm not entirely sure it's friendly."

"Don't be silly," said Liam, "there's nothing else down here. That one," he nodded at the dark tunnel, "has been closed off for decades now."

"Where did it used to go?"

"You don't know?" Liam looked amused. "I'd assumed the Silvertons would have brought you up to speed on everything by now. Oh dear," he tilted his head at me, "do they not quite trust you just yet? Of course," he went on, "that's no surprise. I'd bet good money that you don't trust them, either."

"Just tell me where the bloody tunnel goes," I snapped. "You can keep the monologuing for another time."

"As you wish," he said politely, but I saw the muscles twitching tightly around his eyes. "It leads to—" I never did hear the rest of the sentence. Because right then was when Liam was punched in the face by Gary the Attack Otter.

~

I suppose 'punch' is the wrong word. It was more like a heavy slap, but as the otter had launched itself into the air beforehand, that slap landed as hard and sweet as anything Begbie himself could have managed. Liam went reeling backwards, and I was left standing between two terrified humans and a thoroughly pissed off marine mammal. "Gary?" I said, unable to think of anything else. "Is that you?" Gary's furry brow wrinkled in return. "Don't even think about it," I said to Liam, who was already clambering to his feet. "It's just an otter."

"What the hell is an otter doing down here?" Liam asked. "And more to the point, why did the bloody thing attack me?"

"Probably knows you're a suspicious bastard like the rest of them," I said. From somewhere down by my feet came a noise that sounded suspiciously like a small furry mammal sniggering. "Well," I went on, turning on the spot to look at each of the merry band in turn, "this is turning into a proper little party, innit?" Liam opened his mouth to speak, but a low growl stopped him in his tracks.

"Okay, okay," he said, looking down to where Gary was baring a set of very sharp teeth at him. "I'm not going to hurt anyone."

"No one's going to hurt anyone," I said firmly. "But we can't stay down here."

"I vote we see where the otter came from," said Grenville. I looked at him in surprise. "Well, erm," he mumbled, "it came from somewhere—"

"He," I corrected him. "His name is Gary. He's a boy."

"I dunno," said Derek, "I once knew a Gary who was actually—"

"Shut up," I said sharply. Derek shut up. "It doesn't matter what sodding gender Gary is, his name is Gary, so I'm using 'he' for now. If that's okay with you?" I arched an enquiring eyebrow at him.

"Course," he said quietly. "Just trying to be helpful."

"What I have learned over the past couple of years," I said to him, "is that a lot of people like to say they're helping me when actually they're just helping themselves. So I'd appreciate it if you could just shut the fuck up and leave me to crack on with helping me. M'kay?"

"Course," he said again, before falling quiet.

"You think we should follow the otter?" I asked Grenville. "Like the white rabbit? Cos I'm not sure that ended too well for Alice, when you think about it."

"I always felt sorry for the hedgehogs," said Liam idly. I scowled at him, and he smiled in return. I was ninety-nine-per-cent sure Liam was not to be trusted in any situation. And one-hundred-per-cent sure he wasn't to be trusted when I unexpectedly bumped into him underground. My one woman treasure hunt had turned into a one woman, three men and an otter day trip to the underworld, and it was about as comfortable as you might expect. The sooner we—sorry, I—could get back to the surface of the real world, the better. But I still hadn't found the stupid bloody Grail, and I was still pretty sure it was down here somewhere. If Liam was telling the truth about the side tunnel, then nothing was hidden underneath the Baltic. Because if it had been, he'd have found it and made off with it by now. And he'd thought the other tunnel was closed off, which meant he hadn't been down it either yet. "Gary," I said, looking down at the otter, "I'm going to need you to take us to your leader."

Otterly Ridiculous

Gary turned and headed back the way he'd come, and we followed him. Liam tried to step into the line right behind me, but I stopped him. "Oh no you don't," I said, "you can go at the back. Keep an eye on Pinky and Perky back there."

"Why on earth should I do what you tell me?" Liam said. "I must have missed the memo that said you'd been promoted above me."

"Gary," I called into the darkness, "hang on a minute, would you? Won't be a tick." The soft shuffling stopped, and I heard Gary heave a deep sigh. "Liam," I said slowly, "you are in my territory. I don't care who or what you might have been in a previous life, when you're here, you will do as I say. Is that understood?"

"You forget I am a king," said Liam, "which makes you, technically, my subject."

"Are you seriously going to try arguing ancient politics when we're standing in a mystery tunnel with nothing but humans and an otter for company?" Liam's shrug suggested that yes, he was. "You were a king," I pointed out. "A very long time ago. And—"

"Which king?" We both turned to look at Grenville. "Just asking," he shrugged. "Never met a king before."

"A really old and stupid one," I said. "Now let's get moving." If

Liam wanted the Grail, then he'd have to play the game. We both knew the other's ultimate aim, but it wouldn't benefit either of us to start a fight down here. Especially when we were relying on Gary to show us the way. I didn't think the otter would hang around if things started kicking off, and I really didn't want to end up trapped with Liam. Or Derek and Grenville, come to that. We moved slowly forward, the strangest conga line in history.

This tunnel was pitch black, my torch picking out nothing more than Gary shuffling along ahead of me. He occasionally turned his head to check we were still behind him, his black button eyes shining in the narrow light. It was literally a stone tube down through the rock, the only flat surface a narrow channel of shale beneath our feet. I could hear Grenville moaning quietly behind me as the awkward surface put stress on his damaged knee. But he was still managing to walk, so I suspected he'd just twisted it. As we continued our slow descent, I wondered whether it would be worth asking Mapp to do a bit of memory-sucking on Grenville and Derek, assuming they survived their current adventure. I wouldn't have been so worried had it been just one of them, because it would have been easier to pass their stories off as the confused ramblings of a paranormal enthusiast. But two humans with the same story became harder to disprove. I'd tried asking the city what it thought, but it was noticeably absent. I still wasn't sure what parameters the city existed in. Maybe it was just that the people and memories it consisted of got as scared as any other humans would and chose to stay well out of certain situations. Although that didn't stop it being quick to tell me when it thought I was doing something wrong. The actual City—the old, capitalised heart of it all—certainly wouldn't be scared. I had a vague idea it might actually be with me right now, but I couldn't have explained it. There was just...something shuffling around at the very back of my mind that made me feel less alone.

My thoughts were interrupted by Gary coming to a sudden halt in front of me. I very nearly tripped over him, but shoved my hands out onto the stone tunnel walls and managed to stay upright. Grenville and Derek piled into the back of me, accompanied by a heavy sigh from

Liam bringing up the rear. I'd dropped the torch, and it lit Gary's fat paws as he waited patiently for us to pull ourselves together. Picking it up, I shone it ahead of us and saw a stone wall blocking the way. Before I could say anything, Gary set off again and turned immediately right into the darkness. The tunnel turned at a sharp right-angle, before once again tracking straight ahead. I put a hand out onto the stone and felt the dampness through its surface. "Are we down by the river?" I asked, but no one answered. Which shouldn't have been a surprise, because the people behind me clearly didn't have a clue, and the one member of our party who presumably did know the answer was an otter. As I followed his furry backside through the darkness, I trawled my memories in an attempt to figure out the layout of wherever we might be. Gary stopped again, but this time I was more prepared. "Mind yourselves," I said over my shoulder, "we're stopping again."

"Where the hell are we now?" Liam spoke from behind Derek. "If we don't come up for air soon, we're going to end up in New Brighton."

"Birkenhead," I said. "If we went straight across from here, I'm pretty sure we'd end up somewhere near Hamilton Square." I had a sinking feeling I knew where we were heading. Pointing the torch past where Gary sat gazing implacably up at me, a sudden drop in the tunnel floor confirmed my suspicions. If I shone the light down the slope, I was pretty sure I'd find another, lower tunnel that had clearly been dug out in secret. It would have had to be kept secret, because it isn't normal to run a tunnel right underneath a set of lock gates. And it was going to stay secret, at least for now. I didn't think we had much further to go, and it wasn't going to take Liam very long to figure things out. "After you," I said to Gary, and he disappeared into the darkness. "We're going down," I told the others. "It isn't far," I peered over the edge to see Gary waiting for me at the bottom, "but it's steep."

"Oh brilliant," muttered Grenville from behind me, "just bloody brilliant."

"I thought you'd do anything to help me?" I shone the torch in his face, and he screwed up his eyes against the light. "Support me wherever I go, offer eternal protection and all that?"

"I didn't think it was going to involve so much weirdness," mumbled Grenville. "I thought you were a bit of a faker, in all honesty."

"What?" Derek and I spoke at once. "You didn't believe me?" Derek went on, an aggrieved tone in his voice. "You came to all the meetings!"

"I was bored," shrugged Grenville. "Don't have much to do since I got laid off, do I? Anyway," he went on, "it seemed to be making you happy. And it made a change from playing Warhammer all the time."

"Don't you dare tell me you don't like Warhammer," spluttered Derek. "You've got the collector's pieces and everything!"

"I like painting them," said Grenville. "Not really fussed about the game itself."

"Excuse me," I interrupted, "but right now we've got more to worry about than a stupid bloody game. No," I held up a hand in the face of their indignant expressions, "I'm not discussing it. Get down on the floor and slide. I'll go first." I turned back to where Gary was still gazing up at me. "Out the way then," I said to him. "There's a good fluffball." With that I lowered myself down onto the edge of the drop, before sliding down to where Gary waited. "It's not far," I called up, "only ten feet or so."

"That might not sound like much to you," grumbled Derek, "but it looks a bloody long way from where I'm standing."

"Oh, for christ's sake!" Liam had clearly lost his last shred of patience somewhere along the way. "Get down there before I kick you." With that, he gave Derek a hard shove into Grenville's back, and both men toppled forward. Gary shuffled out of the way faster than I thought an otter should really be able to, and I had no option but to catch the pair of them. What actually happened was that I managed to grab hold of Grenville in a fumbled bear hug and Derek used the pair of us as a crash mat. We ended up in a tangled heap on the tunnel floor. The wet tunnel floor.

"Sorry, sorry," said Grenville, scrabbling to get off me. Derek was sitting against the tunnel wall, looking confused. Liam was staring down at all of us with the sort of expression that mothers give their children a split second before they go absolutely fucking orbital and start swiping at people with wet tea towels. I shoved Grenville out of the way and got to my feet.

"Come on then," I said to Liam, "don't be keeping us waiting." He scowled at me before dropping lightly down into the tunnel and landing neatly on his feet. "No one likes a show off," I snapped, before turning back to Gary. "Off we go, then." I was pretty sure he shook his head wearily at me before turning back to the tunnel, but couldn't be bothered to take offence. All I wanted right now was to get back out without having to fight Liam. Now I'd figured out where we were heading, things were starting to make a lot more sense, but I knew Liam was going to make a move at some point. I just had to hope I was faster than him. It would have been nice to have reinforcements waiting when we reached our destination, but I knew from bitter experience I wasn't going to be that lucky. As I'd expected, the lower section of the tunnel only ran for about thirty feet before we came to a slope back up to the original level. I was expecting Gary to struggle, but to my surprise he scrabbled upwards without missing a beat. "Here," I said to Grenville, cupping my hands, "use your good foot." He silently did as I told him and I propelled him upward towards Gary. There was a muffled squeak as he landed on the stone floor of the upper tunnel, but I could see him getting to his feet. "And you," I said to Derek.

"Nah, I'm okay," he said, "did rock climbing at school, didn't I?" With that, he reached up and found a handhold in the rock, then started scrabbling his way upwards. When I was sure they were both safely out of the way, I turned to Liam.

"I'm going next," I told him, "and you're not to try any funny business."

"What sort of funny business might that be?" His tone was mild, but there was a definite twitch around his eye. He could feel it the same as I could. The Grail was somewhere close by. So much for wondering if I'd recognise it—sheer power was seeping towards us through the stone, and it was all I could do to stop myself from bouncing on the balls of my feet in excitement. It was here, it was close, and it was going to be mine. Fuck Liam O'Connor, fuck Ivo Laithlind, and definitely fuck any humans foolish enough to get in my way. This Grail wasn't holy—it was immortal. And it was calling to me. The ring I'd had made from Liam's ancient crown was becoming warm against my skin, same as it had done when I'd been trapped in Martins Bank with Eve. I wondered if he would be able to feel it as he stood next to me. I looked at him and saw the flash of understanding in his eyes. But before he had a chance to say anything, I leapt into the upper tunnel and began to run. I wasn't just running towards the Grail—there was something else. Another sound rang out over the top of its call, this one real and audible to anyone. It was the sound of someone screaming in anger, overlaid with an air of panic. It was human, and there was more than one. The walls around me suddenly changed back from stone to brick, and I knew where I was.

The basement level of the Albert Dock sits underwater, stamping its way securely into the riverbed via pilings and iron spikes. The lowest level people generally know about is mostly given over to car parking that's accessed via ramps off Gower Street. What I knew—but was pretty sure Liam didn't—was that there was another, even lower level. A tunnel ran around the entire square of the dock buildings, broken only by the swing bridge that opened to allow boats in and out of the dock itself. It had been included in the original plans in order to allow direct access between warehouses without traders having to transport their cargo publicly. The main attraction of the Albert Dock was its security against theft. Once ships had moored safely within the confines of the closed dock and the Hartley Bridge had closed behind them, third party access was restricted and the entrance guarded. Ships and their cargo could be moored in the knowledge that it was very difficult for would-be thieves to get aboard without being seen. And the underground tunnel route only reinforced that security. You could moor your ship and unload its cargo into the safety of the world's first fireproof warehouse, and leave it there until it had been sold to another trader. At which point your workers would move it from your own warehouse bay to that of its new owner, without ever taking their chances in the outside world. I hadn't been able to find any records of the tunnel being accessible past the late eighteen-hundreds, but I'd have bet good money it was still down there. And I'd have won that bet. I skidded to a halt about thirty feet into the brick section and looked around me. The walls were plain and solid and didn't appear to offer any access to the rest of the building. Liam came running up the tunnel after me just as the screaming started up again above me. It was a female voice, and I knew it well. Something was apparently frightening Izzy half to death, and she was making damn sure as many people as possible knew about it. There was another, deeper voice, shouting almost as loud—Damon. He must have got back and gone straight over to see her. Liam slowed as he neared me, looking quizzically up in the direction of the noise and then back at me. Without saying a word, I turned and ran. Grenville and Derek would have to take their chances without me. The worst case scenario was that they'd end up stuck in the tunnel and I'd have to send someone down to rescue them later. Maybe Gary would take them fishing to keep them occupied. Liam was hot on my heels, but I spotted my target and stopped sharply enough that he ran on ahead for a few paces before realising. I was already opening the roof hatch before he turned and headed back towards me. It was nothing more complicated than the sort of loose section used to cover the opening into domestic loft spaces, kept in place by a small latch on either side. Hoping no one was above me and about to have the surprise of their life, I undid the latches and pushed the hatch up into the space above. I had to stand on tiptoe to do it, but just about managed to throw the hatch upward and away from me. It landed with an echoing crash and I'd parkour'd myself up the wall and into the space before the sound died away, Liam close behind me. "Where the hell are we?" he asked as we looked around. We were standing in a small square space with a wrought iron staircase heading upwards. The hatch took up most of the floor and I carefully stepped over it to rescue the cover, which had bounced off the bottom step and wedged itself down the side of the treads.

"Get out of the bloody way," I said, and dropped the cover back into place. Izzy was still shouting somewhere above our heads, so I took the only available option and started running up the stairs. Liam tried to push past me and I kicked out backwards. It was followed by a satisfying crash as he fell and bounced down several iron steps, but I knew it wouldn't slow him for long. As well as the screaming that was presumably coming from Izzy's flat, I could feel the Grail's influence getting stronger. It was as though I was being physically pulled up the staircase towards the source—a magnet tugging me closer, whether I liked it or not. After I got about two dozen steps up, small windows began to break the gloom in what I realised was the outer wall of the dock building. Or rather, the outer section of the wall that faced inward towards the dock itself. This entire section had a false wall, I realised—and it definitely hadn't been on the plans. I wondered if that was something else the Byron Brothers had a hand in. As if to answer my question, I looked up and saw I was nearly at roof level, which meant I was close to Izzy's apartment. And opposite the little window, on the inner side of the staircase, was a door. I hit the door shoulder first without slowing my pace and crashed straight into Izzy's ensuite bathroom. As I rolled across the tiled floor I could hear her yelling from the living room and Damon pleading with her to calm down. There was another voice—Sean? For fuck's actual sake, what was he doing here? I got to my feet just in time for Liam to come flying through the door and bounce off the opposite wall. I could see now that the door to the stairwell was a good eight inches deep and hidden on this side, its shape disguised by mosaic tiling that matched the surrounding wall. Deciding to worry about the apartment's surprise architecture at a later point in time, I headed out into the living space just in time to witness Izzy throwing a saucepan at Sean's head.

"Get away from me, you thieving bastard!" One of her new copper pots went sailing through the air and disappeared into the little reading area in the corner that Sean had been telling me about only a few short days earlier. "I won't let you steal it!"

"Steal what?" Damon was pleading with her. "I don't even know what it is! For god's sake, Iz," he dived to the side as a box of mugs went crashing towards him, "what the fuck's got into you?" It was a good question. Izzy was picking up random boxes and throwing them at Sean and Damon without any apparent difficulty, but I knew only too well just how heavy they actually were. Liam stepped carefully past me into the centre of the room. I didn't bother stopping him—with any luck Iz would make him her next target anyway. Even as I thought it, she turned to look at us. There was a look of surprise on her face, as though she hadn't realised anyone else was in the room. She'd been busy, to be fair.

"What the hell are you doing here?" It was aimed at me. She spat the words out as though disgusted to see me. "How dare you step foot in here, you dirty, undead bitch!" She picked up a metal chair that I knew had been in the John Lewis delivery that the concierge had brought up for her. It was part of a set—a bistro table and two matching chairs, perfect for evening drinks on her fancy roof terrace. I dodged, and the chair disappeared into the bathroom behind me with a crash.

"I'm going to need that necklace back, Iz." I spoke quietly but firmly, keeping a wary eye on her as I stepped forward.

"It's mine," she hissed. "You're not having it!"

Damon looked at me as though only just registering my presence. "Is that what's causing it?" he asked. "The necklace?"

"What necklace?" asked Sean from behind him. He'd clearly decided discretion was the better part of valour at this particular moment in time, and was tucked behind a bookcase that had yet to be stacked with any actual books. "What's going on, Lil?"

"Give it to me," said Liam. He moved forward and would have grabbed Izzy, but Damon was too fast.

"Leave her alone," said Damon, shoving Liam hard enough to make him stagger. Liam turned and I was about to begrudgingly accept the fact I was going to have to help Damon out, when the main door opened behind me.

"Would anyone mind explaining to me exactly what's going on?" said Eadric. He was standing in the open doorway, looking around the room at the confused scene in front of him. For a second, it was like something out of a comedy film—and then Izzy began to scream.

That Way Madness Lies

Once she'd started screaming, Izzy didn't stop. It was an animalistic noise, a high-pitched terrified keening that would have made my blood run cold if my circulation had been up to it. Her gaze was fixed on Eadric, as though he were the cause of her terror. Damon ran towards her, but she flung out an arm and sent him sprawling across the floor. He fetched up against the wall next to the kitchen alcove, staring at her in confusion. As well he might—Damon's a good twelve inches taller than Izzy and probably three times her weight. Yet she'd sent him flying with not much more than a flick of her wrist. Out of the corner of my eye, I saw Sean slowly dropping to the floor and sliding quietly backwards into the furthest corner of the reading nook. I wished I could do the same, but something really fucking weird was happening and I had a horrible feeling it was going to be down to me to fix it. "Izzy," I tried again, "it's okay. I'm here." Her gaze flicked to me and then back to Eadric, as though unable to concentrate on anything else while he was there. Then I saw it. Her necklace was glowing with a pulsing light that cast her face into shadow. The ring I wore—the ring that had been made from the same gold, the gold from the melted down ancient crown that Liam had foolishly given me all that time ago—began to vibrate in time with the light. For a second I thought I could see something else behind Izzy's eyes. Then it disappeared. "I'm going to sort this out," I said, stepping forward with a confidence I definitely didn't feel. "You're safe with me." There was a noise outside in the corridor and I turned just in time to see Eadric running in. Which was interesting, because Eadric was already standing in the doorway. The second Eadric looked exactly like him, but there was something slightly off about the way he moved. It was as though he'd just remembered how to fight and was about to make up for several centuries of inactivity. Ignoring the confused looks on the faces of everyone else in the room, the new Eadric ran towards me, already yelling instructions.

"Grab her," he shouted at me. I didn't need telling twice. Launching myself forward, I rugby-tackled Izzy to the ground, locking my arms around her upper body as Eadric threw himself over her legs. She screamed and kicked with a strength of a man twice her size and it was all I could do to hang onto her. "Don't let go," said Eadric as he wriggled himself around to wrap himself around her knees. I somehow managed to manoeuvre myself so I was sitting behind her, my legs either side of her body and my arms clamping hers to her sides. I looked over her shoulder at Eadric and he winked. Now Eadric is not the winking sort. He's barely the smiling sort, half the time. I risked a glance across to the doorway where the other Eadric stood staring back at us in horrified confusion. His face was wearing the 'unsure of what was going on but my gosh he's going to find out and take charge any minute now, just you watch' look I was all too familiar with after the last couple of years of undead adventuring. Liam was apparently lost for words for the first time in his very long life. I turned back to the person who almost certainly wasn't Eadric and gave him a curious look. Izzy had calmed down a tiny bit now we'd got her pinned down, the screaming reduced to a quiet wail.

"Now what?" I asked.

"Get rid of that," Not-Eadric said, nodding towards the necklace. "We can't let her go until it's off." I leaned forward as if to kiss Izzy's neck, but instead bit down hard on the necklace. I wasn't sure that dental enamel was supposed to be able to cut through gold, but to my surprise I crunched straight through it and ended up spitting bits of gold links onto the hardwood floor. "Don't lose any of it," warned Not-Eadric. The second the chain dropped from her neck, Izzy flopped back against me like a landed fish. I pushed her away towards Damon and he ran forward to grab her just as Liam finally made his move. I'd caught the chain as it fell and for want of anything quicker, shoved it down into my bra as I scrambled to my feet. The missing links would have to wait til later, because Liam was grabbing at me in an attempt to get hold of the chain. I gave him a pleasingly sharp knee to the groin and he fell to the floor with a pained grunt.

"Does this belong to anyone?" Everyone's eyes swivelled to stare at where Grenville was leaning awkwardly against the frame of the doorway to the ensuite. He was holding something in his hand. Behind him, I could see Derek clambering through the gap in the wall. "It was in the door," said Grenville, indicating the false wall in the bathroom. "There was a secret button on the side of it, so I pressed it." He looked sheepish. "Seemed the right thing to do in the circumstances. Anyway," he shuffled sideways to let Derek stand next to him, "I thought it might be important." He held out his hand. In it lay a small goblet, no bigger than a sherry glass. It appeared to be made from pewter, but its innocuous appearance belied its truth. That, if I wasn't very much mistaken, was the Holy Grail. "Oh shit," said Grenville, "it's hot!"

As the Grail fell towards the floor, things seemed to happen in slow motion. Liam forgot his interest in the gold and twisted himself towards Grenville. Derek saw what was about to happen and pulled his friend sideways, the pair of them landing on the floor in a heap of tangled limbs and shrieking. Somehow I pushed myself past Liam and caught the Grail before it hit the floor. It was so hot that I was sure it was burning my skin, but I held onto it for dear life and rolled into a protective ball. A heavy boot kicked me in the back and I gasped. Liam. Thank fuck I didn't actually have to breathe, because I was pretty sure he'd just broken several of my ribs. Gritting my teeth against the pain, I straightened up and got to my feet, already feeling the broken bones cracking themselves back into place. "Lilith!" It was Eadric—the real Eadric, still framed in the doorway. I threw the Grail as hard as possible and he caught it without moving a step.

"Give it back to me," yelled Liam. "You have no right."

"I have every fucking right," I retorted. "You gave up your rights when you gave up the throne, you absolute fucking chickenshit." Not-Eadric stood behind him, looking almost amused. He tilted his head quizzically at me.

"Shall we?" Before he'd even finished speaking, I'd launched myself at Liam and slammed him into the brick wall. Mortar dust flew up in the air and I heard screaming behind me. Sean was clearly not having a good time. Served him right for getting involved in things he shouldn't.

"What are you doing?" Liam yelled. He flung me off as though I was an irritating gnat and I went sprawling to the floor. But as he stepped forward to do whatever the hell it was he was going to do, he was knocked sideways by Not-Eadric, who was showing the sort of fighting skills I was pretty sure the OG Silverton hadn't used in many centuries. His face was flickering like a broken television screen and I saw the disguise fading away even as I scrambled to my feet. "What the hell—" Liam's voice trailed off as he looked up into the thunderous face of a vengeful Ivo Laithlind.

"Think you can trick me, do you?" I kicked Liam in the thigh, and he screamed as the bone cracked loudly. "Think you can pretend to be on my side for just long enough to get what you want?" Another kick, this time to the ribs. Someone started making retching noises behind me, but I was beyond caring. There was a splintering noise that I dearly hoped was the sound of bone piercing Liam O'Connor's cold, dead heart. "Think you can watch as my friend loses her mind?" I kicked out at him again, but Ivo was dragging him upright and it didn't connect. "What the fuck are you doing?" I yelled at Ivo. "Leave him where I can get at him."

"Hang on." Ivo grunted as he pulled Liam to his feet. He dragged Liam's arms behind his back and gripped them hard. "There we go," said Ivo. He was smiling. "Would you like to do the honours?" I didn't need asking twice. Stepping forward, I punched Liam in the face with all my strength. All the fury and frustration that had been building up came out in that punch and I swear I heard the sound of Liam's teeth rattling in his head as it connected. I watched him reel from the blow as if in slow motion, gazing in wonder as ripples spread out from his broken mouth and his eyes rolled upward into his head. Ivo stepped backwards and Liam slumped heavily to the floor.

"Awww," I said to no one in particular, "he's having a little nap. And when he wakes up," I went on, "I'm going to make him an offer he can't refuse."

"I need to borrow your car." Eadric—the real one this time—hadn't said a word since Ivo and I had tag-teamed Liam into submission. He was still standing in the corner of the room, watching silently as Damon carried Izzy off to bed. She was beginning to mumble under her breath and there'd been a couple of quiet farts, so I was reasonably confident she'd be fine after she'd slept it off. I waved a hand in front of Eadric's face. "Are you even listening to me?"

"Yes, Lilith," he said, turning to look at me. "Yes, I'm listening to you. Tell me what you need and it will be arranged."

"Good," I said. "And when I get back, you and I are going to talk."

Which is how I found myself driving north up the M6 with an ancient king of England gaffer-taped and wedged into the boot. Eadric had handed over the keys to his car without a murmur. But that was probably because we had a lot to discuss when I got back to Liverpool. "We have a lot to discuss when I get back to Liverpool," I'd said as he dropped the keys into my hand.

"We do," he'd said.

"These aren't your car keys," I'd said, looking down at the fob he'd given me.

"They are." He gave me a faint smile. "I thought it prudent to suggest Elizabeth kept the old one, given its most recent cargo." I thought about this for a moment, and then narrowed my eyes at him.

"Ohhh," I'd said, "you sneaky bastard." The Alfa had been driven down to London with the rug rolled up in the back. No human would ever guess that immortal remains had ever been in it, but a revenant might. And now it was safely down south, presumably locked safely away in Elizabeth's very expensive garage on a tiny Highgate side street. Or maybe it had already been crushed into a tiny metal block and dumped elsewhere, so Elizabeth herself could never be tied to Eve's sudden and unexpected disappearance. Either way, it wasn't our problem. And now I was driving a brand new and fully-spec'd Guilietta that was easily capable of doing twice our current speed. I overtook an Audi A3 just for the hell of it, and grinned at the look on the driver's face as I sped by.

"You're pretty when you smile," said my passenger. "Do you know that?" I glanced across at him.

"Ivo," I replied, "has anyone ever told you that you're prettier when you shut up?"

By the time we arrived at the spot Eadric had marked on the map, muffled thumping was audible from the boot of the car. Liam might be immortal, but he's restricted to the outer limits of a human body's capabilities, same as the rest of us. And Alfa's are built to last. "Can't we just kill him?" Ivo wasn't happy about any of it. He'd tried telling me several times in the car that he thought it prudent to just lop off Liam's head and dump the remains. He'd been unimpressed when I'd said I didn't want to contaminate the countryside, and suggested we dump him in a handy river instead. But I remembered how upset the Mersey had been when the Grail was merely connected to it, and didn't think that dropping a bad-tempered and very deceased monarch right into an unsuspecting watercourse was a kind thing to do. To the water, not the king. So here we were, parked up in an unremarkable lay-by at the side of a minor country road in Cumbria and about to dump the first official King of England out onto the gravel.

"Someone's coming to get him," I said. "Eadric arranged it. Ready?" We were standing either side of the boot, and I gave Ivo the nod as I popped the lid open. Liam flung himself up and out the second he saw daylight, but we were ready. And so was his welcoming committee. As we grappled Liam to the ground, figures appeared out of the undergrowth on the other side of the road.

"A'right Lil?" Devin grinned as he spotted me. "Brought us a present?" I gaped wordlessly as my ex-boyfriend—and the most recent addition to the netherworld that I knew of—strode across the road towards us. Behind him floated the ghost of his mother, a proud look on her face. And behind her was the biggest man I'd ever seen in my life. At least seven feet tall and almost as wide, he was dressed all in black and appeared to made entirely of stone. Or maybe that was just his sallow complexion. "This is Gav," said Devin, nodding towards the man. "He'll take that for you." Gav—Gav, seriously?—thumped his way over to us, every step making the ground shake. He bent towards Liam and I swear I heard creaking. Then he picked him up by the feet and slung him casually over his shoulder as though carrying a light jacket.

"You're, erm," I really didn't know what to say, "doing okay then?"

"Too right," grinned Dev. "Having the time of my life, girl."

"He's doing so well for himself," said his mother, popping up beside him with a proud look on her face. "My little boy, all grown up!"

"You staying for a bit?" Dev looked hopeful.

"Nah," I said, "got to get back. Things to do, you know how it is."

"Oh I know," said Dev, "it's a busy life being dead." He nodded towards Ivo, who was standing quietly next to the car with a look of polite confusion on his face. "Gonna introduce us to your friend?" Ivo remembered his manners and stepped forward.

"Ivo Laithlind," he said, reaching across to shake Dev's hand. "At your service, as they say."

"Cool." Dev nodded. "Nice to know Lil's got good people on her side."

"Oh," said Ivo, "I'm always on her side." He glanced at me. "Even when she doesn't want me to be."

"Anyway," I said, deciding to cut this budding bromance right off, "we'll be off. You sure you can cope with him?" Dev laughed.

"Oh," he said, "we're looking forward to it! Gav needs some help down the necropolis. I'm sure your," he trailed off, "...associate will make an excellent handyman."

"Yeah," I said drily, "he does like to get involved. Anyway, we'd best be off. Got a job to do on the way back." Ivo gave me a curious look, but didn't say anything. "Have fun!"

"Will do," said Dev. "Come on, Gav," he turned to the big man, "let's get going." Gav had been entertaining himself by jiggling Liam up and down on his back. There was a deep rumbling noise every time Liam gave a muffled shriek, and I strongly suspected Gav was laughing. The trio turned and headed back in the direction they'd come. As they crossed the road and began to push through the hedge, Liam pulled his head up to look at me pleadingly. The gaffer tape was still stuck across his mouth, which explained the lack of yelling.

"See ya," I waved to Liam as they disappeared into the gloom, "wouldn't want to be ya!"

~

"What's this extra job we need to do?" Ivo asked as we got back into the Alfa. I pulled my seatbelt on and started manoeuvring the car round to face back the way we'd come before replying.

"That I need to do," I said as we pulled away. "Not you."

"Okay," said Ivo. "I understand you might not want to tell me everything. Where do I need to wait for you?"

"You don't," I said. "You're the extra job." I glanced across at him and smiled. "I'm taking you home."

I left a very indignant Ivo at the side of a road in the middle of the Yorkshire countryside. I'd offered to drop him wherever he wanted, but he was so quietly furious at being dumped that he insisted on getting out as soon as we were in God's own country. "It's not personal," I said, as he undid his seatbelt silently. "I've got a lot to sort out back in Liverpool and you'll only be a distraction."

"So you admit I distract you?" He raised a hopeful eyebrow.

"You do," I said. "In the same way that having a toddler under my feet would distract me. And mummy's got work to do. So be a good boy and crack on with your own megalomaniac plans, eh?"

"You are utterly insufferable," he grumbled. "I honestly don't know why I even bother."

"So don't bother," I said, grinning at him as he reached for the door handle. "Go sort your own problems out before worrying about mine.

I'll be fine." He shook his head but didn't bother replying. I watched with the engine still running as he got out of the car and turned his face up to the breeze. "You're home, Ivo," I said through the open door. "Enjoy it." I was still grinning as he slammed the door shut and I accelerated away. My smile faded as I turned onto the road that would take me back home to Liverpool. I hadn't been joking when I told Ivo I had work to do. Izzy's life had been put at risk for the sake of a stupid piece of history—and someone was going to pay for it.

Never Trust A Monarch

I'd driven straight back to Liverpool, my good mood fading with every mile that took me further away from Ivo. Or perhaps it was just that I was getting closer to the inevitable showdown. It all made sense now. Actually, no, it didn't make sense—nothing about finding the Holy sodding Grail in Liverpool city centre was ever going to make sense—but I had at least figured out what had happened. Eadric had clearly realised that Eve was secretly too unhinged to be trusted with co-ownership of the Grail any longer, and had taken it upon himself to relocate it before she'd arrived to check up on things. Unfortunately for all concerned, he'd decided to hide it in the walls of Izzy's apartment. Which was something that would have made sense if anyone else had been living in it at the time. The tiny, innocuous little cup could have been tucked away in the secret doorway for decades or more without causing any ill effects to most people. But Izzy wasn't most people. Izzy was the poor sod who was unfortunate enough to be best friends with me—the local head of Undead Anonymous, and the person responsible for giving her a necklace made from gold taken from the true crown of Britain. I'd hoped it would give her protection, but in the end it had damn near cost her sanity. Damon had sent me a cursory text informing me she was fine and just sleeping off what she apparently thought was the tail end of a fever. I'd replied asking him to send her my love, but he hadn't responded. I suspected I was going to be grovelling my apologies to Damon for a very long time.

My priority now was getting the Grail away from the Liver Building and—what? Much as I hated to even consider it, I knew I was going to have to destroy it. Its potential power was also what made it so dangerous. The only person I could trust right now was myself, and I didn't want the thing anywhere near me. Yup, it was a date with a hammer for the Holy Grail.

I stood in the middle of Eadric's office glaring across to where he sat calmly behind his desk. "Hand it over," I said.

"What are you going to do with it?" Eadric asked. "It needs to be kept somewhere safe, Lilith. It can't just be shoved into your wardrobe, or put in the kitchen cupboard where the cats might find it."

"I'll discuss it when you've given it back," I said. "I don't trust you with it." Eadric raised an eyebrow at that. Then he took a small key from his pocket and turned to a little wooden cabinet behind his chair. Opening the top drawer, he used the little key to open what I could only assume was a hidden compartment inside it.

"Here," he said, turning back to me. "But if you take it from here, you also assume responsibility for it." I held out my hand, and he dropped the Grail into it. I hadn't had a chance to look at it properly until now. It was as small and dull-looking as I remembered, and still far heavier than it looked. I turned it over in the hope of finding a useful inscription, but there was nothing.

"This is ours," I said, "isn't it? Not the religious one."

"Perhaps we are a religion," said Eadric. "In some people's eyes, at least." I thought about the goth squad following me around and how eager they all seemed to have someone—anyone—to believe in. I was pretty sure they could do better than me, if they only looked hard enough.

"You nearly killed Izzy," I said eventually.

"No," said Eadric. "It was the Grail taking over her mind, not me."

"It was you who had the bright idea of hiding the bloody thing in her apartment," I said, my voice cold. "Did it not occur to you that you might be putting her at risk?"

"No," he said. "Because I didn't know you'd given her that necklace. You broke down the crown without telling anyone, Lilith. I'm pretty sure that's treason."

"Against who?" I said. "The monarchy? They've had riches of their own for centuries—more than they've ever been rightly entitled to. You're sitting here on their land now, aren't you?"

"I don't know what you mean." But I was pretty sure he did.

"See that out there?" I waved a hand towards the window that looked out across the Mersey. It was the same window I'd once thrown Liam through, back when I first knew him. Aah, happy memories. "That river belongs to the monarchy. Not to the city, or the people, or even you, Eadric. It's divided down the middle, but I suspect you know that already. North side belongs to the monarch, south side to the Crown. So, yeah," I shrugged. "All of it. This city—this city that's been through so much already—has to pay the monarchy for the privilege of living on that poor bloody river. And you," I jabbed a finger at him, "have always been a double-crossing hypocrite."

"I say," muttered Nik from the corner of the room. I hadn't even realised he was there. "That's a bit harsh."

"Tell that to the people he burned to death in my home town," I snapped.

"It was a very long time ago," said Eadric quietly. "And for what it's worth, I've always regretted it."

"Bit late for regrets," I said. "What about all that chopping and changing sides you did back then? Do you regret that as well? Because that's the trouble with you, isn't it," I continued before he could say anything, "you swap loyalty depending on who's winning. You buddied up with Eve until you thought she might not be entirely reliable, then you double-crossed her. And you nearly killed Izzy in the process."

"It wouldn't have killed her," he said. "I keep trying to tell you that. She'd have been fine if you hadn't given her that necklace."

"She's my friend, Eadric," I said. "Not yours. I get to do what's best for her, and I thought that's what I was doing when I gave her the necklace. You get to stay the fuck out of my business. And that means staying the fuck away from Izzy. Do you understand me?"

"I'm her landlord, Lilith," he said calmly. "Isobel is just another human in a very long line of humans I've had to deal with over the centuries. I understand that she is your friend, but the safety of the territory comes first."

"No, it fucking doesn't," I said quietly. "It never comes before friendship. You take that back right now, Eadric Silverton."

"You know I can't."

"Which one of us is in charge, Eadric?" He looked blankly at me. "Tell me now." I took a step forward, struggling to keep my voice level. "Which one of us is in charge?"

"We both are," he said. "That's what we agreed."

"No, we didn't." I swallowed down my temper and managed to make my voice sound far more reasonable than I felt. "We agreed you would show me the ropes and that at some point in the future, I would take over."

"You have made it very clear," said Eadric, "that you do not want to take control of the territory. Has that changed?"

Think very carefully, said the city, ***before you commit yourself***. It sounded worried. ***There will be no going back from this***.

"Yes," I said flatly. "Things have changed."

"May I ask why?" Eadric's tone was carefully neutral. I heard a click as Nik quietly let himself out of the room and closed the door behind him.

"Because," I said, "the only way I can do this is if *I* do this. I need to make my own decisions, Eadric. Right now I'm second-guessing myself all the bloody time and it is doing my fucking head in."

"And you think that prioritising humans over immortals will help us? Help you?" He looked genuinely curious.

"No," I said honestly, "I don't think it will help me. I think this entire situation is a mess of the highest fucking order. But we both know that I'm stuck with this stupid bloody job, whether I like it or not. And that means doing my best for everyone who's relying on me."

"Who do you think is relying on you, Lilith?"

"I don't bloody know!" I yelled at him, my patience finally snapping. "We're the walking fucking dead, Eadric! There are vampires and were-cats and christ knows what else wandering around this sodding city and somehow I'm supposed to keep an eye on all of it, all whilst not being found out by the sodding public. You," I jabbed a finger at him across the desk, "have been sitting up here like sodding Rapunzel for way too fucking long, mate."

"Mate?" Eadric raised an eyebrow. "I remember the first time you turned up here. All fury and impatience and a determination to do what was right for yourself, even if it was dangerous. But you were scared. Weren't you?"

"Of course I was bloody scared," I said, my voice calmer now. "I'd woken up without a fucking pulse! One minute I was bumbling along with life, the next I was dead as the proverbial dodo. But I was still walking around. Do you have any fucking idea just how terrifying that is, Eadric Silverton?"

"Yes," he said, "I do. But it was a very long time ago now. Even immortal memories struggle sometimes."

"Not mine," I said flatly. "My memory's just fine. Every single thing I've ever said or done is still up here," I tapped the side of my head, "and ready to torment me at a moment's notice. But I'm expected to just deal with it, along with everything else. Along with the endless threats to my life, whatever my life even is right now. Threats to my friends, my family, even my fucking cat." Not that anyone would get away with hurting Grimm, not if Grimm himself had anything to do with it. "I was given a vampire guard, Eadric. A vampire fucking guard. Who was killed because of me. For fuck's sake, even the local grannies are trying to off me on the reg! Everyone has a limit, and I've reached mine. I'm sorry."

"Don't be sorry," said Eadric, and I saw he was smiling. "Be proud. Of yourself, of your family, even of your cat. You've got a good team around you, Lilith O'Reilly. It's more than many of us have managed."

"Get out," I said, before I could change my mind. "Get out of this building and out of this city." As I said the words, my confidence began seeping back. "I am taking over, Eadric Silverton. And you will leave."

"Where am I supposed to go?" Eadric's expression was a strange mix of shock, fear and, if I wasn't very much mistaken, excitement. He wanted to leave, I realised. He wanted to run away and not think about it all anymore, to escape from centuries of responsibility and danger and the endlessly boring politics of being immortal. And if he went, I would have to take his place.

You will never be truly free again, said the city. ***You will never be able to leave***.

Until the next one comes along.

That could be a long time, it said. ***Silverton has been here almost a thousand years***.

Well, I replied, *it's not as though I've got much else on*.

"YOU MUST LEAVE," I said to Eadric, the voice flowing through me as naturally as water cascading down a Welsh mountainside. "THIS IS MY TERRITORY NOW." And then I put the Holy Grail in my pocket and walked out, before Eadric Silverton could say a word.

~

I walked back to Harrington Street with the Grail tucked into my bra. Which wasn't exactly dignified for either of us, but at least that way I knew I wouldn't accidentally drop it down a drain and risk the city being overrun by power-hungry mega-rats or something equally ridiculous. Izzy's broken necklace was now tucked into my pocket, and what with the ring that still sat firmly on my finger, I could feel myself almost fizzing by the time I got back to Flora's. Instead of heading up to the flat, I ducked into the carpark and up into the scrubby undergrowth at the far end. After kicking around in the nettles for a while, I eventually found a decent-sized rock. Tucking myself into the furthest corner, I pulled the Grail out of my top and looked at it again. "For what it's worth," I told it, "I'm sorry." It didn't answer. Then I cleared a small space on the ground and carefully put the Grail down. It seemed to get heavier as I did so, as if it was trying to pull away from me. "Like I told you," I said, "I'm sorry." I brought the rock down on it hard, and it cracked with a high-pitched scream. Somewhere in the distance, a dog barked. I smashed the stone down again, and the cup sheared in two. I could hear wailing now, high-pitched and ethereal, as though something just beyond reach was breaking its heart at the destruction of this tiny piece of metal that shouldn't have existed in the first place. There was music, too—a harp, playing a melancholy tune somewhere in the distant past. I raised the rock again and brought it down one final time. Cymbals crashed in my head and the harp—or perhaps it was a lyre—sang one last discordant note, and fell silent. I looked down at the shattered pieces of metal lying on the ground in front of me and tried not to cry. I didn't even know what I'd have been crying for, so it was pointless. Carefully picking up every last fragment, I gazed at them lying in the palm of my hand like nothing more than tiny pieces of scrap metal. Then I closed my fingers around them, and went inside.

"Been busy?" Grimm asked as I walked into the kitchen. I ignored him and headed through the flat into my bedroom, shutting the door behind me. "Nice to see you, too," he called, loud enough for me to hear him. Delving a hand into my knicker drawer, I managed to find a single pink sock. It had a glittery pompom on the back and wasn't exactly the most respectful option, but it would have to do. I dropped the broken pieces of the Grail into it and shoved it into my pocket. Then I lifted the rug and prised up the floorboard that hid the next thing I needed. The small bag was heavy, and I thought I heard music again as I lifted it out. It was probably my imagination.

"I'm going out," I said to Grimm.

"Oh," he drawled, "she speaks! Thought you might have been traumatised by your latest adventures underground. Not that you should have been underground in the first place, of course."

"Shut up," I said mildly. Then I realised what he'd said. "How did you know where I was?"

"Had a chat with Gary earlier," he said, "didn't I? He seemed quite impressed with you, to be fair. Not sure what the Silvertons are going to make of you going rogue, though."

"Not their business anymore," I said. "Things are different now."

"Are they?" He raised a furry eyebrow. "Well now, that's a turn up for the books. Didn't think you had it in you."

"Thanks for the vote of confidence," I snapped. "Nice to know you've got my back."

"Lilith," Grimm said, his voice more gentle than I'd ever heard it, "I've always got your back." It was my turn to look surprised. "You underestimate me," he went on. "I may be cynical, but I'm not unkind. And it's not my confidence you need," he tilted his head and gazed at me, "it's your own."

"What if I don't feel confident but am doing it anyway?"

"Then that's even braver, in my opinion." He gave me what I could have sworn was a faint smile. It was incredibly disconcerting. "The times are, as they say, a-changin'."

"There are a lot of things that need to change," I said. "And I'm starting right now."

To my absolute horror, when I headed out of the kitchen door and down the fire escape to street level, David Mansoor was waiting for me at the bottom. "Hello, Miss Lilith," he said, waving cheerily at me. I actually stopped halfway down the third flight of steps, surprise and confusion freezing my feet in place. I walked slowly down the remaining steps and stopped at the bottom. "I would like to say I am sorry," said David, stepping forward and handing me an envelope, "if you will be kind enough to give me just a few minutes of your time. I have been unwell recently," he went on, his voice apologetically formal, "and I am told I have been inflicting my, erm, problems on you. This is unforgivable of me, and I wish to extend my heartfelt apologies." I looked down at the envelope, which was cream and made of heavyweight paper. Then I looked back up at David, who was eyeing me with the look of a dejected dog who knows it's done wrong and is probably about to get a smack on the nose with a rolled up newspaper. Sliding a fingernail along the top edge of the envelope, I opened it and pulled out the sheet of matching paper from inside. Unfolding the paper, I found a message in handwriting I didn't recognise.

'I can't help very much, I'm afraid,' said the note, 'but this is a start. He doesn't remember anything he's done, nor anything you've done to him in turn. I think it's probably best if we leave it like that, don't you?'

It was signed, and I smiled as I read the name. I wasn't sure what I'd done to deserve someone as helpful as Freya in my life, but I certainly wasn't going to complain.

"Hey Lil," came a voice from behind me. I turned to find Derek standing in the doorway to Flora's. "How's it hanging?"

"It's, erm," I floundered, "yeah," I managed finally, "I'm good, thanks."

"Cool," said Derek, "glad to hear it. I was a bit worried after we lost you in that house up at Canning."

I stared at him in astonishment. "But," I started, "you and Grenville—"

"Derek and Grenville have learned not to go urban exploring in people's houses," said Mapp, appearing beside him. "Haven't you, my love?"

"Aah, errr, yeah," Derek blushed. "Sorry about that. Anyway, I need to get on," he said, his hand on the door to the cafe, "I'm doing the washing up today." With that, he pushed the door open and headed inside without another word.

"What the fuck is going on?" I spluttered. "And you," I turned to David, but he'd disappeared. "Where did he go?"

"Back to work, I'd imagine." Freya popped up next to Mapp and grinned at me. "He's a busy boy. We shouldn't keep him."

I looked at her, then at Mapp, then back at Freya. "I'm going to ask again," I said slowly. "What the fuck is going on?"

"Things are changing, Lil," said Mapp. "We're just helping smooth the way a bit. S'what friends are for, innit?" Before I could think of something to say, Heggie appeared from behind me, making me jump.

"Here, love," said Freya, "let's go finish that stocktaking, aye?" She caught hold of Heggie's hand and the two of them turned to walk away in the direction of Whitechapel. "Oh, Lilith," she said, over her shoulder, "I think a little bit for the river, don't you?" With that, she and Heggie walked away.

"Don't ask me," said Mapp to my unanswered question. "I'm just not looking a gift horse in the dental department. Y'know? Got my Hegs and my Freya and we're all very happy, thank you very much. Although she's still annoyingly independent." He frowned. "Says she's going back to her house over the water soon, and I'll have to start getting the ferry again."

"And you don't mind?" I asked him. "What about Heggie?"

"Oh," he said, "Heggie's happier with me. And he never did like boat trips. Anyway," he went on, "must dash. I've promised to make Freya some curtains. Got some nice velvet for her."

Bloody hell, I thought, she really *is* a witch.

All This I Lay Before You

I headed up Duke Street, hopping off the pavement and walking in the road to avoid gaggles of schoolchildren making their way home. When I got to the entrance of the Anglican cathedral I walked in through the open gates and headed down the tunnel to the gardens below. Now a very nice green space in the city centre, people are often surprised to discover that it doesn't actually belong to the cathedral that looms above it. In fact, the cemetery is a good century-and-a-half older than the neighbouring cathedral, which wasn't completed until the nineteen-seventies. Originally a quarry providing stone for the construction of many of the city's most prominent buildings, a new purpose had to be found for the space once its stone reserves were exhausted in the early eighteen-hundreds. The logical move was to turn it into a cemetery, burial space being much needed in a time of poverty and restricted life expectancy. The resultant burial ground rapidly filled, and it wasn't long before questions were being raised about risks to public health from the sheer volume of bodies that were being packed in. Even so, St James' Cemetery stayed open for burials until not long before the Second World War, when the trustees decided they could no longer justify the funds needed for its maintenance. It was many decades before the neglected cemetery was eventually transformed into the peaceful gardens that are now so beloved of tourists and locals alike, and the bodies stayed where they'd always been. And they're still there today —almost sixty thousand people, all sleeping under the grass on which kids and dogs now play without a care in the world. Most of the gravestones were moved out of the way, many of them stacked along the boundary wall that divides the gardens from the cemetery grounds. I walked slowly along the path next to the wall, reading the gravestones as I went. I knew which one I was looking for. I'd first seen it more than a decade earlier, when I was still at university and liked to spend sunny lunchtimes sitting against one of the many trees dotted around the gardens. Many of the mass burial pits lie to this day close up against the boundary wall, the vast majority of them containing children from the local workhouses. Born in poverty to women who couldn't afford to feed themselves, let alone a child, they'd never stood a chance. Faded names filled entire slabs of stone, propped against the wall in the vague vicinity of the remains of those named on them. Stepping onto the grass, I ran my fingers along the top line of carved writing on the stone I'd been looking for. It bore little detail, just the name of the workhouse followed by a long list of the children lying under my feet. Checking no one was watching, I pulled Izzy's broken necklace out of my pocket. "I know it's too late to help any of you," I said quietly, "but I think you deserve to be custodians of this. You're more important than most people who'd like to get their hands on it." I moved to stand against the boundary wall and peered behind the gravestone. The sinkhole I'd noticed all those years ago was still there. The most logical—and grimly depressing—explanation was that, as the bodies in the pit broke down over the last hundred or more years, the ground was probably dropping with them. Crouching down, I slid my hand behind the stone and dropped the gold chain into the hole. It didn't make a sound as it dropped. It had probably just landed in mud and was destined to be pushed around by slugs and snails for the rest of eternity, but it was better than the alternative. I straightened up, brushed the mud off my jeans, and walked on.

My next stop was at St Luke's on Leece Street. It had been here that I'd first spoken to Ivo properly, not long after I'd died. And it was St Luke's—aka 'the bombed out church'—that hid an access hatch to the more secret of Joe Williamson's beloved tunnels. I wasn't heading down the tunnels today, though. Heading up the front steps and around the side of the church, I stopped at the Irish Famine memorial. Taking the ridiculous pink sock out of my pocket, I dug my fingers into it and pulled out a small piece of metal. "I can't make it up to you," I murmured to the memorial, "and I very much doubt the government ever will. This is just a token." I dropped the metal into the cracked bowl of the sculpture, and it slid down out of view. Then I turned and headed back down to the waterfront.

~

Letting myself in through the plant room door, I pressed the button for the private lift. It took a while to arrive, which meant it must have been up at the Silverton's floor. Oh well—it didn't really matter anymore whether Eadric knew what I was doing. This was my territory, and from now on, things were going to be done my way. I was surprised by my own lack of reaction at this. The prospect of having to take over had been lurking ominously for so long now that I'd expected to at least feel stressed when it finally happened. Even physically sick, maybe. But there was nothing except a calm acceptance of my fate. If this is what I was meant to do, then I was going to do it properly. The lift finally arrived. I stepped inside and pressed my palm against the control panel until the cover dropped, then crouched down so I could insert the little key that still hung around my neck. I should probably get a longer chain for it. Although I supposed the offices up in the clock tower were mine for the taking now, as well. I could keep the key up there. Mind you, Nik would still be there and I wasn't entirely sure I trusted him not to go nosing around when I wasn't looking. Maybe I could foist a flatmate on him, to keep an eye on what he got up to. But that depended first on me being able to find a suitable person, and second on Nik actually deciding to stay. For all I knew, he might leave along with Eadric. They'd been together a long time, and I wasn't sure how well Nik would cope on his own. Anyway, that was a worry for another day. The lift came to a softly thudding halt, and the doors opened—onto complete darkness. I left the key in the lock so the lift wouldn't leave without me, and stepped out onto the stone plinth. The only light came from inside the lift, which did nothing more than illuminate the surface ripples nearest the plinth. Sighing, I stepped down into the water. "You here?" I asked quietly. Nothing. "I've got something for you." I waded further out and stood next to the first stone arch. Putting a hand against the stone, I tried again. "It's gone," I said. "Or at least, its power has. It isn't going to upset you anymore." There was the faintest hint of movement in the air in the far corner of the crypt—a purple swirl in the darkness, edged with fuchsia pink. "I brought you a present," I continued. "No one else will come down here now. It's just you and me. I thought you might like this." I took the heavy gold ingot from its bag and held it out. "It's from the crown," I said. "You deserve to have something valuable, not just the rubbish people drop in all the time. Anyway," I leaned forward and dropped the metal block into the water behind the stone pillar, "this is for you." A strange vibration came from under the water, as though an electrical current was running through it. A bright light appeared and raced towards me, zipping around my ankles. I watched it sparkling through the water as it moved away from me and ran all around the edges of the ingot, as if investigating what it might be. Then it spun off to circle around the base of the stone pillar. A thin line of light trailed behind it, connecting me first to the gold and then to the stone of the crypt itself. I watched it spin back towards me—and then it burst up into the air. A fountain of purple, blue and neon pink pierced the darkness, illuminating the empty crypt. The water was beginning to ripple, as though being brushed by an invisible breeze, rolling slowly back and forth in the confines of the space. The lights began pulling together and forming the shape of what I was horribly suspicious might turn out to be a person. If there was some unholy boss level no one had bothered to warn me about, someone was going to get a shoeing when I got back upstairs. If I got back upstairs. The figure was wearing a long robe and some form of draped headdress. Slowly, as I watched in amazement, the face of a woman appeared, made entirely from light. She smiled down at me.

You will do. For now. It was the same voice I'd heard down here before, but now it was stronger and more coherent. *Thank you.* I stood rooted to the spot, unable to move even if I'd wanted to. The woman leaned down and I could almost see through her. She was one of the most beautiful people I'd ever seen, but not in a human way. There was an air of goodness about her I'd never felt before, a feeling that this woman was the beginning and the end, and the mother of everything. *They call me the spirit of Liverpool*, she said. *You have done well.* Without thinking, I held out a hand to touch her robe. I could see my fingers dipping into the light, but felt velvet and silk beneath my fingertips. Rough cotton and the shredded texture of the tobacco that had brought prosperity to the city—a prosperity that cost others dearly. Suddenly I could smell the sea, and sweat, and the blood of people being beaten into submission. I fell to my knees in the water, overwhelmed by the emotions that were running through my head. They weren't even my emotions. These were echoes of the joy and heartbreak and success and failure across so many centuries. These were the things that had made Liverpool a city loved and cherished by so many. *That's all we can do*, said the woman softly. *We move forward, but we never forget.* I looked up into her glowing face, just inches from mine. She smiled kindly at me. *Give something back to the river*, she said—and then she was gone.

I dripped my way back into the lift and pressed the button for the top floor. When the doors opened, I found Nik waiting for me. "He's gone," he said. "Eadric's gone."

"Already?" I'd half thought I'd be able to see him off, perhaps give him a hug and tell him there were no hard feelings. Pathetic, I know.

"There's nothing here for him now," said Nik. "There can't be two leaders, it never works."

"What will he do?" I felt tears pricking at the back of my eyes and blinked hard.

"Said he's going to look for his son," shrugged Nik. "Assuming he's still around."

"What are you going to do?"

Nik frowned at me. "What do you mean?"

"Well," I started hesitantly, "I thought you might hate me for what

I'd done to Eadric. I thought you might want to go with him." To my astonishment, Nik laughed.

"Oh, my sweet summer child," he said, "why on earth would I do that?"

"Well," I started, "Eadric's your friend, and—"

"Yes, yes," said Nik. "He was also incredibly dreary. I'm thinking I might redecorate the main room into something akin to a Bedouin palace." He paused. "If that's acceptable to you, of course."

"You can do what you like with it," I told him, "so long as you don't damage anything. I'm going up top. Oh, and Nik?" I stopped by the door to the clock tower, and looked back at him. "If you're going to have orgies, at least keep them discreet." I shut the door on his spluttering and headed up to Bella.

"I don't know what I'm doing," I warned the giant copper bird, as we both peered out over the river. "I might look like I do sometimes," Bella's amused creaking suggested she possibly disagreed with that statement, "but I really bloody don't. I've still got pieces of the sodding Grail in my pocket," I went on. "Need to get rid of them somehow. Any suggestions?" Bella made the repetitive staccato creak that meant she had something to tell me, and I looked up. Her big green-blue head tilted towards me in acknowledgement before slowly creaking back up and over to point down to the docks. I followed her gaze. "I don't know what you mean," I said, peering across into the gloom. Then I saw someone waving at me. I hesitantly waved back, and the person pointed to something in the water. "You are fucking kidding me," I said. Bella creaked with amusement. "If this goes wrong," I warned her, "I'm blaming you." Her enormous copper wings winced against their restraints as she shuffled. I was pretty sure she was shrugging. "You," I told her sternly, "are a bad influence." She was still sniggering as I headed back downstairs to finish the job I'd started.

Come Hell Or High Water

"Evenin', miss Lilith," said the man at the water's edge. "Thought you'd be needing me sometime about now."

"Thanks Mack," I said. "Can I ask how you knew what to do?"

"Best not, miss," he said. "Can't be giving away all my secrets, now can I?" He smiled and held out a hand for me to step down into the little boat. It was a small fibreglass dinghy with an outboard motor that was already switched on and idling. It looked like the type used by the coastguard patrol. I checked the hull to make sure there was no logo suggesting Mack might have 'borrowed' it from somewhere, but it was plain dirty white. "It's my own, miss," he said. "Don't you be worrying about it. Now, do you know where you're heading?"

"Yeah," I said, letting him help me down the rusty iron ladder. "I'm pretty sure I can find a good spot."

"Oh, I'm sure you will," said Mack, smiling. "I'm sure you will. Anyway, you just leave her back here when you're done, no worries. She's ready to go, I already dropped the motor." I turned and saw the outboard motor was indeed already down in the water. "Off you go." With that, he untied the boat from its mooring and threw the heavy rope in behind me.

"Thanks Mack," I said. "I really appreciate it." He gave me a mock salute as I turned the boat slowly out away from the river wall, getting a feel for the controls. "Here goes nothing," I muttered, and set off into the dark.

ARE YOU ENTIRELY SURE ABOUT THIS? I'd been half expecting the City to turn up at some point, if only to give me a telling off for the way I'd been handling things, so I wasn't as startled as usual. **WHY WOULD I BE SCOLDING YOU?** It sounded genuinely curious. **HAVE YOU DONE SOMETHING WRONG?**

"You tell me," I said, concentrating on steering the boat. We were heading out into the wind farm, which is a route that is expressly forbidden to unauthorised vessels. I was hoping that, as it was after dark, I'd be less likely to be spotted here than if I steered through the more usual channels. The turbines loomed high above our heads like aquatic aliens getting ready to stomp their way into the city. War of the Worlds, the Scouse edition.

I HAVE TO TRUST SOMEONE, it said, **AND IT MIGHT AS WELL BE YOU**.

"Yeah," I said, "that's not actually as reassuring as you probably think it is."

YOU HAVE FOUND SOMEWHERE SECURE TO DROP IT? the City asked, ignoring my griping as usual.

"As secure as we're going to get," I said. "No guarantees, though."

HOW FAR OUT?

"There's a wreck out past the wind farms," I said. "We'll stop there." I already knew the locations of several historic wrecks out in Liverpool Bay, because I'd spent some time looking at nautical maps after Daisy and her friends had begun interfering with the wind turbines. I hadn't realised how much *stuff* was in the water until I'd found the maps and learned how to read them (two very separate tasks—turns out they're nothing like Ordnance Survey maps, go figure). There were wind farms, power cables and giant warning buoys marking the shipping channels, all sorts of things sat on and under the water of the bay. And then there were the wrecks. So many wrecks. Some ancient, some more recent—and many of them still harbouring the remains of those lost on board. I'd only chosen tonight's target after I was already heading out into open water, but I was fairly confident it would work. The Alarm was an iron-hulled lightship that had been built in the late eighteen-hundreds and was itself used as a floating marker to warn others of obstructions underneath the water. After thirty-odd years of service to the Mersey and all who sailed on her, the Alarm was run down by the SS Pacuare, a steamship transporting bananas into Britain from the West Indies. I wasn't sure whether the fruity cargo had gone overboard, but the Alarm certainly did. The most important thing to me was that no one had died in the incident—the entire crew of the Alarm had managed to escape on her lifeboat. I didn't like the idea of dragging humans into this, however long they might have been dead. And now the Alarm herself was an historic wreck, which meant other boats had to avoid her. And—most importantly—no one was allowed to dive down and disturb her. Deciding I must be at roughly the right spot by now, I cut the boat's engine and looked around to check no one was watching. Balancing precariously in the little boat, I pulled the last fragments of the Grail out of my bag and, before I had time to change my mind, hurled them with all my strength at the dark water. As fast as lightning, a hand shot up from the depths and caught the little pieces before they hit the surface. I had just enough time to see the webbing between its fingers before it disappeared back under the water, taking its prize with it.

WELL, said the City. **THIS WILL BE INTERESTING.**

~THE END~

Author's Notes

I'm almost certainly preaching to the converted by now, but for anyone who isn't already aware, Netherweird is a work of fiction. Any resemblance to anything or anyone (whether living, dead or *un*dead) is not intended, nor should it be inferred. I know, it makes me sad too.

Birkenhead really is known as the 'One-Eyed City', but no one is entirely sure why. There are endless theories ranging from the sublime to the absolutely ridiculous, but any substantiated reason is long lost to the mists of time.

No, I haven't got the name of a well-known high street homewares store wrong in chapter one. You might know it as Home Bargains, but the chain began as a single store called 'Home and Bargain' in Old Swan, Liverpool, back in 1976. Its name officially changed to 'Home Bargains' in 1995, but in the Merseyside area it's still generally still referred to by its original monicker. As the longterm partner of a born and bred Scouser I've long picked up the colloquialism myself, so I strongly suspect Lilith would have done the same.

The 'Kitty' to whom Eadric refers in chapter nine is the legendary

Kitty Wilkinson, often known as the 'Saint of the Slums' for her role in the development of the public wash house system in nineteenth-century Liverpool. Hers is one of the many thousands of bodies that still lie beneath the surface of St James' Cemetery Gardens.

The story about the role of Martins Bank in the relocation of gold stores during WWII is absolutely true. At the time of writing, the building is standing empty and has been for a long time—a sad waste of an enormously important location in the city's history.

The following relates to a small section that was edited out before publication (see also, that time I wrote a history book about vampires which includes a photograph of William MacKenzie's pyramid tomb on Rodney Street with zero context, because I forgot I'd taken the relevant section out of the text) but it still amuses me so I'm leaving the original note intact: Snail farming is a real thing in many areas, but the reasons behind such establishments vary from 'absolutely legit' to 'how the hell hasn't anyone been sued yet'. Search online for 'Dale Street snail farm' for a good example of the more interesting end of this 'industry'.

The Albert Dock does indeed have a deep basement level, but—as far as I'm aware, at least—none of it is currently being used to hide valuable antiquities. Nor is it hoarding 'ancient architects', which is what autocorrect apparently thought I was writing about. This error very nearly got through to publication and I am currently thanking the gods of all that is unholy for my eagle-eyed editing team.

None of my books would be even remotely coherent without the help and support of my utterly brilliant editing champs. Jayne, Sal, Toni - I love and adore you endlessly (and your ridiculous manuscript notes, which would make a highly entertaining book in themselves).

Hugest love and thanks also go to the following (this is not an exhaustive list and I have been awake for more than twenty hours at the time of writing, so do not be getting stroppy with me if I've missed you out):

Sarah Trivedi, who's known me most of my adult life and has

somehow not yet had a Vi-related breakdown (although it's been a close call at times); Cressi Downing (http://www.thebookanalyst.co.uk) who pointed me in the right direction in the first place; Jay Émme, who is clever and funny, and patiently gives endless sensible answers (as well as many ridiculous ones) to my potentially stupid questions; Tracy Whitwell, who Knows; Pixie Purvis, the Dingle Queen; my mother, who doesn't read my books because of the swearing but is still hugely supportive of my potty-mouthed career; my beloved baby brother, Scott; Winston Gomez, possibly the most tolerant man on the planet; and my boys, Jaime and Oscar. Love you to infinity and beyond.

And, as always, to Liverpool. I love you.

Sign up to my newsletter to be the first to hear about upcoming releases and other interesting stuff - and get a FREE short story from Netherweird!
tinyurl.com/netherweirdstory

Printed in Great Britain
by Amazon

50895546R00153